Austen Persuaded

Alana Highbury

Shipsvold Press

Chapter 1

Success! I cheered silently as my toes finally managed to snag the edge of the scarlet cropped cardigan tossed nearby. I dragged my foot across the smooth linen slowly and carefully until it reached my waiting fingers. My eyes slid to the right to see if I'd caused any stir.

The cardigan in hand, I frowned, realizing the hardest part was yet to come. I needed to wriggle out from under his heavy arm, which was lying over my waist. Not cradling me but rather lying *on* me, as though I were part of the bed. Indeed, I realized mirthfully, I was practically a fixture in this executive suite at the Four Seasons.

A half-seated position was all I could manage, but it was enough to slip the cardigan on over my ivory camisole while his thick arm still lay draped over me. But just as I was adjusting the sleeve, I felt a stir. Him.

"Brandon, I really need to…" I started, but his arm only tightened, his breathing still slow and steady. He was still out cold, but it was early. He'd probably dozed off last night as soon as we'd flipped on the movie—just as I had—after our late night on the town.

I smiled, letting my head sink back into the pillows.

Maybe the morning could wait a little longer.

"Just cancel, babe," Brandon grumbled, trying unsuccessfully to reach out and tug me back as I giggled and stepped back.

Fully dressed now, I ran my fingers through my rumpled hair. "I would think you'd *want* me to show up to work, since I do, after all, work for you."

"Ellen can wait." He rose to lean on one elbow, his blue eyes sweeping over me lazily. "What's she ever done for you anyway, babe? Besides giving you the assignments Viviana doesn't want."

My usually playful features settled into a frown. *Was he right?* Sure, my copyediting workload had its share of boring legal and business books, but so did Viviana's. My friend and fellow freelancer had commiserated with me many times on the subject. It was just the nature of the books the company published, as Ellen always said. Then again, Brandon would know better than anyone. He owned Bolder Publishing. Ellen was just the editorial manager.

"Brandon, hon, I'd love some career advice from you, but this is a conversation for another day. I can't just not show up to a meeting."

His cheeks dimpled as he grinned and reclined, displaying his sculpted arms over his head, undoubtedly for effect. "I could write you a doctor's note. Dr. Bolder recommends lots of bed rest. Who could argue with that?"

I felt the corners of my lips tugging upward. He was sure of himself, but not in the condescending way of some men. He knew he was a 10. Maybe an 11.

We were exactly alike in that way.

I sauntered over to him. "I'll make it up to you tonight after Ellen's party." I brushed my lips over his with a light hand resting on his chest and then, with strength I didn't know I had, rose and headed to the restroom to freshen up.

I stared at my reflection, assessing the state of my tangled red hair and frowning slightly. In truth, I felt annoyed that Brandon wanted me to simply skip a work meeting. But just a bit. Whenever I found myself even slightly annoyed with him, I reminded myself I was looking too hard for flaws. Because he must be too good to be true. He *must*.

Because Brandon Bolder was, as much as any man could be, perfect.

I'd certainly dated enough men who were the exact opposite—jerks, all of them, but they were fun—for *so* long I couldn't even remember how long.

Four years.

Since him.

I ignored the tiny voice, barely even a whisper, in my mind.

Men were jerks, but they were fun. And that was fine. Fun was all I needed.

Brandon was fun. Maybe he was even more.

"I'm having a really hard time finding anything wrong with this one, Viviana," I said as I sifted through my friend's closet. "He's, he's ..." Unfortunately, my difficulty finding words was not only due to the topic. As much as I'd tried to ignore it, I'd developed a nasty cough as the day had progressed.

"Your soulmate?" Viviana said, a wide smile on her face. "After all these years, you've finally found the one?"

I rolled my eyes, ignoring the tiniest whisper in my mind reminding me that, once upon a time, I *had* found the one.

No, I hadn't.

"That's so cheesy, Viv. It's not like 26 is *so* old. But I find that—" I paused, staring in the distance as intense eyes from the past stared back in my mind, against my will.

No, I'd never found the one.

A cough rose up in my throat. "Uh, Brandon, I find him so—" I started again hoarsely.

"So perfect?" Viviana flashed an indulgent smile, as we'd had some version of this conversation more than a few times before.

"I'm actually finding it hard to spot anything wrong with him too, I'll admit," she continued. She seemed about to say more, but after I sneezed, she gave me a motherly look. "Hey, don't cough all over my clothes now. Are you feeling OK?"

"Oh, I'm fine. Don't start your worrying thing. Just a tiny cough, probably just a touch of hay fever." I didn't actually know what hay fever was exactly, but it was a common allergy, right? People had allergies in the spring, didn't they?

"Annie, is Gregory coming?"

After blowing my nose as delicately as I could, I glanced at Viviana and grinned. She wasn't even trying to be subtle. She must have it bad for him. "As if Brandon would go anywhere without him. Maybe I shouldn't be telling you this, but he's just as keen on setting up you and Greg as I am. Brandon speaks well of you to Greg."

"Oh, I didn't realize ... well, then." She looked away and laughed softly, though her warm brown eyes showed a touch of uncertainty. "I hope we live up to your expectations."

"We? You're speaking in 'we' now? That has to be a good sign," I said with a grin as I sat next to her on the bed, outfit selection forgotten for the moment. "Tell me everything! I promise I won't cough on you."

Viviana didn't speak at first and instead played with her wavy brown hair, and I frowned. It wasn't the first time I suspected she didn't really trust me. It was as though we weren't truly friends on an equal level but were still mentor/mentee as we'd been in college. I'd been a junior who still hadn't chosen a major when we met, and Viviana had been in the master's English program. We'd become fast friends as she guided me through my newly declared English major and capstone, among other things. Things I'd prefer to forget.

"Well, there isn't much to tell," she said at last. "Gregory is Gregory. Rude, cold, but also unfairly hot." We both laughed. He was definitely all those things and probably worse. He was a snob of the highest degree. But the hot/cold thing was kind of intriguing to her, I could tell. And I couldn't blame her—I'd probably be a bit smitten myself if Brandon hadn't occupied all my thoughts lately. "It's just—"

I didn't hear the rest as I began to cough again.

Stupid, stupid cough.

I can't be getting sick. I just can't.

"Annie, are you sure you're OK to go out tonight? I'm sure Ellen would be fine with you sitting this one out," Viviana said, her brows furrowed as she searched my face, which likely featured a reddened nose and tired eyes by now. She picked up a water bottle from her nightstand and took a sip.

I scowled. "You're changing the subject. You know, you're not as good at that as you think you are."

She nearly spit out her drink and laughed. "Well, maybe, but you really do seem ill. I *am* starting to worry about you."

"I'll be fine." I walked back over to the closet, dodging the piles of clothes I'd discarded on the floor because they weren't up to my party standards. "I would press you for more deets, but I need to focus. I wish we had time to go shopping. You just don't give me much to work with here, Viv. And I—*achoo!*—I still have to do my hair, but we *will* continue this conversation later," I warned. If I was going to find the perfect dress for my friend in this dated, minimalist wardrobe, I was going to need my full concentration and creativity. I sighed, looking again between the discarded heap and what remained in the closet before a series of sneezes overtook me.

Early on at the party, hosted at Ellen's more than comfortable house in the neighboring city of Edina, Viviana looked increasingly concerned as my coughing worsened. She and Brandon traded looks before encouraging—no, commanding—me to go home.

"We haven't even eaten yet," I pouted, though I had no appetite. Honestly, I hadn't been able to taste or smell food all day. Viviana was right; I *was* feeling progressively worse, and it was becoming harder to hide it. But I couldn't bring myself to miss a party with my potential soulmate, could I?

"Annie, babe, I think Viv's right. You should call it a night. You look ..." When Brandon saw me blanch, he backtracked. "I mean, you look gorgeous as always, even sick, but you *are* sick. You should go home and get some rest."

"Oh, I can't just abandon you. I'm fine!" I protested with all the feeling I could muster.

"You're not, love," he said. When he started lightly massaging my shoulders, I couldn't think of anything but his warm hands. "Go home—I'll bring you some chicken soup tonight after we're done here." His breath warm against my face, he added for my ears alone, "and maybe a real massage."

It's a good thing my face was likely already reddened from all the sneezing and congestion. "Oh, if you insist," I said, biting my lip to hide a smile. I sighed and looked at Viviana, forcing the fuzzy-headed feeling to clear before I spoke. "Be sure to keep Brandon company. Maybe if you're sober, you can give him a ride to my place afterward?"

Gregory appeared out of nowhere and offered to take Brandon home himself. "Brandon will be fine without you," he barked. "Go home before you infect the rest of us."

Although Brandon's best friend was being a jerk as usual, Gregory was probably just protective of his friend. I ignored him and pulled Brandon close. "I'm going to miss you so much," I whispered.

"Will you though? You'll be passed out on cold medicine," he said with a pouty expression and then chuckled. His hands roamed down my back until I giggled and pulled them away.

"Not now, hon. Germs, you know. We will have an epic makeup session when I feel better. Which will be tomorrow, if I have anything to say about it." I wanted to kiss him but settled for a forehead nuzzle and stepped away reluctantly.

Sighing, Viviana mumbled, "Probably too late for that."

"What—" I started to ask, but when I saw her glaring at Gregory, I shrugged. It wasn't worth interrupting whatever was going on between those two.

Chapter 2

"**S**he's alive."

"We don't have to pull the plug."

Through the fog of my mind and my blurry vision, I recognized the words and my two roommates sitting at the foot of my bed, looking bored. Rubbing my bleary eyes to clear away sleep, I revised my assessment. No, they were *trying* to look bored.

"Aww, how sweet. You guys were worried about me," I tried to say, though my voice was so scratchy that I doubt it sounded like any human language. Rafael came to arrange pillows behind me while I eagerly clutched the water bottle from the nightstand next to me.

In retrospect, I probably shouldn't have driven myself home last night. I was more than a little exhausted, and I fell asleep within minutes of taking nighttime cold medicine. *This stuff is nasty*, I remembered thinking just before passing out.

"I'll get you some more water," said Rainn, rearranging his Twins hat over his short, messy hair before heading to the kitchen with my water bottle.

"Do you need some, uh, soup?" Rafael asked, sounding uncharacteristically anxious. "Crackers, more meds, or something?"

Rainn pointed at the floor as he returned to hand me more water. "We stacked a few extra boxes of tissues next to the bed."

"At least let me tie up your hair, sweetie," Rafael said, not waiting for permission before he rearranged my matted hair into something resembling a messy bun or ponytail—I couldn't tell.

Rainn started to sit down but then jumped up. "Oh, how about some hot tea? I can go start the kettle."

"Can you guys just ... like, sit?" I asked, exhaling loudly as I grasped the blanket nearby, which was disturbingly damp. "All this movement is exhausting to watch."

They stared at me blankly. With his brow furrowed, Rafael ran his fingers through his black hair, streaked with blue. He glanced helplessly at Rainn, who had that look almost of a deer in the headlights, like when a woman talks about her period.

I rolled my eyes. They were the best roommates and the best friends, but they were such *guys* sometimes. "OK, so you've never seen me sick before. Blah, blah. I'm just like any other person. Stop being so weird." When they looked suitably chastised, I glanced toward the bedside clock. "Now what have—holy crap, it's 4 pm? Why did you let me sleep all day?"

When they didn't answer, I pursed my lips. "What? You both have a weird look."

"You were sick. And sleepy."

"And medicated."

"Well, yeah, obviously," I said impatiently while trying to stretch my achy limbs. "But the meds last eight hours, right? It's been, like ... I don't know how long. I'm still too fuzzy headed to do the math, but at least double that amount of time."

"Yeah, you slept a lot."

"I was asleep all that time?"

Silence.

"Well—" Rainn said slowly before Rafael jabbed him sharply in the ribs. "Pretty much."

I narrowed my eyes. "Out with it. What happened? You're both being ridiculous."

Silence.

Rafael came over to sit closer. "Annie, how about we talk when you're feeling better? I think you're going to feel so much better after some soup and more rest, maybe some trashy TV—"

"Out with it. Now."

He sighed. "I had to try." He looked at Rainn, who nodded reluctantly as he rubbed his square jaw.

"So, this is awkward, honey. But you wanted to know. So, uh, you did wake up this morning, and you were kind of loopy still, from the cold meds, we figured."

"OK," I said, looking back and forth between them. "And I did something embarrassing or ... what?"

"I wouldn't say that. But you saw something on Instagram that upset you, and you started wailing and quickly downed more cold meds. You weren't exactly incoherent at that point, but you wouldn't say a word to us, only buried yourself under the covers until the meds kicked in."

I heard nothing after the word *Instagram*. I wasn't sure how I continued to breathe. It all came rushing back to me. Him. A selfie at an airport. A boarding pass from NYC to MSP. Hashtags I wasn't familiar with. *Block. Block him.* I had to block him out. Nyquil. He didn't matter anyway. He meant nothing now. He *always* meant nothing. He was just a blip. I wouldn't see him if he did visit. If I did see him, who cared? I'd give him a dazzling smile, maybe a smirk. Or maybe I'd ignore him. Better yet, maybe I'd give him an apologetic smile. I did reject him, after all. *He probably hates me. And that's fine. I'd hate me too, if I were him. But I'm not. I'm me, and I'm awesome. Brandon thinks I'm awesome. I should call Brandon. Before this med makes me pass out. Calling Brandon. Grrr, it went to voicemail. Why isn't he answering? He never answers his phone. Well, I know people prefer texts. I prefer texts. But I wanted to hear his voice. I'm sure he'll stop by later. Because he's the one. HE is the one for me. He is, Brandon, not ...*

"So you'll be OK if we head to the gym?"

"What?" I looked up with a dazed expression.

"Rainn and I were going to head to the gym. You'll be fine, right? Brandon just texted that he's on his way," Rafael said, patting me on the head and pointing to the phone in my lap.

"Oh, uh," I mumbled, looking down slowly. "Sure."

"I heard my name," Brandon announced himself, walking into the room. "Rainn let me in. I was just on my way to a work dinner and picked up some soup and stuff for you."

"Aww, that was sweet of you, Brandon," I said, smiling and hoping I didn't look too wretched, having not seen a mirror in almost 24 hours. Thankfully, the light was still somewhat dim. "Maybe we could fall asleep to a movie or something—"

"Sorry, I can't stay." He glanced away briefly as my face fell. "But I had to see you, babe."

I swallowed my disappointment, ever more painful with my raw, scratchy throat. "It's—I understand." I turned to see my roommates waving goodbye as they picked up their gym bags to leave.

"I, uh, brought you some chicken soup, lemon honey lozenges, let's see, what else," he said, looking down into the convenience store bag in his hand. "Cough syrup. You like cherry flavor, right, babe?"

"I like ..." I started to lie.

Since when am I some simpering miss, grateful for a man's every thought? I'm Annie York, and I tell it like it is.

"I'm actually allergic to artificial cherry flavor. It put me in the hospital when I was young." I'd never forget it either. In fact, my mother would never let me forget, as she had to miss a big society party because of it.

"Aww, babe, I'm sorry—" Brandon said, scratching his head of golden blond hair, probably wondering whether he was supposed to have already known this. Yes, I'd mentioned it once before, but we'd probably both been drunk. I tended not to talk about my mother unless I was under the influence. Two bad habits intertwined.

"Brandon, it's fine. I actually really appreciate that you got all this stuff for me. It's ..." I paused, feeling a big sneeze coming on. "It's really thoughtful of you. And I am probably still half drugged from the cold meds from this morning or whenever, but I, uh, have something important to say to you."

His eyes widened a bit, and he straightened his posture. "Uh, OK. I—are you sure now's the best time? I mean, you're not feeling well, and I have this work thing soon."

I smiled, ignoring his protests and wishing I could reach out and grab his hands. "It *is* the best time because you're here with me. We don't have to make a big thing of this right now. But I'm gonna say it anyway: I *think* I'm falling in love with you."

He stared at me, not in the usual way. His lips moved, about to form words, several times. Finally, he pressed his lips together and nodded vigorously. "Babe," he choked out. "Annie, that's—you're so sweet. So beautiful." He drew in a long breath and exhaled quickly while putting his hand to his chest. "For some reason, I'm the luckiest guy there is, Annie. I'm sure I'm not worthy of you. You're—"

"What?" I scoffed. "Of course you are. You're a damn catch, and you know it. We both are. That's what makes us so perfect together." I laughed and leaned forward before forcing myself to stay back, wishing I could soothe him with a kiss.

"Perfect together, yeah," Brandon echoed, his eyes moving to his watch and then back to my face. "Annie, I know this is awful timing, but I have to jet. I can call you later, OK?"

My breath stalled.

Seriously? Now?

"You can, but there's a very good chance I'll be knocked out by some strong cold meds again. It's probably why you couldn't get a hold of me last night ... or this morning." I turned to discreetly wipe my nose before it could make a mess down my chin.

"I ... oh, right," he said quickly, turning to leave. "Get some rest and feel better, babe. Let me know when you're up for hanging out again."

"OK, have fun with the ..." I trailed off. He wouldn't hear me anyway, already out the door.

My face twisted into a grimace. Where were my roommates when I needed them? I wasn't a fan of extended introspection in general, and I definitely didn't want to succumb to it while sick.

There was plenty to overanalyze here.

Was this the wrong time for the confession?

Hmm.

What about his reaction to my confession?

He seemed shocked, as though ... as though this kind of thing wasn't a totally normal next step. At least for him.

But he seemed happy too, didn't he? He said he was the luckiest guy! Suh-woon.

He probably just needed time to process this. Maybe he'd never heard the L-word from a girl, or never even said it! Maybe I was his first. That wasn't a bad thing.

Regardless, why ... *why* did I choose this moment to make the confession?

Am I trying to push aside thoughts about something, someone else?

Trying to forget the past?

No, shut up, shut up, intrusive thoughts!

Was I capable of thinking clearly about anything right now? I sighed, sinking back under the covers.

I was just settling onto the couch with some microwaved soup when I heard a knock at the apartment door.

My heart raced. Had Brandon returned?

I imagined a grand scene with him waltzing into the room dramatically, announcing he'd forgotten to declare that he too was in love with me. I shook my head, smiling half-heartedly.

He probably just forgot his phone or something.

My eyes swept the area as I walked to the door to unlock it. Slowly. *I'd make him wait, just as he was making me wait,* I thought with a slight twist of my lips.

But when I finally opened the door, my face fell. Viviana stared back at me, taking in my gross sick-person look, no doubt. I greeted her, trying not to sound too disappointed, and returned to the couch while motioning for Viviana to follow.

"That bad, huh?" Viviana said, sitting on a nearby chair.

"Ya–yeah, I guess so," I tried to say through coughs. "I'm so embarrassed. This is so not me. I never get sick. Never."

Viviana nodded, her brows drawn together in pity. "That's true. Your immune system is legendary."

Not anymore, I thought, taking a sip of soup. For some reason, I was glad Viviana hadn't seen me at my *worst* worst, which was apparently last night or earlier today when I was heavily medicated.

"I'm glad to see I wasn't the first to bring you soup. Have Rafael and Rainn been taking good care of you?"

"Well, they're men, so not particularly. But they try, or at least they did before they had to go to the gym." I rolled my eyes. In truth, though, I'd been touched by their attentiveness, and not at all surprised. They were my best friends for a reason.

"They mean well."

"It had to be this week, didn't it?" I sighed, only to be overcome by a sneezing fit.

Viviana hid a smile, picking up some tissues from the floor.

"Brandon came by with some sick-person supplies. You just missed him—he came by just 10 minutes ago, maybe 15, I don't know. Or maybe an hour. Did you know that time is all warped when a person is sick?"

"You're lucky to have not experienced sick brain much in your life." Then she frowned and straightened. "Brandon was just here a bit ago? And he didn't stay and take care of you?"

I yawned and shook my head. "Oh, no, I wouldn't let him," I said, stretching the truth. "I didn't even want him to come over at all—he doesn't need to get sick from me, and he doesn't need to see me like this. When have I ever looked worse? Besides, he had an important work thing come up last night after the party, and it's been occupying all his time apparently." I eyed Viviana, who seemed to be watching me carefully, a bit warily. *Something's up.* "Did he mention the work thing to you last night? Oh, and how did last night go with Gregory?"

"He didn't mention ... that."

I noted Viviana's strange pause but shrugged. If Viviana had something to say or ask, she would. "Oh, well, how was the party anyway?" I asked.

"It was fine," she said. She seemed ready to say more but hesitated.

I didn't have the patience tonight. "Viv? I may be sick, but I'm not blind. Did something happen with you and Gregory?"

My impatience increased as my question was met with silence from Viviana and averted eyes. Finally, my friend spoke. "Annie, I don't know how to say this."

What the ...

My brows furrowed. "To say what? What happened? You can tell me anything."

"I know, it's just ... I'm not sure it's my place," Viviana said. She appeared to be on the verge of tears. "And you're already feeling so crappy. I would hate to make you—"

My eyes snapped up to hers. "What the—this is about me?" Just as I was about to demand answers, I suffered another coughing fit. Finally, I sat up straight and looked at my friend as clear-eyed as I could. "What's going on, Viv?"

"It's just ... He was, Brandon was, well, kind of—"

"Kind of what?"

"Flirty." Viviana lowered her eyes.

My first thought was horror, followed quickly by humor. She couldn't possibly be serious. With energy I didn't know I still had, I burst into laughter until I had to blow my nose. But when Viviana still faced me with a grimace, my smile faded.

She can't be serious. Is she?

Dammit, Viv. I don't need this right now.

I rolled my eyes with deliberate calm. "You're serious? Come on, this is Brandon; he's naturally very friendly to women, to everyone. Haven't you noticed that about him before? It's part of his charm."

Viviana chewed her lip, still looking at her lap. "I suppose. But—"

"He comes across as flirty, but I don't think he means it that way. In fact, I know he doesn't. It doesn't mean anything. Trust me, I know the difference. I've *felt* the difference," I said, adding a forced laugh.

My timing was awkward again as I had to stop to blow my nose, with Viviana sitting rigidly and watching me, obviously waiting to say more. "Annie, I … I know the difference too. It was—it was more than that. He was actually coming on to me."

I gasped.

She looks like she believes what she's saying.

"You have got to be kidding. Please tell me you're kidding. You don't seriously think *he* would be interested in …"

OK, maybe that was mean. Why did I go there?

Viviana crossed her arms, beginning to look defensive. "In me? Well, I wouldn't have thought so, but I know what I saw. I didn't imagine this. Gregory saw it too."

A thick silence settled between us before I finally spoke. "Ah, that's it. This is about Gregory, and things are not going the way you'd like." Resentment bubbled up within me. "I can't believe I'm saying this, but *you* … you are jealous."

Viviana recoiled as if struck. "I can't believe I'm *hearing* this. You think I would dream this up just because I'm hurt about what's going on with Gregory? Which I'm not, by the way. Things are going great. My love life is fine!"

I tried to focus on what she was saying, but it was getting harder. Exhaustion was setting in. When had I last taken medicine? I couldn't remember. I stood up, feeling a little dizzy as I headed to the kitchen. "We're done here. I don't know what's gotten into you, but I don't have the energy for it right now."

"I can't even … You don't believe me? Why would I lie? Why would—" She stopped as I turned back toward her. She seemed to be taking deliberately slow breaths, her face reddening in anger. "You know what, it doesn't matter. Forget I said anything. I was trying to be a good friend. I'm *always* trying to be a good friend to you." By that point, I had already turned back toward the kitchen, but I still heard Viviana's last comment: "And it's a thankless job."

In a flash of fury, I turned and pointed to the door. "Just *go*," I said as forcefully as I could, even though my throat was sore and phlegmy. "I think I need a break from this 'good friend' that you think you are." I shot her one last piercing glare before turning to escape to my bedroom.

Before I could decide whether to turn around to ensure Viviana had actually left, I heard the slamming of the front door as it shook the walls.

What the hell was that? What the actual ...

I'd never seen Viviana like that. Ever.

Surely Viviana had never seen *me* like that either.

We'd never really had a fight.

Not really. Not openly, anyway.

I gripped the doorway, feeling weaker and more than a bit dizzy now. Was it the stupid cold, the meds, the argument, or ...

All of the above.

It's a wonder I'm still upright.

Why am I still upright?

Remembering I'd left my phone and supplies on the couch, I walked slowly over to retrieve them. I clutched my head, which was not only spinning but throbbing, and sank onto the couch in relief. Suddenly my bedroom seemed so far away and the well-used couch so comfortable. I could just stay here for a while. Maybe just to snooze a bit.

Hopefully I'd wake up and find that this was all just a terrible dream.

Chapter 3

"**N**o, I don't swim!" A hand gripped my forearm, which was damp from exertion.

"Please, please," I mumbled, fighting out of his grip. "No, I can't swim, get me out of the water, it's so much, these—these sheets of water. It's all over me."

"OK, Annie, I promise you—" said a strong male voice, and I felt a tug in the water.

"No! No, don't pull me under. I ... please. Please help me," I cried, writhing around in the dampness, trying to pull myself out. "No, no, no, not swimming, I can't ..."

Suddenly I felt a tickle. In my ear, of all places. "Annie. *Annie!*"

I stilled.

I knew that voice. I knew this ... this place. Wait, it wasn't a body of water. I was wet. But I was in my bed. My bed was drenched, and my skin was slick with sweat and who knew what other bodily fluids from being ill. I shifted my head toward the voice.

"Rainn?"

"The one and only."

"What is happening to me?" As I looked at him, my eyes filled with tears. "Am I ... dying?"

His face broke into a smile. His reddish-brown hair was sticking out of his hat, as usual, and he looked tired but still as handsome as ever. "Hell no, as if I'd let that happen. Your fever broke. Obviously. Haven't you ever been sick before?"

Confusion washed over me, followed by relief and then embarrassment. I fought the urge to burrow under the pillow. "Oh. Right." An awkward silence ensued as I assessed my surroundings, wet sheets and blankets cast aside in every direction and damp spots all over the bed, especially on my pillow. "I probably need a shower, eh?"

"I mean, maybe? Sure?" He made a face, the I'm-a-guy-don't-ask-me face.

I glanced at the time on the clock. 1:30 pm. More time lost to illness. But as soon as the events of last night came rushing back, I began to wish I were still passed out. I wasn't ready to face, well, anything. Least of all—

"Annie, uh, do you want to talk about the fever dreams?" he asked, scratching his head. "I mean, you don't have to, but they were kind of intense. And not just this one, but this morning and ... last night."

I winced. What I could remember of this dream had something to do with my fear of swimming, not something I liked to admit to anyone. Not even my roommates. And who knew what other fever dreams I'd had but couldn't remember? "Um, can we just, uh, do that some other time?"

Maybe never?

Rainn visibly relaxed, his shoulders down as he leaned back a bit. "Yeah, sure." He crossed his legs on the bed. "So what do you want to do today? I've got the whole day free, so I can keep you company or go buy you soup or whatever you want. Sorry we ditched you yesterday for the gym. We both felt kinda bad after that. But then we figured you'd had a better time with Brandon than your lame old roommates anyway."

I tried to smile despite the queasy feeling rising within me.

Brandon.

Had he tried to call or text me?

Did I want him to?

I knew, I just *knew*, deep down, that there was a slight chance Viviana wasn't making up everything. Wasn't imagining everything. I *knew* it was possible. But I couldn't face that, even the *possibility* of that, last night. Or now.

"Did—did he stop by? Brandon, I mean?" I asked, trying to sound casual while tracing a pattern on the only dry part of the pillowcase.

"Not that I know of—hey, you look like you're going to hurl. Can I get you a bucket, or, like, some salted crackers or something to munch on? Pepto?"

The room did seem a little spinny, now that I considered it. I shook my head, choosing instead to just lay back down on the bed. "I'll be fine. You can check on me later."

"Annie, are you OK? Are you sure you don't need anything?" His own forehead was wrinkled in concern as he put his hand on my face, but I couldn't bring myself to care. I rolled over, pulling some nearby blankets over me. They felt clammy, just like I did, but they would do. I just needed a barrier between me and the outside world.

Chapter 4

I heaved a great sigh under the covers, face down.

Dry.

It was my first concrete thought as I registered the feel of my left cheek buried into the pillow.

A little rough-textured and scratchy.

But dry.

I tentatively sniffed the pillow. It didn't smell like vomit or sweat or any of the other horrific things I'd experienced in the past ... how many hours, or days? I had no idea.

I slowly turned my head and braced myself for the onslaught of light. Reluctantly, I opened one eye at a time. Swallowing felt impossible. I managed to rise, bracing myself with my hands, and then reached over to the nightstand for some water. My brow wrinkled as I saw the ice cubes floating in it.

I stilled. Someone had been in here recently.

After taking a quick sip, I grabbed my phone off the nightstand and sunk back under the covers. If my roommates came in, I'd feign sleep again. It wouldn't be a tough sell, surely, if I'd been passed out for ... how long?

I turned on my phone screen and saw ... Friday, March 26, 9:13 am.

Friday? I searched my brain frantically. I'd fallen ill on Tuesday. According to my phone, it was now Friday.

According to my phone. As if my phone is lying to me. What is wrong with—

Before I could sink into negative thoughts again, I watched as my unread text notifications appeared. I searched the list for one name, and my breath hitched when I didn't see it. Brandon hadn't texted? I looked at the notification list again—no voicemails either? Rainn said Brandon hadn't stopped by, but maybe he'd been at work. Rafael might have seen him.

He must have tried to see me. Or talk.

He cares about me. He does. Maybe even loves me.

Why did I sound like I was trying to convince myself, when there was never any doubt before? I exhaled sharply, my lips downturned in disgust.

Before I could continue this dark line of thinking, my stomach filled with dread as I read one of the waiting messages.

Jacqueline

> Anastasia, darling, you haven't rung me in so long.

I closed my eyes, as though I could shut out the feelings, but it only brought them into sharper focus. My mother was the very, very last person I needed to hear from right now. Or ever. There was no way on earth I'd be calling her back today. She would only make me feel worse about myself and then do what narcissists do best—turn all the attention onto herself.

She was toxic, to put it mildly, and I'd decided years ago to stop indulging her.

But it was easier said than done.

With a grimace, I deleted the message and started scrolling through the rest of the notifications before hearing a knock at the door. I quickly hid under the covers, face down while trying to breathe evenly to feign sleep. I couldn't help but notice how fresh the top blanket smelled. Clearly my roommates had gone to the trouble of laundering everything while I was passed out.

I could tell by the footsteps that it was Rafael. He was a dancer, his steps graceful and dramatic. He always sounded like he was floating across the floor. Besides, Rainn would be at work by now. I sensed Rafael standing by the bed for a moment, presumably assessing the situation, and then he floated out of the room.

After hearing the door close, I breathed a sigh of relief. This was beyond ridiculous, hiding from my roommates, but I needed time. Alone. I couldn't face their questions, their pitying expressions, their advice.

My phone buzzed.

Jacqueline

> Anastasia? You need to get better. I am losing my patience, and you know I'm usually the most patient person.

What the heck? How does Mom know I'm sick?

Annie

> Apparently you're aware I'm sick. I can't control that, Mom.

Jacqueline

> I had to get in contact with your roommate, the flamboyant one. He told me you have the sniffles or something. You always were so melodramatic.

I saw another new text notification but shut off the phone screen before I could read it, placing the phone back on the nightstand.

Burying myself back under the covers yet again, I waited for the tears to fall. I needed to cry, didn't I? What a pathetic state I was in, what a terrible week this had been. But I couldn't feel. My eyes were as dry as my newly pressed top sheets.

When had I ever been so steeped in misery that I couldn't even cry? I had always been an expressive person. I was always—

Well, except *then*.

The other time, when there were no more tears left. No more booze. No more pills. No more love. No more anything, except numbness.

It was emptiness.

It was life without him.

It was life without us.

The biggest mistake of my life.

A life, now empty.

All empty, all agony.

No hope.

But it can't be agony if it's numb, right?

I pushed the searing, long buried thoughts aside and focused on the large ceiling tiles above me, meditating on their dull white pattern. I turned to my side, pressing my cheek into the pillow and giving in to the bleakness of dry eyes, of having nothing left to feel.

Or nothing I had to acknowledge.

Numb.

Good.

Beep.

"Let me try it, just in case you did it wrong."

Beep.

"OK, 98.4."

I swatted their hands away from my forehead.

"Ouch!"

"Our girl has her strength back."

I pulled the covers over my head, burrowing deep within.

If I ignore them, they'll go away. It's worked for, what, three days now? Something like that. Or maybe four by now.

Who knows. Who cares.

"Annie, if you don't come out of hiding, we're coming in."

They wouldn't dare.

But they would. Before I had a chance to rethink my plan, I felt the weight of the two men on the bed, joining me under the covers.

"Hey, girl," said Rafael, cozying up to me on my right, nose to nose, while Rainn arranged himself snugly on my left. It's a good thing I had zero attraction to either of these guys (and the feeling was mutual), or else this would've been pretty awkward for all involved. At one time I decided I *should* be into Rainn, who was straight and admittedly hot and thought the same about me, but our one attempt at dating was a massive failure. Zero sparks. Less than zero, even. He made an awesome BFF though. Co-BFF, that is. Rafael and I went way back, and if friends could be soulmates, he would be mine. But he'd been in a serious relationship for quite a while, so he wasn't available as often now. It had, in truth, been a good opportunity to get closer to Rainn. He and I were like night and day, yet somehow as friends we just clicked. It didn't help that he was the sweetest guy in the universe.

But right now, I didn't want the company of my friends. Or anyone. I needed to be left alone.

"Guys, I—" I coughed, clearing my throat of all the days' worth of sleepy mucus or whatever it was that built up in people's throats when they're sick. "Guys, I mean this in the best possible way, but please, get lost. Leave me to my misery."

Rainn's arms wrapped around me from behind. "Nope."

Rafael spoke softly. "We have left you alone. For too long, I think. It's time to rejoin the world. You don't have a fever, and you're coherent. You're not looking or smelling like death, as far as I can tell, though it *is* hard to see under here. But you still haven't showered, have you?"

I felt panic rising within me. "Guys, please. I just need you to leave me alone. Get *out*—"

And that's when my voice broke, and my eyes burned. Shudders wracked my weakened frame, and I was helpless to do anything but ride them out as Rainn held me tight, as Rafael took my hand in his. With his other hand, he gently wiped the lone tear streaming down my cheek toward the pillow.

No one spoke.

It might have been an hour or two, lying together, just like that. Or ten minutes. I had no idea. When Rafael finally flipped the blanket up, I was relieved to feel the air on my skin. Adjusting to the light was a bit more difficult though. I squinted, noting that the sun was rising and realizing I'd slept another 24 hours. I vaguely remembered taking more cold meds despite not really needing them anymore. At least not for my physical symptoms.

I sat up slowly, relieved to find that my head wasn't pounding. Rainn propped up some pillows behind me as Rafael left the room, saying something about food.

When he returned, he carried in a massive tray of breakfast foods. "They're all cold now, but oh well."

"Aww, guys, you didn't have to ..." I trailed off, biting my lip. "I'm not sure if I'm even hungry."

"Oh, it's not just for you," Rafael said, tilting his head as he eyed the selection. "I'm ravenous."

"Same," Rainn said, grabbing some cold sausage links from the tray. "I forgot to eat before running this morning."

"There will probably be no food left for you, Annie," Rafael said, his eyes twinkling.

My mouth twitched at the corners. "Fine, I guess I'd better take a bite of something before it's too late." I grabbed a piece of toast, nibbling on the edge. What was the last thing I'd eaten? Had I eaten at all? I sighed. So much about the past few days was a blur. But that wasn't necessarily a bad thing.

I'd intended to take only a few bites of toast, but I promptly devoured a whole slice. My appetite now stimulated, I gazed at the tray, deciding whether to have more toast or a boiled egg.

"Talk to us, Annie."

My stomach sank at my oldest friend's words, and my gaze as well as my hands dropped to my lap.

"Fine."

I took a deep breath and made eye contact with each of them in turn. Worried frowns marred both of their faces, as though I was about to tell them someone had died.

I need to put a stop to this now, and stop being dramatic. Yes, I've had a crap week, but it happens.

Directness was always best, right?

The words spilled out. "So, I told Brandon I might be in love with him, Viv told me Brandon hit on her and we had a big fight, I haven't heard from Brandon at all, my mom is awful, my ex—" I shook my head slightly. "Worst of all, I've been sick. I'm never sick. I hate it."

They looked at me, wide-eyed.

"That's it," I said with forced calm. "Satisfied?" I reached out and picked up another piece of toast, proceeding to chew on the crust. "Oh, and who knows what's going on with work. Ellen's probably furious with me for whatever work assignments I'm late on. I haven't bothered checking my messages from her."

"Back up. I don't care about Ellen." Rafael's eyes flashed with suspicion. "Brandon did *what*?"

"Well, according to Viviana, he came on to her at the party after I went home sick," I said, laughing to show them it didn't really bother me. "As if."

When they said nothing, I examined their expressions more closely. Both of them looked shell-shocked, but also angry. No, not angry. Livid. Like they could kill someone.

"You don't … you don't believe her?" Rainn asked, his voice strained.

"Of course not," I said, waving my hand flippantly. "Brandon comes across as flirty, but he'd never flat-out hit on my friend. You know that."

Rafael opened and closed his mouth several times before finally speaking. His voice sounded different, pained. "Annie."

"What?"

His fists were clenched, a rarity for him. "Believe her."

"*What?*"

"You've known her how long?" Rainn asked, his voice tight. "Why would she lie?"

"I—she—" I sputtered. My eyes veered back and forth between my best friends.

"Don't ask me how I know, Annie," Rafael said slowly. "It's not really something I can put into words. But I feel certain Viv's telling the truth."

There was a sharp intake of breath, and I thought it was from Rainn, but it might have been my own. I was faintly aware of a tremble overtaking me. I might have said, "No," but I couldn't be sure my voice was even audible.

"Annie, I know this sounds super blunt and ... not what you want to hear," Rafael said, his eyes pleading with mine when I dared to look at him. "I'm really sorry for that."

"You deserve better, dammit!" Rainn's fists were clenched. "I'm going to find him and beat his—"

Rafael put a calming hand on Rainn's thick, tense forearm. "Settle down, muscle man. She probably doesn't need that right now."

"Not yet. Let me have my pity party first. Then you can beat him up for me. Or call for a duel." When Rainn's eyes widened, I added, "I'm kidding, of course. About both things. Violence is for the weak."

Suitably chastised, Rainn looked down, trying to relax his fists. After a long moment, I said, "But what am I, if not weak? I mean, look at me."

My heart sank as I flopped down sideways onto the pillow and turned my face into it. Somewhere inside, I knew they were right. He was a player, and I hadn't seen it.

How did I not see it? Weak, weak, weak.

"You, weak?" Rafael laughed. "She's still high on cold meds."

"You guys!" I sat up, brushing rumpled hair out of my eyes. "I told him I *loved* him. The night after he tried to cheat on me. Or—" My eyes widened. "Oh no, Raf, what if Viv wasn't the only one?"

Rafael's features were filled with sympathy. Pity, really.

"What am I saying?" I shook my head. "Of course she wasn't the only one. Not with a guy like that. What an idiot I am. How could I ... I didn't see the signs. How did I not see it? I never see it coming. I mean, maybe sometimes there are hints and I just, like, don't care because I'm having fun. But I really didn't see any hints. Were there hints of him being a jackass player?" I looked between the two men, my eyes vulnerable and full of unshed tears.

They looked at each other.

Rainn shrugged. "I thought he seemed like a nice guy, honestly. I didn't spend a ton of time with him though."

Rafael didn't speak at first. "He did seem like a nice guy. There was ..." he trailed off, looking at the ceiling thoughtfully. "There was something about him that always seemed a bit off to me. Maybe a bit false. Or, I don't know. I have no idea how to put it into words, so I guess that's why I didn't. I thought, I hoped, I was wrong." He frowned.

I stared into his dark brown eyes before nodding. Rafael occasionally had a vague sixth sense about a person, and he couldn't explain it. He was *always* right though, about these impressions. That's why I'd immediately believed him when he told me that Viviana was likely right about Brandon. Even though, with every fiber of my being, I hadn't wanted to believe it. I'd wanted to resist the truth—almost like I'd rather hate my good friend than lose a love so new, so promising, so full of hope. Was I that desperate?

No, I'm Annie York, dammit. Men always flock to me, more than I know what to do with. The opposite of desperate.

And yet ...

"So, violence is out," Rafael said, interrupting my thoughts. "How are we going to get back at him?" He and Rainn looked at me eagerly.

I shook my head slowly. "Not necessary. I think I made some wrong assumptions. That we were exclusive. That he was interested in anything serious. That's on me."

"Annie, please tell me you're being ironic."

"I'm not."

"Annie! You can't possibly think—"

"Don't give me some stupid spiel about how I deserve better and blah blah. I've heard it all before, many times. Usually from Viv. Maybe she was right about Brandon but wrong about me."

Rainn scratched his head. "That's ..."

"Total B.S.," Rafael said, clenching his jaw.

I crossed my arms. "Look, I appreciate everything you guys have done for me, but I know myself and I can take responsibility for my own role in disasters like this. I can ... put on my big-girl pants."

There was a moment of silence before Rafael said quietly, "You've been doing that far too long."

"Excuse me?"

His eyes flashed, but his voice was barely audible. "You heard me."

"What do you mean?" I shook my head. "Never mind. Case closed. This is—"

Rafael took a deep breath. "Jacqueline has been telling you to put on your big-girl pants since long before you were a big girl. You never had a chance to make mistakes, to have someone take care of you ... everything was always your responsibility, *always* your fault. Enough! We need to get her toxic, soul-sucking voice out of your head once and for all!" By the time he'd finished, he was shouting.

My breath caught as I reared back. Rafael and I had, of course, talked about Mom many times in the many years I'd known him, but he'd never erupted like this before. *He's right*, a voice inside whispered, faintly.

"I hope I never have to meet this woman," Rainn said menacingly. "Actually, she'd better hope that *she* never has to meet *me*."

After a beat, we all dissolved into slightly pained laughter. Despite Rainn's tough talk and muscular frame, he was a softie through and through. Born and raised in the South, he still had his Southern manners too, though he'd mostly left the accent behind.

I laughed until my sides ached, until I forgot what I was laughing about, until we all did, probably, until we forgot whether the tears streaming down our faces were tears of joy or sadness. Likely both.

"You guys, oh my gosh, what was that?" I asked between gasping breaths and giggles. Finally after some deliberately slow breaths, I steeled myself.

It was time to face this.

"You're right. Brandon's a jerk who treated me badly. So, how should I dump him?"

Chapter 5

"She's awake, showered, *and* making waffles?" Rainn said, walking into the kitchen to set his gym bag on the floor. He grinned, grabbing a steaming waffle off the plate. "My trainer isn't going to love this, but she doesn't have to know."

"She?" Rafael said, eyebrows raised. "Since when is your trainer a she?"

Rainn's cheeks turned pink. "Oh, I don't know. A while ago. Last Monday or something. Anyway—"

"What's her name?" I asked while pouring more batter into the waffle maker. "Bertha?"

Rafael bit his lip to keep from laughing.

"I'm not telling!" Rainn said. He shook his head with a lopsided grin. "And I just realized how sixth grade that just sounded. Whatever, guys. It's just the gym. No big deal." He turned to head out. "Annie, I'm so, so glad you're feeling better. Catch you guys later!"

I waited until Rainn had closed the door and the remaining waffles were plated. "Hey, Raf?" I sat on a stool next to him and licked syrup off my fork.

"Yeah?" He took his first bite of the largest waffle, closing his eyes with satisfaction. "These are amazing as always. You *look* amazing as always. Of course, only you would recover from a hellish week like this in such, well, amazing form. But I wonder if you feel as amazing as you look. Maybe not?" He put his fork down and frowned, eyeing me closely.

"Eh, I've been better. Not great, not terrible, I suppose," I admitted. It was the truth. I was glad to be 80% over the viral symptoms, with only a few lingering nasal congestion issues, which I now knew (after a lot of internet searching) was normal after the first few days of a cold or flu. I was still a little tired but had most of my energy back. My appetite was low; the syrupy waffle tasted good, but I was nearly full already. There was no trace of the fever, chills, nausea, or aches that made me feel like death earlier in the week. How did people survive getting sick all the time? I thought of my friend Jenn Weston, who got sick all the time because of her two young children who brought all the germs home. Well, Jenn was really Viviana's friend. She was friendly to me—and actually a lot of fun—but we only knew each other through Viviana.

Viviana ... that's what I needed advice on.

"I am wracking my brain about how to deal with Viv. Like, I know, logically, she was right. I mean, she was *wronged*, in a sense. Brandon was a slimeball to her, apparently. Probably Gregory isn't much better, if I'm really honest. Maybe he's worse. He doesn't even pretend to be nice. But at least that makes him honest ... maybe? I don't know."

Rafael raised his eyebrows and tilted his head. "So, what's the issue?"

With my nostrils flaring, I tried to figure out how to ask what I needed to ask. "Well, I don't know ... what to do about her. I mean, do I need to, um, tell her she was right? Apologize? Beg her to stay friends with me after the awful way I threw her out?"

He searched my face for a long moment and then took a few leisurely nibbles of his waffle. "I get the feeling you don't want to apologize, or maybe you aren't sure you need to. Are you thinking that your ... reaction to her was somehow justified?" he asked, doubt written across his face.

My brow wrinkled.

Maybe this was a mistake.

"Hey, I won't judge," he said, "or I'll try not to. I promise you, I'm always on your side. As if I even have to tell you that." He punched me lightly on the shoulder before swallowing another bite of waffle.

"I know." And I did. My sigh was long and pained. "I'm just not even sure what to say, honestly. I was super harsh to her, and that wasn't cool. She didn't deserve that from me, and she didn't deserve to be propositioned by Brandon either. I'm sure that made her really uncomfortable, knowing her. She doesn't pull off casual flirting well even under the best of circumstances. And normally I don't have a problem apologizing when I mess up. Right? Like, I'm cool with that usually. And yet ... I feel like I'm not ready to talk to her. I don't know why. Or at least ..."

"You don't know if you know why."

"Yes!" My eyebrows shot up. "How can you know me that well?"

Rafael gave me a dazzling smile before running a hand over his dark hair with the royal blue streaks. "How can I not? I'm fabulous and so are you."

I tried but failed to produce a smile, so I stabbed the waffle on my plate. "Not feeling so fabulous though. So ... do you have any theories?"

He bit his lower lip. "Hmm. I do, but I want to hear yours first."

"All right," I said uncertainly. "I think I'm ... um, feeling some resentment ... from the past. Some unresolved stuff. It's actually kind of a vague feeling that's hard to really nail down."

He nodded repeatedly. "Yes, yes. I was getting that vibe. I think we can be a little more specific than that though, can't we?"

"What—what do you mean?" My voice shook as I feared what he'd say next.

What if he brings up ... no, why would he suddenly bring up Kylan? He wouldn't have seen the Instagram post, would he? The one with my ex, flashing the plane tickets next to his face. The tickets that looked like round-trip tickets, but it was hard to tell, even zooming in. They had to be, right? He wouldn't want to come back here. Maybe he's already gone by now. And his face.

Oh, man, his face.

That strong jaw, his lips curved in that tiny almost-smile he wore when he thought no one was looking, his short yet fluffy hair, the steel eyes that somehow managed to look both intense and amused at once.

I shook my head.

But surely Rafael wasn't following him on socials, right? He wouldn't have seen the post.

My stomach twinged with regret. I wished I hadn't brought up any of this. At all.

Rafael studied me for what felt like hours until he seemed to make a decision. "You resent her for meddling in past relationships, and you've never really addressed it with her, so it's finally come bubbling to the surface. You don't feel like you can express the feeling now because it's not that relevant to the current situation. This time, she wasn't meddling, like, pushing you toward or away from Brandon, but rather telling you something that you really needed to know."

I sighed. It was annoying how spot on he always was. "You get it. Yeah, it feels really unfair to bring up a bunch of old issues that have nothing to do with this Brandon thing, which wasn't her fault at all."

Yes, Brandon. This is only about Brandon. No one else. Not some old fling.

In his eyes, I saw something, a hesitation, a serious look that suggested he wanted to say more, but he closed his mouth before taking a long swig of apple juice. Fearing what he might be afraid to say, I filled the silence instead. "So what do I do?"

"This is a tough one. I feel like you should say *something* to her. To let her know you're not mad, that you're not *that* crazy—" He yelped when I punched him in the shoulder. "I mean, not crazy at all. *A-hem.* Anyway, I do think you need some space from her, and that's your right, girl. Maybe eventually this resentment stuff has to be brought out into the open. Or not, whatever you decide, but you don't have to decide right now." He eyed me for a moment before adding, "Just have some space, girl."

I bumped shoulders with him. "It's like you read my mind and knew exactly what I wanted you to say ... before I even knew myself."

He pursed his lips before nibbling on another waffle. "Of course. It's one of my many talents."

I grinned. "Any plans after class today?"

"Lunch at Joel's parents' house," he said after swallowing a mouthful. "Why do you make this stuff so delicious? I'll never fit into my leotard."

My eyes widened. "His *parents'* house? That's new, right? I know you've met up with them, but is this your first invite to their house?"

Rafael nodded, turning to me with an anxious expression. "Oh, *Annie.* How do I not bungle this?"

"As if you could," I said, giving him a reassuring smile. "You can charm anyone. *Anyone.* If anyone should be nervous, it's them. They should be trying to impress *you.* You're a 10, Raf."

He twisted his lips in a thoughtful manner and then nodded. "Yep, you're right. I am. Thanks, girl." He flashed his winning smile, the one that charmed everyone he met, and then sashayed away to clean up the dishes. After a moment, he glanced back at me, still facing my plate of barely eaten waffles. "What about you? Any plans for today?"

"I should check in with work emails and dig myself out of whatever hole I'm in with Ellen. I think at least one editing job is late, or maybe she's reassigned it by now. I should probably text her." I groaned just thinking about having to deal with all of that. My job was OK. I didn't hate it or love it. I liked Ellen, most of the time. But it didn't inspire passion, and it wouldn't give me the strong distraction I needed right now.

Rafael stilled, his only movement in his eyes, which also stilled once they met mine. After a long moment of silence, he suddenly laughed. "Oh, you're joking."

I tilted my head in confusion and smiled weakly. "Uh ... sure?"

He stared at me, and then his jaw dropped. "*Annie!* You can't work for that Bolder trash. What are you thinking?"

I gasped. "Oh, I ... it didn't even cross my mind. I guess in my mind I've kept work and my personal life so separate for the longest time that I didn't connect the dots ... well, they've never been connected before." I scowled. "Rafael, it's my *job* though. Like, my source of income."

"Girl, I'd rather pay your rent than see you spend another day, another minute working for that garbage human."

"I'm touched."

"I mean it, Annie. You need to cut ties, and this is part of it. You can find another job. And, I mean, you ..."

"I what?"

Rafael sighed, sitting down on the kitchen stool next to me again. "Maybe this isn't the right time, or maybe it is," he said in a gentle tone he didn't use often with me. Or anyone. And then, he suddenly shifted to a blunt tone. "You don't even like that job. Admit it. You never really have. It's just a paycheck, a decent one, but that's it."

How many times was I going to be blindsided this week? I blinked and drew in a deep breath. "So many truth bombs. Good thing resilience is my jam. Oh, man, what a dork I've become, editing so many psych books lately," I said, with a slight chuckle. I rested my chin on my hands and digested what he'd said.

He's right.

Being a copyeditor was OK. I didn't hate it, but I didn't love it. I didn't even like it much. It really wasn't *me*. I was good at it, I supposed.

"I wonder if Viv will quit contracting for Bolder too," I wondered aloud. "I didn't get the sense she was flattered by Brandon's attention. She seemed pretty disgusted actually. But then there's the thing with Gregory, so I dunno. Well, that's her issue, not mine."

"Exactly, boundaries," Rafael said, holding up both hands briefly. "I always wondered if she's the reason you stayed there so long. I get that you needed some work out of college, and I thought it was awesome for her to hook you up with that gig, but I never expected you to keep doing it for more than a few months. I mean … did *you*?"

I shook my head slowly. "I don't know what I expected, really. I just … knew I needed to finish my degree and get a job and—and not let anything get in the way."

"Or anyone."

"Or anyone," I whispered, trying unsuccessfully to think of the half-smile on the face of that unfairly handsome man holding up the plane tickets. I drew in a deep breath. I hadn't told anyone this before. "You have to understand. I didn't want to be like my mother and just … just blindly follow men around the world. I needed to do something for me, get an education, a career, a life, for myself. That's all that mattered."

Rafael nodded sympathetically, as though none of this was a revelation. Either he knew me so well he'd guessed at this or I'd confessed these thoughts before while intoxicated—both highly likely. "So instead of doing what your mother wanted or what some man wanted, you did what … Viviana wanted."

I sighed. "Yes and no. I needed guidance, I really did. She gave me a path, and maybe it wasn't the best one, but it was better than the alternatives at the time. She was trying to help. I just … I don't know why I stayed on the path this long. Four years, I think?"

As my mentor when we both attended the University of Minnesota, Viviana had made me realize that I was actually pretty good at editing and writing, which is what led me to the English major and then to the freelance editing gig for both of us at Bolder.

And away from a life of unknowns with Kylan.

Viviana talked me out of making a huge mistake, throwing my life away to follow him across the country on a pipe dream.

Rafael looked like he had a burning question he was holding back. Then, he suddenly turned to the clock and gasped. "Annie, you're going to make me late! I need to dress for class."

"Sorry," I said, rising to finish cleaning up the kitchen. "Good talk though."

"We can keep talking," he said as he darted into his bedroom. Then he swung his head back out. "Hey, want to come along? The Saturday ballet class is my favorite, actually."

"Oh, I'm so out of practice—"

"You haven't visited the school lately," he said, with pouty eyes and lips. "Anyway, it's a beginning class, so it's not like you'll need to demonstrate a fouetté. Though, knowing you, you probably could."

One of the few things I didn't resent my mother for was forcing me to take ballet as a child. It was grueling at times, and sometimes I hated it, but I grew to mostly love it, and devotion to the art was one of the things that had gotten me through some of the harder years of adolescence. Of course, by that point, my mother wasn't very supportive of the pursuit, as she realized it was claiming my attention and thus suiting her daughter's needs rather than serving her own goals. *That* was never something Jacqueline could handle very well. Fortunately, Rafael's parents had helped support my love of dance when my mother would not. For a while, they even helped me pay for lessons and drove me to class when my mother refused—but only until Jacqueline found out, because then she was horrified and refused to have anyone think she couldn't afford ballet class for her own daughter. The monthly checks were never an issue again after that.

Rafael had been such a natural at dance that he'd gone on to co-found and co-manage a dance school, which he continued to teach at, even on weekends. I had occasionally joined him for a class here and there, but it had been months. Maybe even a year or more. I was beyond proud of him for his ingenuity and success at such a young age—we were only 26. What had I accomplished in that time? Besides a string of casual relationships, a party girl image, a job that paid the bills and not much more, and a couple of amazing best friends who were roommates now but would eventually get married and leave me all alone?

"I'm going to pass this time, Rafael," I said, averting my eyes. "I am still recovering from the worst cold ever."

After he furrowed his brows and ducked into his room, I shouted, "I promise you, next time!"

When he came out, dressed in his black and pink tank and purple tights, he walked over to me and enveloped me in a hug that nearly stole my breath. "I'll be dragging you there next time. You relax here and get better, do you hear me? I love you, girl." When he released me, he jogged to the door, mumbling about being late.

Once the door closed, without realizing what I was doing, I started taking steps toward the center of the room. Of their own accord, my legs arranged themselves in fourth position and then into a plié, and then I executed a perfect pirouette. Or nearly so. *Might as well try a fouetté. I'll probably land on my butt, but no one's around to see.* But again, my muscle memory proved intact, and I managed a fouetté turn, stumbling only a little. But I began to feel dizzy and … oh, right. I was supposed to be taking it easy, a little, since I was recovering from a viral illness. I sighed. It was probably time for another nap. At least the guys had been thoughtful enough to wash all my bedding, so it wasn't quite as abhorrent to return to that bed yet again.

Settling into my room, I realized I wasn't that sleepy, though I knew the nap would be good for me. At least, my mind wasn't sleepy, though my body probably was. My eyes wandered over to the bookshelf in the corner of my room. I rarely made time for reading anymore. Between working, socializing, adulting, and spending time with Brandon, there wasn't much time for reading, as I often told myself.

But the truth was, reading was somewhat bittersweet for me. I absolutely loved to read, always had. I'd discovered this wasn't the most common trait among extroverts, yet I was a book-loving extrovert. But sometimes reading brought back painful memories that were hard to deal with.

Reading reminded me of my father. Anders Martin was often away on business or working long hours, but when I did see him, he always read to me. Reading was our thing, whether just the two of us or attending a library reading group for kids. He died of a heart attack when I was only six years old, and ... my world shattered. As if it wasn't hard enough to deal with my mother before that, I'd truly loved my father and felt his loss keenly. Shortly after his death, my mother changed both our last names to York, her maiden name, because she said it was more sophisticated than Martin. I wasn't even allowed to express my grief, as my mother wouldn't tolerate it. She insisted on happy moods, fun, and pleasantness at all times—except of course when she was annoyed, and then I knew to stay far away from her.

Before I knew it, I was standing in front of the bookcase. I felt a pull I hadn't in a long time. Blinking back a bit of moisture in my eyes, I began to slowly scan and lightly touch the shelves, looking at old favorites and some unread ones. I expected a layer of dust on my fingers as I brushed the spines, but none appeared. Rainn or Rafael must have been more thorough in cleaning my room than I'd realized. I really owed those guys. Sure, they were my best friends, and that made them kind of obligated to make sure I didn't, like, die of a cold virus, but they went above and beyond. Dusting books? Who does that? I smiled.

I couldn't decide what to read; it had been so long. So I did what Dad and I used to sometimes do. He'd say, "Pick four randomly off the shelf, and then choose the one that calls to you the most." I closed my eyes and picked four off the shelf, one by one, selecting from different rows, and then carried them to the nightstand. I resisted the urge to reveal them and dive in to make a choice now; it was probably a good idea to get some rest first. For the first time in days, I felt excited about something, but my body was putting on the brakes. Fine, I'd slow down ... for a bit.

I was half asleep the next day when my phone buzzed repeatedly with text notifications. I'd forgotten to put it on silent; it wasn't something I'd worried about the past few days while I'd slept like the dead. If my phone was even on, I hadn't heard it.

I rubbed my eyes and yawned as I reached over for the phone on the nightstand. Instead of grabbing it though, I must have knocked it over, as it clattered loudly to the floor along with the books I'd set on the stand. I grunted, face-planting into the pillow and pulling the covers back over my head. By this point, though, I was awake enough and eventually climbed out of bed and looked at my phone. My eyes widened when I saw who sent the texts.

Brandon.

He wanted to know if I was feeling better and if I was free tonight.

I took a deep breath and sat cross-legged on the bed. This was it. Before I could second-guess myself, I fired off a quick text asking him to call me.

He called surprisingly quickly. "Annie, how are you doing? I was worried. You're not still sick, are you?" He did sound concerned.

Probably wanted to make sure I wouldn't pass anything on to him.

But his tone sounded sincere, I thought with a lump in my throat.

"Not really, I'm doing better. Pretty awful for a few days, but I feel like myself again," I said.

"Oh good, good," he said quickly. "So listen, I was going to be in your part of town and wondered if I could come over tonight?" He paused. "I would've come sooner, but I got dragged to this literary convention in Duluth with Gregory. Wish you'd been there. I missed you, babe."

Doubt began to rear its ugly head.

What if he was genuinely serious about me and just had a momentary lapse?

What if Viviana misinterpreted his intentions?

What if he realized he made a mistake and wants to come clean and apologize?

What if he realized he's in love with me too?

What if...

Be cool, dammit.

"I'd love to see you tonight, Brandon. I'm actually feeling a lot better, thanks for asking. Do you want to come over around 7 or 8 tonight?"

"Oh, babe, no, I have a work thing. It'll run late. I was thinking I'd stop over around midnight or so. Is that OK?"

Nope, he's a scumbag. Definitely a booty call.

And he'd done this before … how many times? I felt sick thinking about it. And then I had an idea. "Sure." I lowered my voice an octave. "I'll be waiting for you, babe."

"Wear the red bow thing. You know the one. I'll unwrap—"

"I just might," I said. "Later." And then I hung up, before I started to feel truly ill.

What had I seen in him? Had I been that oblivious? Or was he just a master player? I'd dated these types before, but usually I could spot them sooner (or Viviana spotted it for me), and we were using *each other*. Rarely was I *this* completely blindsided.

Rafael had seen it coming, but he had a weird sixth sense, so he didn't count. Viviana had seemed genuinely surprised, as had Rainn. Maybe Brandon *was* just really good at hiding his duplicitousness. So I wasn't just an idiot for falling for him.

I shook my head, trying to clear out the thoughts of that man. After tonight, I wouldn't think about him anymore. He wasn't worth it. Just like all the others in the past. Well, most of them.

Picking up the books that had fallen onto the floor, I lovingly placed them on the bed and leaned back against the headboard to look through them. I'd managed to select *Great Expectations* by Dickens, *The Love Hypothesis* by Ali Hazelwood, *Untamed* by Glennon Doyle, and *Persuasion* by Jane Austen.

Ugh, Austen. Another reminder of Viviana. She was obsessed with Austen. It was hard to think about Austen without thinking about Viv. *No thanks*, I thought, setting that one aside. Definitely in the "no" pile for now. The question now is whether I wanted a re-read or a new read. And then fiction or nonfiction? I'd read *Great Expectations*, of course, and loved it. I hadn't read Hazelwood's rom-com book yet, but I'd heard excellent reviews. Could

I really handle reading a love story right now though? I'd heard great things about Doyle too, though *Untamed* was a nonfiction, personal growth type of book—not really my usual style. But maybe my life was about to take some different turns.

Facing indecision, I set the books down and decided to venture out of my room to see if the guys were home.

"Hey girl," came Rafael's distracted voice.

"Guys."

"Hungry?"

"Starving, actually. Um. What are you doing?"

"Playing a game."

"Yeah, I can see that, but ..." I was at a loss for words. The guys never played board games. We didn't own any. None of us were board game-playing people. Viviana and her friends were. But not Rainn and Rafael.

And this game didn't look like Monopoly or Checkers. It looked like the nerdy kind of game. The kind I wouldn't touch with a ten-foot pole. Or ten-sided dice. Or whatever they called it.

It wasn't that I looked down on board game nerds. They were fun people, when they weren't playing their games. I just wasn't interested in those games myself.

Because of him.

I closed my eyes to try to shut out the memory—but it rushed in uninvited anyway.

His bedroom had smelled faintly of cedarwood and laundry detergent, with a tiny plastic dragon perched on his windowsill and stacks of hardcover books lining the floor like some kind of chaotic border. I'd sat cross-legged on his bed, laughing throatily as I tugged at his sleeve, hoping to distract him.

"Come on," I'd purred. "You seriously expect me to care about imaginary goblins right now?"

He'd just grinned—that maddening, dimpled, focused grin—and handed me a set of colorful dice that clicked together like candy. "You will. Trust me."

And, annoyingly, I had. Against all odds, I'd actually listened. I'd asked questions. I'd created a character. I'd even made up a ridiculous voice for her. He'd guided me through a battle scene so vividly that I forgot we were in his room and not trapped in some mythical forest with an enchanted sword.

By the time I looked at my phone again, it was almost 11 pm.

We hadn't kissed that day. He hadn't even touched me. But somehow, it had felt more intimate than anything else we'd ever done. And that—that was the problem.

No.

There is absolutely no point in thinking about that. About him. About a time long ago. About freaking board games. But ...

"Well, what brought this on?" I asked tentatively, resting my arms on the back of an empty chair.

"Oh, some guys at my new job play it every day at lunchtime. They invited me to play a few days ago, and I'm kind of hooked," Rainn said.

"And now he's forced me to play," Rafael said, rolling his eyes before they eagerly returned to study the board.

Rainn laughed. "You're the one that wanted to play a third time."

"Shut up, you dork."

"You're both nerds now," I said with exaggerated disappointment in my tone. "I should have seen it coming. You were both watching that *Star Wars* show last week, mandarin, or whatever it is."

Rafael looked outraged for a moment and then took a calming breath. "*The Mandalorian*. Whatever, Annie. I saw you with a big stack of books on your nightstand today. Maybe you're not as much of a party girl as you'd like us all to believe, eh?"

"Oh, that's way below the belt, Raf." I punched him in the shoulder lightly. "But as it happens, I do plan to do some reading. I have hours to kill before Brandon stops over tonight."

Both of them turned sharply toward me with eyebrows raised.

"Yeah, he called. For a booty call. And he's going to get ... the *boot*," I said, cackling as I kicked my foot out.

Rafael jumped up from his chair and hugged me, spinning me around. "That's my girl. I wish I could sit and watch, with popcorn. But you'll want it to be private, won't you?"

I nodded. "I was hoping you could send him into my room when he arrives. Make him think I'm waiting in there for him."

"Sure, what time?" Rainn asked, cracking his knuckles.

My lips twitched. "He said around midnight. And don't get any crazy ideas. I'm going to deliver the news Annie-style."

"Play the next game with us?" Rafael asked with pleading eyes, pointing to the empty chair. "We'll be done with this round soon."

"And now you're not even pretending to not be hooked," I said, shaking my head. "As appealing as that is, or isn't, I am going to read."

Rainn frowned. "But Annie—"

"OK, because I know you guys miss seeing me, I'll read out here on the couch." I flashed a dazzling smile, running my fingers through my hair while I turned to go fetch my books.

Pip had only just discovered he would be meeting Miss Havisham when my phone buzzed beside me on the bed. I drew in a steadying breath and looked at the text message. Brandon was on his way. I scanned the area for my bookmark, which I'd brought with me when I'd gone to read in my bedroom an hour ago. Finally, I found it and placed it lovingly within my worn-out copy of Dickens' classic. I'd decided to read *Great Expectations* after all, as I couldn't handle a romance happily ever after right now, and I definitely needed fiction. I couldn't recall every detail of the novel I'd read many years ago, but I was pretty sure Pip's love story didn't end well. And that was perfect.

Soon I heard voices outside my room, followed by a brief knock before he entered.

Brandon walked in, closing the door behind him quickly. I'd dimmed the lights, so it took a moment for his eyes to adjust. "Annie, hi. Oh, you … aren't wearing the red thing."

I steeled myself. I'd prepared for this conversation. I would play it cool if it killed me.

I kept my expression and my tone neutral. "I am not."

He shrugged and took a few steps forward. "Eh, it's OK. You're in bed. You know I like that." As he came closer, I could see even in the dimness his tongue licking the back of his teeth as his eyes glazed over. I was surprised he wasn't salivating. And I could smell the liquor on his breath, and something else too. Probably some woman's perfume.

He was disgusting.

"Brandon, I was hoping we could talk first."

His brows furrowed a bit, but he nodded. "Sure, yeah, of course." He sat on the bed, the dazed look in his eyes clearing a bit. "What's up, babe?"

"I didn't see you much this week." I watched his face for a reaction and paused to see if he'd offer any excuses for not checking in on me. He simply ran his fingers through his slightly tousled hair and stared at me, waiting for me to say more. "When I last saw you, I made a pretty big confession. Do you remember?"

He glanced at his lap and scratched his head. "Ah, I … I'm not sure—"

"I said I might be falling in love with you." I narrowed my eyes slightly as I watched him.

A look of shock or maybe panic crossed his face before he quickly pasted on his winning smile. "You did. Of course I remember. I'm such a lucky guy. It's, uh, it's part of the reason I came over."

"Oh?"

"I mean, yeah. Had to show my appreciation," he said with a grin.

"Your appreciation? That's an interesting way to put it." I kept my voice even and pretended to examine my nails before looking him square in the eye. "Usually when one person uses the L-word for the first time, a different kind of response is expected."

He couldn't hide his discomfort now, though he still tried. He quickly pasted on another smile and put his hand to his heart. "Well, of course, babe. You're so gorgeous, it was love at first sight for me."

I swallowed the disgust threatening to overtake me.

He reached out then to stroke my calf, while I forced myself not to immediately pull away in revulsion. "So, do you want to—"

"Not yet. I was wondering, are you in love with Viviana too?"

He sharply drew his hand back to his lap. His mouth opened and then closed, and his eyes were wary. "Hell no. I don't even like her that much. Why?"

I bristled at this. Even though I wasn't on speaking terms with Viviana right now, I didn't want to hear this jerk disparaging her. "Oh, she paid me a visit the night after Ellen's dinner party."

Brandon stood up, his blue eyes flashing in anger. "I'll bet she did." He paused for a moment with a calculating sneer. "She was pretty forward with me, and she didn't take my rejection well. Whatever she told you—"

I rose from the bed and stood in front of him, finally allowing him to see the full force of the fury in my eyes. "How *dare* you. You are not fit to say her name, you ... you snake."

His expression morphed from disbelief to brief regret and then to a sneer, transforming his face into something I didn't recognize. Who was this person I thought I'd been falling in love with?

He must have seen the horror pass over my face at that moment, as he said mockingly, "Don't worry, we can still have a quickie before I go."

Ice ran through my veins as I purred, "That's the one thing I will miss. The bedroom. You gave almost as good as you received. *Almost,* but not quite." I spun on my heel before commanding him over my shoulder, "Now get out."

There was a beat before I heard him shuffle his feet. As he opened the door, I heard his loathsome voice again. "Girls like you are a dime a dozen, Annie. You're a pretty redhead, a hot lay, nothing more. It'll take me five minutes to replace you."

Before he could close the door, I was flying across the room, slamming it in his face and then sliding down, down, down to the floor.

Through gasping breaths, I stilled when I heard what sounded like … bone on bone? I quickly rose, opening the door quietly, just a crack. Brandon was holding his nose, fuming and stomping out the door.

Once he was safely out of the apartment, I stomped out of my room to find my roommates there, panting and red-faced. "Rainn!" I thundered. "I told you not to touch him. I'm not … I don't like violence. Even with a bastard like him."

And then I saw Rafael's hand, bloodied and starting to bruise rapidly as he headed over to the sink. I gasped. "Rafael?" Never in a million years could I see *him* hitting someone.

Rainn went over to help him wash and then bandage his hand. Once they were finished, they walked back over to me, heads hung low. "Sorry, Annie. I'm as surprised as you," Rafael mumbled.

"No, it's … it's fine." I felt a strange squeeze in my heart.

These guys loved me.

That was more important than anything.

"Don't do it again, but … I'm touched."

"Don't be mad, Annie, but I also hacked into some accounts on his phone, since he left it in his coat on the rack when he got here," Rainn said, wincing because he apparently thought this would upset me.

"Oh, you did? And what did you find?" I couldn't hide a smile. Rainn was a pretty talented IT guy, which had definitely come in handy for nefarious reasons more than once during our friendship.

"Let's just say, it's enough to make sure he doesn't try to hurt you, like give you bad job references or spread rumors or anything like that. And I let him know it."

I lunged forward and embraced them both. "I'm sure I don't deserve such amazing friends, but I am so glad I have you guys. Thank you, again and again and again. Now, excuse me while I go spend the rest of my life figuring out how I can make all this up to you guys. You've both been godsends all week. Forever, really."

Rafael shook his head. "No, no, no. Don't you dare talk like that. *As if* you don't deserve us. Give yourself some credit, girl. We might have been listening a bit at the door tonight, and that was an epic takedown of an epic jerk."

"We could go on and on all night about how much we love you, Annie," Rainn said, "but we're guys and, well, love fests aren't really our thing. At least not that kind."

Rafael and I laughed, but then he sobered. "But seriously, Annie. I heard his parting shot. He's full of BS, you know. You *do* know that, right?"

I thought his words might be burned in my brain forever, except that they were words I'd heard many times before, from many other men and some women too. They were already imprinted there, had been for years, maybe my whole life. It was practically my birthright, as a daughter of Jacqueline York.

"Right, I know," I said with a smile that didn't reach my eyes. My tired eyes. It was well past midnight by now, and I was exhausted.

Thank goodness for sleep. It was my only refuge of late.

Chapter 6

"Oh no, Joel, have my degenerate roommates converted you too?" I asked, covering a yawn as I padded out of my bedroom toward the table where my roommates sat, along with Rafael's boyfriend.

Joel leaned back in his chair with a grin that showed both dimples. "Hi, Annie." He stretched his long legs, finely sculpted from years of dancing with a professional ballet company. Although they met while dancing together with the company, Rafael had chosen to shift careers to teaching a few years ago after a chronic condition—fatigue and a finicky heartbeat—made the long hours of professional dancing excruciating.

Rafael smirked as he laid down cards on the table. "Hardly. Joel was a closet gamer as a teen, apparently. Why I'm just finding this out *now* is a question I'm asking myself ..." he trailed off, a pouty expression on his face.

Joel leaned over and stretched his arm around Rafael's shoulders. "I have to keep some air of mystery if I want to keep you interested, don't I?"

Rafael smiled at Joel, his eyes showing a tenderness I'd never seen in him before he met Joel. These two could make almost anyone believe in love, cheesy as it sounded even in my own mind.

After a long moment of enduring their pining-for-each-other eyes, Rainn cleared his throat. "I think it's your turn, Joel."

Joel reluctantly turned back to the game and made his play. "You should give it a try, Annie. You never know—even you might like it."

"She'd rather die," Rafael said dryly.

I pursed my lips. Feeling contrary, I heard myself say, "Well, I don't know. Maybe I would."

"So, Mythic Forge is a card game, but it's a bit like Dungeons & Dragons. Have you heard of that before? That's classic roleplaying, but in this game, it's more structured ..."

My heart suddenly lodged in my throat, and I didn't hear a word as he continued talking about whatever game they were playing. I tried to look at the game box for the name, but my vision was fuzzy. I placed my hand on my chest, trying to catch my breath. Thinking I might be swaying, I grasped the table with my other hand.

In the next moment, someone was guiding me downward into a chair. I looked behind me slowly, and it was Rainn, worry etched in his features.

Rafael clasped my hand. "Annie, girl, breathe." He led me through some exercises to slowly count breaths. We'd done this before, so many years ago, though I couldn't remember exactly why. Slowly I felt my body return to calm and my mind start to clear.

"I ... wow, sorry about that."

"Hey, don't apologize," Joel said, turning to me, and the other guys nodded. "I've had panic attacks before, Annie. Used to have panic disorder pretty bad actually. Long time ago, but I remember what it was like."

"Panic attacks? No, I don't ... this wasn't ..." I protested. *Is that what this is?* "I don't know."

"Did we say or do something to upset you?" Rafael asked, looking at me intently, holding both of my hands now.

I swallowed. It was coming back to me now. Again. D&D. Hearing Joel talk about the game threatened to plunge me into those memories best left hidden. Memories of the man who ... Well. Memories I *needed* to keep buried, so *this* didn't happen. How mortifying. I took my hands out of Rafael's grip and used them to hide my face. "I don't know, but this is embarrassing. Please, can we just forget this? I'm *so* not a panic kind of girl."

Silence descended upon the table for a few long moments. When I uncovered my face, they were all looking at me with curious eyes, as if expecting me to explain. But I raised my chin and met their eyes defiantly. "Well, are you going to teach me this dorky game or not? Mystic Forge? So cheesy—"

"Mythic," muttered Rafael.

I felt the shadow of a smile. "Whatever. Also, I hope you bought enough muffins to share with me, Raf."

I watched as they finished their current game and listened as they described the particulars. After the game ended, Joel rose to go brew more coffee.

"Hey Annie, if you don't want to talk about this yet, just say so, but have you thought about finding work yet? Like what you might be looking to do? Raf here said you wouldn't be editing for Bolder anymore, and I couldn't agree more. We couldn't let you work for that bastard again." Rainn flexed his hands over his head. "Are you wanting another editing gig or something else?"

I let out a long exhale. "I haven't really given it much thought yet." *None, actually.* "There's been a lot to think about the past few days, you know?" I bit my lip and looked at Rafael. "I mean, I don't plan to mooch off you guys forever. Don't worry—I'll find something. And I do have a little savings, so you don't have to pay my bills or anything like that."

"We weren't worried about that," Rafael scoffed. "We just ... want to help you find your passion, Annie. Your true calling wasn't fixing punctuation, girl."

"Hey, don't knock proper punctuation. Doing it *well* is a rare skill, I'm telling you." I grinned briefly before my face fell. "Maybe editing isn't really my passion, but is that so wrong? Why does passion need to be associated with a paycheck?"

The three men stared at me, seemingly unsure how to respond. "OK, I guess I'm asking the wrong people. All of you get paid to do the jobs you love. But not everyone has to. Maybe I'm meant to live a passionate life outside of work, and work just ... pays the bills?"

After a beat of silence, Rafael spoke cautiously, "Sure, that can work. If you live your passions outside of work."

He's implying I don't!

Resentment rose as a bitter taste in my throat, but not necessarily toward him.

He's probably right. What am I passionate about? Buying a new outfit? Going to a party? Meeting a new guy?

Yet I knew the answer.

Passion was not for me.

Passion led to pain.

Passion, even the memory of it, led to ... well, apparently, panic attacks.

Passion never did me any favors.

Passion is better left to others. I have no use for it.

"Meh, I don't know about all that," I said breezily. "Don't worry. I'll find something." When they glanced at me and then at each other with some doubt, I smiled through clenched teeth. "Seriously, it'll be *fine*."

As Joel and Rainn started to set up the next game, Rafael gazed at me thoughtfully, and then his eyes brightened. "I have it! You can teach a few classes at the school. I've actually been wanting to hire a new part-time teacher for some ballet and contemporary classes."

"Oh, I don't think—"

"I mean, just for a while. You're a fantastic dancer, Annie, but I doubt teaching students is your true passion. I could be wrong though. Probably just a temp thing until you find something full time elsewhere ..." Rafael trailed off, looking into the distance as though already making plans in his head.

"Raf, I'm really rusty—"

"Shush, I won't hear it. You can do jetes and pointe work in your sleep. You're not saying no."

When I narrowed my eyes and pursed my lips, he sighed, and his shoulders slumped. "OK. Please, please don't say no, Annie. You'd be doing me a favor, you know. At least think about it?"

I sighed and then nodded reluctantly.

"If it helps, I'll keep an eye out for openings at the agency. So far it seems like a good place to work, though I'm still pretty new there," Rainn offered. "I did make a friend in HR already though. Robin, remember him? He's a runner too."

My frustration mounting, I nonetheless pasted a smile on my face. As I started pushing my chair back from the table, I looked at each of them in turn. "Thank you, Rainn, all of you, actually. I know your hearts are in the right place. I'm just ... ugh, I need some escapism, you know? After the week I've had, you know. I think I'm going to my room to read."

They glanced at each other as though wondering whether they should protest. When their eyes met mine again, they all nodded with resigned expressions.

I laughed lightly before turning on my heel. "I'll just be on the other side of that wall. Not leaving the country. Have fun with your nerd games, boys."

As I shut my door, I breathed a sigh of relief. But before stepping away, I paused to listen to the voices that carried through the door.

"Is she OK? I've never seen her like that," Joel said.

"Rough week, to put it mildly," said Rainn. "But she's tough." For some reason, I felt a little bitter about that assessment.

I'm tough?

I've never had a choice.

What if I'm tired of being tough?

Finally, Rafael spoke, his voice a bit somber. "She isn't OK now, but she will be. She needs time." He could always see right through me.

I'd made an effort today. Whatever day it was, maybe Thursday. Lunch eaten, face washed, a bit of laundry sorted, and … I was ready to go back to bed. I'd finished my book last night and hadn't yet started another because, well, how do you follow Dickens? And what on earth could a person read when in a mood like this?

I just needed my bed. The soft covers, the bliss of being asleep, oblivious to everything and everyone.

Except when the dreams came. Then I *had* to wake up. To get out of bed. Or just to lie in bed and not think, not sleep, not feel anything but the soft covers.

The dreams of humiliation, of betrayal, of infidelity, of resentment, of all the things I felt because of Brandon, and some because of Viviana, and then the dreams in which I was small, insignificant, yet somehow always in my mother's way … all of them haunting me and making me wake up in a cold sweat, sometimes with tears burning my eyes and blazing a path down my cheeks onto my already damp pillow or tangled sheets.

These were nothing, though, compared to the dreams of him.

Of Kylan Quinn, the man whose love I desperately needed to forget but somehow couldn't, *still* couldn't. Why was he still haunting me, years later? Why did it feel like every time I thought of him, my heart broke again and again, as fresh and raw as the first time?

And I just … shut down.

Was this all because of the stupid Instagram post? He might have come and gone already. And why would it matter anyway? It's not like our paths would cross, and even if they did, so what? It was so far in the past. Four years was forever ago. Well, maybe not that long, but I'd dated many guys since then. Surely he'd been with many women too, if his Instagram photos were any indication.

I hadn't allowed myself to open Instagram since the day I'd seen that photo. Not that I'd been on my phone all that much in the past week anyway, but when I had, I'd resisted clicking on the photo app. It would do me no good to learn any details about where he was, whether he was still in town, why he was here in the first place, *who* he was with …

I felt a stab of pain in my chest and curled up into a ball under the covers. By now there must be a permanent imprint of my body on the mattress in the fetal position. Why *now*, of all times, was Kylan the only thing I could think about? I had far more devastating things happen to me lately. Heck, I'd rather think about the womanizer Brandon. Yet I couldn't. It turned out ... he was nothing to me. Had he ever been? Had any of them? It was almost as though nothing had mattered—nothing had been real—since Kylan.

What? That's insane. Am I going crazy?

Maybe I had a fever again. Could that happen after someone has already recovered?

Some indeterminate amount of time later, Rafael was peeling back the covers and pinching his nose. "Girl, I'm sorry, but you need to shower."

I ignored that. I was holed up in my room with no responsibilities and nowhere to be. Why shower? But I sat up slowly, brushing some oily red strands behind my ears.

"Raf, do I have a fever again? Am I sick? I feel like I have a heavy weight on my chest, on all of me really, holding me down. I don't want to get out of bed. But when I sleep, my dreams are ... dark." I sniffed. "I must be sick."

He came very close and then reared back, pinching his nose again. "Well, you badly need to brush your teeth, but I don't smell booze. Just wanted to make sure you weren't drunk."

I glared at him. "I wish. I asked Rainn to pick me up some vodka yesterday, but he seems to have conveniently forgotten about it." I crossed my arms and frowned. "Do you think I'm feverish again? Another viral thing or the same one?"

His knowing look told me I wasn't going to like what he had to say. But it was better to know, right? "Uh, well, I'm not a doctor, but I'm pretty sure these are not viral symptoms. It's called depression."

"What?" I blinked a few times. "Oh. I guess so." I sat up, running my fingers through my rat's nest of hair. "But I'm having some crazy thoughts, maybe delirium, fever dreams? Maybe you should check my temperature just in case?"

His lips twitched, but he nodded and searched the nearby table for the thermometer.

A minute later, he pronounced me fever-free, but instead of smiling, his look was full of sympathy. "Do you want to talk, Annie?"

"What's there to say, Raf? My life is a mess right now. I'm having a pity party, a party for one. Something stupid like that. You know everything already, nothing more to talk about. Just get me the vodka I asked for."

"Are you sure, Annie?" As he studied me, I had to avert my eyes. He was trying to see into my soul, and I couldn't let that happen.

After all, there's probably nothing there.

"Of course I'm sure," I said, starting to lie back down. "It's just—"

Suddenly my phone rang somewhere nearby. It was on the bed somewhere rather than on the nightstand. I felt around for it with my hand. Lately, I'd been more apt to let calls go to voicemail, but taking this call—any call—might be better than continuing this conversation with Rafael. However, it was proving hard to find the phone. The caller tried a second time, and I attempted again to locate the phone, this time finally finding it wedged between the headboard and the mattress.

My face fell when I saw the name on the screen. Jacqueline.

Rafael saw it at the same time. "Annie, *no.*"

I felt torn, but at the moment, talking to my mother felt like a better option than dealing with Rafael's prying and eventually finding out the source of my current emotional strife. "She's my mother," I whispered just before answering the call.

He shook his head with a pained expression and turned to leave the room.

"Hi, M–mother," I managed, my voice already shaking.

"Anastasia, why have you been so difficult to reach?"

I swallowed with some effort. My mother wouldn't understand, yet ... "I had a really terrible week, Mom. I was sick, a man betrayed me, I quit—"

"Anastasia, calm yourself!" she exclaimed, her tone harsh. "I did *not* raise you to be hysterical. How do you think it makes me feel, hearing you speak like this, and after making it so hard to contact you!"

I was at a loss for words, as usual.

"I'm astounded that you could be so careless with my feelings," my mother continued. "Though perhaps I should be accustomed to it by now."

"I'm sorry, Mother," I heard myself whisper.

After some silence, my mother spoke in a more delicate tone. "There, there. I forgive you, as I always do. But you can't expect men to always be so forgiving, my darling, which is probably why your man has left you ..." and on she went.

She knows nothing of the situation with Brandon, but she assumes I'm at fault. I should be livid, but ... could she be right? Did I somehow push him into other women's arms? Was that even possible?

Some saner part of me wanted to ask why on earth I was letting my mother get into my head at all, but it was drowned out.

"See, this is a perfect example where you could improve, Anastasia. I've called you to tell you my news, yet you've monopolized the conversation, haven't you? And I've allowed it because I am a kind, adoring mother. It's always been my weakness, I suppose."

I bit my tongue, hoping I didn't draw blood.

"I called to give you formal notice of our visit in the near future."

"We?"

"Yes, to *Minn-e-sota*." She said Minnesota as though it were a foreign word to her, never uttered before, something strange and perhaps even unsavory. As though her only daughter hadn't lived there for her entire adult life. "It's as I mentioned earlier, though Alcott has decided he wants to move sooner. Dear Caroline needs to find a position and a new home in St. Paul before the end of this year."

"Mom, hold on," I said, frustration rising above the meekness that had taken hold earlier in the conversation. "What are you talking about? I have no idea who Alcott and Caroline are, for starters."

My mother gasped. "Anastasia, you—I—" she sputtered. "I can only assume you're still suffering from severe illness. Dear Caroline is Ricardo's lovely daughter, just finishing her residency at Johns Hopkins. Alcott is her dear husband. Surely you remember."

I remembered nothing of the sort, but the name Ricardo sounded familiar. I searched my brain as quickly as I could. "Ricardo ... the drug company guy?"

"Yes, he owns a pharmaceutical company," my mother said testily. "Anastasia, you are severely trying my patience."

I exhaled slowly. It would be easier to just play along. "Sorry. So what can I do for you, Mother?"

"We expected you could provide assistance to Caroline as she looks for suitable positions and of course a new home in St. Paul."

"I ... well, I'm not a medical recruiter or a real estate agent, Mother."

"I'm aware, dear. What is it you do again?" My mother paused. "Never mind. I only meant that you could provide any assistance that Caroline requests, perhaps serving as her virtual assistant as she arranges their new life from afar. Surely even you could manage that."

I swallowed the wave of nausea rising in me. I couldn't speak. Couldn't. Shouldn't.

"But I could have informed you of this by text message or email, darling. The true reason I called is to inform you that I'll be visiting. We all will, actually. I wanted you to be one of the first to know, as my daughter. We want to make sure you have plenty of time to make due preparations for our visit. When I have the exact dates, I will let you know."

"Oh, uh, I—wh—" Something like a word salad came out of my mouth.

"I had thought to ask if you had a sufficient number of guest rooms in your home with Brendan, but if he's left you, I gather that is no longer an option. Or is it? After all, you didn't inherit my stunning beauty for nothing ... perhaps you will lure him back."

Oh, so now she remembers his name, does she? Well, almost. But not the name of my best friend for over a decade.

My stomach turned, and I felt a slight wave of dizziness as her words echoed through my mind. Finally, I replied, "Brandon doesn't even live in town, Mother. He—he was only visiting. Staying at the Four Seasons. And no, we're not together anymore and never will be. He's a terrible person. He cheated."

I heard a clucking sound. "Oh, darling. You still have much to learn. It's fortunate I'll be visiting soon, and we can work on your ... perspective, among other things." And then she *giggled*. I nearly expired from shock. "But I'm getting ahead of myself. As I said, we shall let you know when we have firm dates for travel. The Four Seasons is exactly what I had in mind. Thanks for the suggestion, darling. I will be in touch—"

"No!" I croaked. "Not, I mean, I'd rather you didn't stay at that hotel. I don't know how long Brandon will be there, and I'd hate to run into him—"

"Nonsense, dearest. Ricardo will want only the best for dear Caroline and Alcott and, of course, for me, the love of his life." Her tone turned accusing. "Not everything can revolve around you, Anastasia. One would think I erred greatly as a mother in indulging your feelings far too much and too often when you were a child. But I could hardly be to blame. I've only done the best that any mother could, under the circumstances. If I indulged you too much, well, it is only because I am such a loving person ..."

And on my mother droned. I didn't hear any more but merely set the phone down on the bed next to me. Jacqueline would end the call eventually, none the wiser.

I stared at my nails, but not really seeing them.

There were no tears. I was somewhat numb, but not numb enough.

If the guys won't bring me the liquor, I'll just go find some.

As the second shot of whiskey burned a path down my throat, I realized this stuff tasted much worse now than it did in my teens and early 20s. Jack Daniels was no longer my drink of choice, but it was all I'd been able to find in the kitchen, besides beer and wine, which were obviously far too weak for a day like today.

Just like I was.

But even as my throat burned and my taste buds objected with each shot, a calming, pleasantly heavy feeling began to spread through my core and then my limbs. Eventually, I could barely taste it, and I knew from experience that meant it was time to slow down.

I wanted numb. I wanted to not feel. But I didn't want to be violently ill.

I knew my limits. Or at least I thought so.

In the last couple years, drinking hadn't held nearly as much appeal as it once did. Sure, I drank at parties and bars or occasionally threw a few back to relax with my roommates. I was the consummate party girl, so of course I drank socially. Sometimes a lot. But I almost never drank when alone or sad.

Not since ...

Well, him.

Not since I ended a relationship with the man who'd been head over heels in love with me. The man who was everything good in a person—the man I had never deserved. The man I couldn't forget ... the one whose love I couldn't put out of my mind, couldn't erase from my body's memory, couldn't eradicate from my dreams.

"Kylan," I said hoarsely. I rarely allowed myself to even *think* his name, much less say it aloud.

My fingers were shaky as I unlocked my phone screen and swiped to the Instagram icon, which I'd hidden on a distant home screen that I rarely used. My fingers hovered just above the screen, over the icon.

This is a mistake.

I should delete Instagram. Or unfollow him.

But my fingers apparently had a mind of their own, tapping to open the app.

After a brief moment of mindless scrolling in which I convinced myself that was all I'd do, I sighed heavily. I might as well just do what I *knew* I was going to end up doing: Go to his profile. Look for updates.

Taking one more shot for courage, I typed his name in the search and opened his page.

No new photos. The most recent one was from last week, from the airport.

Does that mean he's still here? Or he just didn't feel the need to announce his return?

The latter was more likely. He wasn't the kind of guy who posted constant updates to narrate his life; in fact, his posts were infrequent and typically didn't reveal much about his life. This was both a relief and a frustration, of course.

Feeling a little disappointed by the lack of new photos, I then noticed the videos section on his profile.

Two recent videos, from this past weekend actually.

Did I dare watch them?

Yes.

No!

I flopped down on the bed, my breathing faster as I imagined seeing a video of him.

It could be, like, his dog. Or his dinner. Or a sunset. Or a girlfriend.

My stomach churned.

Or it could just be … him.

The room was spinning now. I squeezed my eyes shut to block it out: the room, the phone, him. Especially him.

Chapter 7

"Annie, I resent this cliché BFF role you're making us play, but you're getting up. And out. Now," Rafael screamed as he barged into my room.

I felt around for a pillow to put over my head and moaned. "Shhh, don't yell."

When Rainn laugh-screamed right in my ear, I opened my eyes to tell him to back off, but he was several feet away.

Opening my eyes was a mistake.

Pain.

"Here, we brought coffee."

"Oh, I—" I started before clearing my dry throat. "Thanks, but I'm just going to stay—"

"Oh no you don't," Rafael said in a booming voice. His hands were on my upper arms this time, gently pulling me up into a sitting position. He was strong for such a lithe form as his, but then, ballet *was* one of the most physically demanding forms of exercise. "You're getting out of this room if we have to kidnap you. You've done your wallowing. You excelled at it. A-plus. It's over now. *Fini.*"

Rainn chimed in, his voice also loud as he sat on the bed on the other side of me. "You can make this easy or hard, Annie. Sip the coffee, take a shower, get dressed, have a light dinner, and come out with us. OR fight us every step of the way, but still the endpoint is the same."

"Friends don't let friends wallow for more than ... what is it, Rainn, almost two weeks now?"

Rainn shook his head in wonder, like he couldn't imagine doing that himself. "Something like that. It's time to get out, see people, be yourself. If you're going to drink, let's do it at the bar or club."

"Are you two done?" I crossed my arms over my chest, which was covered in some kind of sticky fabric that I didn't have the stomach to look down at. I actually didn't feel *that* queasy, though my head was definitely going to explode. Then again, I'd only been awake for a few minutes. Was I even awake now, or was this another nightmare? But when I pinched my own arm, I winced in pain. "Stop shouting, boys. And even if I did want to get up and do something, I wouldn't want to go partying."

The two men looked at each other, worry creasing their foreheads.

I sighed. "I need to cut back on drinking. Obviously. And ... it's sad you think that partying is the only thing I can enjoy. You know, I like to watch movies and do other stuff. Not just party." It hurt, actually, that even my closest friends saw me as merely a party girl, but I didn't want to admit it aloud.

Rafael bit his lip as he communicated silently with Rainn for a long moment. When his sharp eyes returned to me, he took my hand. "I know. We both know that. It's just ... I wanted to wait and tell you later, but I guess I can share it now. I want to go out and celebrate with you guys tonight because I have some kind of big news."

Rainn grinned. Whatever it was, clearly he already knew.

I sat up straighter, my eyes widening as I forgot my own misery for a moment. "You're—"

"Oh, don't you dare steal my dramatic announcement, girl." Rafael playfully flicked me on the arm with his finger. "Yes, I'm engaged. Joel asked me to marry him last night."

"*Raf*, this is so wonderful!" I squealed, not even caring how much my headache worsened at the sound coming out of my own mouth.

"I know, it totally is!" he squealed in return. "I want to tell you everything, but in exchange, you have to come out with us."

Rainn cut in then. "Annie, I know you just want to keep wallowing, but celebrating Raf's engagement is totally worth getting out of the house for."

I nodded slowly. "You're right. Raf ... I'm really happy for you. I'm sure I don't look it. But I am. You and Joel are everyone's relationship goals, but you already knew that. Will he be coming tonight?"

Rafael frowned. "No, he has a show tomorrow. It's local, but you know how he is." Translation: Joel took his career seriously, and he would never go out drinking the night before a performance. Being a professional male dancer was so physically demanding that he had to maintain top form, especially around performance dates. I admired Joel's dedication, even if it did sometimes spoil our fun.

"Bring him over for lunch or something soon so we can all congratulate you guys together," I suggested. "But for now, please give me that cold coffee and some time to shower. It may take a while to clean off all the grime I've accumulated from the last few days or however long it's been." I laughed because, well, it was the only thing I could do. I needed to smile and put on a brave face for my friends. And, really, for myself.

"I didn't want to cry tonight. Dang it, Raf!" I accused him, carefully dabbing at my damp eyes, surrounded by dusky grey eye makeup that supposedly highlighted my green irises.

Rainn punched Rafael lightly in the arm. "He doesn't even feel bad—look at him. The lovesick eyes. It's like he doesn't even see any other guy in the room."

My lips twitched. "If you'd asked me a year ago, I wouldn't have believed it possible for us to be sitting here taking shots and listening to the most romantic proposal story ever from *you*, of all people."

"I mean, the part about the fountain and the music ... I've got to say, Joel has outdone himself," Rainn said. "Are you mad that he beat you to it? I know you'd been mulling over some proposal scenarios yourself—don't pretend you weren't."

Rafael pursed his lips. "I'll never admit it."

"Let's drink to that!" This had been my refrain every 5–10 minutes. And it had worked. I felt relaxed, and I could pretend I was having fun—that living it up at the bar was really what I wanted to be doing.

Pretending.

As long as the drinks kept flowing.

Rafael's smile slipped a bit before he picked up his drink, and he eyed me closely. I pretended not to notice. I wasn't going to be fielding questions tonight.

This night wasn't about me.

That's what made it bearable.

Until it wasn't.

Not five minutes later, Rafael looked at Rainn in astonishment. "Rainn, I can't believe you blew off that girl just now. Are you feeling OK?"

"What? I didn't notice a girl." He glanced around, genuinely confused.

"He didn't notice her," Rafael said slowly as he turned to me. "Annie, you know what that means?"

"Yep. He's either crushing hardcore on someone else or having some diarrhea issues," I said, swirling my drink.

Rainn spit out some of his drink. "I am—" he sputtered. "My digestive system is fine, thank you very much."

"Then it's a woman," said Rafael with a sly smile, nudging me as I nodded distractedly.

Rainn crossed his arms and shook his head. "No. I don't know ... maybe. It's too soon to tell."

After a moment of silence, Rafael laughed. "OK, you have your secrets for now, but we'll expect progress reports, all right?"

"Not agreeing to that," Rainn mumbled. "I PR'd today, and all you can do is rib me about some girl you don't even know?"

"A-ha, so there *is* a girl!" Rafael said with a gleeful smile at me.

I giggled and then abruptly halted. "Wait ... you set a personal record? Was your half marathon *today*?"

"I've got the sore plantar fascia to prove it," he said, pointing to his left foot. "But it was worth beating 1:30 finally."

"That's amazing, Rainn! Congratulations," I said, throwing my arms around him and nearly knocking us both off our bar stools.

Rafael sighed, surveying the two of us with a resigned smile. Likely he'd already congratulated Rainn earlier in the day. Unlike me, wallowing in my own drama, Rafael probably hadn't completely forgotten about our friend's big race. He had probably been there to greet Rainn at the finish line. "Fine, you're off the hook for now, man. You'll tell us about the new girl soon though."

Rainn flashed us both an enigmatic smile.

"And what about you, Ms. York?" Rafael asked, angling his stool to better face me.

My brows lowered and drew together. "What about me?"

"I know what you're thinking, girl. How dare he ask me, since I've had my heart broken so recently, blah blah," said my supposed best friend.

So he wanted to push my buttons. I said nothing, not willing to appease him by agreeing.

Why's my damn glass empty?

I raised my hand toward the bartender.

"Annie," Rafael said, more gently this time as he put a hand on mine. "I know you liked Brandon, but I don't think you loved him. I feel like there's more to this. More than you're telling us."

My mouth set in a thin line, I looked away. "Tonight's not about me."

"No, tonight's about *me*, and *I* want to talk about you."

I crossed my arms and then heaved a great sigh. "Well, you know my mother called."

Rafael squeezed my hand. "And that never ends well."

"She—she's coming here. Not to visit me, of course, but to help her latest boyfriend's med-school daughter get settled into a new place here. Or some crap, I won't bore you with the details. I tuned out after a while."

"Did you tell her you'd had some personal struggles, uh, with Brandon, illness?" Rainn asked. He understood my mother less than Rafael, who knew better than to ask that question.

"I did, but she has no sympathy. She's chronically incapable of it. She assumed Brandon had—had left me because of something *I* did and then accused m-me of being hysterical and making everything about me. Typical Jacqueline," I said shakily. I tried to laugh flippantly but croaked instead.

I watched as both men's expressions turned angry, their fists clenched and faces red—or was it the alcohol and heat of the bar?

Why am I telling them all of this? It's nothing new, nothing they haven't heard before.

"Guys, you know this is just how she is. Calm down. Nothing shocking here."

"I've said this before, but seriously, Annie ..." Rafael paused, a pained look on his face. "I know it's easier said than done, but you *need* to cut her off. Completely."

Rainn nodded, his posture tense.

I opened my mouth to speak and then closed it. "I ... I know. I think I will, someday." I drew in a deep breath. "But for now ... I'm actually OK, mostly."

I stared at my lap for some time, hoping they'd change the subject. But when I raised my eyelids, Rafael was staring at me intently. My right eyebrow shot up.

He merely asked, "What else?"

"What do you mean?"

"What else is going on with you, Annie?"

"You mean besides having a nasty virus, a terrible breakup with a cheating jerk, and then a falling out with a good friend, followed by a reminder that my mother is a horrible person and will never approve of me?" My tone was bitter, and I wondered again why my glass was empty.

Rainn came to my rescue, putting an arm around my shoulders. "That's certainly more than enough for anyone, Raf. Let's leave her be."

"No."

I glared at him for a moment before looking away.

Rafael sighed and leaned back. "There's more to it."

I bit my lip too hard and then winced at the sharp pain. Rainn was silent but pulled me in closer.

"Annie."

I swallowed the lump in my throat. "I guess ... we never did talk about whatever came out of my fever delirium, did we?"

"I mean, *we* talked about it," Rafael said, motioning between himself and Rainn, "but not with you." When I narrowed my eyes, he grinned. "*Kidding*! Mostly."

"Can I at least get, like, five more shots first?" I asked, my lower lip jutting out. "It's the least you can do if you're going to make me talk."

Rainn looked uneasy. "I don't think more booze is what you need, girl. In fact, I'm a little concerned about how much you've already had."

I rolled my eyes, tapping my foot against the bar stool leg. It was then I realized I'd lost my shoe on the other foot. How long ago had it fallen off? I bent down to find it on the floor and then bumped my head on the counter, nearly losing my balance.

"I rest my case," Rainn said with a cocky grin.

"I know, let's go to a greasy diner place and eat like lumberjacks!" Rafael said, grasping us both by the sleeves.

We both looked at him in surprise.

"What?" he asked defensively. "It's not like any of us wants to dance or socialize or meet someone new here tonight, and we're all past the point of drinking too much. Besides, it'll give us a quieter place to listen to Annie's troubles."

My lips curved into a frown. "I'm just fine here, actually—"

"Come on, I want 2 am pancakes. And it's my night to celebrate, isn't it?" Rafael turned his pleading eyes toward me.

"I could go for a lumberjack breakfast," Rainn said. "Come on, Annie. It's Raf's night—let's do it."

I gritted my teeth and squeezed my eyes shut. Gorging myself with my besties at a greasy spoon restaurant actually did sound kind of wonderful, but there, I'd have no opportunity to escape the interrogation I knew was coming. At least here, at the bar, I had options.

I could catch the eye of some guy. There were no rules, right? I could dance and find someone to have fun with for the night. And escape my roomies.

But I realized, to my surprise and increasingly to my horror, that the thought of being with anyone, even casually, held no appeal at the moment.

Why? A good rebound can be so fun!

I didn't want to think about why this time might be different. Still, it could be worth a try, and if I drank a little more, I might not care who was who or what was what. I could just tell the guys I'd meet them later ...

But then I looked at Rafael, my best friend for over half of my life, and there was no question. "Anything for you, Raf."

I licked my slippery lips, sighing with pleasure. "How did I go 26 years of my life without ever trying Becky's amazing waffles?" The surprisingly delicious fare was doing its job of soaking up some of the alcohol I was now ready to admit I'd overindulged in ... not for the first time lately.

"Comfort food at its finest," Rafael said, wiping egg yolk off his chin. "I'm so glad you convinced me to get both the runny eggs and the pancakes. And the biscuits. Though the server probably thinks we're high."

"She probably thinks *you* are, Raf. But look at him," I said, pointing to Rainn. "She's had her eye on Rainn the whole time. And he looks like ... like he eats like this every day."

Rafael and I dissolved into a fit of giggles as Rainn shifted uncomfortably in his seat. To be sure, part of his athletic good looks was genetic, and part of it was hard work lifting at the gym and running on the trails. I loved that he was modest and even awkward when anyone talked about how well-built he was. Every other guy I'd ever met who looked like Rainn had been anything but modest. It was initially part of their appeal, but it quickly soured when I realized they were usually not nice human beings or had nothing in their brains other than exercise plans. Though I hated to stereotype, of course.

Because I hated being stereotyped myself.

I was the fun, perky, hot redhead party girl to most people. I often leaned into it. It was practically my birthright, or so my mother had drilled into me since, well, always. But sometimes I was just so tired of it all. It *was* me, but it wasn't. I frowned. That made no sense.

"Jokes aside," Rafael said, putting his fork down. "Annie, talk to us."

The time had come, and there was no use avoiding it. I could try, but it would only delay the inevitable, and then it would probably just seem like I was making an even bigger deal out of it. Which ... maybe it was too late for that already.

I inhaled and exhaled slowly and then slammed my juice for fortitude. "I'm guessing I mentioned an old flame in one of my fever dreams. Is that right?"

Rainn nodded as he finished chewing his silver dollar pancake. "More than once."

I swallowed the embarrassment down. "Right. Well, I—I'm pretty sure that's only because I'd happened to see an Instagram update from him. One of the days I was sick, I think I was scrolling mind-lessly or something and saw his post. And then it got stuck in my head. That's all it was. Case closed."

Rafael could always see into my soul, so I tried to look away. "Annie, can you even say his name?"

My lips parted and then wavered. "Of—of course I can." My breath felt shallow as I forced myself to say it. "It's … Kylan." My voice, saying that name, sounded strange to my own ears. "Rainn, he's just an old fling from college, so maybe I haven't mentioned him to you. Pretty insignificant, really—"

"Annie, stop," Rafael said, his eyes piercing through my shield. "We're your friends. I don't know the whole of what you felt or what you still feel, but to say it was insignificant … *puh-lease*. Don't lie to us or to yourself."

Rainn looked from Rafael to me. His brows were creased, as though he expected me to lash out at Rafael in return.

But I only dropped forward, my face in my hands and my hair just barely avoiding touching my greasy plate.

"He's coming to town. Here." I raised my head briefly to add, "I mean, he's probably already here."

The guys nodded sympathetically, instead of looking surprised. "You knew?"

"I did," Rafael confirmed.

I looked back and forth between them, my mouth struggling to form words. "Wha—how?"

Rafael glanced down at his recently manicured nails, painted royal blue with thin black and green stripes. "I saw him."

I nearly jumped out of my seat. "You *what*? You saw him and didn't tell me?"

"I would have told you," Rafael said calmly, "but you've been holed up in your room for days, and you didn't want to talk, espe-cially about him."

"It's true. He did—" Rainn started.

"Where did you see him?" I asked slowly, still in shock and feeling pretty sober by this point.

"He was at the little park just across the bridge, with his bike."

I paled, remembering our long weekend bike rides back in college. And trying not to. And then it sank in—*across the bridge?* I gasped. "The park that's like three blocks from our apartment?" I watched in disbelief as Rafael nodded. "You can't be serious. He was that close to where we live?"

Oh no, oh no, oh no.

"Don't hyperventilate, girl," Rafael said in a soothing tone. "He had a bike, so he probably isn't staying anywhere near here but just happened to be on a long bike ride. But who knows. I didn't talk to him, so I don't know where he's staying."

"Or why he's in town?"

"No, I don't know that either." Rafael paused. "I mean, I'm sure we could find out, if you want to do a little digging—"

"*No!*" I burst out, eyes wide. I took in a steadying breath and tried to compose myself. "I mean, this is ... it's not a big deal. Not worth the effort."

"Totally not a big deal," Rafael said as he turned to Rainn, and they shared a chuckle.

I crossed my arms over my chest and sulked for a few minutes, picking at what was left of my buttery toast. Finally, I asked quietly, "Did he see you, Raf?"

"Doubtful. But it doesn't matter anyway, right?" Rafael smirked, while Rainn openly laughed.

"Since when is it OK to laugh about your dear friend's misfortunes?"

"Is it a misfortune? I thought it was no big deal," Rafael said, not even trying to hide a smirk.

"I'd say it's a fortune. Your true love's back in town, Annie!" Rainn said with a wide grin.

"He's—you don't understand, Rainn." I shook my head. "There's a lot more to the story. I sort of ... broke his heart. And my own, in the process. Our relationship was never going to work. We just—we wanted different things, and the timing was bad. I *broke* him. Trust me, he'd never in a million years want anything to do with me now. I know this because I've heard *nothing* from him in four years. Not a single message."

As they watched me, I was dangerously on the verge of tears. How did this happen? I'd wanted to keep this conversation quick and light. Surface level. I tossed my hair back and shrugged for effect. "And that's the way I want it. It's over, and it's for the best."

"Right," Rafael said, holding out the vowel in the word. He dabbed at his mouth with his napkin and then sat back. "I don't think I can eat another bite."

"Me neither," Rainn agreed.

"I was going to ask if either of you wanted the rest of my chocolate chip muffin. I don't want to burst the seams of this dress I squeezed into tonight," I said wryly.

When they both grabbed for the muffin at the same time, I giggled. "You can share, boys."

As they devoured the remains of my giant muffin, Rafael's eyes met mine again. "Do you know what Kylan is doing now? Career-wise, I mean?"

My heart skipped a beat.

So we're still doing this, talking about him.

I can handle this. Not a big deal.

"He's actually pretty successful in the publishing industry, I think." I lied. I didn't think this; I *knew* he was successful, against the odds. He'd had a difficult upbringing in a low-income neighborhood. It was one of my mother's many objections to the idea of my dating Kylan. "I'm not sure exactly what he does," I said truthfully. I had stuck to Instagram only, steadfastly avoiding any other social media or even Googling, so I didn't know exactly what he did for a living. But it was clear from his photos that he'd made it big, and he was often tagged in photos with publishing executives or even occasionally celebrities.

"You don't want to know?" Rainn asked as he wiped chocolate off his lips. "I'm sure it wouldn't be hard to find out. Even if he's the private type on social media, I could find some info for you."

I shook my head rapidly. "Please don't. I find …" I grasped for the right words. How could I explain that I needed to keep the distance? It was how I'd survived. "I find comfort in not knowing."

"I can see that," Rafael said, looking thoughtful. "If Joel ever ghosted me—"

"But he wouldn't," I said firmly. "Because you guys are in love. He's the *one*, Raf." Then, with some difficulty, I added hoarsely, "Kylan, he … he wasn't the one. He was just a guy I dated and then dumped. Among many others." I offered a wry smile.

"He was a guy you *loved*, Annie. Maybe the only guy you've loved? And Viviana convinced you to give him up."

I stared at my best friend, my eyebrows raised. "Well, she wasn't the only one who disapproved." Rafael had never told me explicitly not to follow Kylan to New York to pursue his dreams, but I knew he'd agreed with Viviana on that.

With his brows furrowed, he put his napkin over his plate. "I'll leave you alone about Kylan for now. But this may not be the end of the conversation, Annie."

"Yeah, I mean, you could bump into him any day," Rainn said, and then he palmed his forehead. "Oh, crap, speaking of bumping into someone, I forgot to mention I saw Viv today, at the race. We chatted for a bit."

I exhaled slowly. "Oh, did she … did you …" *Just ask him already.* "Did she ask about me?"

"Ah, not that I remember. She seemed distracted, like she was looking for someone but nervous? I don't know. It was quick." Rainn shrugged and took a sip of water. "No big deal, just wanted to let you know. It wasn't weird or anything."

It sounded as though Viviana had been alone at the race, which was odd. She always ran with her best friend, Jack. I wondered if there was a story there.

"Back to Kylan, we don't know how long he's in town, do we? A bike ride in the park suggests an extended stay," Rainn said.

I frowned. I'd started to fear this too. What was he doing in the Twin Cities anyway?

No, it doesn't matter.

I don't need—or want—to know.

He just needs to wrap it up and go home, so I can go back to living my life pretending like ... like I didn't meet the love of my life four years ago and then push him away, forever.

Chapter 8

S miling dreamily, I savored my second bite of the crab cake in front of me.

"Divine?" Joel asked.

"It's ... almost beyond words," I said breathily. The crab cake was rich and buttery, with a lemony zing and just a whisper of crispness around the edges, with the aioli adding a creamy, tangy kick that perfectly balanced the flavors. "My favorite appetizer has never tasted so good. And you know I love aioli. Rafael, why haven't you taken me here before? Such a tiny place, I've probably driven by hundreds of times before and not noticed it."

"I didn't know it existed until recently."

"Well, thanks for taking me out to lunch, guys. This is already a thousand times better than the plain sandwich I would've eaten at home."

We ate in silence for a few minutes, and then Joel spoke up. "So, Annie, what are you up to this week? Free as a bird, must be nice, eh?"

I inhaled softly. "I hadn't thought of it that way. I don't really know what I'm going to do this week ... or any week, for that matter.

No plans." I stuffed the rest of the crab cake in my mouth and closed my eyes to savor it.

At least he waited until I'd finished my last bite. "Have you given any more thought to my offer to teach part time?"

I licked my lips and then smiled as I saw the server approaching with our entrees already. After the food was arranged in front of us, I looked at him thoughtfully before picking up my utensils and diving into my stir-fry. "Not really." After a few bites, I exclaimed, "OK, this dish is amazing too. Please take me out to lunch every day."

Joel smiled. "It is delicious. But you should really consider his offer, Annie. I've seen you dance ballet, and Raf tells me you've done contemporary too. In my professional opinion, you're phenomenal, for someone who doesn't train regularly."

That gave me pause. He *was* a professional. He was also my friend—well, my best friend's fiancé to be specific—but also a very talented professional. He knew dance talent when he saw it. I'd always felt like a natural on the stage, though pursuing it as a career had never interested me. Still, I had nothing else going on right now. "Oh, what the heck. Sure, I'll teach your little dancers, Rafael. Temporarily."

Rafael's face lit up as he literally squealed and bounced out of his chair. "Yay, I'm so glad. The kids are going to *love* you. Or hate you, but sometimes that's a good thing in a dance teacher," he said with a laugh. "But actually, I can arrange it so you have some teen and adult classes too, not just little kids."

"Sure, I'm open to whatever. I've never been good at tap or hip-hop though. I can handle ballet or maybe contemporary. Possibly jazz if you're in a pinch."

"Let's go over the schedules this afternoon and figure out what classes would work best. The other two teachers have some flexibility and probably wouldn't hate us too much if I shuffled some classes around. Are you around this afternoon?" Rafael asked. "Wait, what am I saying? Of course you're around. You have literally nothing to do."

I opened my mouth to utter a sarcastic retort and then laughed instead. "You're right."

As we continued to eat and the two lovers began discussing wedding ideas, my mind began to drift. I was kind of excited to actually get paid to teach dance, just for fun for a while, though it wasn't my true calling. But what was? I needed to keep thinking about what I truly wanted. I had no idea.

"Annie, are you listening?"

I jolted, looking at the two men. "I, uh, sorry. Daydreaming. What's up?"

"We were just discussing the wedding. Big, flashy wedding, small cozy one, or elope. What do you think?"

"Uh, I really can't make that kind of decision for you. What are you leaning toward?"

Rafael looked exasperated. "We just finished talking about that. You didn't hear any of it?"

"Sorry, guys. Wedding stuff isn't really my thing," I admitted. When they looked at me with brows furrowed, I held up my hands. "What? Just because I'm a woman, I'm supposed to love weddings and be all about wedding planning?"

They sighed, and Rafael said, "Fair enough."

"So what *are* you guys leaning toward as of now?"

Joel grinned at Rafael and then at me. "Let's make it a surprise for now, eh, love?"

"That suggests eloping, but that would be too obvious. So I've narrowed it down to *not* eloping."

Rafael narrowed his eyes. "Are you suggesting we're predictable in our unpredictableness?"

I smirked. "Something like that. Hey, we're going to order dessert, right? Because you know that's why I'm here."

"Meanwhile, she's just regular old 'predictable,'" Rafael said to Joel, tongue in cheek. "Only Annie can turn any discussion into a conversation about dessert in a matter of seconds, all while looking like *that*." He gestured toward my figure, reclining against the chair.

It was true—I could eat anything and stay slim. Society's idea of an ideal figure, slender with the hint of an hourglass shape, was one of the few things I'd been lucky to inherit from Jacqueline. My mother also liked to point to our lush red hair, sea-green eyes, heart-shaped faces, well-formed lips, and fashion sense—as silly as it sounded—as if they were accomplishments. As if we'd done anything to deserve them. Of course, I knew that it all meant essentially nothing. My body wasn't better than anyone else's, despite what society said. Sometimes, it even made me feel strangely inferior, though I never bothered to analyze why. My socially approved beauty had opened doors, but I had learned it meant little in the grand scheme of things.

"Well, I, for one, can't eat another bite," Joel said.

Rafael leaned in for a dramatic whisper. "He actually means it."

I smiled. As we waited for the server to bring the dessert menu, my thoughts returned to my situation. What did I want in life? At least, career-wise?

Why was it so hard to figure out? After we placed our dessert orders, I stared out the window at the blustery spring day, trying to envision what my ideal life would be. At first the vision was ... empty. Then hazy. Then ...

"*Books.*"

"What?" I turned to see Joel looking at me.

The crease between my brows deepened. "What?"

Joel studied me with an amused expression. "You were staring into space and then said 'books' out of nowhere."

"Quite decisively, I might add." Rafael eyed me curiously.

I pressed my lips together. "I said that aloud? Oh—" And then the server arrived, and all words escaped me as my eyes lit upon the strawberry shortcake that Rafael and I were going to share. "I can see why you wanted to share, Raf. This is massive."

We both dipped our dessert spoons into the cake and then sighed in unison. When our spoons nearly collided for the second bite, Joel smiled, shaking his head with mirth. "Watching you two eat dessert is almost better than actually eating it."

After several more bites, Rafael slowed down. "So, Annie, did you have some kind of revelation about books?"

I set my spoon down reluctantly. "I'm not sure. Maybe this will sound silly. No, it definitely will—"

"Say it," Rafael said, rolling his eyes.

"I was asking myself, what do I want to do with my life? I know, deep stuff for a casual lunch," I said with a half-smile. "And then I thought, something to do with books. That's all … that's as far as I got, before I apparently blurted it out to you guys."

"You've always been better with talking things out loud rather than doing the internal debates, girl."

"That's true." I was an extrovert through and through. Most of the time, I'd much rather talk about things than think about them. And I'd been stuck in my head far too much lately. "I don't mean editing dull nonfiction books like I've been doing since college. I mean, well, actually … I don't know. Like, I have no idea. But not what I did before."

Joel looked thoughtful. "Books … hmm. What about writing books? Novels? Are you interested in that?"

I shook my head slowly. "I don't think I'd have the patience. I love to read books, but I don't think I could write them. I could maybe edit fiction, but I'm sort of leaning toward moving away from editing at the moment. Or at least taking a break from it."

"Maybe you could be a professional book reviewer," Rafael offered. "Is that a thing?"

"It is a thing, but it's not an entry-level thing. People have usually built up respected literary careers first before their opinion can be trusted as a professional reviewer. Well, at least the good ones." I took a long drink of my iced tea. "I probably need something entry level." When Rafael made a face, I added, "It's fine, I'm only twenty-six. I don't mind starting over."

We were all silent for a while. Finally, Joel asked, "Something in publishing?"

"I really don't know … maybe."

"Just tell me you won't be a cashier at the bookstore," Rafael said, waving his hand imperiously. "You can't go *that* entry level."

My eyes widened ever so slowly as the idea took hold.

Yes!

The voice inside was quiet but firm. I took another sip of iced tea. "Hold up. I like that idea, Raf. Don't be a snob. What's wrong with working the bookstore counter? I could learn more about book sales. You're right that it's entry level, almost like *pre-entry level*, but I'm fine with that. Everyone has to start somewhere."

Rafael's nose wrinkled in distaste, and Joel nudged him. "Hey, she's right. Don't be a snob, love." Then he turned toward me with an encouraging smile. "I think it's a great idea if that interests you!"

Rafael sighed. "All right, sorry, it's snobbish, you're right. I just have such grand plans and dreams for you, girl. But everyone has to start somewhere, or so the cliché goes." He clasped my hands, pulling them across the table towards him. "You'll be amazing at this, and before you know it, you'll be running the place. Or, like, starting your own."

With a playful tilt of my head, I flashed a brilliant smile at him and then Joel. "Oh, heck yes."

"Bye, Fatima!" I called out to the receptionist while swinging the door open to leave. I'd just finished teaching a grueling advanced ballet class, and for the second time this week, I felt chastened that I was far more out of breath than the teens in this class. I was heading home to shower because even though Rafael's studio had a shower that the teachers and a select few dancers could use, I much preferred bathing in my own home. Besides, it wasn't a long walk home, maybe a mile.

I slid my sunglasses over my eyes and felt an ache in my legs, so I stopped to do a quick quad stretch. Once I started walking in the direction of home, my mind started drifting to Rafael's happy news.

Despite sharing a love of dance, not to mention talent, he and Joel were so different. Sometimes it was hard to see how they'd found love, but I was so glad they had. Rafael deserved that. So did Rainn, and I hoped that he'd find it someday.

A pang of guilt stabbed me in the chest as I remembered how I'd refused to help with the wedding planning. Not my kindest moment, but Rafael deserved the best and more, including from me. I resolved to talk to Rainn later that night to see how we could help Rafael with the wedding. I didn't know a thing about wedding planning, but I'd thrown many amazing parties, so surely that would count for something.

With a self-satisfied smile, I started to round the corner at the end of the block.

I'll plan the most gorgeous wedding, and they—

The upper half of my body slammed into something solid, unforgivably hard, and then it bounced back, and so did I.

Trying to catch my breath, I glanced upward with wide eyes at the thing—no, the person—I'd collided with. Upward because he was tall. And panting, just like me. As my eyes traveled upward above his wide neck, a slightly tingly feeling pulsed through me. I noted first his strong set jaw, covered in at least a few days' worth of stubble, and his tanned skin, complementing his head of short, dirty blond hair. He wore a winter hat pulled low over his eyebrows, almost concealing his eyes, whose color was in shadow.

"I'm sorry," I managed, still out of breath, putting my hand on my heart. "I was a little lost in thought."

As soon as I started speaking, the man froze in place, his full lips open slightly as if he'd been about to speak. Then, before I could blink, he mumbled a curt apology and brushed past me.

I'd never seen a man run away from me so fast.

Or at all, actually.

What the...

I turned to stare at him as he speedwalked away. Sure, I was a little sweaty from dance class and maybe not looking amazing, but surely I didn't look horrific.

Ignoring the tight feeling in my chest, I shrugged, about to turn back and continue on my way when I saw his steps slow, and he turned around.

Time ... stopped.

It can't be.

I'd know those steel-grey eyes anywhere.

Kylan.

This time, with his face out of the shadows, I could see his features more clearly even though he was farther away. The full lips I'd kissed, so many times. The fluff of hair at his neck that I'd always liked running my fingers through. The nose he thought was too big. The eyes ... I could drown in their beauty, shining with the love he'd had for me.

Past tense.

Oh, Kylan.

My throat made a sound.

His eyes were on me.

I moistened my dry lips and tried to form a thought. Anything coherent.

It's him. And he's looking at me.

The next thing I knew, I was nearly tripping over the icy front steps into a store, my senses instantly overwhelmed by the smell of cats and dogs. Dazed and desperate, I glanced around. It was a pet store. I walked in slowly, seeking a place to hide where I could still see out the window.

What the heck am I doing? Why did I run in here like an idiot?

The cats for adoption were arranged near the front windows, so I pretended to be looking for a new pet while watching until the coast was clear outside.

Probably a stupid plan, but the only one I've got.

When I found a place that seemed relatively safe where he wouldn't likely see me unless he came really close (and why would he?), I peered outside. From here, I couldn't spot anyone, but I'd keep watch for a while until it was likely he'd moved on.

Smooth plan, you lunatic.

My self-recrimination was rudely interrupted by a young man's voice nearby. "Hi, can I help you?" he asked, startling me. "Interested in adopting a kitten?"

I turned to the man, more of a boy. He couldn't be more than 18 or 19 years old. "Oh, I don't know. Maybe just looking today."

"Looking ... for a cat?" he said hopefully.

So this kid fancied himself a salesman, did he? "I'm not sure yet," I mumbled, a hint of irritation in my voice as my eyes darted back toward the window.

"You look like you're window shopping, but from the wrong side of the window," he said with a laugh.

I turned back to him with narrowed eyes, but when I saw the friendly look on his face, I sighed with a slight smile. "You know what? That's actually more reasonable than the truth, sadly."

The young man smiled back. "I won't ask. As long as you take a moment to look at these adorable little guys and girls. Maybe just hold one of them? Then if you still want to walk away and go home kitten-less, I'll let you."

I raised an eyebrow. He was shrewd.

"I'm Franco, by the way. Would you like to meet Charlie?" he asked, pointing to the little cat in front of me.

I nodded reluctantly, anxiously eyeing the window again before turning to the cage.

Franco handed me the kitten. "He's a Siamese, healthy as can be, and he's just four months old. He won't last more than a day or two before someone adopts him because he's just so cuddly and—" Charlie started purring and immediately climbed up to my shoulder to tug at my ponytail. "Well, you can see. He's freaking adorable."

I rubbed Charlie's fluffy cheeks and gazed at his little face as he rubbed it against mine. For a moment, I forgot about the threat outside; I forgot everything except this adorable ball of fur.

"I'll take him back now," Franco was saying as he tried to take Charlie out of my arms.

I clutched him a bit tighter before realizing what I was doing. "Oh, of course."

"I'm sure you want to get back to your window shopping in re-verse," Franco said. Then he lowered his voice. "I won't tell anyone."

I looked at Charlie, back in the cage and gazing at me with his gorgeous little blue eyes, his paw against the cage wall closest to me. Franco turned to leave.

"Wait."

He turned back, a grin spreading across his face. "Should I get the paperwork?"

I narrowed my eyes. "Man, you're good. And yes. Go."

Am I really doing this?

Apparently I was. As I waited, I stepped back over to get a clearer view out the window but saw nothing. Kylan was surely gone by now. He'd probably left as soon as I weirdly disappeared. Maybe he hadn't even recognized me in the first place but merely turned around to make sure the woman he'd nearly knocked over was still standing up.

But I felt it, something in his gaze even from a distance ... he knew it was me.

How could he not?

Before I could dwell on it further—there would be plenty of time for that later—Franco returned. "If I can tear you away from the window, we can go to the table in the back of the store to go over the paperwork."

"Wait, can we bring Charlie back there with us?"

"Sure," he answered with a smirk. "Do you have a pet carrier to bring him home in? I'm guessing not ..."

I blanked. "Oh, uh ... no, I have nothing. No pet supplies whatso-ever. Oh, this is going to be a great day of commission for you, isn't it?"

He grinned again. "It'll all be worth it when Charlie is snuggling up and purring in your lap tonight."

A smile tugged at the corners of my lips. "I've always liked cats, actually—"

"And then chewing on your toes tonight while you're trying to sleep."

Chapter 9

Strolling through Loring Park the next day, I scanned the early spring scene around me. Winter wasn't over yet—this was Minnesota, after all—but there were signs of rebirth all around. It wasn't freezing today, and some children were even running around without coats on. I'd worn a coat, but only because it looked so perfect with my outfit. I glanced in the other direction toward some still-bare trees near a bike rack.

My heart skipped a beat when I spotted him turning around, his eyes shaded as he removed his helmet.

When he slid his sunglasses off, I exhaled sharply and nearly tripped on a rock in my path.

It's not him.

I tried to calm my racing heart as I focused on putting one foot in front of the other.

Of course it wasn't him. What were the odds I'd see him two days in a row?

I bit my lip, shaking my head at the ridiculous thought. I'd managed to avoid dwelling on yesterday's encounter too much. It had been surprisingly easy with a new kitten to deal with. Like most kittens, Charlie was fun but exhausting to take care of. And obviously adorable. Though he kept me up most of the night, I'd been a little sad to leave him with Rafael today for this lunch meeting at the park.

I refocused my attention on the path in front of me, being sure to avoid any rocks or branches left by the recently melted snow and ice. When my eyes landed on Jack Normandy, I nearly lost my footing again, and my heartbeat quickened a bit. I wasn't interested in Jack, not like *that*, but I was anticipating some tension with him today. Maybe a lot.

"Jack!" I said, coming toward the picnic table where he sat, his lunch set out in tidy containers around him.

"Hey, Annie, it's good to see you," he said with a genuine smile.

Relief coursed through me. So far so good. He didn't seem angry. Not that Jack was the angry type—he was the most even-tempered man I'd ever met, even to a fault. He should show *some* feeling once in a while, I'd always thought privately. "Same to you," I said, sliding into the bench across from him and putting down my lunch bag. "Thanks for agreeing to BYO lunch at the park. I'm unemployed, so I need to save my pennies."

"Are you kidding? I love eating at the park. I always ask myself why we don't—why I don't do it more often." He ran his hands through his wavy brown hair in a little gesture of what I could only gather was nerves. The "we" slip was interesting. Was he referring to himself with a love interest? He'd always been so mum about any lovers or girlfriends. I knew next to nothing about his love life, actually; I wasn't even certain if he was straight. Except ... there was something about the way he looked at Viviana that made me wonder sometimes. They had been best friends forever, yet sometimes in his gaze I read something more than platonic feelings. I shivered.

It's probably my imagination—it's not like I've been great at identifying real *romantic feelings lately.*

"Well, thank you, nonetheless." I dug into my packed lunch. "I will admit I have an ulterior motive, though hanging out with you is always fun, Jack."

"Sure it is," he said with a lopsided smile. "Fun is what I'm known for."

I peered at him for a moment before shrugging. He was giving off a kind of strange mood, but I couldn't put my finger on it. He was his usual pleasant self, yet there was something different, maybe an edge that I hadn't seen before. *Interesting.* Making a mental note to probe later, I unwrapped my PBJ sandwich. "Then I hope this won't be too disappointing. I've come on business, sort of. That is, I want to learn about your business."

"My business? You want to know about *Randall's*?" He was a highly esteemed writer for a well-regarded literary publication, as well as being the author of several books. During and after grad school, his success had come fast, and he was already well on the path to peaking in his career, if he hadn't already. I wondered how it felt to be a writer who'd reached such heights in his career already. He couldn't be more than 35 at the most, if his classic good looks and toned physical form were any indication.

"Not *Randall's* specifically, just ... publishing, books, all of it." I paused to chew a mouthful of sticky-sweet PBJ.

"Are you interested in becoming a writer?"

"Me? Not a chance." I laughed. "I should back up. In the past weeks, some things have happened ... kind of a lot."

He nodded as though he understood that feeling. I wondered again what was going on with him, but I could try to wring it out of him later. No distractions now.

"Some good things, like Rafael getting engaged. But some not so good." I drew in a deep breath. "So, this is a little bit mortifying, but it must be said. The short version is this: Brandon turned out to be a cheating jerk. So I had to quit Bolder. Now I'm, well, I guess you could say I'm exploring my options. I think ... no, I *know* I don't want to look for another editing job."

His eyes widened. "That is a lot. And from the look on your face, I can tell it's not even the half of it. I have to say ... well, never mind. It's not my place. Let's talk about the career move—"

"Wait, Jack. You can say anything to me."

His blue eyes stared into mine, and he gave me an earnest smile. "I was going to say Brandon didn't deserve you. I will admit I'm a little surprised. He did seem decent, unlike his friend Greg. I knew *he* was a jerk from the start. I only wish Vivi had seen it sooner."

The very last thing I wanted to talk about was anything adjacent to my falling out with Viviana, but the look on his face contained such anguish that I couldn't just bypass the subject. "Jack, what ... happened?"

"You don't know?"

I shook my head. "I haven't been in touch with her or with Brandon. Didn't Viv mention we had a huge fight? Probably my fault."

"If she did, it was vague," Jack said, his brows furrowed. "Sorry, I can't recall the details."

I bit my lip. It wasn't really relevant right now, was it? "It doesn't matter. Suffice to say, we fought, bitterly. And haven't talked since. I need to call her, but ... I haven't yet. I have been going through a lot of other stuff, I guess, is my only excuse."

His face was full of sympathy. "It's all right, Annie. You don't need an excuse for me."

I wanted to hug him, but we weren't that close. "Thanks, Jack. That means a lot. It's been a hell of a week. Or two weeks. I've lost track. Anyway ... I feel bad about Viv, but I don't know what to do about it. I've never been awesome at friendships with other women, for some reason. *And* I don't know why I'm telling you that." I laughed self-consciously and took a sip of water to distract from my embarrassment.

He looked thoughtful for a moment. "Hey, not sure if it's your thing, but Jenn and Kieran are having one of their board game nights on Sunday. Vivi usually comes. Might be a low-key way to break the ice. Interested?"

I glanced up, surprised, and then I winced. I'd been invited a few times in the past but had always declined because, well, board games. Not my thing. So they'd given up on inviting me at least a year ago. "Well, I—"

Jack put his forkful of salad down and raised a hand. "No pressure, Annie. None at all. I was just throwing that out there. In fact, don't even answer. Just think on it."

I nodded slowly and smiled. "Thank you, Jack. That's really nice of you. You're right, it's not really an interest of mine, but ... I will at least think about it." I chewed some grapes and then frowned. "But will you tell me what happened with Greg? Did he hurt her? I'll kill him."

"I've contemplated bodily harm to him myself." Jack grimaced. He was the furthest thing from a violent person I'd ever met. The idea was laughable, except that this must mean that Gregory had been really awful to Viviana. "I don't want to share a lot of personal details that aren't my business to share, but basically he was using her to get information about her father. And she found out in a pretty awful way, overhearing him talking about her to Brandon."

My heart rate quickened, and I felt the flames of fury rise. I couldn't even think of Brandon with sadness or humiliation anymore; I felt only loathing.

He knew.

The bastard had been in on Gregory's scheme this whole time.

How could I have been so oblivious?

I was so angry I could barely speak. "So, in addition to playing me, all the while he was supporting some sick goal of Gregory's to exploit Viviana and her father? Brandon *had* to have known the whole time. Maybe dating me was even part of the plan. Either that or I was just a fun way to pass the time," I said, feeling the heat on my face as rage mounted.

Jack lowered his lids for a moment before looking up with a pained expression. "I'm so sorry you were part of this whole betrayal too. I blame myself in part. I knew Gregory was no good. I had no evidence, but I knew. Yet I stood by ... I should've been more vocal about it."

"Do you think she would've listened?" My voice rose. "No, Jack. I'm at fault. I saw them together quite a bit. I saw how he treated her ... and even how he talked about her if I asked when she wasn't around. I wanted it to work out between them, maybe for selfish reasons. I wanted to see Viviana happy, and the moments where Greg *wasn't* being a jerk, she did seem happy."

Jack made a face but nodded slightly in acknowledgement. "I know what you mean. I suppose that's why I didn't say anything. I didn't want to ruin her happiness or her excitement."

"She seemed to really like him, at times. I hoped ... well, I should've known it wouldn't go anywhere with someone like him. But I wanted that for her. I don't think I've ever seen her truly in love before." I sighed. "For that matter, I don't think I've seen *you* in love before either, Jack."

He paused momentarily in chewing what appeared to be a home-made trail mix. The pause was very brief, and I wouldn't have noticed if I hadn't been watching him carefully. When he finished chewing, he folded his hands in front of him and looked at them for several long seconds. Finally, he looked up with a slight smile. "We're not here to talk about me, are we?"

I laughed, feeling some of the earlier anger and tension dissipating. "Fair enough, Jack. Though I do want to hear about your work. Tell me everything you know about book publishing, book sales, anything adjacent to that."

Appearing relieved, he sat back with ease, popping another hand-ful of raisins and nuts in his mouth. "That I can do. Anything I can emphasize in particular?"

"I want to know how the business works, what kinds of opportunities there might be for someone just starting out, willing to work her way up, that sort of thing," I said, my voice slightly shaky at the end. Inexplicably, I felt a little nervous. Perhaps because I was finally thinking about—and ready to start talking about and hearing about—something I might actually grow to care about and build a life around. My true calling. Maybe. "I don't think I want to edit, and I don't think I'm cut out for writing books. But I want to be ... near books. Involved with them somehow. Or other kinds of publications, I don't know. Tell me everything. Educate me, wise master."

His wide smile set me at ease once again, and he proceeded to do just that. Though he worked for a periodical, not a book publisher, he had in fact written several published books and knew a lot of people in adjacent industries. He was easy on the eyes too, I observed as he spoke animatedly about his passions. But I also reconfirmed that I felt nothing more than friendship for him.

Which was a bit of a relief, but also disappointing ... ugh, why *wouldn't* I be attracted to someone like Jack?

Not because of ...

Freaking Kylan.

Get out of my head.

And out of my city.

Chapter 10

Standing with my hands on my bare hips, I examined my options laid out on the bed. First was a crisp, navy blue pantsuit, which I'd worn only once before, for my Bolder interview years ago. Next to the pantsuit was a blue and yellow floral dress with a sash at the waist and a long flowy skirt that nearly reached my ankles. And on the right was a baby blue ribbed sweater and newish jeans.

What does one wear when going to an interview at a bookstore? Well, possibly an interview. I hadn't even applied yet. But I hoped that by appearing in person, I could ask to speak to the manager and sell myself as someone to hire on the spot. Or at least as someone to interview. Surely they needed someone in some area of the store, whether working at the cash register or stocking the shelves. Wrinkling my nose with distaste, I thought I might even agree to clean bathrooms if that's what it took to get my foot in the door. I was committed to finding my destiny. And I was going to do it. Today.

Bookshop was the natural place to do it. It was my favorite bookstore by far.

So I needed to dress for success, right? But I didn't want to seem presumptuous. How silly would it be if they were hiring for cashiers and I interviewed in an expensive pantsuit? They'd never hire me.

Still, I couldn't bring myself to go to the interview in jeans, even designer ones that fit me like a glove.

I picked up the floral dress lovingly. I didn't wear it very often and wasn't sure why, because it was beautiful. My eyes swept over the soft fabric. It would be perfect for today; the choice of outfit said, *"I took the time to look nice today but didn't want to look pretentious."* And I should know. Fashion was my thing. Or at least it used to be. I'd barely given it a thought lately, but perhaps that was for the best, given that fashion was an expensive habit and I needed to be a little frugal. At least until I had regular paychecks streaming in.

And with that thought, I smiled confidently and slipped the dress over my head. It seemed looser than usual. But the dress was designed to be loose, so no one would notice but me. I slipped into the bathroom to brush my teeth, apply my favorite cherry-red lipstick and black mascara, and brush my hair. I studied my reflection. It was a low-effort look that seemed just right for a bookstore interview. I flashed a brilliant smile in the mirror before turning to leave.

A short while later, walking up to the Bookshop sign with its fancy, old-style lettering carved into a dark wooden plank, I took a calming breath.

This is it. My destiny awaits.

I chuckled at my own dramatic words, drawing an amused look from an older couple walking by.

Once I'd stepped inside, I breathed in the books. The spines, the pages, the worlds within them, the stories, the characters, the people reading them, the tall shelves on which they sat, the ladders placed strategically throughout. Bookshop had an old-fashioned feel, with its wood floors and wood-paneled walls, many thick patterned rugs and upholstered chairs and wooden tables. It even boasted a small European-style cafe in the corner area, with some shockingly good coffee, tea, and pastries. Yet somehow the place didn't feel old and dusty; it was also large and thoroughly modern at the same time. I had no idea how they achieved that effect, but I'd love to find out. I meandered over to the registers, lightly touching the books I passed on their special display shelves.

"Can I help you?" asked a girl who looked about thirteen years old, but she had to be older because, well, labor laws. She had jet-black hair and a bored expression, and her arm was in a cast.

"Hi, I'm Annie," I said, flashing my winning smile. At least it was usually a win. This girl didn't even blink.

Sigh. Teenagers.

"I'm Sai." The girl pointed to her name tag, which read *Sayaka.* "Can I help you find something?"

The girl's unblinking stare was somehow a bit unnerving. I bit my lip.

Snap out of it. She's just a kid.

"Uh, yes. I'd like to speak to your manager."

Sai's eyes widened, and she opened her mouth to speak, but no words came.

"Sorry," I said, feeling compassion for the terrified teen. "I just realized how that sounded. Not what I meant at all. I'm here about a job. Is your manager in this morning?"

Sai's expression transformed from fear to relief to suspicion. "*You* are here about a job? What job?"

I tried to ignore the doubt in her tone.

She's just a kid. Be professional.

"Well, to answer your question, that's what I'd like to speak to the manager about."

A deep voice from behind jolted me. "I'm Sai's manager. How can I help you, Ms. ...?"

I turned toward the voice. The man a few feet away from me was tall and broad-shouldered, dressed in a crisp button-down that made him look more corporate than bookish. His dark skin contrasted with the pale shelves behind him, but it was the stillness in his posture that caught me—not unkind, but measured—like someone who didn't offer trust easily, especially to strangers walking in uninvited.

"I'm Annie York. It's great to meet you." I stuck out my hand, and he took it with reluctance, obviously unsure what to make of me. It was time to shine. "I'm actually here to talk about how *I* can help your store, Mr. ... ?"

His lips tightened almost imperceptibly. Perhaps he didn't appreciate my showing up uninvited. I knew that bothered some people, as my roommates had told me repeatedly. But I was prepared. I had a secret weapon. Myself.

"Hakeem Carter. Sorry, Ms. York. We're not currently hiring." His voice was flat, as though the conversation were over.

I heard a scoff, and I knew it was Sai, probably gloating. Why didn't the Bookshop staff seem to like me? Had I lost my touch? It was way too soon to give up, so I raised my chin. "Mr. Carter, I'd love to have 30 minutes of your time. Can we sit somewhere and chat?"

"I'm a busy manager, Ms. York. If you're looking for a job selling books, perhaps try the Barnes & Noble across the street. Or Amazon." Looking at me dismissively, he started to pivot on his heel.

"Mr. Carter, please," I pleaded. The slight disdain in his eyes told me that I hadn't fully succeeded in hiding my desperation. I took a deep breath. "Even 20 minutes would be nice. I could wait a bit, if you're busy right now. I'd be happy to sit and wait."

He observed my practiced smile and casual flipping of hair off my shoulders. But instead of feeling confident as I usually did, I got the uncomfortable feeling that he was seeing right through me now, though I didn't know how. I was so good at this! Performing. Winning people over. Wasn't I?

Finally, after a long silence, he nodded and said gruffly, "I'll give you 10 minutes. I need to finish something first. Wait over at the cafe. And we don't take loiterers, so I hope you can afford to buy a cup o' something."

I nodded, too fast, and smiled, this time genuinely. He was going to give me a chance! A real chance. I murmured a thank you as he turned to walk away, back toward his office presumably.

"You really impressed him," Sai said in that flat tone. She was probably being sarcastic, but I wasn't sure. Neither of them seemed the least impressed.

I simply smiled as best as I could manage and walked calmly toward the cafe, hoping I had enough cash in my purse for a coffee. I didn't typically bring my credit cards everywhere, as I was too prone to overspending, usually on clothing.

Two and a half long hours later, the manager finally appeared in the cafe, catching sight of me and then strolling over to the counter, apparently to get his own coffee, or annoy me, or both. My annoyance level was already sky-high, not only because of the ridiculous wait but also because he'd never once appeared to tell me he was delayed or to apologize. I'd asked Sai at the register several times and even a very elderly-looking man stocking books, but neither of them knew their boss's schedule, apparently. The last time I'd asked, I even detected a trace of sympathy from Sai before she quickly hid it with a smirk.

As I watched him chat with and even smile at the cafe workers, I grudgingly noticed he was objectively attractive. There was almost something a bit familiar about him, but I was probably imagining it. Handsome jerks were a dime a dozen, and I felt not a shred of attraction as I eyed him from a distance.

Finally, he appeared before me. "You're still here."

I smiled and gestured to the chair across from me. If he thought he could intimidate me, he was in for a surprise. I wasn't Jacqueline York's daughter for nothing.

He hesitated and then sat in the chair, placing his elbows on the table. "Ms. York, you wanted to meet?"

"Yes. I know you said you're not hiring. But I was hoping I could tell you a little about myself and what I could bring to your business, before you just dismiss me."

"Ms. York—"

"In fact, I insist. You said I could have 10 minutes, so I'm going to use them." This was bold, even for me. But I wasn't going to get anywhere with this guy without being demanding. I learned long, long ago that women who didn't stand up for themselves didn't have a chance in this world.

He waved his hand at me and grunted. "Go on then."

"Pleased to make your acquaintance, sir," I said, flashing another smile to smooth things over. "So, you could say I'm going through a rough patch in my life. I had to quit my work as a freelance editor recently for personal reasons. I have a bachelor's in English, and I'm good at editing, but I want to do something different, something that excites me. Something with books or publishing. I love reading. I don't exactly know the exact career path I want, but I'm willing to start at the ground level, learn about the business of books, and find out what my path should be. If you need someone to mop your floors at night for minimum wage, I'd even do that. And I don't want to work at Barnes & Noble. I want to work *here*. This place is amazing."

He was silent for so long that I assumed he wasn't going to respond. Finally, he spoke. "We have a cleaning company that comes in after hours." After another long pause, he added, "Even if we had a cash register or floor stocking position open, which we don't, I can't see you being a good fit."

I swallowed the lump in my throat. "Why not?"

"Look, I guess I applaud your willingness to work your way up in this business. But it's not going to work out, at least not here. I can't—"

What is it with this guy? Why does he hate me?

"Mr. Carter, may I ask you a question?"

He rolled his eyes. "I doubt I could stop you."

I ignored the sarcasm and looked him in the eye. "Why do you so obviously dislike me? You don't even know me."

He looked back at me for a long moment before looking away. "Oh, but I do."

I felt the anger rising, even while telling myself this was *not* the time to get angry. I had to keep my cool. I *had* to. "I hope you're not stereotyping me—"

"I'm not ... OK, you really don't remember, do you?" he said, exasperated.

I tilted my head in confusion. "I don't ... have we met?"

He pulled out his phone and swiped across and punched the screen with jerky motions. Then, he shoved it in front of my face so I could see a photo.

"Wait, that's *me*!" I squinted. "And ... I remember him! We had an awesome time at a friend's bachelor party, but ... why do *you* have this photo?" I looked at him, and his eyebrows were raised. "Wait, don't tell me that's *you*?"

He just stared at me, and the confirmation was in his eyes. I glanced between his face and the photo. It *was* him. The haircuts were very different, and he had a goatee now. "It is you. Hakeem Carter?" I whispered. "Now it all makes sense."

"What does?" He looked at me accusingly. "That you said you *had* to see me again but then never bothered to message me?"

"No, I tried looking you up the next day. I'd typed your name into my phone so I'd remember, but I was probably drunk and got either your first or last name really wrong because I remember not finding anyone on Facebook with a name even close to what I'd written down. Not anyone who looked like you, anyway."

He eyed me doubtfully.

"I was crushed, actually. I'd had an amazing time that night. I was actually furious that you didn't try to look *me* up."

"Well, I ... I mean ..." he fumbled for words. "Fine, point taken." He let out a long sigh and buried his head in his hands. When he finally raised his eyes to mine, his face looked a little friendlier. "Let's leave the past in the past. I shouldn't have been so petty. I'm sorry. And I'm happily married now anyway, so, yeah." His mouth curved into the smallest smile.

"Leaving the past in the past sounds like a wonderful idea," I concurred. Was there any way to salvage this potential job situation? "Listen, about the job thing—"

"Annie, is it OK if I call you that?" When I nodded, he continued, "I truly don't have the budget to hire anyone right now. I'm sorry. You're almost making me wish I could."

I tapped my nails on the table for a moment, my brain sorting quickly through all the ideas swirling around. "What if ... maybe you don't have to pay me." When he was about to interrupt, I stopped him. "No, hear me out. It could be like an internship. Or an actual internship. Think about it ... what do you wish you could hire someone for but can't get a budgeted position for?"

I sensed he was uncertain about the idea of an internship at all, so I pressed forward. "Who handles media, events, and communications for Bookshop?"

"Uh, that would have to be me or my assistant manager," he said with a grimace. "What little we have, that is. We have very little time or budget to organize things like that, so very little of it happens. So there wouldn't be much for you to do there, I'm afraid."

"But what if I coordinated all of it? I could be, like, your event coordinator intern? Or communication planning intern? Or something like that. If it's something you think could benefit the business and I handled it and you didn't have to pay me, it's a win-win-win." *Well, other than the lack of paycheck.* I had to force myself not to bounce up and down with excitement.

His brows were lowered, his expression skeptical. "I don't know. I can't imagine it would be that easy. I'd have to talk to corporate HR."

"Talk to them then."

He rubbed his trimmed beard for a moment before speaking. "I do believe this kind of stuff would increase sales, have always thought that. But I feel like we'd be exploiting you."

I beamed. "Don't you see? It's a win for me too. Because it lets me gain experience and exposure to this world of books that I'm dying to get into."

He started nodding slowly. "That's fair." A long moment went by, while he seemed deep in thought.

My heart was racing. This was the moment of truth. Would he go for it and give me a chance?

He met my eyes with an almost friendly expression. "Well, you've got some good points, actually. I need to think about this a bit and run it by HR. Can I get back to you in a day or two?"

I jumped out of my chair and nearly squealed. "I would hug you if not for all that weirdness of the past!" He sent me a dubious look. "Oh, and also because I'm a professional and you may be my boss, soon."

He nodded awkwardly then and rose from his chair. "I'll be in touch, Annie."

"You won't regret this, Hakeem."

"Um. We should probably exchange contact info this time," he said, his mouth twitching.

I bit my lip to keep from laughing. "Yes, sir."

"Actually, here's my email address. Just send me your resume for HR."

I rubbed my feet after removing my ballet flats, grateful that the classes I was teaching didn't require pointe shoes. Still, my feet weren't used to dancing this often; they hadn't been for years. Suddenly my phone buzzed.

Unknown number

Annie, this is Hakeem. Got HR approval.

Annie

YAY!

I mean, thank you. I'm so grateful for the opportunity.

Your internship starts today. Send me a summary of your ideas and a proposed description of the intern position by tomorrow morning.

Yes, boss.

I couldn't suppress my squeal of excitement, not caring that a few dancers and their parents were still in the building.

This could be it, the big break.

I was going to start by organizing a book club—maybe several—and for that I needed publicity. Maybe local authors. Book signings. A book festival? Kids' events with costumes for their favorite characters?

Oh, I know, how about a local writers' group? Writers love hanging out at bookstores and talking about writing. Like Jack and …

I felt an ache in my chest.

Viviana.

I miss her.

I sighed as I finished gathering my things to leave.

Would showing up at board game night tomorrow help or hurt the situation with her?

I needed to make things right.

Chapter 11

W e were face to face.

Viviana stood in the doorway, clutching the edge of the smooth wooden door tightly.

I stood next to Jack, who was smiling brightly, probably trying to ease the tension he no doubt anticipated. We were about to enter Jenn's townhouse for Sunday game night. From his other side, a slim arm stretched across Jack's shoulders, and his sister smiled. I'd honestly never seen two siblings get along as well as he and Belinda did. Sure, they teased each other a bit, but I'd never seen them arguing or angry with each other. Not for the first time, I wondered what it was like to have a loving, caring family. I used to like to believe my father was a wonderful, loving parent, but long after he was gone, I finally admitted to myself: Nope, he wasn't a great dad either. He didn't even love me enough to stay. And I didn't care if my thought was unfair.

Focus.

Say something!

Don't make it weirder.

Jack spoke first. "Jenn said to invite Annie, so—"

Before I could overthink it further, I stepped forward and smiled. "So here I am!"

Viviana looked uneasy and merely motioned toward the coat rack, avoiding eye contact.

I tried but failed to keep the smile on my face.

She's not going to make this easy, is she? But why should she? I was a real jerk to her.

"Uh—" I stopped to clear my throat. "I hope it's OK that I'm here."

Viviana stilled and turned toward me. "Sure, I mean ..." As she spoke, I attempted to communicate an apology with my eyes, but she lowered hers too quickly. "I didn't think board games were really your style."

I winced and glanced at Jack, wondering if this was a mistake. Was he thinking the same thing?

"This is our chance to show Annie what she's been missing all this time," Jack said in his light, soothing tone.

Viviana choked out a laugh and abruptly turned to Belinda and then to her husband. "Great to have you join us, Choua! I call dibs on your team."

Choua chuckled and rubbed his chin. "You and everyone else. I think it's time I picked my own team." He was ridiculously good at board games, especially strategy games. He smirked, and Belinda elbowed him with a fake scowl.

Belinda Vue was not only Jack's sister but Viviana's oldest friend along with Jenn. I liked Belinda and Jenn well enough and had spent time with them on many occasions, yet I'd never really felt like one of the girls. They were fun and friendly to me, but I wasn't close with them. It felt more ... surface level. The first time I'd noticed that, I'd let out a self-deprecating laugh as I reminded myself that the surface level was the only one that worked for me anyway.

I wondered if they were serving alcohol tonight—that tended to blunt the feeling of being an outsider in my friend group or others. Though I knew I should probably cut back on drinking.

As we proceeded to the living room, the tension between Viviana and me felt thick, but everyone else seemed unaware at first, laughing and joking with each other.

"Jenn, so sorry to hear about your leg," I said, sitting near her on the couch, where her leg was propped up near her crutches. "Jack filled me in. And Kieran's layoff. How's he doing?"

Crap. Is it rude to refer to someone's layoff in such explicit terms?

Jenn smiled at me. "Thanks, Annie. You know me, ugh, I hate being immobile. And stuck at home."

"As a fellow extrovert, I have the utmost sympathy," I said, my hand on my heart.

"I knew you would. The only people I see are Kieran and the kids, who have been *so* whiny. But they're probably just always whiny because they're little. As for Kieran, you can ask him yourself."

As soon as Kieran walked into the room, everyone peppered him with questions and unsolicited advice about the job market. From the start, though, I could see in his eyes that he wanted to forget about it for the night. I could relate, obviously. How often lately had my friends forced me to talk about the very last thing I wanted to talk about?

Fortunately, Jenn knew her husband well and steered the group conversation away from Kieran and toward the first game we'd be playing. I felt some of the tension melt away until realization struck: This meant an actual board game. That I had to play. It had been years.

Four years, to be exact.

Please, please let it be nothing like D&D...

Lucky for me, the first game involved drawing and guessing. I liked to draw and was decent at it. I could do this. It was a pretty funny game too, and that, along with some beer, helped loosen the tension aching from a dozen places in my body. Occasionally I eyed Viviana, who seemed a bit more relaxed too, though only slightly. Granted, she wasn't the most relaxed person in general. As the night progressed, I noticed that Viviana was acting a bit stiff around Jack too. Of course, I was careful to observe them covertly.

Or so I thought until Jenn whispered in my ear, "So you're noticing it too? Something's up with Viv and Jack."

"Things do seem a little off." I placed my finger on my lips thoughtfully.

Before we could say more though, Kieran announced a switch to a roleplaying game, and my heart rate quickened.

I can do this.

I can do this.

It's not D&D, it's not Kylan, and who cares anyway? That was forever ago.

Jenn must have noticed my grimace. "Are you all right, Annie?"

"Oh, I'm—I'm fine," I stammered before gulping down the rest of my beer. "I'm so thirsty though, anyone else?" I forced a smile, the party-girl smile I'd mastered and used hundreds if not thousands of times before to show the world that I didn't care about anything serious, that I was all about fun and good times.

But my cool-girl facade couldn't withstand the tension soon to come as Kieran and Choua set up the next game, which required partners. With the two married couples pairing up, that left Jack, Viviana, and me. "Oh, I didn't even think about the uneven numbers until now," Jenn said, biting her lip. "Ugh, I'm usually so good at planning to avoid that."

"No problem. I can sit this one out," Jack said, leaning back as if to suggest he welcomed a chance to rest.

"No! I'll sit out," Viviana said almost forcefully. "I, uh, I was the last-minute addition to this party anyway, I think."

Wow, she won't even pretend she doesn't want to avoid partnering with me.

As Viviana avoided eye contact and I tried to figure out how to respond, Kieran cut in. "Don't be silly. We'll just play something else. If you haven't noticed, we have a number of other games to choose from. A ridiculous number, actually."

I leaned back in partial relief and started to put my practiced smile back on until I glanced at both Jenn and Belinda giving Viviana meaningful looks. Surprisingly, a stab of envy lodged itself somewhere in my chest. What must it be like to have such close female friends—and for most of their lives? The one female friend I'd managed to hang onto for any length of time now seemed to hate me and was no longer speaking to me.

Well, you need to actually talk to her. Apologize, make things right. Not just awkwardly show up to game night.

But I couldn't face the voice of reason in my head right now. I just needed to survive this evening. I nodded pleasantly to everyone and pretended to be engaged in whatever they were talking about.

I glanced down in my lap, running slightly sweaty palms over my tweed skirt.

Since when do I wear tweed?

I sighed, remembering I was far behind on laundry. Then again, I could always go shopping ... retail therapy was my favorite kind.

The only kind, as far as I was concerned.

"Wow, you look ... fancy for a Monday morning," Jack said, a polite questioning look on his face.

I sighed, setting my purse down as I sat down at the table at the Krumkake Cafe. Its sweet and savory fare was top-notch, especially the scones. But I was too tired to appreciate it. "Sorry I'm so late. So, it turns out combining two of my favorite bad habits in one night isn't the best idea, especially if I'm going to agree to a super early breakfast with a friend." I winced while finger-combing my hair. "I may have just woken up 10 minutes ago. I barely even glanced in the mirror, so I'm hoping my face isn't a disaster." I hadn't worn eye makeup yesterday, so I had no black streaks running down my face. Probably.

Jack smiled, amused. "No worries, Annie."

"So I don't lose my reputation as having amazing fashion sense, I went shopping last night at Karla's, you know that trendy new clothing store with the bar and crazy hours—well, maybe you don't.

Anyway, I tried on some dresses, and I … might have had a few more drinks, so I ended up passing out wearing one of them. I didn't bother to change since I was running so late." I gestured to the very short (but somehow still classy) red dress I was still wearing, rather overdressed for a cafe breakfast meeting with a friend. "That's probably more than you cared to know. It's gorgeous though, isn't it?" I asked with a grin.

"It looks very nice, Annie. I'd expect no less from you." Jack nodded.

"But so much for penny pinching," I said, frowning. "I should probably just order a water. That's still free, isn't it?"

"I don't think so," Jack said, laughing. "Don't worry about it. Breakfast is on me."

"No need. I'm not *that* poor, Jack. Yet. I actually have a little savings I can dip into." When he raised an eyebrow, I sighed. Why was everyone so surprised that I was capable of saving money? As though whatever stereotyped categories they'd placed me in excluded the possibility that I could be halfway decent at managing money. Instead of being defensive though, I said smoothly, "I've spent years splitting rent and expenses with two roommates." I didn't mention that I'd learned to save at a young age. Because of Jacqueline. Not that my mother had taught me to save—of course not, my mother had no notion of what saving meant. I didn't want to be anything like her, and I'd realized early that independence meant having your own money, not relying on others to support you.

He nodded. "That makes sense. Renting, in the right situation, can be a good way to save money," he said, a bit cryptically. Was that why he still lived in that apartment building just down the hall from Viviana, even though he surely earned much more money than she did and could afford something far better—was it because he was saving for something, a house perhaps?

I rose from my seat. "I'm going to go place my order. Be right back."

As I ordered a bacon cheese croissant and fruit, the woman behind the register looked me up and down with a somewhat resentful, calculating gaze. I pressed my lips together. It was that *She needs some meat on her bones* look that I often got from older women. As if she hadn't *tried* over the years.

Or maybe … it was something else. When the woman looked over to Jack and then back to me, I began to suspect it had something to do with Jack. After all, he was a regular here, he'd said.

"You can have a seat. We'll bring it out when it's ready," the woman said flatly, placing a coffee on the counter and then turning away.

When I slid back into the seat at our table, I asked Jack, "Do you know the cashier?"

"Melanie? Oh yeah, Vivi and I come here all the time, so we're all on a first-name basis. Mel's fantastic."

"Huh," I mumbled. Then what on earth was that? Did this Melanie somehow disapprove of me as a friend for Jack? How ridiculous did that even sound? I shook my head to clear my thoughts. "So, Jack, how are you doing?"

"I'm fine. How about you?" he said, studying me. "I'm sorry if last night wasn't great."

"It … wasn't. I shouldn't have come," I admitted. "I mean, Viv and I have had a serious fracture in our friendship, and showing up randomly to put her on the spot while playing board games? I should've known that was a dumb move."

"Well, you can blame me for suggesting it. I'm sorry, Annie," Jack said, frowning.

"You were just trying to help." I sipped my coffee and gazed at him thoughtfully. "Viviana did seem troubled by something else though. Maybe it wasn't just me." When he didn't reply, I asked, "Did you notice that?"

"I … did," Jack answered. He looked past me then and gave a polite nod to the server on the way to their table. As the server arranged the food in front of me, I took the opportunity to watch Jack. He appeared uncomfortable, which struck me as peculiar—he was always so at ease. Still, I could postpone any further questioning for the moment.

"So, I have news," I said, my tone rising with excitement as I picked up the buttery croissant sandwich in front of me. "I'm officially doing an internship for Bookshop. I've got my foot in the door!"

Jack's face lit up, all traces of his previous mood vanishing. "That's wonderful, Annie! What is the position?"

"We're calling the position the literary events coordinator. So I'll plan book clubs, book signings, and other special events to be hosted at the store. It sounds like a dream, doesn't it?"

Jack laughed heartily. "For the right person, yes. And I do believe that person will be you. When do you start?"

"I already did, the day after I walked into the store insisting they give me a job." I laughed. "My boss is pretty demanding and wanted me to start immediately."

"Sounds like a great match then."

"Yes, but it was an uphill climb. It was really hard to convince him to give me a chance. Turns out he was a guy I'd been briefly involved with years ago, but I hadn't recognized him ... It was a mess." I shook my head but then smiled. "I convinced him I'm worth a shot."

Jack smiled admiringly. "I'm not at all surprised. Congratulations, Annie. Can I come to the book club? It's been years since I was part of one, but I'd love to join." Then a frown marred his face. "Under normal circumstances, Vivi would come too, but ... well, you know. Maybe someday."

"Yeah," I said wistfully. "But I'm not here to mope. I'd love to pick your brain for ideas about events. Maybe you could be our inaugural guest author!"

Jack scratched his head, making a face. "I sure could, if it would help you out, but surely people would be more interested in an author with a recent release. I haven't published any books in a couple years. And maybe an author with a bit more mass appeal."

"So modest, Jack." I grinned. "We'll see. So for the book club, I'm thinking of organizing around themes that change on a quarterly basis. For example, historical fiction for a quarter, or even more specific, Victorian literature. Or if that's too academic, then modern mystery or romance, YA, books with social justice themes, that sort of thing. And then each quarter, we'd select a handful of books within that theme to discuss. I'm still organizing the ideas before writing them up for Hakeem—he's the manager. Do you have any thoughts? I'm particularly wondering if—"

I closed my mouth when Jack's eyes widened as he seemed to spot something beyond me.

Viviana was standing near the front counter, smiling in our direction until I met her gaze. Her face immediately fell, and she gasped audibly.

Then, with no subtlety whatsoever, she simply spun around and turned her back on us. A woman behind the counter—not Melanie from before—came over to give her a coffee. I stared for a moment and then turned back to Jack, whose face was a mix of emotions.

"What—"

"That's—"

We both sighed and eyed one another with sympathy.

"Jack, I don't know if I should stay—"

His throat cleared loudly, and he looked pointedly over my head. Even as I turned, I knew what I'd find. Viviana was standing a few feet from our table. I studied her closely. She looked tired, physically and emotionally. Her usually cute, wavy brown hair looked limp, her eyes tired, and her posture slumped.

"Vivi, I never thought I'd see you here so early!" Jack said, still looking shocked but not unhappy to see her.

Viviana was clearly trying very hard to be polite and maintain composure, but I could tell something was bothering her. Tension was radiating from her in waves. "Well, that makes two of us. Or three, I guess." Her eyes darted to me for a split second before turning back to Jack.

I should speak up. Why not try to mend things? Maybe this wasn't the best scenario, but there might never be a perfect time. "Hi, Viv. Would you like to join us?" I asked in a quiet, friendly tone.

Jack added, "Yes, Vivi, pull up a chair."

Her eyes met mine but then drifted down, if I wasn't mistaken, to my dress, and she was quick to decline. "Oh, no, I can't. I have a *lot* to do today."

Jack was still smiling, but the light in his eyes seemed to dim a bit. "You do? I thought you were free for another week until you started that new job."

"Oh, you got a new job? Congratulations!" I offered a generous smile.

"Yes, is that so hard to believe?" Viviana snapped at me. Or us. I wasn't sure. "I do have a new job starting soon, *and* I do have things to do today."

I reared back, and Jack looked stunned as well.

So much venom in her tone.

Is this still about Brandon, or something else?

Jack inhaled slowly. "I'm sure we didn't mean to imply—"

"It's fine," Viviana interrupted. She closed her eyes and massaged her temples. "Sorry, I didn't mean to snap. It's just, I do have a busy day ahead, so I don't really have time to chat. And I wouldn't want to interrupt your ... well, whatever this is."

I eyed Jack, who looked troubled, maybe even hurt.

And well he should. Viv is his best friend. What the heck?

She still refused to look at me. Still, I needed to try again. "Viv, I—"

"You two have a lovely breakfast," Viviana said, her smile a little too bright, before spinning on her heel and making a beeline for the exit.

My jaw dropped as I watched her nearly collide with an older man in her haste to reach the exit door. When she was out the door, I swiveled back to face Jack, who looked stricken. That was my best guess, anyway. It wasn't an expression I'd ever seen on him before. "Jack, are you all right? I'm—I'm so sorry. I think this is all my fault."

He shifted his gaze from the cafe window slowly to my concerned face. "What? No. How could it be? You were friendly, just as you were last night."

"She seemed really upset, much more so than last night," I said quietly, eyes focused on my lap. "Do you think ..."

"Do I think what?"

I opened my mouth and then closed it. "You don't think she got the wrong idea, do you?" I gestured between the two of us with a grimace.

His eyebrows rose. "I hadn't thought of that. Vivi *can* be prone to leaping to conclusions a bit too quickly. But that seems far-fetched even for her." He frowned and shook his head. "Sorry, I shouldn't speak of her so. That's unfair."

He was unnerved in a way I hadn't seen before. "I agree it's unlikely. Even if she did jump to that conclusion, it's not like she'd be jealous." I laughed for effect, watching his reaction closely.

He shook his head slowly. "No, of course she wouldn't." His eyes were downcast, and I began to seriously wonder if he had feelings for his best friend. But then he sighed, replacing his expression with a more neutral one as he leaned back in his chair. "Odds are she's just a little annoyed that I'm hanging out with the enemy—not that you're the enemy, but—"

"I know what you mean," I acknowledged. "Yeah, that's probably it. Like you failed a loyalty test." I tried not to laugh at the absurdity of it. I loved Viviana, but she could occasionally be petty. She probably had every right in this case though. "In any case, I hope my presence hasn't caused problems between you two. I've messed up enough already when it comes to her."

Jack's face was full of sympathy as he shook his head. "Say no more about it. I've made mistakes too. I for one have enjoyed catching up with you. It's great to hear about your internship. Did you mention last night that you're teaching dance too?"

I grinned. "Yeah, Rafael roped me into it, likely temporary. At least it's a paycheck for a little while. The internship is unpaid. Between the two gigs, I'm actually staying pretty busy, which is ... well, let's just say I needed that. Too much time stuck in my room, alone with my depressing thoughts, was not working out well for me."

He nodded. "I can't imagine that being alone with depressing thoughts is great for anyone, but especially not for you." He sipped his drink and smiled. "I'm glad you've found some things to not only occupy your time but also make you excited about life. That's important, you know?"

I smiled before taking the last bite of my sandwich. I could see why Viviana had treasured his friendship all these years. Though I suspected something was brewing there beyond friendship, I'd keep my theories to myself for now. I didn't know Jack as well as Viviana did, but surely if he wanted to confide in me as a friend, he would.

"So, Jack—"

I paused as my heart nearly stopped.

My breaths became shallow as I gazed out the front window.

Is that ... no, it can't be.

It's a huge city. Twin Cities. What are the odds?

I stared at the tall, broad figure standing on the sidewalk outside the cafe, looking at his phone.

Squinting, I tried but failed to see the man's face from this distance and side angle.

Is it him? If—what if he comes in—I can't—

"Annie, are you all right?"

I jolted, snapping my gaze back to Jack. "Oh. Uh ..."

"You look like you've seen a ghost." His brow wrinkled as he peered at me closely.

I forced myself to take a few slower breaths and snuck a glance back at the window, but the man was gone. My eyes frantically scanned the cafe, but he didn't appear to have entered. He was just gone.

Good.

Right?

I took a steadying breath. "Yes, I think ... something like that. OK, now that *that's* behind us." I shook my head slightly and nearly laughed. This was ridiculous. I *was* chasing a ghost. That was all Kylan was.

But my friend Jack was real, and he was right here. I'd be an idiot to not take advantage of breakfasting with a successful writer and get his feedback on my book club publicity ideas. "Let's talk about books, baby."

He laughed. "All right, Annie, just no more Salt-N-Pepa for the rest of the meal, OK?"

Chapter 12

"Do you think you can tear yourself away from that adorable ball of fur for a night?" Rafael demanded as he danced into my room.

I looked up from where I'd been taunting the kitten with a mouse on a long string. "I can't leave Charlie for a whole night, Raf."

"He'd survive, Annie." Rafael rolled his eyes. "Not sure our sofas would, but that's another issue. You need to trim his nails again." Then, he leaned down to pet Charlie, and in a baby voice, he said, "What a troublesome brat, the cutest ever though."

"He's not ready to be on his own at night," I said firmly. "Besides, where would I go?"

"Rainn wants to go out, but I had to tell him no because Joel is sick and I'm playing nurse."

"You want me to babysit Rainn at the bar?"

"Hey, I heard that!" Rainn said, coming into the room and sounding annoyed. "He's lying. I don't even want to go anyway."

"You need to go," Rafael insisted. "Both of you do. You're stuck here far too much." He sighed dramatically. "Fine, I'll have Joel come over here, and we'll babysit the hellcat, I mean, Charlie."

Rainn and I looked at each other and sighed. He was thinking the same thing I was: The energy we'd expend arguing with Rafael wouldn't be worth it. We might as well go out. "I guess maybe it could be fun."

"Right then. Let me just go text Joel, and then I'll watch this guy while you go have fun without us. And you'd better have fun. I don't want you home early, you hear me?" He smirked at us and winked at Charlie.

"Tell me you love my cat without telling me you love my cat," I called out as Rafael strolled out of the room.

Rainn sat on the bed with a thoughtful expression. "He is pretty darn adorable. Who wouldn't love him?"

"I know, right? That'll be my future litmus test for the guys I date. Love me? Love my cat!" I laughed. "Well, I suppose I'd better start getting ready. Getting you drunk is actually going to be fun, I think."

"Uh-uh," he said, elbowing me. "I'm getting *you* drunk. I'll drive."

"I'm driving," Rafael said, poking his head in. "So you can both get drunk. Laid too, if you want."

I rolled my eyes as I rubbed under Charlie's chin, which he enjoyed immensely until he started to bite. "You just want the apartment to yourself for a whole night. But it might not be as fun as you think, with this little ball of energy." I put Charlie down and stood up. "Also, why is it that everyone hears everything that's said in my room? Twice you guys have overheard each other's conversations in here within the last, like, 10 minutes."

They looked at me blankly, and then Rainn groaned. "We didn't plan this, if that's what you're thinking. I'm as reluctant as you to go out. But I'll be a good sport. Let's do this. I'll take one for the team," he added as he walked out of my room, presumably to go change and do whatever minimal grooming he needed to do.

"Uh-oh, it's a sports metaphor kind of night," I said. "Now look what you've done, Raf."

Rafael smiled. "You can handle it. You might even have fun." Then his expression became more serious. "I'll be straight with you,

Annie. The run-in with Kylan last week and then the thing with Viviana this week—well, they've been messing with your head a little. You have been trying your very best not to let it, by burying yourself in work, but I can see it. You know it's there. I think getting out and having fun, maybe meeting someone new, may help. At least for the night, you know?"

"I sure hope so," I said. There was no point denying it. He was partly right. Though not so much about Viviana. I'd decided to give her a bit of time to cool off before approaching her again, but approach her I would. I missed my friend. I was the new and improved Annie, right? I could figure out this female friendship thing—could it really be that hard?

But as for Kylan, Rafael's assessment was spot on, as usual. I had managed to devote most of my time, energy, and attention this week to working on bookstore plans and ballet choreography, but in the rare moments of quiet without work or roommates or social media to distract me, *he* came rushing into my thoughts, his face burned into my mind, memories rushing back, feelings coming to the fore. And mortification too, given my ridiculous behavior of escaping into a pet store of all things. "All right, are you going to help me choose an outfit or not?"

Rafael sighed in relief as he picked up Charlie. "I thought you'd never ask. I have to go pick up Joel soon, so we do have to make this quicker than usual. No time for a montage, unfortunately."

"First world problems, Raf."

"Shut up."

I leaned on the bar and nudged Rainn, nearly cheek to cheek. "What about that tall, black-haired goddess with the hot guy in the grey striped top?"

"Uh, they're awfully close. I think they're *together*," he said, a slight slur in his words.

"Nope," I said. "I'm sensing friend vibes. Maybe even brother/sister. Go talk to her." I tried to shove him sideways off the chair, but he was too bulky.

He grinned. "Nice try. If they're just friends, then why don't *you* go approach the guy?"

"Well, I ... is ... " I paused. "Words are hard."

"Have we had too much to drink already?"

"Oh, we definitely have. But not enough to go hit on some random, apparently."

Rainn threw back another shot. "There might not be enough alcohol in the bar for that."

I draped my arm across his shoulders. "Aww. That bad, Rainn? Please tell me about her."

He grunted and then waved to the bartender for another. "There's not enough alcohol in the bar for that either."

"Oh, come on." I stuck out my lower lip. "It's just you and me. I won't tell Rafael. If you won't tell me her name, tell me something about her. Anything."

He was quiet for a long time, and I didn't think he was going to indulge my curiosity. But finally, while staring into his glass, he muttered, "She's way out of my league."

That was not at all what I expected him to say. "What? Impossible. You're a catch by anyone's standards. *Look* at you. I constantly regret the fact that we're not attracted to each other at all." We'd tried one awkward date, not long after being introduced through Rafael. After dinner and a chaste goodnight kiss, both of us had admitted to feeling a total lack of romantic potential. But great friends we had become. And I was certain he'd make a perfect partner for the right woman someday. He had dated here and there, but rarely did his relationships last very long.

Rainn put his head on my shoulder. "Thanks, Annie, but trust me on this one. I don't just mean she's out of my league in terms of looks, though she's beautiful too."

I looked at him quizzically. "I don't get it. It's not like you're all brawn and no brains. You're the new IT manager, and you have a master's in software engineering—if that doesn't make you smart as hell, I don't know what does."

He waved his hand dismissively. "I mean, I'm good at what I do. But this is a literary agency. Some of these people read, like, James Joyce and Faulkner, I can't even remember his first name. It's a whole other league, you know?"

"Hmm, I don't know. I wouldn't consider myself in a different league from you, and I read those authors in college. I even liked some of Faulkner."

He looked at me doubtfully and sighed. "You just need to trust me on this one. Even if somehow she was attainable, she's probably not available."

I gasped. "Wait a minute, go back to the agency thing. She *works* with you? That is a fairly important detail!"

"Uh, I thought I mentioned that to you guys before."

I searched my memories. "Hmm … it's possible you did. I might've been distracted. But that's a whole new level of interesting."

"I mean, we both work at the agency, but we work in different departments. No regular interactions."

I nodded. "Because her job is …"

Rainn shook his head with a lopsided smile. "Not falling for that. I'm not *that* drunk. But it's cute that you tried."

"I had to try."

"And what about Kylan?"

My smile faltered, and my words slurred a bit. "W—w—what about him?"

"What are you going to do?"

I stared at Rainn. "I don't know what you're asking. What is there to *do*, other than hope we don't run into each other again? I can't guarantee that unless I … like, move to another country or become a hermit. It's tempting, but a little extreme, even for me."

He searched my face and stared for a long moment. "Annie, is that what you want? To just hope you never cross paths?"

"I—well—"

"Haven't you even thought about trying to reach out?"

I swallowed with some difficulty, beginning to wish I had some water to drink instead of another shot. "I don't ... no, I haven't." I shook my head, feeling a bit queasy. "No, I haven't considered that. What's the point?"

"The point," Rainn said, studying me far too closely, "is closure. This stuff with him has been tearing you up for years. It's driving you crazy even now. Maybe talking to him would help bring you some peace, finally ... I don't know." He chuckled. "I mean, I'm no expert, just an IT guy, and a drunk one at that, but closure is what you're supposed to find in the rom-coms, right? Worth a shot."

I shot him a dubious look. "I—I don't know. I really think he'd just refuse to talk."

"But would that really be worse than where you're at now?" he asked.

"Oh, it could definitely be worse. If he did agree to talk, it wouldn't be some magical healing conversation but just something to open old wounds and make me feel even worse. I don't know. I haven't really thought about it. Let's just ... talk about something else." I shook my bracelets on my wrist. "Tell me about the agency. What's it called again?"

"Franchersantz Agency."

"Fran–cha–what?"

"It's a made-up name that combines all the founders' names. Kind of cool but also kind of unfortunate, if you ask me. Franchersantz." Rainn smiled. "It's a cool place to work though. I like it so far. You know, I've actually been meaning to ask if you've thought about agency work. You're interested in book publishing, and obviously literary agencies are a key part of that. I don't know all the ins and outs of what positions and duties there are, since I'm just an IT guy, but I could find out if there's anything that might interest you. Or you could go on the Franchersantz website under the Careers page. No, scratch that. Let me find out for you—I've got a good friend in HR, the one who referred me to the place. Remember Robin Johnson? You met him a few months back. Anyway, maybe with my connections, I can get you an interview faster or something." He scratched his head. "Sorry, that was a ramble and a half. Don't mean to be pushy."

My jaw was nearly on the table. "No, I ... can't believe I never thought of that. You work in a freaking literary agency. This could be an amazing connection for me, *Rainn*! Yes, please do whatever you need to do to hook me up with something there, however menial. I'll do third-shift toilet cleaning if I have to."

"Anything for you, my sweet," he said. "Ugh, why couldn't *we* be soulmates? Not even a tiny spark. Stupid fate." Then his eyes widened in alarm. "And don't you ever tell Rafael I got drunk enough to think about a 'soulmate,' much less utter the word. I'd never live it down."

I stood up and started bobbing my head as I tried to pull him off his stool. "Come on, Rainn. I think this calls for some of our hot BFF moves."

"Can we even stand up straight enough for this?" he asked doubtfully as we clasped hands.

I bent back and spun around, and I smiled. "We don't have to stand up straight—that's the great thing about dancing."

Chapter 13

My fingers shook a bit as I unlocked my phone, cursing my poor choice to wear a casual, thin-cotton yellow dress today. Today was a bit colder than I'd expected, but April in Minnesota was notoriously unpredictable. By the time I'd realized how cold it was, I was already on my way to Target and didn't feel like returning home to change. Charlie was fairly well adjusted at this point, but leaving him was still tough—I'd rather not do it again so soon.

Scanning the notes app on my phone, I opened the shopping list. I needed supplies as part of my book club project, specifically the publicity part. I'd decided against asking Hakeem for a budget for such things, wanting to show him I could do a lot with a little. I scanned the crafting aisle, a bit bewildered. Maybe I should start in the paper aisle instead? Where was the posterboard anyway? Why didn't I think to go to an office supply store? I palmed my forehead in regret.

Be reasonable.

I could pick up a few things here and then head over to the office supply store later. Maybe I could rope Rainn into coming along; surely he had some experience with this sort of thing. With that in mind, I started browsing and grabbing a few things that caught my interest. Before long, I realized this was kind of fun.

"... Besides, he has *her* now. Oh—oh no, Jane, I'll have to call you back."

I knew that voice.

I took a deep, calming breath and walked toward the voice. "Viv!"

Viviana inhaled sharply and made a face that wasn't quite a smile. "Annie ... hi."

"I'm surprised to see you here," I said, giving her a friendly smile. I felt nervous, somehow sensing that this was my opportunity. We were alone. In a public place, but not among our friends.

"Why?" Viviana demanded, eyes flashing. "Can't I shop like anyone else?"

Whoa, I bring out the worst in her.

I stepped back. "Of course, sorry, I just meant that it's a strange coincidence because, well, I was just thinking about calling you." I smiled a little. "And here you are."

Likely realizing she was overreacting, Viviana bit her lip and lowered her eyes slightly. "Sorry. I ... didn't mean to be so defensive."

"It's fine. I get it. Things did not end well between us." I sighed.

Just own up to it, Annie.

"I was a total jerk, actually."

Viviana burst into laughter. "Sorry, I shouldn't laugh. That was just so *blunt*."

"Yeah, that's me." I shrugged and then grinned.

She looked down and said quietly, "I miss that."

"You do? I've been realizing of late that it's not one of my better traits. I can't believe it took me this long to figure that out."

"Well, bluntness has a time and place. Sometimes I wish ..."

"You wish what?"

"I wish I could be like that. Sometimes."

"Oh. Well, maybe I could teach you." I smiled hesitantly. "I could be the mentor for once."

Viviana actually smiled in return. "I'd like that."

I wasn't sure what to say next. My female friendships had usually just fizzled out with little to no effort to revive them. What did one do next? So, I looked into Viviana's eyes with the most sincere expression I could muster. "Can you forgive me, Viv?"

She nodded, her eyes hopeful. "Only if *you* forgive *me*."

"I was the awful person, not you. It's the damn redhead temper, right? No, I don't have an excuse. You were just looking out for me and trying to protect me from another jerk, as always." With a heavy shrug, I let out a long exhale. "I sure know how to pick 'em."

"But I could've tried to get in touch with you after that. Instead of giving up on us so easily," Viviana said.

That's true, I thought. *That's cool she can admit that.*

She swallowed visibly and continued, "I just ... I don't know. Maybe I needed space. Not from you necessarily, but from every-thing. Things weren't going well with Gregory, and that ended ter-ribly. I'm sure you know that. They both played us for fools, and I was just as gullible as you were, maybe more so because Gregory made it pretty obvious from the start that he was not a good person. And—"

"Viv, I'm so sorry I wasn't there for you and that I pushed him on you. I was a little too wrapped up in myself to see what was happening or what *could* happen with a guy like that." I frowned.

Wow, I owe her an apology for lots of things. More than I thought.

I squeezed my hands together, trying to refrain from jumping at her with a huge hug. "I wasn't being a great friend either."

"OK, so ... let's stop being crappy friends. Deal?" Viviana smiled, sticking out her hand.

I laughed, putting both arms out to pull her into a hug. "Bring it in."

Even though I could feel the tension in her body as well as my own, the hug was immensely calming. It struck me how much I'd suffered from having little contact—physical or emotional—for weeks with anyone other than occasionally my roomies. "Well, this is playing out like a scene in a Hallmark movie," Viviana said. "And we're in the Hallmark aisle."

"Oh, the horror," I said with a giggle. "At least it's not a Christmas movie. Speaking of horrors, you have heard about poor Ellen, right?"

"*Poor* Ellen?" Viviana's tone was doubtful.

"I know she kind of took advantage of us, and she didn't take my quitting very well. But I feel bad for her, don't you?"

Her face clouded over with resent. "Why would I?"

My eyes widened. "Oh my—you didn't hear? Have you been on social media, like, at all?"

Viviana shook her head. "I needed a break. I didn't even read any of my emails or messages from Ellen as I was so furious at her."

My jaw dropped. "I'm in awe ... I tried to go off the grid for a while, but I was too weak." It had been easy to avoid social media when I didn't care about anything and had been holed up in my room, but once I'd returned to the living, avoidance wasn't as easy. I'd heard about Ellen's self-destruction by texting another Bolder editor I'd occasionally gone drinking with in the past. "OK, but anyway, so she was having an affair with some no-name guy at the gym. Her husband found out and not only confronted the gym guy but also got in touch with the gym guy's wife. The wife just happened to be one of those influencers on Instagram and TikTok with literally millions of followers. Within hours, the story was everywhere. Ellen had to resign, and she's said to be taking a spa vacation somewhere. Can you believe it? I mean, I feel for her, but ... I also don't."

"Wow, that is insane. I actually wondered if there was a gym guy on the side. There was a weird late night in the office one weekend ... but anyway, just wow. She kinda sold me out to Greg by telling him my dad was a famous writer, but still, I do feel sorry for her. That's a hefty consequence for one bad decision." Ah, so *that's* why Viviana was furious with Ellen. I was just relieved that she didn't suspect *me* of divulging her father's identity to Greg—I might not get the friendship thing right all the time, but I knew better than to do *that*.

"No kidding. If only all the two-timers paid such a price. Like the jerks we dated. But let's not go there ... Hey, are you ready to check out too?" When she nodded, I added, "Good, because I need to update you on my life. I finally found a good guy, if you'll allow me a humble brag. It's been hell not being able to talk to you all this time!" I smiled. I couldn't wait to tell her about Charlie, because he was surely better than any boyfriend.

But my friend suddenly looked pained.

"Viv? Are you OK?"

Shaking her head, Viviana sputtered, "Yes—I mean—no. That is, yes, I'm OK, but I just remembered I'm not done shopping."

I offered a gentle smile, trying to set her at ease. Something was off. "Oh, no problem. I can tag along while you finish and gush about my new guy."

"No!" She looked truly alarmed now. "I mean, I would love that, but I, well, it's just not really the right time. I still have a lot of things to buy."

Realizing I was staring at her small shopping basket, Viviana mumbled, "I should probably go get a cart, actually. Since I need a ton of stuff."

I spoke slowly, trying to keep my tone even. "It's fine, Viv. You can just tell me if you don't want to talk. Remember, bluntness? You can start now."

"No, it's, it's not that ... I just—it's not the best time. It's hard to explain." She looked flustered.

I stepped forward and enveloped her in another hug. "It's *fine*, Viv. We'll catch up another time, I hope. I'm just glad we got to talk. Really glad."

She offered a small smile. It looked painful, but she was trying. Really hard. And that's what mattered. This might not be easy, but we were both trying and *that* mattered. I smiled back in relief—our friendship might not be great right now, but we would be OK.

I smoothed my skirt as I strolled down the hallway, giving one last smile to Rainn as we approached the HR offices. For this interview, I'd elected to wear the navy-blue pantsuit, but I'd sprung for a new pair of heels. It was a professional investment, I'd told my roommates (and myself). I looked amazing. Well, as amazing as anyone could look in a business-style suit that was almost never flattering to anyone.

"You're going to kill it, Annie," Rainn said, turning to grin at me as we stopped outside the room where I'd be interviewing. He pointed to a small waiting area with several chairs.

"I think I'll stand, actually," I said, smoothing my skirt again. I was a *little* nervous. Confident but nervous. If this job didn't pan out, there would be other opportunities.

The most exciting thing at the moment wasn't this agency per se. It was the job. Literary agent. I'd spent the last 24 hours researching what agents do—and what their assistants do—and I was enthralled, to say the least. It was everything I never knew I wanted. I was born for this job. I just *knew* I had to do this.

Now I just had to sell myself to some strangers. I was pretty good at that.

"Thank you, Rainn. This means a lot." I smiled and gave him a partial hug. "Now go. I've got it from here."

No sooner did he walk away than the door opened, and a tall, athletic-looking woman opened the door. "Annie York?"

"I am she," I said, smiling.

"We're ready for you. Come on in," said the woman. "I'm just going to pop down to the kitchen for a moment."

"Oh ... sure," I said, maintaining my smile. Odd, but OK. I walked into the room, and before me sat eight people on one side of a long rectangular table, all staring at me.

"Wow, OK. A lot of you today. I mean ..." I said. *Foot in mouth. Foot in mouth.* "You'll have to excuse me. I'm not normally this eloquent." Pause, blank stares, dead silence. "Hi, I'm Annie York."

"Hi, Annie" and "Nice to meet you" came a chorus of voices and polite smiles, even a few laughs.

Whew, not a total bomb yet.

An older woman stuck out her hand. "Hello, I'm D'Elaina, but people just call me Laina. I'm the senior agent on the team." She pointed to her left. "This here is Sofia Jackson. We're the two agents who recently lost our assistant, so the open position will be working closely with us."

Sofia smiled at me. "Please, have a seat. We'll get started soon, when Jardin returns."

I returned the smile. My face was going to hurt by the end of this interview. Why were there nine people in the room? I wasn't applying to become the CEO, after all.

The tall woman returned, a Gatorade and a pack of wheat crackers in hand. "Ms. York, sorry about the wait. I'm Jardin Floquet, HR director. We spoke on the phone after Robin passed along the referral."

After I stood to shake her hand, I carefully smoothed my skirt and sat back down. "It's wonderful to meet you, Ms. Floquet, and all of you."

"Call me Jardin," she said, sitting in the vacant seat to the right of Laina across from me. "It's nice to meet you too, Annie. I want to explain first why you're going to be grilled by a nine-person interview panel. We do tend to accelerate the interview process for referrals and of course internal candidates, when applicable. Perhaps just as important in this case, though, is that we are looking to fill a vacant seat rather quickly. The man holding this particular assistant position had to relocate very suddenly, and the person we were looking to replace him with did not pass the background checks, leaving us in a tough spot where poor Sofia and Laina have been without an assistant for close to two months now."

"To their credit, our other agents' assistants have helped fill the gap in the meantime, and they've been amazing in doing as much as they can," Sofia offered.

"But they have their own busy workloads, including some co-agenting, so everyone's been stretched thin. Work–life balance is impossible to guarantee in a business like this, but we do try to set up our team for success," said Jardin. And then she smiled widely before taking a long drink of her purple sports drink. "I sound like an HR handbook, don't I? I'm actually going to be quiet and let the agent team take over most of the interview from here."

Everyone looked at me for a response, so I smiled graciously. "I appreciate the explanation. It is great to meet all of your agents and to get a sense of the makeup of your team."

So far, so good. I could fit in here. And they need someone ASAP—I just need to seal the deal.

I considered telling them I'd start tomorrow if that would help, but ... no. That sounded desperate.

"So, Annie," Laina said, "I do want to introduce you to the rest of the team first. Starting from that end is Jessa, then Caroline ..." I tried to mentally associate the names with faces quickly, but I found myself forgetting many of the names as soon as I heard them.

When Laina finished, I said, "It's great to meet you all," hating how cliché that sounded but knowing it was the normal response.

"We do our interviews a little differently here. We're going to mostly avoid the typical 'why do you want this job' and 'tell me about yourself' questions and jump to some more specific but perhaps nontraditional ones, because we want to get to know you and because, as you know, we already asked the generic ones when you submitted your application. So, with that said, we're going to do a round robin of questions, like a typical panel, if that works for you," Laina said.

As if I have a choice.

I nodded, almost giggling at the absurdity. Did anyone ever say "No, that doesn't work for me?" Probably someone did; Rainn's HR friend had said some people were just completely clueless about interview etiquette or even just common sense.

Near the far end of the table, an agent named Abi asked me the first question. "Who are your top three favorite authors?"

I blinked in surprise. "That is specific, but I'm happy to answer. I'll admit to some recency bias here, but I'm going with Ali Hazelwood, Charles Dickens, and Sally Rooney."

"By recency bias, do you mean that they're your favorites because you read them recently or because they're relatively recent authors (compared to, say, Dante or Aristotle)?" Abi asked.

I smiled. "Ah, they've been recent favorites. I change favorites fairly often because I become very passionate and engaged in the books I read."

Laina spoke up. "Do you think that's a good skill for an agent or assistant to have? Or could it set a person back, becoming too emotionally involved in what you're reading?"

I tilted my head slightly as I gave this some thought. "Good question. I think it could go either way, and a person needs balance. Too much emotional involvement in a book could make it difficult if not impossible to notice fatal flaws that would be crucial for an agent to spot, but too much emotional distance would mean we couldn't get into the minds of our readers and couldn't do a good job of anticipating what would sell."

I scanned all their faces anxiously. It was a good, safe, and maybe smart answer, but it was perhaps a risky one since it could be, well, wrong. Most panelists smiled, except for Laina and one other agent whose name I'd already forgotten. Laina hadn't smiled much, actually. She did not appear to be the overly smiling type.

Abi nodded in thanks at my answer, and the woman next to him took her turn. The next few questions were fairly straightforward, not requiring particularly difficult or controversial answers. They asked about my favorite and least favorite genres, the novel I'd hated most in college, the current author I'd most like to sign as an agent, what kind of book I'd write if I ever wrote a book, and so on.

When it was her turn, Laina asked a bigger-picture question, with a shrewd look in her eye. "The agent assistant role is ideal for developing talented individuals to become agents, and we like to hire assistants who are interested in that career trajectory so we can promote from within. So I'm going to ask you bluntly: is it your career goal to become a literary agent?" A couple of the agents glanced at Laina with raised eyebrows, as though they weren't quite prepared for her blunt words or sharp tone. Jardin merely continued eating crackers while looking intently at me for a response.

After a brief moment of hesitation, I smiled and looked at Laina first and then around the room at the others. "That's a great question, and I'll answer it honestly. My answer is yes, I want to be an agent. But I only discovered this recently. Just a few weeks ago, I was a freelance copyeditor for a small nonfiction publisher, and I had no notion of wanting to be an agent. I realized though, long overdue, that the solitary and often dull work of nonfiction editing wasn't for me. I didn't belong in that world. I don't hate editing, but on its own, it wasn't fulfilling. I love reading, I love fiction, I love variety and new challenges, and I love *people*. I'm an extrovert who adores books. Learning about what a literary agent does, I felt like ... it was love at first sight. I fell in love with the job description. As cheesy as that sounds. I want to work hard and learn this business and make it my life."

Everyone stared at me, mostly with what seemed like respect in their eyes. They all seemed to be waiting for Laina to respond. Laina cracked a small smile, finally. "Thank you, Annie."

"On that note," Sofia said, running her hand over her shiny, black styled hair, "we do also want applicants to be aware that a substantial portion of the assistant job is administrative support. We do have a full-time office manager, Ernesto, but most of the support specific to agents comes from the agent assistant role. So, for example, if we ran out of staples or needed brochures printed, we'd probably contact Ernesto, but we'd rely on you to take care of meeting planning, royalty payments, social media, that sort of thing."

I nodded. "I did assume that would be the case, and I'm eager to take on any and all responsibilities that will give me more insight into the whole process from start to finish. I do like a variety of tasks too, so I think juggling all of these different kinds of things will be perfect for me. I think you mentioned co-agenting as well?"

"Yes, that doesn't happen right away, but as you get more experience, you may be able to take on clients of your own in collaboration with an agent." Sofia smiled and added, "It's sort of a stepping stone to a full agent position."

"That sounds wonderful," I said. My cheek muscles were starting to feel tired.

When they asked whether I was currently employed and when I would be able to start if offered the position, I debated on whether to tell them about my Bookshop internship. Should I continue doing the internship if I become an agent assistant? Would that be taking on too much? I would look like a flake to Hakeem if I quit already, and that was a terrible start to my new career path. Plus, I wanted to do it—the internship was kind of my baby, and I wanted it, almost as much as this agent position. And I should be open about it with any prospective employer.

With that in mind, I told them about the internship and my plans to continue doing it, on the side. Clearly, the agency would be my first priority; the unpaid work at the bookstore would have to work around important agency business. If it became too difficult to manage both, I'd quit the bookstore role or delegate more of it to Sai or someone else. Sai, despite her initial frosty reception, seemed surprisingly interested in hearing more about my book club ideas lately.

After nearly two hours of questioning, the interview was over. Everyone stood to shake my hand as they filed out, and I was so sweaty that going home and showering seemed more appealing than it had in a long time. I noticed that Sofia was quite tall and Laina was quite short. This was interesting, as Sofia was a bit soft-spoken and Laina seemed anything but.

As I left the building, I reflected on the people I'd met. The two of them would be interesting to work with. I felt like Sofia could become a friend. Laina seemed almost hostile or at least reserved, which was a little concerning; I would need to get to the bottom of that. I really didn't enjoy letting conflicts with friends and coworkers linger. I'd dealt with that long enough with my family over the years. Well, one person in particular. Ugh. Thinking about my mother was never a good idea, and today of all days, I didn't want to dwell on that.

Ah well, it was a beautiful day, and I'd had a stellar interview ... at least I thought so. *And* I had my very first book club to look forward to tomorrow night. I was so excited I'd almost forgotten about baking cookies until late last night, when I remembered and wrote a reminder note for myself.

Mmm, cookies.

Chapter 14

As I placed the last chair in the circle, I watched Sai rearrange them unnecessarily. "I'm so glad you got your cast off in time to help me."

Sai gave me a side-eye glance but said nothing as she continued arranging the chairs until they were perfectly spaced.

"I really appreciate your help. You don't have to be here, so it means a lot," I said, standing a bit closer.

Sai sighed loudly and stood upright. "Stop. It's not about you, drama queen."

I'm the drama queen? I suppressed a chuckle. "Right, it's about ... the store. Bookshop will benefit from this in sales, exposure—"

Sai rolled her eyes. "It's about literature. Why do you think I work here? I'm not like you. I don't care about money. I care about *literature*." Then, she dramatically turned in the other direction toward the snack table.

I pinched the bridge of my nose. Being around Sai was difficult even on a good day, and she seemed agitated today. And her accusation—*Do I seem like I just care about money?* I had never felt like that sort of person. My mother was, certainly. But not me.

Of course, the business of books was a *business*, so there was that. Books had to be sold, and that involved money. I wanted to help authors make money. And all the people involved, but especially authors, because they were the real magic. And maybe they wouldn't become rich—most of them wouldn't—but they could make enough to live on, perhaps. Or enough to make them want to keep writing and producing their art for the world to read and enjoy. The real magic.

Lost in my reverie, I didn't notice when a short, round woman walked up to the edge of the circle of chairs where I was still standing. "Hi, is this the book club?"

I smiled and stuck out my hand. "It is. I'm Annie, and I'm the host tonight."

"Carlina," said the woman, probably in her early 40s. "Oh look, I'm the first one here! I'm always early to everything. I like to get the best seat."

I checked my watch and frowned. It was only one minute before 7:00, the starting time.

Shouldn't more people be arriving by now?

Reading my mind, Carlina put a hand on my arm and then drew it away. "Sorry, I'm a touchy-feely type. Don't worry, darling. I bet you'll have a full house, but no one wants to be the first one to arrive since it's a new group. Well, no one except me." She cackled and sat down.

Sai returned and scanned the area. She gave me a scathing look and took out her phone.

At 7:01, two women wandered over with full shopping bags and excitement in their eyes. "Oh, are you having a book club?"

My face fell a bit when I realized they weren't intended participants. "Yes, it is ... the first meeting of a new book club. We're waiting for everyone to arrive."

The women looked at each other, communicating with their eyes and joined hands. Then, one of them said, "Do you have room for a couple more? We would *love* to join. We were just talking about this the other day. We love books and we love talking."

I nodded, trying to appear cheerful. "I think we'll have room. We can always get more chairs."

Or remove some, so it doesn't look so pathetic.

How did I fail so spectacularly at marketing this simple FREE thing?

Finally, at 7:04, people started streaming in, some with coffees or other drinks purchased from the cafe. Most didn't even ask if this was the book club; they just took a seat in the circle. I exhaled in relief and gazed around at the diversity of people in attendance. Only one man though. Well, more of a boy, actually. He looked about Sai's age.

Speaking of Sai, where is she?

I spotted her off to the side, her eyes darting between her phone and the young man. Very interesting. A crush? Then she disappeared.

As people filled in the seats, my smile widened. I decided to go in search of Sai and more chairs. But first, I introduced myself quickly to those gathered and told them I'd return soon.

I found Sai lingering in the back room where the extra chairs were stored. "Sai, what are you doing? You disappeared rather mysteriously. And now you're just standing around?"

Sai glared at me. "I'm not ... I ... the chairs." As her voice faltered, her eyes went downcast, and she mumbled, "Sorry. Just got distracted."

I narrowed my eyes but softened my tone. "It's OK. Are you all right?"

"I'm fine!" she snapped, her old fire returning.

"OK then. Let's bring out some more chairs. Lots of people have shown up. I'm so excited!"

Sai rolled her eyes but helped me grab as many chairs as we could. When we returned, I asked her to fix the chair arrangement because I'd forgotten my contact sheet and needed to retrieve it from the back office. Hakeem had wanted me to pass along a sheet so everyone could sign up for the bookstore's email list.

Contact sheet in hand, I was walking along a row of bookshelves close to the book club circle when suddenly my heart caught in my throat, and my feet stopped moving.

It can't be.

That's ... that's ...

My chest felt tight as I tried to breathe and form a coherent thought.

What ... is ... he ... doing here?

I guess he's buying books.

He's by the circle. My circle.

No, not the book club. NOT MY BOOK CLUB!

Why is he so damn attractive? I'm not the only one staring at him.

Oh no. I'm ...

Staring.

At him.

And he's watching me stare at him.

Besides my bulging wide eyes, I couldn't imagine what awful expression he was seeing on my face at that moment.

Deer in the headlights? Hungry like a wolf? Lovestruck like an ...

In panic, I dropped to the floor and pretended to search through the books on the lowest shelf. I prayed no one would come over and see that they were pregnancy books. Taking some deep breaths as best as I could while crouched down, I tried to calm myself and think through the haze.

Most people were likely looking at him, not at me. I can just grab one of these books and then casually walk over, like it's no big deal, probably. Maybe.

I can say the book is for a friend. Or—

I inhaled softly.

Can I even do this? With him here?

Does he have to ruin this *too? Just like he ruined the ...*

But a tiny voice inside reminded me that *he* hadn't ruined our relationship; I had. I'd ended things when I wasn't ready to commit to uprooting my life for him. When I wasn't ready to give up everything. Even though he *was* everything.

"Annie?" said a feminine voice above me.

I glanced up, eyes widened, as Carlina stood above me and knelt down. "Are you OK?"

"Oh, hi. I was, um, you see, this friend of mine—"

Carlina shook her head. "No need to explain. If you're pregnant or not, or if it has something to do with that guy who joined the circle or not, you don't owe anyone any explanation. I just came over to see if you need any help."

I felt a little moisture well up in my eye, which I quickly dabbed away. "Carlina, you are too sweet. We've only just met. But thank you. It's, ah, a long story."

"It always is." She nodded. "If you ever want to get a coffee and talk about it, let me know. Or not, that's cool too." She took my hand. "In the meantime though, let's get you up and back to the book club you're going to lead. How can I help?"

My eyes darted around, not knowing what to do. "I ... uh ... a few people might've seen me hide behind the shelf like an idiot, so ... um ..."

"Oh, I have an idea." Carlina stood and extended a hand to pull me up surprisingly quickly. "Just follow my lead," she whispered with a sly smile.

I was about to protest, but the words died on my lips. I had no good alternatives.

As we entered the book club area, Carlina squeezed my hand and said a bit loudly, "Thanks so much for finding this for me, Annie. My partner insisted all the other pregnancy books were written by quacks, and there's no convincing her otherwise."

I hid my surprise and gave Carlina a warm albeit shaky smile. What a lovely woman. I was definitely going to take her up on the coffee offer. "Anytime, pal."

I winced.

Anytime, pal? Really, that's the best you can do?

I strode over to my chair and sat down, noting that Sai was next to me. I tried to smile at her, and she was staring at me oddly. Was that pity? Kindred spirits we were, perhaps, hiding from our love interests.

What? No, Kylan isn't a love interest. That's firmly in the past.

But before I could analyze Sai's face further, the look vanished, replaced by her bored expression.

I took a deep breath and scanned the perimeter of the circle, with all the eager faces. I skipped over his, of course. He was sitting on the opposite side of the circle. There were probably nearly thirty people in attendance, so it was a large circle. Still, I felt so exposed, like he was right in front of me, seeing everything.

I cleared my throat. I would be professional, and I would ignore him. "Hello, everyone! I'm Annie York, and I coordinate events for Bookshop. Welcome to the inaugural book club meeting! I'm *so* excited to see so much interest in this, and I hope you all have as much fun as I know I will in this club. Since we haven't started reading a book yet, I thought we'd spend this meeting getting to know each other and then discussing what books we'd like to read in the future. I want this to be *your* book club, so I'm not going to merely make selections from somewhere on high. We're going to decide together, vote, and all that." There were smiles around the room, mostly. A few people looked disappointed. "Although if the group decided we wanted to have a surprise pick chosen by the leader or someone else, that's within the realm of possibility too. This is *your* book club." I smiled while scanning all the interested faces again, except of course his.

I wouldn't meet his eyes again. I couldn't.

"So, let's start off by introducing ourselves. I know some people don't love introductions, so if you're one of those folks, you can keep it minimal. Tell us your first name and one thing about you. Anything. Could be your pet's name or your favorite author. Or if you like talking about yourself, tell us something else, including what you like to read. Sound good?"

Many heads bobbed up and down. Not everyone was nodding, but that was OK. I didn't like to put anyone on the spot, but a book club did require discussion, so people did need to speak up a little.

Then again, maybe there were ways to make it more inclusive for people who were shy. I frowned, wondering if I might have bungled things already; book lovers were probably statistically more likely to be shy, after all. Or was that just a stereotype? I had no idea, as shyness was as foreign to me as Antarctica.

I quickly recovered my smile. "I'll start. I'm Annie, as I said, and I'm interning here as an event coordinator. I'm looking to get more involved in the world of books and publishing. I worked as an editor for nonfiction, but my real love is fiction, so that's where I'm looking to transition into, career-wise, somehow. I don't want to drone on about work, but it does overlap with my interests so much because, you guys, I have loved books for as long as I can remember. I'm the most extroverted book lover you'll ever meet, probably. Well, maybe besides Carlina." I glanced at my new friend, who laughed and winked.

"I like a variety of fiction. I have a degree in English so I've read and enjoyed a lot of the classics, but I also enjoy genre fiction, especially rom-coms. Let's see ... for random stuff, I also teach ballet, I love fashion, and I have a kitten named Charlie." I blushed when I thought of the reason I had a kitten, remembering how I'd ducked into the pet store. Was Kylan even now connecting the dots? I didn't dare look at him and find out. "I think that's enough about me. You don't need to say that much about yourself unless you want to. We'll get to know each other better as we talk about the books we read, naturally. OK ... Sai, how about you go next?"

Sai scowled in my direction and then looked at the floor in the center of the circle. "Hi, I'm Sai, and I work at Bookshop. I like literature."

I waited for her to say more, but she seemed to be done. Disappointed, I forced a smile anyway. "OK, Sai, thanks. And we'll move on—go ahead and just continue around the circle one after another."

As the women around the circle spoke, I smiled and nodded, making occasional comments in response to what they'd revealed about themselves. But I began to feel increasingly anxious as Kylan's turn approached.

How could I bear it? To not only look upon him but hear him speak. To hear that slightly gravelly voice that once spoke of love, of forever, of promises that I'd never given him a chance to keep. And that same voice that, because of my choices, began to speak to me with pain, with brokenness, and eventually with coldness.

Could I bear it? No? But I had to.

I *had* to. This book club was important to me. It was part of my new life, the one I was crafting for myself. I could be polite, professional, even friendly.

Sai stiffened beside me as a different voice began to speak. It was the boy, introducing himself as Zachary, a college freshman intent on majoring in literature and women's studies. I snuck a glance at Sai as he spoke. She was staring open-mouthed. So the grumpy teen girl had a crush on a bookish college boy. *A tale as old as time.* My mouth twitched as I imagined how cute they would be together, how satisfying it would be to nudge them together through the book club.

My smile wavered as a deep voice jolted me, reaching deep inside me, filling me with an awareness that was both terrifying and exhilarating. I tried to steady my breathing as he began to speak. "Hi, I'm Kylan Quinn. I work with a big literary agency in New York, but I'm in Minneapolis on a rather extended visit."

"You *work with* the agency? Aren't you its head?" said a pretty brunette raising her eyebrows a few seats to his left. "I've heard of you. You're a big name in New York City!"

Kylan ran a hand through his sun-streaked hair and chuckled. "I don't like to toot my own horn, but I do lead the agency, yes. I wouldn't call myself a big name though."

"And he's modest too," said a blonde woman next to the brunette, nudging her friend. His gorgeous full lips formed an easy smile that the women lapped up.

I began to seethe inside.

Was he going to steal the whole damn show?

I was about to prompt the next participant to introduce herself when another woman spoke, this time on the other side of the circle. "What do you like to read, Mr. Quinn?"

"Oh, call me Kylan. I read a little bit of everything, really," he said thoughtfully as he absently stroked his angular jaw, which was stubbly as usual. "And yes, my career will tell you I'm obviously invested in traditional publishing, but I read indie published books too. If I had to choose, hmm, let me think on that a moment ..."

I dared myself to glance at him just briefly, just to acknowledge that he was speaking and then I could go on ignoring him. A jolt of shock passed through me as I found his eyes intently focused on me, and I couldn't move.

He has to stop doing this to me.

He has to stop.

I need to find a way to make him leave.

"I like literary fiction," Kylan continued, "but lately I've been on a fantasy streak. Really, I will read or represent almost any genre. Well, except romance. Can't stomach it."

There were audible gasps in the room, and I hoped mine hadn't been one of them. He was still looking at me, as if daring me to look away. Or maybe to keep looking.

He hates the entire romance genre because of me? Is that what he's saying?

Or am I making a giant leap? Flattering myself, really. I probably didn't mean enough to him to have such an effect ...

Finally, he broke contact and flashed a casual smile to the others in the circle. "Don't get me wrong. Romance is an amazing genre. I love selling it, I love that people enjoy it, and as a businessman, I obviously love how much money it makes." Laughs erupted around the circle. "It's just not for me."

I noted some disappointed looks from some of the younger women but not from the brunette, who looked ... determined? How odd. Well, maybe she was into that sort of difficult man.

She can have him then.

I tried to ignore the lead ball feeling in my abdomen.

When the introductions were finally over, I announced a 10-minute break. "Go get some water, have a cookie, or whatever. I'll see you back at 8:00, and then we'll spend the last half hour discussing our future book selections. The cookies are nut-free, by the way."

Most people rose from their seats and wandered off. A few people stayed in their seats to chat or look at their phones. Carlina immediately started chatting up the woman next to her. Before I had a chance to worry about what Kylan would do and where I would hide, I was surrounded by a group of three mid-30s-ish women who wanted to know where I taught ballet. Two of them were looking to enroll their children in ballet and looking for recommendations.

Before I knew it, the break was over, and I called for everyone's attention to sit down again. I had no idea where Kylan had spent the break time, but when I stood up to speak, he was already in his seat, his long legs stretched out in front of him as he chatted with the boy next to him.

Who cares where he was during the break? Why am I even thinking about this? I'm not his keeper.

He's nothing to me now.

And I'm obviously nothing to him.

After recapturing everyone's attention, I described the plan to focus on a certain genre or theme each quarter and choose a handful of books per quarter matching that theme. No one had any objections, so I went on. "So now we just need to choose a theme. We can go broad, or we can be really specific." Nods all around, and people looked thoughtful.

"I'll just throw out an idea first, and you can all feel free to jump on board or disagree and suggest something entirely different." Desperation surged in me, and I plunged forward with the only idea I could think of to get rid of him. I couldn't suggest the theme of romance tonight, since he'd made such a big deal of hating it; it would only make me look bad. "So, I was thinking we'd start with something broad, since we're just getting to know each other and it's a larger group. How about women's fiction?"

All was quiet except for a child's tantrum nearby near the pregnancy book section. A few people in the group opened their mouths to speak and then apparently thought better of it. All were looking either at me or at Kylan and Zachary.

His deep voice arrested me once again, and I felt shivers through my body. "I'm in. I love women's fiction." As I reluctantly made eye contact, his face broke out into a wide smile, though not at me. He was grinning as he looked around the room at the women practically ogling him. "As long as it's not a romance novel. Romance in a plot I can tolerate, as long as it's not the main plot."

He'd stabbed me once again with his diatribe against romance. I wasn't the only one who looked stricken; a few women pouted openly at his declaration.

Kylan looked over at Zachary, who was nodding in agreement. "Zachary here is majoring in women's studies, so it seems like a great fit for us guys."

"Well, the men have spoken, so I guess that's what matters," I said irritably as I tossed my hair back.

Heads snapped in my direction, and jaws dropped.

What was that?

They're going to hate me already on the first day.

He brings out the freaking worst in me.

"Women's fiction was your idea, Ms. York," Kylan said, crossing his arms over his broad chest as his mouth twitched at the corners.

Is he trying not to laugh at me?

Pressing my buttons on purpose? How dare he—

I stopped the stream of thoughts in their tracks. I needed to get myself under control.

While smoothing my hair that didn't need smoothing, I smiled as serenely as I could. "You're right. I'm sorry."

He nodded slightly in acknowledgement but said nothing, his expression revealing nothing. No one else spoke, with the air so thick with tension.

Once again, Carlina saved me. "You can't have a good book club without some heated discussions and passionate exchanges, I've always found." I laughed in relief, and many others joined me, nodding in agreement.

Kylan seemed like he was going to say more but didn't. Instead, he studied me with hooded eyes, his legs outstretched and crossed at the ankle. I asked myself once again why I was looking at him and found it difficult to catch my breath. This was ridiculous. I'd seen and dated plenty of guys since him, many of whom were objectively just as attractive as Kylan, if not more so. But there was something about him. Or something about *me* that was reacting to him in such an annoyingly strong way. I had to put a stop to this somehow. I'd have to strategize later.

Once I'd facilitated the discussion and eventual decision of which book to start with and how to find a copy—Hakeem would be very pleased with the resulting sales tonight—I asked if anyone had questions.

When no one seemed to have any, I added, "Oh, I almost forgot to mention, I've already set up a Facebook group for us, so we can discuss and debate outside of our weekly meetings too. In particular, we could discuss online and vote on the next books we'll read, so we'll have more time in our in-person meetings for talking about the books themselves. It's a private group, so just look me up on Facebook, and I'll add you to the group."

Crap.

Oh, crap. I don't want Kylan contacting me on socials. No, no, no!

Maybe there's another way; I could direct them to contact Sai instead—she's a younger person anyway—

My thoughts stilled when one petite young woman raised her hand and spoke softly. "Have you thought about having a Zoom option? For those who ... can't attend in person, for one reason or another?"

I glanced at the woman, whose face was red and fingers were white as she clutched a purse in her lap tightly. Perhaps the woman was shy or agoraphobic, or maybe she had an illness that made it difficult to leave home frequently. I felt a wave of sympathy and then admiration for the woman's courage in asking this question in front of a large group. "I actually haven't looked into an online option, but that is an excellent idea. I feel silly for not considering that before—thank you so much for bringing it to my attention. I do want this group to be as inclusive as possible. Annalise, right? I *love* your name." I smiled widely at the young woman, whose rigid pose relaxed just slightly.

I checked the clock. "And that, my new friends, is our first book club! It's 8:25, so I'll let you all leave a few minutes early. Feel free to eat more cookies or take them with you." I smiled and then turned to thank Sai for helping out, but the girl ran off before I had a chance. Shaking my head, I leaned down to gather some things I'd left under my chair, including my phone and some notes.

I noticed the blinking notification and unlocked my screen quickly. A message from Rainn. No, *lots* of messages from Rainn.

Rainn

Annie!

Annie, come on! What are you doing that you're too busy to text me?

Oh wait, sorry. Book club is tonight, right? I'm an idiot. This is a big night for you.

Still, I can't wait to tell you … Robin heard the interview went well!

Said he'd be shocked if you weren't offered the position

You should check your email and voicemail - maybe they called or left a message?

YOU'RE GOING TO BE AN AGENT!! Probably!!

I laughed as I reread his messages. A big dopey grin decorated my face when I turned off my phone screen and stood up. I was surprised to see the area empty. Everyone from the group had left.

Good, I thought, sobering a bit. But I smiled again, remembering my great news.

"Annie."

Hearing the deep baritone behind me, I closed my eyes.

No, it couldn't be. He's still here? And now …

I opened my eyes and looked around frantically without turning my head.

Now we were alone, apart from a few stray bookstore customers and an employee or two far off in the distance.

I needed to turn and face him. But how could I? I willed my feet to move, but they wouldn't. It was taking all my energy to just breathe and stay upright.

"Annie?" Kylan said again, his voice a bit scratchy. "Do you need some help cleaning up?"

Turn around before you melt into the floor!

I exhaled shakily, and I hoped he couldn't see or hear—but he probably could, because he sounded like he was close to me, far too close.

Finally, I turned, and my eyes immediately found his piercing grey ones, highlighting a face that was far too handsome for any man, let alone this one. Time hadn't altered his physical appeal at all, I realized as my eyes roved over each of his facial features, all of them perfect except for the two days' worth of stubble. And even that was somehow perfect. I lowered my eyes as my cheeks heated. He must have noticed I was staring. But … maybe he was too.

I cleared my throat. "I can handle it. Thank you." I immediately started to turn back, but his voice stopped me. His voice …

It was deeper than I remembered it, and yet there was something else too. Though it was still a bit gravelly, he spoke now with the tone and manner of a successful, confident man. Of course, given how fast he'd worked his way up from his working-class roots, he had every reason to feel confident.

"Don't be silly," he said, his voice clear yet casual. "There are a lot of chairs, and your bookstore friend ditched you. I'll just help and then go. For the bookstore's sake." A look of annoyance marred his perfect face.

I swallowed with some difficulty. "Well, I—fine." I walked to the other side of the circle and started folding the chairs. When I started carrying them to the back of the store, he followed me silently. I felt his every move, his presence consuming the air around us. I needed air; there wasn't enough air in here. I vowed to lift more chairs next time so we could get this done as fast as possible.

Finally, only the snack table remained, and we had to carry that together. As we neared the storage area, he finally broke the silence. "I'll walk you out. It's pretty dark out by now, not safe."

"Oh, that's not necessary—" I protested, terrified at the thought of being alone with him any longer, especially in the dark. Who knew what idiocy would come out of my mouth in those conditions?

He scowled as we put down the table. "Don't be a pain, Annie."

I scoffed. "Don't be ... a *pain*?"

"You heard me," he said curtly as he propped the table against a wall.

Fuming, I crossed my arms, daring him to meet my eyes.

His eyes landed on me briefly and then rose toward the ceiling, his jaw rigid as he sighed. "Come on, let's just go."

After a long moment in which I continued to glare at him, I realized this was counterproductive. I needed to get out of his presence, and if letting him walk me out was the quickest way to make that happen, so be it. "Fine," I forced out.

His lips seemed to twitch, so I started walking ahead without him. Fast.

But his legs were long and powerful, so he caught up easily.

So we walked side by side in silence, for which I was grateful. Once we exited the store, I cursed my choice to not bring a coat, as it was freezing outside. "My car is this way," I mumbled while pointing. "See, not that far from the door. Not that dangerous. I'll be fine."

He made a sound that almost seemed like a laugh but probably wasn't. Surely he was in too foul a mood for that. And he didn't seem to find me funny or pleasant in any way anymore.

Just before we reached my car, he spoke up, his tone softer. "Annie, do you want me to bow out of the club?"

With wider eyes, I turned to him and scanned his earnest expression. "I ... well ..."

"I'm only in town for a visit, but I thought it would be fun to join a book club while I'm in town. I should have said 'hello' first. Uh, hello. I had no idea you were the host ..." He cleared his throat. "My presence here is innocent, I swear."

I gazed into his eyes and felt, for a moment, that time hadn't passed. That it was Kylan from long ago, the one who liked me. Adored me. Before I could take that thought any further, I bit my lip and nodded. "OK. I believe you. And ... you don't have to bow out."

Something flashed through his eyes, and I didn't know what to call it, but it might have been relief.

"Unless you want to," I added, staring at the ground. My shivers intensified, and I wasn't sure if it was from the cold or from his proximity.

"I don't want to bow out," he said easily, and for a moment his face hinted at a smile. Then something less pleasant passed over his face, and his eyes were steely. "I like to stick with things. See them through."

Unlike me. That's what he's thinking. "Right, OK," I said stiffly, my eyes downcast. "Thanks for the help."

"Bye, Annie."

And off he went.

I didn't bother saying goodbye, as he was already striding off at a fast clip and likely wouldn't hear me over the wind whipping around us. Digging my keys out of my pocket, I unlocked my car and quickly climbed inside.

As soon as the door closed, I let my head fall into my arms on the wheel.

I'd survived.

Somehow.

But would I again? And again?

Then came the creeping realization that he'd given me an out. And I hadn't taken it. I'd basically invited him to keep coming to the book club. To keep torturing me.

I was a survivor. But this?

This, I didn't know how to survive.

Of course ... I had no choice.

Taking a few shallow breaths, I turned on the car radio with shaky fingers.

As if on cue, Sia's "Chandelier" started playing—one of my favorite songs. It might as well have been written for me, the ultimate party girl, using alcohol to numb the pain. But everyone loved a party girl, right?

Yes, drink.

That's what I need.

Chapter 15

While opening my bedroom door cautiously, I peeked around the corner to see if the coast was clear and then took some hesitant, quiet steps out of the room.

Rafael's head popped up over the back of the couch.

Busted.

"Girl, I saw you!" he shouted.

I covered my ears and closed my eyes. "Why are you yelling at me?"

He stood and sauntered over, pursing his lips. "I'm not, but I should be. You got wasted last night, didn't you?"

I stared at my best friend, my *best* best friend. If my head didn't hurt so much, I'd glare at him, but it hurt to make facial expressions right now. "First of all, lower your damn voice. Second ... are you *judging* me?"

His hands were on his hips as he nodded and then turned to start the coffee maker. "I'll take pity on you though and get you some coffee and toast."

Misery replaced my indignation, and I just nodded, ambled over to a kitchen stool, and then rested my head on my arms. He was probably right anyway—I've been relying on alcohol too much lately.

After a few minutes in silence, he placed a much-needed steaming coffee and buttery toast in front of me. "You went out with Cory and Stacy, didn't you?"

My mouth full of toast, I shook my head.

Rafael narrowed his eyes.

When I finished chewing, I mumbled, "Just Stacy. Cory's been sick or something."

"Probably with liver disease," he snickered.

I glared at him, even though it worsened the splitting headache I'd woken up with. "That's not funny."

"Sorry, you're right." After a moment of what appeared to be sincere regret, he scrutinized me with scrunched brows and demanded answers. "But what the hell, Annie? Why'd you call them instead of us? Rainn and I were sitting here in the apartment with nothing going on when we got your text that you were going out with a friend."

Stalling, I took a sip of the coffee and then a few more.

Going out with Stacy last night had been a stupid idea, as it always was. Stacy and Cory were the friends I called when I wanted to party hard, to drown my sorrows or work off some rage, to get completely wasted and forget everything and everyone. In college, we were all friends, but Rafael and Rainn had started distancing themselves a year or so ago, claiming they'd outgrown the lifestyle of constant drunkenness and recklessness. I mostly agreed; I felt too old for this crap. But every now and then, the old life pulled at me, sucking me back in. It wasn't the alcohol so much as the life of just … not caring, pretending nothing really mattered except having fun. The life my mother lived, basically. I flinched at the thought, and not for the first time. This was always my thought the morning after. But this time, drinking with Stacy hadn't been fun at all. I hadn't blocked out any of the feelings I wanted to forget, I couldn't muster any desire to hook up with a new guy, and I couldn't even look back and say the hangover was slightly worth it. Not even a little.

Rafael reached out slowly and took my hand, squeezing it briefly before letting it go. "It wasn't even worth it, was it? Sorry, girl."

"How are you a mind reader?" I asked, shaking my head in disbelief.

"I'm not. But I know my girl." He sat on the stool next to me. "What I don't know is what led to this. Last night was the book club. Was it that bad? I don't see how it could go that wrong—"

"It was a success by all measures. Twenty-eight people showed up. By and large, everyone seemed engaged and interested," I said flatly, using my finger to gather up the crumbs left up on my plate.

"OK, then ..." his voice trailed off as he eyed me patiently.

"He was there."

"Who?"

I raised my eyes to meet his.

"Oh," he said quietly. "*Oh*."

"Yeah."

"How—why—"

"It was just chance. He wasn't following me or anything weird. He likes books and so do I. Just my bad, bad, bad luck," I said, punctuating the last "bad" by stomping my foot on the ground as I rose to put my plate and cup in the sink. But I winced, realizing that although the food and caffeine had begun to help my headache, it hadn't vanished.

"We don't have to talk about it," Rafael said casually. "Want to talk about my wedding instead?"

I turned and leaned back against the counter, regarding him thoughtfully. "Yes, please."

An hour later, we were eating chocolate on the couch, laptops perched on our laps. "Oh, Raf, this is classic you and me. What's Joel going to think when we tell him we spent the morning finding your honeymoon destination instead of your wedding venue?"

He gasped, and for a moment, he looked worried. Then, we both broke out into giggles. "He'd expect nothing less."

"So true, and that's how you *know* it's meant to be," I said, smiling a bit wistfully. Before I could dwell on that thought, I returned to my laptop screen, scrolling through more honeymoon locales, when my phone started ringing.

"Unknown number," I said, setting it back down on the arm rest.

Rafael sat up a little straighter and spoke through a mouthful of chocolate. "Annie, you should answer it. What if it's the agency? Or the bookstore?"

"Or what if it's ..." I wouldn't let myself finish the sentence. "No."

"Fine, I'll do it then."

"Raf, no—" I shouted as he grabbed my phone and slid the Answer slider to the left.

"Annie York's phone. Can I help you?" he asked, sounding like a receptionist.

A few seconds passed as he listened. "Yes, of course. She's right here."

As he handed me the phone, I glared at him, making the meanest face I could muster. "Hello?" I said reluctantly.

"Hi, Annie. This is Jardin from Franchersantz Literary Agency. How are you doing today?"

My heart racing, I stifled the desire to scream and motioned to Rafael a thumbs up. "Hi, I'm doing well. It's great to hear from you."

"That's good. I'll get right to the point. We'd like to offer you the agent assistant role. Though most of our previous new hires for the assistant role have done an agency internship or something similar, we felt that the combination of your editing experience, your drive, and other factors indicated you'd be likely to succeed in this position. And, of course, you come highly recommended by an internal staffer as well as by your past colleagues. All in all, we'd like you to take on this role, if you want it. The starting salary is only $40,000, which isn't negotiable since it's entry-level. You'll have full benefits, and I can send you all of those details in an email later today. Are you still interested in the position?"

When Jardin stopped talking, I released a heavy breath. "I am," I croaked. After clearing my throat, I added, "Yes, I am *so* interested."

"Fantastic," Jardin said briskly. "Can you start Monday? Our standard background checks take a while, but we've started people earlier on occasion."

"Oh, um ... yes!" I was surprised, but why not? After all, this was a real job, perhaps my destiny.

Once the call ended, Rafael was sitting there with arms crossed, and I was frozen in place. When his face broke out into a grin, I started jumping up and down and screaming, as I'd wanted to do while on the phone. As I felt my head pound in protest, I sank back onto the couch. "Whew, I really needed to get that out of my system."

"You got the job. Rainn told me last night you would. I was like 'obviously,'" he said, rolling his eyes. "So, what about your ... other commitments?"

I waved my hand dismissively. "Oh, I've already decided I'm going to keep doing the Bookshop internship. I even mentioned it during my interview at the agency, so they're aware. It'll just be on the side. Hakeem will be fine with me scaling back slightly from the original plan, I think."

Rafael opened his mouth and then closed it for a moment. "And the school?"

I gasped. "Oh, I—I ... sorry, I totally spaced it."

His frown deepened for a moment, and then he sighed and extended an arm around me. "I know. You've had a lot on your mind, girl. It's fine."

I laid my head on his shoulder, silently thanking the universe for this wonderful, moody friend of mine. "I think I'd like to keep teaching, actually. But I'll need to scale back. Could I do just the late evenings and weekends?"

He squeezed my shoulder. "How about just Saturday mornings? I'll need to hire another part-timer, so I can give them the weeknight ones. And you never know, your agency job might not be a 9-to-5 one. I wouldn't want you disappointing our little dancers by not showing up if Diana the diva writer decides she needs you to babysit her chihuahua."

I burst into laughter. "That's not a real thing."

"It's not?" Rafael looked disappointed. "Then I'm not sure I want you doing this agency work. The movies made it look interesting. You're going to become downright boring, aren't you?"

I elbowed him in the ribs before we both dissolved into laughter.

I was going to miss this, just relaxing with my friend on a weekday. Working a full-time job plus two part-time ones, I was going to be busy, beyond busy. But I needed that. Busy meant less time to think and to dwell on the past, what might have been, what never would be.

"Annie, please, no!" Rafael whined, sinking into the couch dramatically.

I stood with my hands on my hips. "What's wrong with you?"

"My fiancé is a professional dancer, and even *he* lets me rest!" my roommate whined.

I sighed. "Move over, or I'll sit on you."

As I sat next to him, he groaned in pain. "See, even just that little movement. My abs are killing me. My thigh just screamed at me."

"I didn't hear anything," I said, grinning at him.

"Seriously, Annie. Couldn't you find something else to distract you until your first day at the agency? This is insane."

"You of all people should approve. We're dance teachers, and it's practice we preach."

"This isn't practice. It's torturing ourselves," he mumbled. "I'm going to take a nap, but I'm too tired to get up. Go dance in your room or somewhere else."

"But I don't have a barre in my room!" I protested. One of the coolest things about living with Rafael—and likely one of the only reasons I'd stayed in dancing shape over the years—was that he'd installed a barre along one living room wall, as soon as we'd moved in.

Both his eyes were already closed, but he opened one. "Then find something else to do?"

"Easier said than done," I huffed. But he was right. We'd been working out nearly nonstop for several days, working on new choreography and challenging leaps and turns. I'd claimed it was prep for a new advanced class we were going to start co-teaching on weekends soon, but he saw through that after the first four hours, when I felt inexhaustible. I needed to move, to stay busy, to be so exhausted I couldn't obsess about my new job. Or the other thing I needed desperately not to think about.

I found a nearby blanket and placed it over him. After gently inserting a throw pillow beneath his head, I whispered, "Sorry."

He opened one eye again and flashed a small smile. "What are you wearing for your first day tomorrow?"

I blanked. "What am I ... I don't know!"

With both eyes firmly closed, he pulled the blanket over him and rolled over. With a muffled voice, he said, "That's what I thought. You have my permission to go shopping."

He knew, of course, better than anyone that retail therapy was my favorite kind. I didn't hesitate and was out the door after a quick shower.

After thoroughly reviewing the newest fashions in my favorite store and reluctantly even looking through some older styles on clearance, I gathered an armload of outfits to bring to the changing room. As soon as I hung them in the room, my phone buzzed, and I smiled when I saw who'd sent a text.

Viviana

> **Hey Annie! how are you?**

Annie

> Hey Viv! I'm doing amazing, have some big news actually

Viviana

> I have big news too, would love to catch up when you have time

Annie

> How about today? I could stop by your place this evening

Viviana

> Can't wait! :) Just text on your way over

I put my phone away and started trying on the outfits I'd chosen. But I felt distracted and then eventually shocked to realize my heart wasn't in it.

Hell must be freezing over if my heart's not into shopping.
Do I not love shopping anymore?
Fashion was always my first love!

But that wasn't it. I was just excited to talk to Viviana. To tell her everything. To hear whatever it is that Viviana wanted to share with me. I missed my friend. With this thought, I smiled and tried on the outfits quickly. Realistically, I knew most of the outfits looked great on me; I was just lucky in that way. Fashion designers *designed* clothes for people who looked like me. It wasn't fair, but ... well, it was another problem for another day.

I scanned over all the clothes again. My eyes gravitated toward the emerald green and white dress. It was flattering but also classy enough for an office setting. Or at least I hoped so. Deciding not to dither any longer, I grabbed the dress and left the rest.

Viviana's apartment wasn't far, so I decided to just head straight over there. She was a homebody through and through, so the odds were she'd be there, even though it wasn't yet evening. Still, I fired off a text saying I was on my way.

Standing in the apartment lobby not ten minutes later, I noticed she hadn't texted back yet, so I headed upstairs. There was no response at the door either. Maybe she was showering. Or running. Or napping. Viviana liked to nap. A lot. I smiled, remembering my friend's quirks. I missed her.

I shrugged and retrieved the key she had given to me. I'd used it countless times in situations like this, and I would wait on the couch if need be. Of course, this was a bit different in that we'd had a pretty major fight recently, but still, I was fairly confident my friend would be happy to see me.

Once I let myself in, I absently slipped off my shoes by the door as I called out Viviana's name. There was no answer, but I heard what sounded like the shower. I smiled in relief. She was home.

I sunk into the soft depths of her couch and put up my feet, tossing my phone and keys onto the coffee table.

Rafael was right, we worked way too hard. I'm going to be sore in heels tomorrow.

As my mind wandered, my eyes swept the room and landed near the door, on the floor. Two large black objects took shape. Shoes. Loafers, more specifically. I started to sit up slowly. *No way were Viviana's feet that big.*

As my mind sluggishly connected the dots, I realized the shower had stopped, and I heard the low hum of voices. My jaw sunk to the floor.

This is not the way to reconnect with her, you idiot. She's going to be so embarrassed.

Go, go, go!

I scrambled to my feet and tripped over them as I ran toward the door, only to realize I'd left my things on the table. I dashed back to retrieve them, panting.

A sound of shock interrupted me, followed by my friend's familiar voice. "Annie!"

I winced, squeezing my eyes shut as I felt around for my phone while leaning down. "I ... so sorry, Viv. I was in the neighborhood and wanted to surprise you, and thought I'd just wait and ... I'm just going to go."

"Ah ... It's OK, Annie," said Viviana warmly. "Stay."

"I mean, don't leave on my account," said another familiar voice, followed by a chuckle.

I looked up in astonishment, dropping my things. My lips formed an *O* before breaking out into a massive grin. "You guys are—oh my gosh, I'm so happy for you!" I ran at Viviana and Jack full speed, pulling them both in for a group hug.

Too late, I realized they were wearing robes, barely dressed, so I stumbled back quickly. "Oops, sorry, I was just … I can't believe this. You two! I mean, well, actually I can. You know what? I totally saw this coming."

My friends' wide smiles turned to confusion. "You did?" Viviana asked.

"Well, in him, at least," I said, smiling and pointing at Jack. "We'd had lunch a couple times, and I kinda got the sense he was in love with you." Then I covered my mouth with my hand. "Oh no, sorry, the L-word. Is it too soon?"

They both laughed. "Not at all," Viviana said. "I just found out he loved me yesterday. This is, obviously, the big news I wanted to share."

With eyes twinkling, I said, "Well, I guess you did, in the most dramatic way. I love dramatic, so A plus for you."

"Well, there's also my new job. But that's not nearly as exciting as this guy finally falling in love."

"Not just falling in love, Vivi. Falling in love with *you*," Jack said, his eyes full of adoration. I just stared in amazement. I'd never, ever seen this side of him—or even any hint that there could *be* a side of him like this. I felt a glow of genuine happiness for them as he smiled at us both and started to head to the bedroom. "I'm going to finish getting dressed and then go back to my place. I want to get a run in before dark, and you two probably want to catch up without me hovering around."

"I'm not going anywhere, so I don't need to change," Viviana said, pulling me over to the couch. "So tell me everything! Wait, have you eaten? Should we get food? Drinks?"

A burst of something warm and wonderful bubbled up inside me. It was this. Friendship. My face glowed with happiness as I nodded. "Yes to the food. No to the booze. I'm starting my dream job tomorrow, so I can't be hung over. And honestly, I need to cut back anyway."

She stopped before heading to the kitchen. "Wait, hold on—I need to know about the dream job!"

I laughed. "Well, a stepping stone to my dream job, but still. Yeah. I'm on cloud nine."

"Hold that thought. Just let me get some *nonalcoholic* beverages then and order some food," she said, practically skipping the rest of the short way to the kitchen. I smiled, getting comfortable on the couch and grabbing one of the comfy pillows. *Austen themed, of course*. Viviana was an Austen fanatic. I didn't mind Jane Austen, but the themes of love and romance and happy endings, well ... they just didn't suit me at the moment. I frowned, thinking of my Kylan drama and looking over at my friend. Talking about that with her would be risky, so I decided not to bring it up. It wasn't worth risking the recovery of our friendship right now, which seemed back on track so far.

Besides, I didn't *want* to talk about him now.

Or maybe ever.

Chapter 16

"The agents sometimes work from home, though you'll see them in the office a lot," the chatty blonde assistant said while leading me on a rapid guided tour of the office suite. Ambrose had taken me past the executive and HR offices—glass-fronted and sparsely modern—before gesturing down a very wide hall lined with mostly closed doors and a tidy cluster of cubicles in the middle. The whole space had a minimalist, functional vibe: neutral walls, light wood accents, and abstract art prints that felt like they were chosen to offend no one. "Sofia and Laina are here most days, though Laina's been around less lately. Abi and Ryla have offices right over here, and they're here most days too." Outside the offices were the four back-to-back cubicles with low walls. "This is you," he said, pointing to the only unoccupied desk. "And this is me. All four assistant desks are here."

Ambrose swung around a bit to point toward a side hall. "Further down is Francis's office—I imagine they'll stop and say hi today because you technically report to them, though you won't have a lot of 1–1 contact with them. Don't get their pronouns wrong, or you'll never hear the end of it. Francis manages all of us assistants and agents." And on he went, pointing to the other agent offices that were across the hall. I just took it all in, smiling until my face hurt, breathing in an air of something unfamiliar but exciting, a restless energy coursing through me at the feeling of entering this new world, where I knew so little except that *I belonged. Here.*

"Are you all right?" he asked, looking at me quizzically. I must have looked dazed. I kicked myself inwardly. I could be blissfully happy but still needed to look professional.

I quickly offered a gracious smile. "I'm great. What's next?"

"Just a couple more areas, and then we'll come back and get you settled into your desk before you start the HR orientation. Follow me." He walked off down another hallway, much narrower than the other.

I hurried to catch up. Ambrose wasn't even that tall, but I'd never met anyone who walked as fast as he did. It had to be an occupational hazard. "How long is the HR orientation?"

"Sixteen hours."

At that reply, I almost tripped in my heels. I must have misheard. "Pardon?"

"Sixteen hours, split up over your first three days."

My heart sank. "Oh, that's ... fun."

Ambrose turned toward me and walked a little slower. "Oh, suck it up. You'll be getting Laina's coffee and drycleaning in no time, never fear." At my raised eyebrows, he laughed. "Kidding, mostly. It's not that kind of position. Well, usually. Laina can be demanding though."

Relief washed over me. If getting coffee for the agents was going to help me reach my goals, I was definitely willing, even if it wasn't my first choice. I wanted to dive into the world of books and publishing and authors and royalties and everything else I needed to learn about. Getting someone's coffee seemed like such a waste of time when there was so much to do and learn! Still, I'd suck it up as he suggested, just like the HR training. "Of course," I said, lifting my chin. "This isn't my first job, you know."

"Right," Ambrose snickered, a glimmer of amusement in his eyes. As we came to a stop, he pointed to the left. "Here's the IT offices. We'll just stop in for a quick introduction."

I smiled widely. As soon as we walked in, I spotted Rainn in a cubicle in the corner of a large room full of computer and server equipment. Instead of waiting for an intro from Ambrose, I ran over to his desk, where he looked up and smiled.

Ambrose followed, disapproval on his face.

"It's all right, I know her," Rainn said, grinning as he stood and enveloped me in a giant hug. "She's my roommate."

Ambrose's jaw dropped and then closed quickly. I felt a sense of unease but then dismissed it. "I just wanted to say hi to Rainn. Please do continue with your tour, Ambrose."

After I gave Rainn a helpless look and waved goodbye, Ambrose nodded and curtly led me to meet a few others in the room. Once we were back in the hallway, Ambrose pointed out a few more rooms in the same hall, including the break room, nursing room, and meeting rooms. His tone was as brisk as his walking pace.

Just before we returned to the open area where the assistant desks were, I pulled him aside. "Ambrose, I'm sorry about that, back there."

He looked at me impatiently. "What?"

"About ... running into the IT room without waiting for your introductions. It was unprofessional. I'll do better, I promise."

He sighed. "We have a lot of big personalities around here. I don't care about that."

"Then ..." I trailed off, a questioning look on my face.

He stood in stony silence for a long moment and glanced at his watch. "You're the direct type, aren't you?"

I nodded, sucking my cheeks in to avoid a smile or a cringe, I wasn't sure which.

"I have to respect that," he said grudgingly, gazing up at the ceiling before looking back at me directly. "I'm the same way. So, I'll be frank. I fear you're going to be a nightmare to train because you're underqualified and only got the job because you're, uh, 'rooming with the IT guy.' And I have a heavy workload, so ... that's just more work for me."

"Wha—" I sputtered. "I ... honestly, I don't know why they picked me. You're probably right that my *friendship* with the IT guy—and *his* friendship with a guy in HR—had something to do with it." When Ambrose smirked, I took a step in his direction. I wasn't going to be intimidated. "But that does *not* mean I'm underqualified. I'm going to be amazing at this job. I'm going to be the best damn assistant this agency has ever seen."

His scowl slowly turned into a grin. "Except me."

I raised my eyebrows in challenge. "Game on?"

He laughed and linked arms with me. "This is horrid: I think I might like you. But also hate you. All right, let's get you set up at your desk before you head to the HR snoozefest, I mean, orientation."

I smiled and relaxed my shoulders but not my determination. One battle won, probably many to go. I could do this. I was born to do this.

"I'm taking you to brunch," Sofia announced the next morning when she waltzed over to my desk.

"Oh, I—"

"You do not want to cross me when it comes to brunch," she said, hands on her hips. She flipped her long black hair behind her shoulders and grinned. "Annie, I'm so excited you're going to be my new assistant! I knew from the moment you stumbled into the interview that you were the *one*. I love you already. Sorry we didn't get to chat yesterday, but my day was ridiculous, buried in calls and emails. I'd much rather be meeting a client in person, but lately it's been a lot of phone and texts and stuff."

"I'm the same way," I said. "We'll have a lot in common. So, what time for brunch?" I glanced at the schedule on my computer screen. "My HR orientation is 11–4."

"Blah, OK. We'll go around 9:30 then, so we have plenty of time."

"That's ... soon. OK!"

"Are you too busy?" Sofia said, laughter in her tone as I shook my head. "I thought not. You will be soon though, so let's take advantage of this time to chat. I'll pretend I don't have a mountain of messages to return and manuscripts to read today."

I smiled in spite of myself. That—the phone calls, the emails, the manuscripts in the slush pile, the work of agenting—was what I couldn't wait to start doing. Sofia was busy, but she looked *alive*. Everyone here did. I'd never experienced that while doing freelance editing. There was nothing wrong with that job, of course, but it hadn't been right for me. Why had I continued doing it so long? I shook my head in wonder.

Sofia was talking though, and I felt bad, realizing I hadn't heard everything. I heard a change in Sofia's tone as she pressed her lips together. "Right, IT guy's here. Well, I'll leave you to your busy Day 2 schedule for now and see you in half an hour. I can't wait!" She smiled brightly and headed back to her office just as Annie turned to see Rainn standing a short distance away, thick arms crossed over his chest. He was glowering.

My roommate never glowered.

"Rainn? Hey, what's up? Have you come to install the database, or ... what's wrong?" I frowned.

"Nothing," he grunted. I stood up so he could take my chair and use the computer. As he began doing his IT magic on my computer, I noticed he was sweating a bit and frowning.

"What's wrong?" I repeated.

"I'm working," he snapped.

I reared back and sat in shocked silence for over a minute. Finally, he swiveled in the chair toward me with his eyes lowered. "Sorry, Annie. I don't like her."

"You don't ... you mean Sofia?" I asked, shocked. "You don't like Sofia? She seems awesome."

How could anyone not like Sofia?

"Well, not to me," he said, turning back to the computer.

"Did she do something to you?"

He didn't answer.

"Rainn?"

He sighed. "Just because I know you won't ever give up ..." he leaned closer, whispering, "I overheard her saying I was 'just a muscle man' to another agent. I can tolerate 'IT guy,' but 'muscle man,' really?"

I tilted my head. "Are you sure it was her? She seems really great. I can't picture her saying that."

"Of course I'm sure it was her. I have eyes." He scowled.

I shrugged. "Is it possible she didn't know you worked here yet? Maybe she thought you were the water cooler guy or something?"

"Is that supposed to make it OK?"

"Hmm, nope," I admitted, feeling suitably chastised. "You're right, not cool. What matters is impact, not intention, and obviously it had a pretty negative impact on you."

He shifted uncomfortably in the chair. Of course he wouldn't want to admit to the insecurity underlying this. He'd dated a few girls before who'd treated him like man candy, seeing only a muscular, attractive guy rather than the kind, funny, intelligent, awesome guy inside. I'd wanted to punch those old girlfriends in the throat, actually, but he'd reminded me it wasn't worth it. "It's ... you know, it's fine. I don't want to talk about it. She's your colleague now, so I'll play it cool." The look on his face left me in doubt though.

I leaned forward to turn the volume down on the annoying pop song that Rainn had been blasting in the car. "Thanks for driving me to the bookstore, Rainn, and agreeing to pick me up. If you could come meet me inside, that would be even better. That way, I won't have any awkward walks to the door with Kylan this time." I sighed. "If he even shows up. Hopefully he won't!"

"No problem," Rainn said with a grin. We didn't usually drive to the office together every day, despite working similar schedules so far, simply because I wanted to make sure I was available to stay late if the agents needed me to. It was far too soon for that kind of longer hours yet, but I wanted to be prepared and show I was committed. But today we'd carpooled.

"You know, maybe Sofia was just having a bad day when she said that about you, Rainn, because she is amazing. Seriously, I couldn't be happier working with her."

Rainn said nothing, but he gripped the steering wheel a bit tighter.

Continuing, I added, "She said she might even come tonight. She's already read the book we selected, of course, since it's basically her job to read what's current and know what's selling."

"How nice for her," he said flatly.

"Are you going to hold that one comment against her forever?" I demanded. "You know, women face far worse and far more frequent comments from men *all the time*, and we're expected to just *get over it*. Move on. No big deal."

"And that makes it OK?" He glanced at me briefly with a challenge in his eyes.

"No." I sighed. "I bet if I talked to her about it, she'd apologize. I bet she'd be really embarrassed and want to make it right. She's really sweet—"

"*No*. Absolutely not."

"But, Rainn—"

"Don't say anything to her."

"Rainn, I—"

"No."

I stayed silent for a moment. This had struck a bigger nerve with him than I'd realized. I said quietly, "Fine. Sorry."

"Not your fault."

We rode the rest of the way in silence, other than the quiet hum of the radio in the background.

When we arrived, I asked him if he wanted to stop in.

"Oh, I'm not ... the book club type."

"You don't have to stay. I just ... I could use help setting up the chairs and stuff. I don't know if my teenage coworker will show up, and she's so moody."

Rainn looked at me, not yet responding.

"OK, fine ... the truth is, I'm terrified of facing Kylan alone, in case he shows up early. Are you happy?" I buried my face in my palms.

"Yep," he said, turning off the engine and getting out of the car.

"Finally, I get a smile from you," I muttered, "but only at my own expense."

He put a broad arm around my shoulder as we started walking toward the door, and he didn't hide a wry smile. "We've both had a bit of that tonight, haven't we?"

I needn't have feared, as Kylan didn't make his grand appearance until five minutes after we'd started. I was actually quite annoyed, as we'd already started discussing the book. I'd started relaxing enough to enjoy myself, thinking he'd abandoned the idea of attending altogether. But so much for that hope. Sofia showed up too, but on time, so she sat next to me. Yet again, I had to resist the urge to bring up Rainn and ask what the deal was.

At the halfway point, I announced a five-minute break and turned to Sofia. "You've been quiet. Are you all right?" Usually Sofia was just like me, the furthest thing from shy.

My new friend and colleague smiled. "Oh, I'm fine, girl. I'm just feeling out the room. As an agent, I'm trying to figure out what kind of role I should play in a conversation like this, you know? I talked to Jardin earlier, and they didn't see my attending as a conflict of interest per se, but they wanted me to be thoughtful in my approach. So I'm just trying to, you know, be thoughtful."

"I'm glad you talked to Jardin about it." I winced. "I hadn't even thought of that."

"Laina suggested it."

I was about to say more, but a deep voice intervened. "Another agent in the room, eh?" Kylan stood in front of us, sticking out his large hand in front of Sofia as I watched him warily. "I'm Kylan Quinn, from Elliott Literary in New York. I was kind of thinking along the same lines. Getting a feel for how the discussion goes. Sorry, I didn't catch your name last time?"

"Sofia. Jackson. I wasn't here last time, so that's why you didn't catch it," she said, smiling at him and smoothing her black hair while looking him up and down.

Is she flirting with him?

And why on earth would I care?

I wouldn't.

I don't.

In what was becoming a pattern now, Carlina came over to save me, yet again. "Annie!" she said loudly. "Introduce me to your new friend here. I don't think we've met yet, but I overheard you saying she's an agent."

Sofia's eyes lingered on Kylan just a bit longer before swinging over to Carlina, whom she flashed a friendly smile. "Hi, I'm Sofia Jackson. Annie just started working at our agency and brought me along tonight."

"I have a memoir I want to publish, so maybe you're the one to talk to?" Carlina said, pulling Sofia aside. "I'm only joking. I'd never subject anyone to reading that, much less publishing it for all to see. But I'd love to hear more about your work."

Unfortunately, this left Kylan just standing there near me, and when I dared to look up, he was staring at me, his expression impossible to read. Half a minute passed. He might have been about to speak, but I couldn't bear to listen.

"Everyone, let's get back to our discussion," I called out loudly, waving my hands in the air to usher people back to their seats. A muscle ticked in his jaw just before he returned to his seat on the other side of the circle.

Whew, dodged another bullet.

But I couldn't do this forever, could I? Eventually we'd have to talk.

Nope, nope, nope.

Chapter 17

I blinked several times slowly, trying to counteract the eye strain I'd been trying to ignore. I had spent the last three hours poring over contracts and royalty statements for several of Laina's authors. My senior colleague had thought it best to introduce me to the technical and legal side of my job first, reasoning that legal or financial errors were extremely expensive. I couldn't argue with that. I'd been out of work for a few weeks though and was no longer in the habit of staring at a screen at a desk for hours on end, so my poor eyes, neck, and other stiff body parts were paying the price.

Fortunately, Sofia had given me some interesting tasks to dip my toe into agent work. I was able to tag along to a lunch with one of Sofia's best author clients and then listened in on a conference call with a few editors that she said I'd get to know eventually. Before Laina tasked me with the contractual review, I'd even gotten a preliminary training from Ambrose on query handling.

Truthfully, I was buzzing with excitement—even with a sore neck—and even a bit sad it was already Friday so I'd have to wait until Monday to learn more about my dream job.

Smiling, I forced my attention back to the long clause still waiting to be read on my screen, but then an email notification flagged as

Important! appeared in the corner of my screen, followed almost immediately by a hum of voices from every direction.

I opened the email quickly. It was from Lucas Mantz, agency president, calling a company-wide meeting immediately.

My heart sank. I'd heard of this happening before. The company was being shut down, or there'd be layoffs. More likely layoffs. And I'd be the first person cut.

I was shaking slightly as I rose to join the other assistants who stood nearby, eyeing me with what was probably pity. Before I could join them, Sofia was by my side, linking arms with me and leading me to the large conference room. I looked up at my tall, usually confident friend, who also looked nervous. We walked in silence, but it was comforting, and I squeezed her arm in gratitude.

Once we reached the conference room, Rainn found me as well and immediately came over. "Annie, hey." He didn't speak to Sofia, but he didn't glare at her either. Sofia in turn didn't seem to notice Rainn, seeming distracted. I sat on the floor, as there weren't enough chairs for everyone, and they sat on either side of me. A handful of people in the room were openly chatting, but most people were either silent or whispering. Many were fidgeting or using their phones.

Lucas and the other leadership, including Jardin and others I hadn't met yet, arrived soon after, taking seats near the podium. Then, Lucas left the room for a moment and returned, followed by another man.

And that's when my heart dropped into my stomach.

What the—

Why—

He…

He can't be here.

I tugged on Rainn's sleeve desperately and looked at him with wild eyes. He tilted his head in concern and mouthed, *What?*

Sofia leaned over, and I tried to conceal my distress. "Annie, is that …" she whispered. "It looks like that guy from the book club. Kyle?"

I nodded numbly, unable to tear my eyes away now. Kylan wasn't looking at me, probably hadn't spotted me. He was talking quietly to Lucas and the others in the front, smiling and looking dashing in a suit and tie.

Oh my god, he's handsome. I'd never seen him this dressed up, had I? No, I would remember if I had.

"Good afternoon, everyone," Lucas spoke, his voice naturally carrying across the room. A few people still streamed into the room, but he was a busy man and wasn't going to wait all day, his tone said. "Thanks for gathering so quickly. We have an important announcement to share, and I wanted you all to be the first to know, before it goes public."

The pit in my stomach grew. As if it weren't traumatic enough that Kylan was here inexplicably, this was sounding even more ominous for the future of my new job that I already loved so much. I wasn't the nervous type normally, but I bit my trembling lip and tried to breathe steadily. Rainn squeezed my hand in my lap.

"Franchersantz is being acquired by Elliott Literary." Gasps circulated around the room, but Lucas put his hand forward for silence. "Elliott is a much larger agency headquartered in New York, one of the top agencies in the country if you somehow haven't heard of it." He extended his arm toward Kylan. "I want to introduce Kylan Quinn, who heads up the agency. Elliott has brokered countless deals with the biggest publishers and has been acquiring some smaller regional agencies like ours." I heard Rainn gasp next to me as I leaned into him for support.

Kylan was smiling politely at Lucas with what seemed like a genuinely humble expression. I was starting to suspect my ex was actually a lot more successful (and richer) than I'd ever realized ... to think he'd started from nothing, or almost nothing! Viviana had thought me too good for him—which I'd never really believed—but now *he* was far too good for *me*. How on earth had he traveled *that* far up the ladder in just four years since we'd known each other?

Not that it matters, since that was long in the past. Just pay attention, dammit.

"... so this is great news for our business," Lucas was saying. "With more resources and contacts within our reach, we can grow and

succeed beyond what we could do on our own. We're really excited."
My face scrunched in confusion.

Was Lucas spinning this acquisition as a good thing? Was it actually good, or was he just trying to smooth things over for the moment?

"We're going to have a Q&A session early next week," Lucas continued, "as well as some other resources to help our team with the first part of this transition. For now, I'm going to give the floor over to Mr. Quinn for a bit, and then to Jardin to discuss the human resource perspective."

Kylan shook Lucas's hand as though concluding a business transaction right then and there. Then he turned to the rest of the room and smiled. If he saw me, it wasn't obvious. Rainn squeezed my hand again in support, and I gave him a weak but grateful smile before turning back to Kylan. I tried to focus on his words instead of ... him. In a well-tailored, expensive suit, simple but perfect haircut, strong, clean-shaven jaw, and a confident smile, he *looked* the part of the man taking over a company. It was hard to imagine I'd known him just four years ago as the sweet and passionate college guy with a lot of dreams and no money. Again I reminded myself to pay attention to the speaker.

"I'm all about growth," Kylan was saying. "I want to grow my company, but I want to grow your company too. Ours. Together. I've been in town for a few weeks now, and I plan to stay here in the Twin Cities for at least a few months to make this a smooth transition. I'm committed to helping us all succeed. Every single one of us. I don't plan to lay off anyone." I heard someone behind me sigh in relief. "Lucas is choosing to step away from his post and move to a board position, but other than that, every one of you still has a job, if you want it. We'll even be looking to make transfers or hire for a few new positions and asking you for referrals. Your HR director will be able to answer more questions too—she's great, by the way. I'm looking forward to meeting with all of you in the coming weeks and getting to know your business. I like to be hands-on, but I also have a lot of trust in the people we employ. We have a great transition plan mapped out that we'll share and kick off next week."

He paused, scanning the room and flashing a massive smile.

He must not have seen me yet.

After clearing his throat, he continued, "This will be an amazing union for all of us. We'll be able to help more authors than ever before and help bring more books to market and sell more than ever. And hopefully—this goal is close to my heart—through those books, inspire more people and instill in them a lifelong love of reading."

Some people clapped, and I rolled my eyes. Unfortunately, Kylan chose that moment to finally notice me, and a muscle in his jaw tightened slightly before his eyes darted away.

Oh crap.

No ...

He's going to be ... my boss! Or my boss's boss's boss, or something like that. He could fire me.

And I've just started this awkward new phase by rolling my eyes at his cheesy but probably well-intentioned line.

Not to mention being frosty every time I've seen him.

He could ruin me. Ruin this dream.

Just like I ruined his.

No, I didn't ruin his dream. He's living it, here, now. Look how successful he is. This was his dream, not some silly college romance with me.

Rainn squeezed my hand again, and I looked up first at him and then at the woman now speaking. Jardin was giving a brief overview of what to expect next week from HR.

Ugh, how could Kylan do this to me?

I can't even pay attention to an important meeting, one of the most important of my life, possibly.

I could ask Rainn for details on what I'd missed later, but this did not bode well for my future with the agency, whatever it was going to become.

When the meeting was finally over, I turned to Rainn, who gave me a sympathetic smile and quickly started leading me out of the room. What had I ever done to deserve such amazing best friends?

He had to be worried about his own position, but he was more concerned about me. Just before we left the room though, I stopped. "Wait, Rainn, I just realized we should wait for Sofia—" I started saying but then stopped as I spotted her, standing close to Kylan. "Oh, she's talking to him a–a–and ... and they're laughing."

My eyes burned. Why, I didn't know. The sight of Sofia standing so close to him, both of them smiling, made speech difficult. I managed to swallow with some effort. "Is she flirting?"

Rainn's tone was monotone. "I don't know. Maybe."

I looked at him, surprised to see his face look stiff, his usually full lips set in a thin line.

When he noticed my gaze, he shrugged. "Or maybe she's just being strategic, making friends with the new boss right away."

My gaze landed on Sofia and Kylan again. "Maybe. That's something she would do. And they've met before, at the book club, so I guess it's not all that strange that she'd go say hi."

Rainn agreed, "True. That's probably it then. But, Annie ..." He paused, pulling me gently out of the room and waiting until we were in the hallway away from most of the others. "Does it really bother you that much? I mean, if he were flirting with someone here? It could happen, you know."

I opened my mouth, which made some shapes but no sound.

He sighed softly. "OK, I get it."

"Rainn, I—" I started, recovering my voice and turning to him with eyebrows raised.

"Your secret is safe with me," he said, putting his arm around me for a quick squeeze before we went back to our respective desks to pack up for the day. It was nearly time to sign off for the day—thank goodness, as I couldn't handle the possibility of another encounter or even a distant sighting of Kylan today.

"So, Annie," Sofia said while spearing some salad onto her fork, "what did you think of Debbie, now that you've met her?"

I finished chewing my chicken pesto sandwich and then wiped my mouth carefully. "Well, I know you had some reservations about signing her, but I think you made the right choice. She seems really open to the changes we're asking her to make, at least."

Sofia nodded. "Yeah, she is. She's sweet, and we need a lot more Black women authors. Above all, her writing was good. It's just ... well, Laina told me I was making a mistake, and sometimes I let her get in my head."

"What's the saying? Never let others live rent-free inside your head, or something like that," I said with a sympathetic smile. "Easier said than done, I know."

Sofia smiled and shook her head. "So true. All right, I promised we wouldn't talk about work this whole lunch, so I'll shut up about this."

I smiled. "I don't mind. I have no life outside of work right now."

"Oh," she said, wincing, "sorry to hear that. I can help you with that—"

"No, it's actually just the way I want it. For now."

Sofia eyed me thoughtfully. "Ah, I see. Just ... don't burn out, OK? I really like you, lady. The last thing I need is to find a new assistant."

I laughed. "No danger of that. You'd have to drag me out, kicking and screaming."

After a few moments while we continued eating, Sofia said, "Oh, I meant to tell you, when I had my first meeting with Kylan this afternoon, we talked a little about you actually."

My heart rate seemed to triple as I feigned only mild interest. I'd known Sofia was meeting with him, of course. As Sofia's assistant, I knew everything about her schedule, as well as Laina's. Kylan was making the rounds and meeting with all the agents early on to get the lay of the land. With a forced calm, I asked, "You met with him?"

Sofia nodded. "I like him. I didn't want to. I mean, he's the rich, hot, privileged, white boy coming in to shake things up here." She shrugged. "But there's something about him."

"Well, he wasn't always rich," I said, before I could stop myself.

"Oh?" Then she sat back in her chair and took a sip of iced tea. "That reminds me. You never told me you had a history."

My heart rate quickened as I forced a smile. "Oh, I didn't? Well, not much to speak of. I know he grew up poor though, worked his way through college."

"You dated though, didn't you?" Sofia raised an eyebrow. "But it's not much to speak of?"

Crap.

He told Sofia that?

"Uh, I—well, it wasn't ..." I grasped for words. "I'm sure he said it wasn't that serious—"

Sofia laughed. "I suppose, in so many words. He did say he barely recognized you at first, and this was the last place he expected to see you working."

As my heart shattered into pieces, I arranged my face into a careful smile. I was good at that. "Right, I–I was a bit aimless in college. I'm surprised he even remembers me."

"Not your soulmate then. Got it." She chuckled after taking another sip of tea. But her face sobered. "Well, I ..." she trailed off, looking hesitant.

I didn't really want to know what she was going to say, but I made myself ask. "What? Just say it."

With a somewhat guilty expression, my new friend sighed. "I can't say I'm not interested myself. I did feel some heat when we met last week at Bookshop. Would you mind if ..."

I shook my head rapidly, trying to focus on breathing before I uttered in a raspy voice, "No, but ... it might not be a good idea, professionally. During the transition, at least."

She winced. "True. As a woman of color, I can't afford to risk mixing personal and professional. It's not fair, but that's the way of things. At least, I've never found anyone worth the risk before." She winked at me. Was she saying Kylan might be the exception? My heart sank further as my mind filled with dread.

The only thing worse than working under Kylan as a boss would be watching him fall in love with my coworker and new friend. I'd have to quit.

I can't quit! I love this job.

Think, Annie.

I raised my chin and pursed my lips. "Sofia, no man is worth that risk. And I'm going to remind you of that as often as I need to, just as you'll do the same for me."

"Aww, girl, of course I will. I've known you for like a week. Or two? Whatever. I already want to get bestie tattoos." At my surprised face, she laughed. "I'm joking, of course. I don't do pain. But you're awesome, girl."

Not two hours later, I was pouring my special caramel coffee blend into the coffeemaker as the accounting manager was standing near the microwave making popcorn. Despite my usual habit of making small talk in the break room, I wasn't attempting to chat at all, in part because voices would've been hard to hear over the popcorn and in part because Sandra would've ignored me anyway. I'd said hello to the woman every day and never received anything in response except an icy glare, if that. At first I'd wondered what I had done to offend her, but Sofia assured me it wasn't personal. Apparently Sandra was just an unpleasant person, but she was related to one of the agency's founders and thus had been working here forever.

I tapped my foot, wishing I'd thought to bring my phone as I waited for the coffee to brew. I sighed as I considered all the work remaining on my to-do list for today. I had at least a dozen emails to reply to, and Laina had a meeting she needed me to schedule. I was trying to remember the other to-do when a familiar deep voice startled me.

"I just had to find out who the office popcorn lover is," said the owner of the voice, flashing a charming smile as he rounded the corner into the room. Kylan's smile wavered just a bit when he saw me, but he recovered quickly. Me, not so much. I had to lean back against the counter to steady myself.

Thank goodness I'm not in here alone.

I glanced over at Sandra with reluctant gratitude. But I frowned, noting that Sandra was pulling the steaming popcorn bag out of the microwave.

"It is only I," Sandra said in a high-pitched voice, followed by a giggle. "I can share." I stared at her, wide-eyed. Who was this woman? She had to be at least 50 years old, as stern and frosty as any woman I'd ever met, but she'd transformed into a flirty schoolgirl just like that?

Kylan gave her a winning smile. "Any other day, Sandra—it's Sandra, right?" When she beamed, he continued, "Any other day, I would, but I'm still stuffed from lunch. I just came to get some coffee."

Sandra sighed. "Your loss, Mr. Quinn. Maybe another time then," she said in almost a whisper as she sashayed past him with her popcorn.

I stared after her in disbelief, jaw nearly on the floor. But when the door closed, I jolted back to reality and found my ex walking toward me. "I, uh, I was just waiting for my coffee."

"OK," he said in a pleasant voice.

"I don't like the office coffee, so I brew my own."

"Cool."

Why am I explaining what I'm doing in the break room?

I'm not doing anything wrong.

I shook my head as I warily watched him pour some of the normal office coffee and then add sugar.

Instead of turning to leave though, he leaned against the counter and took a sip. And then another. "No wonder you bring your own. Can I try it?"

"Uh, well, it's... uh—"

"Forget it, if it's a big deal—"

"No! I mean, yes, you can. It's not ready yet though. I do a slow brew."

He was quiet for a moment and then said, "OK."

Silence reigned for the next two and a half minutes while it finished. A painful silence that I kept debating whether or not to fill. I was very talented when it came to filling silences. I loved doing it, actually. But *this—this* silence was one I wasn't sure should be filled. It was better this way.

Finally, the coffee was done, and we each poured a cup. I waited while he took a few sips. Slowly, his lips turned up at the corners, and at such close proximity, I could see the slight crinkles around his eyes.

I swallowed with some effort. "You like it then. Good. Some things are worth the wait, right?"

Oh my—I did not *just say that.*

He's going to think—oh no, I just said ... that.

He sipped the coffee and met my eyes for a moment. "Perhaps you're right."

I averted my eyes first, getting a lid for my coffee cup and handing him one. "Well, I need to go back to my desk."

"So do I," he said, sounding distracted. As he followed me out of the room, he suddenly called to me. "Oh wait, Annie."

I whirled around, my heart fluttering. This job, being here with *him*, was going to be the death of me.

And my name.

On his lips.

Those lips.

"Yes?"

"I almost forgot. I can't make it tonight. I have a work thing with Lucas. I told him I'm busy on Wednesdays, but apparently this meeting *had* to take place tonight. Sorry," Kylan said, actually looking apologetic.

I stared into his eyes, surprise on my face. Why was he telling me this? "Oh, it's ... I'm ... thanks for letting me know. Um, have a good time at your meeting."

With that idiotic closing statement, I gave him a polite smile and turned to leave.

I'd survived another encounter with him, but at what cost?

Chapter 18

A few days later, my friends and I had barely started on the famous Bennie's appetizers when the dreaded questions came.

"So tell us all about your new job and the agency!" Viviana said, dipping her crusty bread into the artichoke dip that she'd claimed for herself.

"Yeah, we've been dying to hear more," Jack chimed in. "What's the name of the agency?"

I dipped my tortilla chip into the salsa that had won Bennie's a local foodie award three years in a row. After taking my time to savor each bite, I exhaled slowly. "I was hired at Franchersantz, but the company is being acquired—" At the sharp look of concern on both my friends' faces, I paused. "No, my job is fine, it seems. He said—I mean, they said everyone's jobs are safe, and they'll probably expand the staff rather than downsize. Anyway, I'm an assistant to two literary agents, one of whom I really, really like. I'm going to have to introduce you sometime because she's becoming a great friend already. The job is ... amazing. I love it so much."

"That is so wonderful, Annie," Jack said, his eyes crinkled at the corners. "I knew you'd find your niche."

"I'm so excited for you!" Viviana said, smiling. "I never heard you describe work as amazing before, so this is huge for you. So, was it hard to break into this field? I always imagined it would be, but you weren't jobless for very long and ... well, you do have that Annie charisma."

I grinned. "Aww, thanks. Well, I had help. Rainn already worked there, and he had a good friend in HR too."

"Ah," Jack said, nodding as he speared another piece of vegetable tempura. "It helps when you know people."

My smile faltered a bit, thinking of the person at the agency I wished I *didn't* know, or at least I wished I didn't have to face him there nearly every day. "It does, though I think my instant connection with Sofia helped. She's the agent I made quick friends with."

Jack took a long swig of his drink and then crossed his arms over his chest. "So tell us about this acquisition. How does that even work anyway?"

I bit my lip. "It's actually a New York agency that's been acquiring smaller agencies around the country. He tried to sell it to us as a positive for our regional agency, that we'll have better access to bigger publishers and more power in the collective. That remains to be seen, but I suppose it makes sense." I sighed. "Still, such a massive shakeup at the company almost right after I start a new job—a new *career*—is a bit harrowing, you know?"

"Who's he?" Viviana asked.

"What?"

"You said 'he' tried to sell this vision of the acquisition as benefiting you guys ... Who? The acquirer? Or your agency's old leadership?"

My cheeks heated. "Oh, uh, I guess both."

Viviana peered at me closely. "Annie, are you OK?"

"I'm fine," I rushed to reply. "Well, I, uh—"

"You don't look fine," Jack said in his usual gentle tone. "But if you want to talk about something else, that's OK." He turned to Viviana with a pointed look. "We don't mind."

My gaze swung from Jack to Viviana and back again before sighing in resignation. "Oh, why not? I'll probably have to tell you eventually," I muttered. After a deep breath, I raised my chin and began, "Viviana, do you remember Kylan Quinn from college? The guy I was kind of serious about?"

Her eyes widened and lips parted, and she nodded slowly. She and Jack exchanged a strange look.

"Well, he's the acquirer. The big New York agency is his."

Silence.

"He's *what?*"

"Yeah."

"That's impossible!"

"It's not."

"How could *he* ... how could *anyone* go from nothing to ... to such a prestigious position in, what, five years?"

"Four."

"It does sound quite impressive," Jack finally weighed in. "And how are you doing with that, Annie?"

I pressed my lips together, full of resolve. "I'm fine. I obviously moved on, long ago."

Viviana nodded, with an approving smile. "Good. And so has he, I'm sure." When my lips quivered a bit, she added softly, "He didn't deserve you anyway."

"I'm not sure about that. It seems like the other way around, actually. He's the big shot, and I'm the lowly assistant." I forced a laugh and flipped my hair back as though it mattered not at all.

Viviana raised her eyebrows. "What? No. He may have a fancy job title now, but that doesn't mean he's good enough for you."

"Well, it doesn't matter because I–I, well, I'm not interested in him anymore. It's just a temporary work situation that we have to endure, and then he'll go back to New York and ..." I paused. My friends were studying me intently. What could I say? I hadn't thought that far ahead. I'd just focused on how much I wanted him out of my life because ... it was excruciating. But *did* I really want him out of my life? Could I handle saying goodbye again? Losing him again?

He's not yours to lose.

"And that's that," I finished with a shrug.

Viviana opened her mouth to speak, but Jack's hand entwined with hers. "Vivi and I are here for you if you ever want to talk, but it sounds like you're handling everything just fine on your own. I'm really excited that *you're* so excited about this new career. You deserve that, Annie."

My friend nodded slowly, reluctant to give up the subject of Kylan. "Just ... be careful. He's the boss now, and this job means a lot to you. Jack's right, you *totally* deserve an amazing career that you love. And I want to hear all about what agents do. After all, I'm going to need one at some point myself!"

My brows were scrunched together in confusion. "Are you going to write a book?"

"I am!" Viviana said, a brilliant smile lighting her face. "I have, actually."

"Viv, that is amazing! I can't wait to read it. I didn't even know you were interested in writing. I mean, I knew you were writing for the feminist magazine now, which by the way is awesome, but writing a novel? That's just ... wow. I can't imagine the diligence that would take. So when can I read it?"

"Well ..." She looked at Jack. "I was just talking to Jack about how I probably need some beta readers. I've gone through a few drafts myself, and Jack's read it, but he's so far from impartial it's laughable." At my questioning look, I added, "The book is loosely based on our own love story. It's Austen-inspired."

As the two of them stared at each other for an awkward length of time, I cleared my throat and forced out the words. "Of course. Austen."

"Well, you know Vivi," Jack said, smiling as he tore his eyes away from her.

"Would you like me to beta read?" I heard myself asking. "In a totally non-professional capacity, of course. I would not be your future agent. I imagine that would be a conflict of interest or something, at least at my early career stage, but I'd love to help you out as a friend."

"You would?" Viviana's eyes lit up. "Oh, that would be so, so great if you did."

I laughed. "I mean, I can't promise that my feedback is worth anything anyway, but I'd love to read it."

"I'm going to send it right now," Viviana said, pulling out her phone and typing away on the screen.

"Oh," I said, surprised at her haste. "OK, sure."

"Vivi's just a bit eager for readers," Jack said with a laugh. "So, Annie, are you still working at the bookstore and dance school too, or did you quit to make time for the agent role?"

"I'm doing all three. I just came from ballet before this, actually. I almost had to cancel because my ankle was killing me, but some ice and a wrap fixed it. I'm only hobbling now."

"All three?" Jack's eyes were wide. "Wow, you must have ... zero time."

"I did scale back on the dance classes, and the bookstore events happen only whenever I decide to do them, so I can plan them at a relatively slow pace. But yeah, I'm pretty busy," I conceded. "I like it ... or maybe I need it, right now. I was sort of in a dark place a month ago, and becoming busy really helped, you know? I'll probably have to scale back eventually, but for now, it works for me."

Jack nodded, sympathy in his clear blue eyes. "I'm glad it's helping." And then he added softly, "And I hope the darkness has passed."

I smiled. "Mostly, yeah. It sounds crazy, but finding myself in this new job is ... well, it's everything."

"It doesn't sound crazy at all," Jack said.

"I only caught the tail end of that," Viviana chimed in as she set her phone down, "but it doesn't sound crazy to me either. I'm so much happier after finding a new job, exploring new options." She rose from her seat and sank down next to Annie's seat to embrace her. "Oh, Annie, I'm so happy we're both so much happier now!"

I hugged her back. I was probably happier, it was true. Not as happy as Viviana, who'd found her true love. But that was OK. Not everyone could have that, and that was fine.

It was *fine*.

When Viviana had returned to her place next to Jack, her face lit up. "Annie, you should come over tonight and watch rom-coms. You haven't come over for takeout and wine for, like, forever!"

"That sounds fun," I lied. Watching a rom-com as a third wheel with these lovebirds? No, thank you! "But Rainn and Raf have been complaining that they never get to hang out with me anymore, so I promised I'd be around tonight."

Viviana frowned. "But they're your roommates. Surely they see you a lot more than we do—"

Jack put his arm around her shoulders and smiled. "We'll take a raincheck. Annie, it's been really fun catching up. We should do it more often."

Viviana extricated herself from his embrace and went around to hug me again instead. "For sure. I missed you, girl."

My eyes filled with tears, inexplicably, and I hugged Viviana tighter as I tried to covertly wipe my eyes. "Same."

A gentle tug on my hand came before the faint, feminine voice. "Annie ... hey, girl."

"Ms. York, wake up," came a deeper voice. Firm, commanding, but sexy. It was the one that haunted my dreams, waking and asleep.

A giggle from the other voice. "Annie! We kind of need you to wake up now," she said, louder this time.

It was Sofia, I realized, turning my head toward the voice and immediately regretting it as my neck screamed in response. I opened my eyes slowly to find two pairs staring at me. Sofia and Kylan were crouched with the car door open, and I was slumped at an unnatural angle in the backseat. "I—" I croaked before clearing my throat. "I am sorry, I must have dozed off for a minute or so."

Sofia's rich laugh filled the small space. "More than a minute or two. We let you sleep a bit longer. But it's time for you to go run the book club meeting now."

"It's almost 7 o' clock," Kylan said, sounding irritated. But when I met his eyes, I saw something that didn't look like irritation. It looked like ... something. I had no idea. Interest? Was he showing *interest* in me? My brows furrowed in confusion, and then my spirits deflated. If anything, it was probably interest in Sofia. They'd let me sleep a while, so who knows what they'd been doing in the meantime.

I rubbed my eyes, sitting up slowly, when his words suddenly clicked. "Seven? You guys let me sleep this long? I have to set up!" I said frantically, wild eyes darting around as I launched myself out of the car.

"Relax, Annie. We got you, girl. We saw Sai arrive a while ago and told her to set up. And then we told her little boy crush Zach to go help her," Sofia said, smirking. "She should be thanking us."

I couldn't help but grin at the idea of that. I hurried toward the door, the other two on my heels. Kylan overtook me just before reaching the door, opening it for both of us.

"Such a gentleman he is, Annie," Sofia said to me, but her soft smile and shining eyes were on him. Gritting my teeth, I forced my eyes forward, toward the gathering book club crowd.

"You're late," Sai declared with her usual scowl as I claimed the empty seat next to her.

It was 6:59, so not quite late, but it wasn't worth arguing about. "Sorry, Sai. Thanks for setting up. You did a great job."

Sai mumbled a sullen-sounding "Thanks," but I thought she was biting back a grin. Could Sai be won over with praise? I'd been wondering if Sai might want to co-lead the book club with me or at least facilitate some book discussion meetings herself, but I wasn't sure how to bring it up.

Maybe I could ask her when she's—

"Annie?" Carlina whispered loudly from a few seats away. "I think we're all here."

My face felt warm. How long had I been lost in my thoughts? It was 7:04 now, and everyone was looking at me expectantly. I cleared my throat and pretended to look at my small notebook. "Yes, right. Sorry about that, I was just ... thinking about the, uh, effects of women's fiction on our society. I ..."

What the hell am I saying? I sound like a total idiot.

"Well, let's dive into part 2 of the book discussion following up from last week, shall we? Mental health is certainly a theme in this book, both with the main character and her mother. How do you think the setting of this book—outside the U.S.—affects how the issue of mental health is handled here? Or maybe it doesn't?" Fortunately, I always came prepared with question prompts written beforehand, exactly for situations like this where my brained ceased to work.

I'd almost forgotten to prepare the questions though. What with beta reading Viviana's book, tux fitting appointments, and long hours at work on some impending manuscript deadlines and contract negotiations, the past two days had given me almost no time to think, let alone sleep. I could've asked Viviana for an extra day or two, or even more, to read her story, but I hated to go back on my word, especially given that we'd just reconciled in our friendship.

Carpooling to the bookstore with Sofia and Kylan had been the *last* thing I wanted to do, but we were all working late at the office that evening—and every other evening that week—and Sofia had insisted on driving us, since we'd all planned to return to the office after the book club anyway. I was too tired to argue against it, so I'd reluctantly agreed. Despite my embarrassment at falling asleep in the back seat of Sofia's car, a little part of me was relieved. It was kind of my worst nightmare to ride as the third wheel as the two of them chatted and flirted and laughed in the front seat. And flirt they did. A vile sensation filled my stomach at the thought. There was a growing awareness that Kylan might actually be interested in

Sofia and that—worse yet—I would have front-row tickets to their courtship.

Courtship.

I almost let out a laugh, but my eyes felt too heavy.

This isn't a Jane Austen novel.

But if it were, I'd be the sad, lonely one ... the—

"What do you think, Annie?" Kylan's voice suddenly cut through my disjointed thoughts. His eyes were curious, his expression serious.

Panic set in. I had not been following the discussion at all. "I think ... well, I always—" Some non-word sounds came out, and I desperately glanced at the clock over his head. It had been nearly 40 minutes, and I'd been spaced out the entire time. "It's actually a great time to take a break. Let's return in five minutes, everyone, and then come back to discuss some more and decide on our next book, OK?"

As soon as I stood up, Sofia and Sai were rising with me.

"Annie, are you OK?" Sofia asked, her brows furrowed. "You seem a little distracted. Or maybe really tired. Are we working you too hard? You can tell me, you know."

When I shook my head and started to respond, Sai raised an eyebrow. "Are you high?"

I sighed. "No. I ... all right, I'm a little tired."

Sofia crossed her arms. "A little? You fell asleep in a 5-minute car ride on the way here."

"Maybe more than a little."

"OK, I'm bored now. I'm going to sit back down," Sai said, pulling out her phone and sneaking a glance at Zachary, who was sneaking a glance at her.

Just then, I felt a certain heated masculine presence directly behind me, perhaps just a few inches. I sidestepped a few inches, my breath catching.

"Annie, I've called Rainn to take you home. Sai," he said in a commanding voice, staring down at the teenager. "ou can facilitate the rest of the discussion, right?"

Her mouth gaping, Sai just stared up at Kylan for a moment. "I guess so. Can't be that hard," she mumbled.

I felt dizzy as my gaze bounced between them. "Wait, what? You called me a ride ... home? Wh—why would you do that?"

He gave me a look of impatience before sitting down to talk to Sai quietly for a brief moment, and then he rose again. "Rainn should be here soon. He concurred that you likely need rest."

"What—how—you don't get to decide that for me," I sputtered. "In what universe do you think—"

Sofia put an arm across my shoulders and spoke in a soothing tone. "Yes, it's a bit heavy-handed, but it's sweet. We're just worried about you, girl. You look really pale, and your eyes, well, it's not you. Go home and rest. Take care of you. Work can wait till tomorrow."

I wanted to protest, to scream that Kylan of all people had no right to decide this for me, but my outrage was dwindling along with the last of my energy. I couldn't deny that I was bone-tired. At least it was Rainn driving me home and not Kylan. I couldn't resist glaring at him for good measure before turning to leave, but he didn't seem offended. He looked somehow ... grateful? OK, so *maybe* he cared about my basic well-being at some rudimentary level.

So what?

As if that mattered.

Except it does.

Oh, it does.

On Friday morning, I was considerably more awake, having slept like a rock for the past two nights, but my embarrassment lingered as I avoided eye contact with Sofia and then Kylan when they entered the conference room. Fortunately, we were surrounded by many others, as this was the weekly agents' strategy meeting, which meant that all agents and assistants would be there as usual, along with our manager, Francis, and apparently Kylan too.

Francis, who hated when people arrived to meetings late, didn't wait for the two latecomers and simply started without them. Ambrose and Jessa were only half a minute late, but their eyes clearly conveyed their nerves and regret, which Francis ignored as they spoke of some general company business first.

My nerves were so high in my new boss's presence, which had been relatively rare so far, that I hardly paid attention to my former lover in the room. I was starting to become used to his presence at work—if you could call not having a panic attack becoming used to it.

After speaking for a long while, Francis paused and pinned Laina with a stare. "And now, Laina has an announcement to share."

"Thanks, Fran." Laina's mouth curved into a half-smile. Only she could call Francis by the nickname; apparently the two of them went way back. "I don't want to make a fuss, so I'll just say it: I'm retiring." Gasps were heard around the room, but before anyone could respond, she added, "In July. You have two months."

Once again, I forgot that Kylan was in the room.

Laina's leaving.

Laina's leaving!

I could ...

"Two months for one of you assistants to prove yourself capable of being an agent," Laina said, giving a cursory glance to each of the four of us. "If *any* of you are."

Kylan frowned and cleared his throat. "I've no doubt they are. I'd actually like to help—to support the team, which is part of the reason I've joined you for the weekly meeting today."

Francis's lips curled in distaste. Although they were often distant both literally and figuratively in my day-to-day work, it wasn't the first time I'd found myself thinking that my boss was one of the few people who didn't like Kylan. Despite being one of the "bad guys" acquiring our precious agency, he was almost universally liked. Either that or people were very good at pretending. He knew how to turn on the charm though.

I know that better than anyone.

Clearly Francis was immune though. "Yes, thank you, Kylan. Now I'm going to assume all of you assistants are eager to move into an agent role. Our optimistic new leader here has convinced me not to open the position externally, at least not yet, and to give you four the chance to fight for the position first. You have two months. In that time, you will need to persuade us you can do this job and do it well. Our agents are top notch here, and they don't just learn on the job. You need to be top notch on Day 1. Spend your time in the next two months well. If you're not already co-agenting some projects, you'll be at a serious disadvantage." At this news, my heart sank. Of course I hadn't started doing that yet, as I was still so new. Two of the other assistants smirked, while the other newer one looked about as happy as I did.

"But as Francis said, you have two months," Kylan said smoothly. "You can do a lot in that time. If you work hard. Many of the agents are already great mentors to you, from what I've heard. And I'll be here to support you and the agents, as well as the leadership. I'm rooting for all of you." He flashed an encouraging smile as his gaze traveled to everyone around the large table. I thought his eyes paused just slightly when landing on me, though I might have imagined it.

After Francis concluded the meeting indicating they would be sending the job posting and interview process details via email shortly, I rushed back to my desk, eager to read all the information. This was my chance! The chance every agent assistant was always waiting for. But was it too soon? Before I could sink into self-doubt, Sofia came over and pulled me into her office.

"Annie, we are getting you that job," she hissed. I had never seen a more determined look on Sofia's face, and she was one of the most driven people I'd ever met.

I smiled and looked at the open door as I sank into a chair in Sofia's office. "Should I close your door?"

Shaking her head, Sofia sat down at her desk. "No need, this will be quick. I just thought you might need to know you have my full support."

"Thank you. It means so much," I said, my voice trembling a bit. I'd known Sofia only a short time, and she was already such an amazing friend and colleague.

"Seniority isn't everything. Don't let that issue get to you, Annie. You have what it takes."

"Well, it's not so much seniority I'm worried about as lack of experience, knowledge ..." I floundered. "I—you know, the stuff I just haven't had time to acquire since I'm brand new."

"We'll get you there. I'm not worried. At all. This job is yours," Sofia said breezily.

Our heads both turned at the sound of heavy footsteps. Kylan strode into the room noisily, wanting his presence known. "Sorry, I couldn't help but overhear." He didn't look pleased.

"Really, you couldn't?" Sofia raised her eyebrows, and her lips were curved into a slight frown, unlike her usual lightly flirting expression around him.

"Well," he said, clearing his throat. "This agent opening isn't anyone's to claim. Ann—uh, Ms. York will have to work just as hard as anyone else to get this position. Probably much harder. It's rare for a brand new assistant to be promoted to agent so soon. Nearly unheard of."

The gentle ticking of the clock was suddenly the loudest sound in the room.

"But not quite unheard of, right?" Sofia asked, her tone deceptively calm as her gaze narrowed. "After all, you went from college grad to owning and acquiring agencies in, what, four years? Clearly some people can move up the ladder quite quickly."

I wanted to high-five her, especially as I noted Kylan's grimace as he shuffled his feet. Instead I inhaled slowly. "I'm aware I'll have to work harder than anyone else," I said quietly. Before he could respond, I added, "But I'm up for the challenge. I can't wait for it, actually. It's why I joined the agency."

Sofia smiled at me, and even Kylan's stoic expression started to curve into a grin until he caught himself. He covered his face with his large hand, pretending to yawn instead. "All right, good luck to you," he said gruffly. "Sofia, I'll get in touch later about the client dinner."

Once he was safely out of the room, Sofia let out a bark of laughter. "That man is wound so tightly sometimes, and then other times he just morphs into the most easygoing, charismatic guy ... so confusing. But I think I like that about him, you know?"

Fortunately she was turned toward a window away from me and didn't seem to be expecting an answer. I probably couldn't have given her one because, well, what did one say in such a situation?

"Yeah, I like that too, everything about him actually, well, more like I used to love him, but now I—"

So stupid, stop it, Annie.

"So anyway, we're going to make this work. In a few months, you are going to be the newest agent, and I'll be the brilliant agent just next door," Sofia said, spinning in her chair back toward me. "Can Sayaka handle book club for a while? The more time we can put into mentoring you, the better. Get ready to eat, breathe, and sleep agenting, Annie."

"I can ask Sai and Hakeem. She'll probably roll her eyes but say yes." I couldn't stop smiling if I wanted to, but of course I didn't want to. "Curious, what's in it for you—to put so much effort into helping me, that is—other than just being an awesome friend?"

"Hmm, good point. I'd actually lose a great assistant if you're promoted. Maybe I should rethink this ..." She grinned as I threw a stick of gum at her.

Chapter 19

"Hey, Annie."

Even now, after three weeks of being in the same office building with Kylan almost daily, I still couldn't handle it like a normal person. And if I had to see him, even from a distance conversing with someone down the hall or in an office as I passed by? My heart skipped a beat, or several. Serious efforts were needed to calm myself whenever I heard his voice, even when it wasn't directed toward me and even if I couldn't see him.

But on those rare occasions he was speaking to me, in front of me? I was a bumbling idiot. Not to mention a klutz.

And that's how, moments later, I ended up face-down in the hallway but perversely glad of it, if only so I could escape interaction.

But of course he couldn't have the decency to leave me alone in my mortification, could he? I looked up and sideways at his bulky thighs crouched down and his hand hovered above me in uncertainty. "Annie? Are you OK? Can I ... help you? I think I misheard you."

No, you didn't mishear.

I just said something completely incoherent about tea and peaches and then venetian blinds before inelegantly tripping over ... probably nothing.

Why can't he just go on his way and pretend I'm not here?

Step over me and move on?

He let out a bark of laughter. "I'm not going to step over you and move on. Geez, what do you think of me, Annie?" When I buried my face in my hands again, he chuckled again. "Never mind, don't answer that. But let me help you."

I squeezed my eyes shut, wishing he'd go away. When I heard no footsteps, I exhaled heavily and started to raise my upper body with my hands. One of his hands was braced on his thigh, and the other was outstretched toward me.

Oh, no.

Noooo, no.

The last thing, the very last *thing I need is to touch him. In any way.*

But this job mattered to me, and I couldn't completely blow off the boss. Gritting my teeth, I let him take my hand and tried to ignore the current that passed through me. As he helped me rise, he also put a hand on my waist and then my back, steadying me gently.

And ... I couldn't think.

Those hands, innocent though they were, and that heat ...

When he deemed me steady enough, he released me and stepped away as though the contact had meant nothing to him. The only emotion in his eyes was concern. "Are you all right, Annie?"

"I'm fine. I—" I said hoarsely. "I just ... I was—" I said before coughing.

He was staring into my eyes so intently that I had to look away. But I found my eyes drifting back, such was the pull of his gaze. He hadn't looked at me that closely since he'd been back, since ... since he'd gazed at me like I was the only woman in the world. But this look wasn't love. Surely, he was simply worried about me.

"OK," he said, his voice a bit gruff. "Let me take you home. You look pretty pale."

"What?" My eyes widened. "No, I'm fine. Why would you—"

"You don't seem fine, Annie," he said. Without warning, he stepped a little closer and gently placed the back of his hand on my forehead. After a moment, he removed his hand slowly, and his face relaxed a bit. "You don't seem feverish, at least. That's good. But I think—"

"Kylan," I started. His name on my tongue felt strange. When had I last spoken his name *to him*? Everything felt strange. He had just touched my face; his hands had been on my body; he was staring at me. What was I going to say?

"Yes?" His voice was quiet.

I opened my mouth to speak, and for a moment, no words came. Finally, I took a steadying breath and managed to say, "I'm OK, really. I just ... I was just flustered because you ..."

He was still, his voice still quiet. "Yes?"

Save yourself, Annie!

"Because I fell on my face. It's embarrassing, you know? And more embarrassing to admit, so thanks for making me do that."

But far less embarrassing than admitting the reason I fell—that I can't be normal around you and my feelings and thoughts make no sense when we're near each other.

Kylan stared at me before his lips twisted into a teasing smile. "You're welcome."

That smile! I can't handle it ...

Is he—is he joking around with me?

Maybe he doesn't actually hate me anymore.

But that theory died when I saw his smile morph into a frown.

"Well, I'm sorry about the peaches in the breakroom. And the other stuff you mentioned," he said, scratching his head although trying to remember all the details of the rambling I'd done before tripping in front of him. "But I just wanted to ask if you'd planned to cancel book club tonight."

I tilted my head, drawing my eyebrows together. "Why?"

"Because of the snow," he said, as though it were obvious.

"The ..." I started to say before giggling. "The snow?"

A faint smile appeared briefly before he frowned again. "Uh, the blizzard warning. You can't not know about it."

I suppressed another laugh. It wasn't even 8 o'clock yet, but the sun was already up on this beautiful spring day. "Right. I'll get right on that." Interesting that Kylan was showing a sense of humor with me—it was the first time since, well, four years ago. It was probably best to leave the conversation on this high note, so I started to walk past him to return to my desk.

But he put his hand out, and I stopped just before he could touch my arm. For self-preservation, of course.

Responding to my questioning look, he sighed. "Annie, I'm not joking. I know it's a sunny morning, but there's a blizzard tonight. You know as well as I do that such things can and do happen in Minnesota sometimes, even in May. And it's happening. I have a meteorologist friend who gives it 97% odds."

I stared at him in disbelief and crossed my arms. "Well, even if it's going to snow, I wouldn't necessarily cancel book club. We're Midwesterners—we can handle it. I bet most people would still show up."

It was his turn to cross his arms, and he took in my defiant stance. Finally, he said, "Fine. Well, we'll see what happens. I just wanted to warn you." Then, without another word, he turned and walked in the other direction.

I blew out a long breath. As uncomfortable as that had been, I was shocked to find it was also a bit exhilarating to spar with him. Could it be OK between us? Could we get to a place where interacting with each other could be only 90% painful and awkward instead of 100%? With this silly thought, I shook my head with a little smile and walked back to my desk.

Once logged on to my computer, it didn't take long to confirm Kylan's prediction on the weather websites. I swiveled in my chair in disbelief for a few moments before shaking my head briefly to clear my thoughts. It didn't matter. This was Minneapolis. A little snow was no big deal. It did make my choice of spring outfit rather undesirable—a short, high-waisted pleated dress with short sleeves and strappy sandals. In my defense, yesterday it had been seventy-nine degrees, and I'd been sweating profusely in my jeans and sweater. The city hadn't seen snow for weeks, as far as I could remember. Shrugging, I turned back to my computer screen and pulled up the latest manuscript I'd offered to read for Sofia. Although reading through the slush pile was part of an assistant's job to some degree, it wasn't a large part, since there were so many other duties. But Sofia had insisted I needed to get more active in the content of our submissions, including reading, editing, and deciding whether to represent an author. After all, I'd need to demonstrate I could do all those things to get the job—and, if Francis's warnings were to be heeded, to demonstrate I could do all those things *expertly*.

I sighed. The next few months were going to mean a lot of sleep-deprived days and nights, but it would all be worth it. It was *already* worth it. I loved every minute of this.

"This snowstorm is such a freaking nightmare! I need to get home. My sister is in freaking labor—*in my house*. I can't be stuck here. I can't!" Sofia wailed, her arms flailing before she clenched her fists in front of her face with a grimace.

I bit my lip, unsure what to say. Usually unflappable, Sofia never made a scene. Staying calm and professional was a must in this career, given how many different and sometimes difficult personalities we deal with.

Rainn stepped around the wall from Ambrose's cubicle, his usually easygoing face curved into a grim expression. "What's all this commotion?"

Sofia's jaw dropped, and she seemed to momentarily forget her dilemma. "What's all this rudeness?"

He crossed his arms over his thick chest and took his time in responding. "This is a professional office, is it not? Or did I step onto the set of a soap opera?"

They stared at each other for a moment, seething. "I can't handle Mr. Grumpy right now. I'll be in my office," Sofia snapped, turning to me briefly as she spun on her heel.

But I called out to her to wait.

Sofia turned around reluctantly, closing her eyes briefly. "What? I have a disaster to deal with, Annie."

"I know. And this may not be ideal, but ..." I glanced sideways at Rainn, who was zipping up his thick winter coat. "Rainn looks like he's about to go home. We don't live that far from your apartment. Maybe he could drop you off?"

"*No*—" said both Sofia and Rainn simultaneously, their eyes flashing in protest.

"As I said, it's not ideal, but—" I started.

I halted, sensing a warm presence by my side, his arm an inch away from mine. "It sounds ideal to me," Kylan said in his deep, commanding voice. "Sofia needs to get home, and Rainn is going home. Nice and simple."

Sofia looked at him in alarm. "But it's ... he's ... we don't get along," she said, her voice becoming quiet when she realized she had no rational reason to protest.

Rainn's lips were clamped shut, and he stared at his feet for a long moment. Finally, without looking at her, he said, "Fine, I'll take you. Let's not drag this out further. Meet me at the front door." With that parting note, he turned and walked away. I stared after him. I'd never known Rainn to act this way. Yes, there was a little resentment between them, but I'd had no idea the animosity ran this deep. And Sofia appeared as though she could murder him. She didn't look too happy with Kylan either, I noted with a twisted sense of satisfaction that I quickly stifled.

"Sofia—" Kylan started.

"I'll see you tomorrow, Kylan. I have to go gather my things to meet my *ride*." She glowered at him.

"I'm sorry, Sof, but at least now you can be with your sister," I said in what I hoped was a sympathetic tone.

Her face softened, and she nodded. "Well, I hope you both stay safe. Don't stay at work long—for real, girl, cancel the book club if you haven't already, Annie."

As she left, Kylan turned to me. "Have you?"

I shook my head, trying to ignore his nearness. "I told you, I'm not canceling. Minnesotans don't stay home every time it snows."

"You're not a true Minnesotan though," he said lightly.

I pursed my lips. He was right—I'd only moved here for college, but I fit in here better than I ever had when living in California with my mother. "Still not canceling."

My phone buzzed, and I unlocked the screen to see a text from Hakeem. Kylan's arm brushed mine as he leaned over, and I fought the urge to shudder from the delicious warmth of it.

"Oh, good, now you don't have a choice."

"What?" I mumbled, disoriented from his touch as I focused on the words on the screen. "Oh ... Bookshop is closing early. Ugh, seriously?"

Kylan smirked. "Oh, darn. Well, get your work wrapped up so you can head out before the worst of the snow comes."

"Is that an order, boss?" I asked, narrowing my eyes.

He frowned, something unreadable in his piercing grey eyes. "No. Just a friendly suggestion. I know you've been working late because you want the promotion, and I wouldn't stop you. But I may decide to close the office if it gets bad enough because, you know, safety."

With a huff, I turned on my heel to go ... somewhere. To the vending machine, maybe. Why I was angry, I didn't even know. But I wasn't about to let him, or a little snow, dictate my day. Or my evening, as it happened. I might as well work late since book club was canceled.

But snow had a way of dictating a great deal of life in Minnesota. Hours later, it was dark, and I was out of options. I hadn't even wiped the snow off my car yet when I dropped my car keys in the fluffy white stuff. Lacking winter gloves or anything sensible to keep my fingers from going completely numb, I was forced to take frequent breaks in my search for the keys to try to warm my shaking hands. But this was a losing battle. I was freezing and shaking and wet and on the verge of tears when I heard a low voice cut through the furious wind and swirling snow that extended in every direction around me.

At first I couldn't make out his words or even see him as my eyes darted around desperately, my teeth chattering and eyelashes coated with snowflakes. At least I'd found some stylish boots and a sweater in my bottom desk drawer—a forgotten stash—so my feet weren't frozen in sandals. When a thickly gloved hand landed on my shoulder, I knew the warm, wet breath so near my face could only be *his*.

"Annie, I'm going to carry you back inside."

Before I could even begin to protest, I was off my feet and nearly lost my breath. His arms cradled my slender, wet, shaking form as shock coursed through me. "K–Kylan," I mustered.

"Shhh," he said into my ear, his hot breath on my skin the best thing I'd ever felt. "You can yell at me when we're back inside."

I pressed my lips together and relaxed my head on his shoulder as we made the short but arduous trek back to the building through several feet of snow and ice.

Warm air surrounded me as he carried me under the eave and through the open door and then quickly deposited me on a nearby chair in the lobby. "Stay here," he ordered, an edge in his tone.

Too weak to argue, I simply nodded, not that he noticed, as he was already jogging away toward the offices. He came back quickly with a blanket and a duffel bag. I eyed the blanket as a starving person eyes a meal, and he arranged it around me, his eyes hard as he watched me shaking.

Was he angry?

I began to form more coherent thoughts as the warmth began to slowly return to my body.

Great, his anger is just what I need right now.

I closed my eyes and buried my head under the blanket.

"Don't go to sleep," he warned. "We're not staying here."

Is he going to kick me out of the office, knowing I can't very well drive home?

What the heck is the point of bringing me in from the cold only to toss me back out there?

My fury began to rise as my body temperature did. "I don't—see how—my car—lost my keys," I managed, teeth still chattering.

When he didn't reply or even acknowledge me, I added, "There's a sofa in—office library—"

"We're not staying here," he repeated, sounding annoyed as he strode toward the window, which was nearly impossible to see out of.

"Are you ..." I hesitated. "Are you going to, uh—take me home?"

He turned back, a blank look on his face. "Yes. We'll have to go back out there, of course. Are you ready, or do you need to warm up some more first?"

I wanted to protest that I couldn't walk in these flimsy boots, that we'd never get out of the parking lot, that it was far easier to just stay here. But his jaw was set with determination and probably annoyance, so I decided not to bother arguing with him. I simply nodded and said, "I'm fine. Ready."

He looked at his phone for a few minutes and then stuffed it in his pocket. As he inhaled and exhaled slowly, his eyes were on the ceiling before he strode over to me. "Let's go."

I stood as quickly as I could, since his face bore a look of impatience. But before I could take a step, I was again swept into his arms as though I weighed nothing. "What—Kylan, what are you doing? I can *walk*!" I sputtered as I grasped his shoulder tightly.

He glanced at me with raised eyebrows and then fixed his eyes on the door. Before I could blink, we were back outside, and I braced for the shock of the swirling cold nightmare around us. His arms tightened around me, and he said something I couldn't understand as he began trudging through the snow, which was higher than his knees in some areas.

After a few minutes that felt like an eternity, I tried to get his attention. "Hey." When shouting his name didn't seem to work either, I tried punching his shoulder.

Finally his eyes, shaded by brows and lashes covered with snowflakes, met mine. "Yes?" he asked with an edge in his voice.

It was probably the worst thing to ask any man, but this was kind of a dangerous situation, both physically and emotionally, for us both. "Are we lost?" I dared to ask.

He couldn't have parked *that* far from the door to the office, and we were walking somewhat slowly by necessity, but not *that* slowly. I'd given up trying to see anything in the whiteout around us, but I knew we'd taken quite a few turns.

"No."

"If we can't find your car, we could just go back inside. It's not ideal, but—"

"I said, no." He turned his face away from me once again.

My jaw hung open until I realized I'd be swallowing a lot of snow that way.

Why is he dragging me along with him if he's so annoyed with my presence?

So infuriating!

Not a minute later, he'd taken more steps to who knows where, and we were suddenly under a kind of shelter. I scanned the area, startled. We appeared to be at the entrance of some kind of business or residence. Maybe a hotel?

I gasped. "What the—Kylan, you said you were taking me home," I said as I slid out of his arms to the wet ground just outside the door to the building.

"I did."

"This isn't—"

"I couldn't very well drive in these conditions, Annie."

"Well, why didn't you just say that? You said—"

"I said I was taking you home," he said.

He smiled, catching me off guard. Way off guard.

His smile, it's—I can't even—

"Which I did," he added.

My eyes skipped around wildly as I tried to understand what was going on and tried to avoid that smile, the one that told me to forget everything else and just ... melt. Run to him and melt.

He waved his hand in the direction of the doors. "This is home, Annie. My home. For now, anyway. I'm staying here with my sister while I'm in town. It's just a couple blocks from the office, and I didn't really see any other viable options to get us somewhere safe tonight."

Us? I wanted to ask, but didn't. Instead, I followed him shakily through the double doors into what I hazily began to suspect were some fairly high-end apartments, if the uniformed security guard and well-dressed reception staff were any indication. I had a million questions, but they all died on my lips as I looked around, astounded by the opulence in everything from the massive chandelier to the soft leather seats in front of a stately fireplace. This was where he *lived*? Or his sister, rather. I knew they'd both grown up without wealth. Perhaps his sister had married rich, or they'd come into some kind of inheritance.

I shook my head. It didn't matter. I'd grown up with wealth, and I knew the kind of people who had it. Most of them I wanted nothing to do with, but I tried not to judge everyone based on my mother's lifestyle and those in her orbit.

As the elevator doors closed on us, I dared to glance up at Kylan. His piercing eyes were sweeping over my shivering form, and he cursed before tearing the blanket away from me. "This is soaked. It's only making you colder!" he barked.

"That's ... I guess that's true," I said, my teeth still chattering. After a long beat of silence where he stared at the doors until they opened and then strode out of the elevator like the devil was after him, I spoke up. "Hey." When he didn't seem to hear, I found the energy to speak a bit louder. "*Hey. Kylan.*"

He halted and waited for me to catch up, saying nothing and looking in my direction but not *at* me.

"You could have just *suggested* I take off the cold blanket. *Told* me where we were going. *Asked* if you could haul me like a sack of potatoes." My anger rising, I placed my shaking hands on my hips. "Show some d–damn respect."

"Well, when you show up wearing *that* in a snowstorm and then expect to—"

"Since when is it your business what I wear and, for that matter, what I do?" I demanded, my voice becoming louder. "If I want to die in the snow, it's my prerogative, dammit."

He eyed me and said coldly, "You're right. Fine." He spun around and walked quickly, stopping at a door farther down the hall.

I attempted to calm my breathing as he unlocked a door and disappeared through it. "Wait!" I shouted, but it was futile, as he'd already closed the door. I walked slowly toward the door, dread but also resignation growing with every step. What had I been thinking?

Sure, he'd been a total jerk, but I do need his help.

Crap.

Just as I was about to knock on the door, I noticed it wasn't fully closed and took a steadying breath of the blissfully warm air around me before slowly pushing the door open.

He was sitting on a chair near the door, removing his wet winter gear, and he didn't look up.

"Kylan," I started, trying to stop shaking, only partly from the cold at this point. "Thanks for helping me. I, uh, I know you meant well."

His response was something like a grunt, and he glanced up only briefly before gathering up his wet things.

I swallowed with some effort. He wasn't going to make this easy. "I have no way to get home, and I ... well, I wouldn't ask a friend to pick me up in this weather." My brow furrowed. "I just realized I don't even have my phone. I must have left it in my car just before dropping my keys into the snowy abyss."

He slowly rose from his seat and stared at me. He started to turn, and I realized he was going to make me ask.

"Kylan, wait—" I called out. "Can I ... stay here for a bit? Until it's safe to go? Not too long." I tried to remember what the weather forecast had said. Snow until 3:00 am, I thought, but I couldn't trust my memory now.

He halted but didn't turn around fully. "It's fine. Kelly's out of town. I'm going to bring the wet things to the laundry," he said in a tone with forced civility. As I wondered if that was an invitation to follow, he said, "Don't follow me."

I stared after his retreating form as he disappeared down the hallway.

His sister's name is Zophie, so who the heck is Kelly?

And why can't I bring my wet stuff to the laundry too, if I'm to stay here?

I folded my arms over my drenched chest and sighed deeply. It was perhaps fortunate that I was fuming; the flames of indignation were the only thing keeping me warm.

Minutes later, Kylan finally reemerged, only to disappear into a different room from the hallway. I scoffed and considered shouting his name. What did he expect me to do?

Before I could vocalize my discontent, he strode out of the second room armed with a fluffy pink robe and oversized thick blue slippers. "Here, put these on," he said as he placed the slippers on the floor in front of me.

I raised my eyebrows as our eyes met.

He sighed in frustration. "Please put on the slippers," he said slowly, as though talking to a wayward child. "Then, I'll show you to the bathroom, where we'll draw a warm bath." When my eyes widened, he added quickly, "For you. A bath for you. We need to get you warm as soon as we can. I worry about hypothermia. I'm surprised you don't have frostbite."

"Well, how would you know?" I asked, biting my lip. "You haven't asked."

He narrowed his eyes. "Do you?"

I shook my head. "I am so cold though. I feel like … like I'll never be warm again. Like the cold has seeped into my bones, my very soul."

Seeing his alarmed expression, I tried to laugh. "I mean, I'm half-kidding. Not quite that bad, but I don't think I've ever been this cold before. I didn't grow up making snow angels as a kid, after all."

He nodded, a serious expression on his face, and gestured toward my feet. "Do you need help removing your boots and putting the slippers on?"

The last thing I wanted was for him to touch my feet, or touch me *anywhere* again, and he surely wanted to avoid further contact as well. I shook my head as I bent down and peeled the boots—which were really more style than substance—off my numb feet.

After I followed him to the bathroom, he sat on the edge of the large tub and turned on the faucet, testing the water temperature until it was slightly steaming. I stood there, still shaking … it must be from the chill. Though it was quite warm in here. I bit my lip hard, trying to see if it was still numb. "Can you, um, leave?"

He rose to his feet and eyed me briefly. "Yes. Obviously." Before he crossed the threshold though, he pointed toward the linen closet. "Towels are in there."

"Thanks," I said, thinking that was unnecessary. Towels were usually in linen closets.

He said nothing as his eyes focused on the floor. Finally, he cleared his throat. "Do you need any assistance?"

"No," I said quickly.

Just as rapidly, he said, "Right." He dashed out of the room before closing the door firmly.

I blew out a long breath before walking over to the tub. I was still shaking as I pried off my thin, soaked dress and underthings, leaving them in a heap on the floor. A quick glance in the mirror told me I looked like the dead. My usually shiny red hair was a cold, wet rat's nest, and my skin was damp and mostly pale, with some blotchy red areas. I squeezed my eyes shut to clear out the hideous image and stepped into the steaming tub.

These are the fires of hell. I winced as I sank into the hot water. The last thought I remembered being conscious of before my body just took over, succumbing to the healing and relaxation, was *Paradise.*

Some time later, in a vague region between wakeful bliss and gentle dozing, I heard tapping. My senses slowly reawakening, I realized it was the sound of knocking and was growing louder and faster. As I started to gather the strength to sit up from my reclining position, the door burst open, and my eyes met Kylan's, which were frantic.

I gasped softly, and he averted his eyes. "You weren't answering, and it had been a long time. I was worr—uh—" He stopped to clear his throat. "I wanted to see if you were still alive."

I laughed, because ... why not? This night could not get any stranger or more uncomfortable, could it? "Quite alive."

"Ah, that—" he started, and his eyes met mine for a half a second before he turned away. "I'm going to go," he said, flattening his lips as he turned to leave.

I watched the infuriating man walk out the door again. Sighing, I grabbed the soap nearby and finished washing up before rising to towel off. A thick robe was on a wooden stool nearby, complete with matching pink fuzzy socks and slippers. Realizing I'd be spending time in Kylan's presence without underwear or a bra, I shivered, whether from the cold or not, I wasn't sure. I didn't even know what time it was. Hopefully I could just rest on a couch for a couple hours until my clothes dried and the weather settled down.

I found a hairbrush and even some makeup. The hairbrush appeared unused, and I was desperate, so I used it. Still, I wasn't about to try another woman's makeup, and it would look odd if I wore makeup now anyway, wouldn't it? I sighed, examining my reflection, still pale but a bit less so.

After leaving the bathroom, I clutched the robe tightly to my chest, despite tying it in a double knot at my waist, and wandered slowly to an open area with dim lighting. It appeared to be the living room, where Kylan was staring into the fireplace.

"Hi," I said. What else could I say?

He turned his head slowly and waved me over. "How are you?" he asked with a guarded expression. His eyes swept over my face and any bit of exposed skin. Appearing satisfied that I wasn't at death's door, he sat back. "You look a bit better."

"Uh, thanks?" I said with a wry smile. "The bath was heavenly. I still feel like I got run over by a truck made of ice, but I think a little rest will help. Do you mind if I, um—"

"Rest and warmth will indeed do wonders," Kylan agreed. "But I'd like to see you get some fluids, food, check your temperature. Can you stay awake for a bit?"

I frowned. "I don't know if all that's necessary."

"I just want to make sure you're OK. Humor me," he said with pleading eyes.

My own eyes softened. He did look genuinely worried, and I was ready to concede for the moment.

Before I could speak though, he added dryly, "Can't have an employee dying at my house now, can I?"

Ouch.

He seemed to realize immediately it was the wrong thing to say, observing my lips pressed together in a thin line and my eyes downcast. "I was joking," he said, sounding contrite. "I'm ... uh, not great at the caregiver thing. Sorry. I'll be right back with some food and drink. You like hot chocolate, right?"

I nodded. He remembered that? But then I shook my head.

Nearly everyone likes hot chocolate, dummy. It doesn't mean he remembers anything.

While I waited, I stretched my legs out and sank beneath a soft blanket draped over the arm of the sofa. My gaze swept the large room, with its high ceilings, enormous fireplace, soft, recessed lighting, variety of plants, and minimalist but expensive-looking earth-toned decor. This place must cost a fortune. My eyes landed on the coffee table near the couch. Beneath the table was a bookshelf, and I leaned forward to glance at the titles. Mostly naval reference books ... one military romance book I'd seen at the bookstore recently in the new release section.

I searched my brain to put the pieces together. Zophie, Kylan's sister, had rarely been around when I'd dated him. Had she been in the military? I scratched my head, frowning at my inability to remember. My memory was usually pretty good, but it had been a long day, to say the least.

A more recent memory stirred then. He had mentioned Kelly earlier. Did he have a girlfriend no one knew about? I tried to ignore the sharp pain in my chest at the thought.

My body's been through a lot tonight, almost freezing to death—that's all it is, surely—I'm not jealous or anything stupid like that.

I was certain Kylan and Sofia were at the very least flirting and possibly dating, and he didn't seem like the cheating type. Of course, the thought of him with Sofia didn't make me feel any better. By the time I heard footsteps, a rather stormy expression had taken over my face.

"Hey," he said, "I brought a few different things, not sure what you'd want. Oh, uh ... are you all right?" he asked, noticing my scowl.

I forced a polite smile. "I'm fine. And thank you, you didn't have to do that." Obviously, letting me into his home was the very last thing he wanted. And now, serving me food? He had to be hating every moment of this. Understandably.

"Yeah, well," he said, his voice sounding gruff as he set out the tray of food options and hot chocolate on the coffee table. "I have some lasagna, rice pilaf, banana, and ... well, you can see everything. Hopefully you can find something here that looks edible. You need to regain some strength."

My breath caught when he said lasagna, and my face softened as memories flooded my vision. Memories of the two of us, eating at our favorite little Italian place, right off campus, nearly every weekend. It was cheap but good. He wasn't really adventurous with food back then, but lasagna was something we could always agree on. It became our go-to order for dates or even for ordering in.

Surely he remembered.

I dared to raise my eyes to his.

Or maybe not.

He looked as disgruntled as he always did in my presence.

"Eat," he said sharply as he perched on the other end of the sofa.

I drew in a breath and sat up straighter. "All right, geez."

He said nothing while pushing the tray closer to me. But I was incredibly thirsty and took a sip of the hot chocolate first.

A sound escaped my throat, and it was probably a bit inappropriate in front of my boss, but I didn't care. The drink was absolutely delicious.

The perfect blend of hot chocolate, marshmallows, and caramel—wait a minute.

He has to remember.

Everyone likes hot chocolate, but not everyone puts caramel in it.

He remembers how I like my hot chocolate!

I took another sip, closing my eyes to savor it before opening them and daring to meet his eyes.

He was staring. But likely unaware he was doing so. I lowered my eyes and set the cup down. "This all looks delicious ... lasagna, always a favorite," I said casually, my glance sliding back up to his.

He sat further back against the cushions, nodding slightly while watching me.

After taking a few bites of everything, I sighed. I hadn't realized how hungry I was. When I set down my utensils, he barked, "Keep eating."

My eyes flashed as I turned to him with rising ire. "Excuse me? I'll stop eating when *I want* to stop."

He opened and closed his mouth and then crossed his arms over his chest. Focusing on my anger was hard though because ... *those arms*. He'd always had a nice form, but had he been so muscular back in college? I didn't think so—I'd remember if he looked like *this*. He hadn't been a gym type. But the new Kylan had to be a gym type. His biceps were fairly bursting to escape the sleeves. I frowned, realizing the totally pointless direction of my thoughts and feeling my cheeks heat up.

"Well, at least you're getting some color back. You were so pale and clammy before," he observed quietly. "I ... sorry if I've been a little overbearing. I've just been worried. You are ... you were not in a good way."

My lips curved into a small smile in surprise. "Thank you for that. Overbearing is putting it mildly." When his brows furrowed, I added, "I'm so glad you were there to help though. I don't know what I would've done if ... well, I don't want to think about it." I sipped more hot chocolate, which was more like warm chocolate by this point but still delicious. "I just realized drinking hot chocolate might not be the best idea if you're about to take my temperature. Unless you have a forehead or ear thermometer?"

"It's no matter. We won't be taking your temperature for a while yet anyway. Kelly told me it's best to wait at least a half hour after bathing, ideally longer, to take someone's temperature."

"Oh, uh, OK," I said, my brain scrambling to keep up.

So we have to sit here longer and make awkward small talk before I can take a nap. Great.

And who is this Kelly?

The last thing I want to do is ask, but it would be weird if I didn't, right?

"Kelly? Is she your, uh ..."

His mouth twitched. "I'm just now realizing you probably know her as Zophie Croft, right? My sister changed her name a couple years back after dealing with a stalker situation. It was a whole thing, a long story. But anyway, she's Kelly now. She's in DC at the moment presenting at a naval engineering conference."

My shoulders relaxed as I let out a breath. "Oh, I see. So she's a bigshot engineer now, huh?"

Kylan laughed, rich and deep. He'd so rarely laughed recently that the sound—and the smile that came with it—caught me off guard, and I had to avert my eyes. "Maybe someday, but no. She's still slogging through her PhD work now."

I gasped. "Wait, what?" I looked around the grand, spacious apartment or condo or whatever this type of home was. "How does a PhD student afford this house?"

"You don't have to remind me I wasn't born into money." Kylan looked at his lap for a moment, as though uncomfortable or unsure what else to say. Finally he simply said, "She deserves the best."

And then it dawned on me. This spacious, sophisticated home—and everything in it—was all from him. He'd made sure his sister lived in luxury. He must be even richer than I realized. "Ah. She's lucky to have such a generous brother."

He waved his hand dismissively. "I'm the lucky one. She's amazing."

I looked away.

"Something wrong?" he asked.

Shaking my head, I studied my hands and then squeezed my eyes shut.

"Annie?"

Breathing out shakily, I turned toward him partially. "Nothing, really. I'm really happy you guys have each other. Sometimes I–I wish I had a close family member like that, that's all. My ... my mother is still a horrible person." I didn't dare make eye contact with him. I knew how he felt about my mother—he blamed her, along with Viviana, for persuading me to break things off all those years ago.

After a long silence, he said, "People like her rarely change."

"I know," I said quietly.

Finishing the decadent drink, I set the cup down and leaned back against the sofa, tucking my feet under the blanket. I needed to lighten the mood, so I said the first thing that came to mind—which may or may not have been the best idea. "So, look at you."

His eyebrows rose slightly as he gazed at me. "Look at me?"

"Kylan Quinn has made a name for himself," I said with a small smile. "How does that feel?"

He gazed at me uncertainly, but seeing that my smile was genuine, he started to grin. "Not going to lie, it was pretty intoxicating at first. I mean, who was I? Nobody, right? It was all parties and money and … a little fame … well, you know, like a dream for a humble kid from Minnesota, I guess. I suppose the novelty wore off after a while. I'm leading a quieter life now, though in this line of work networking and image do matter, of course, so I can't just hibernate. I probably would if I could though," he said with a chuckle. "Sorry, rambling."

"Not at all." I bit my lip. Had he been drinking? That was by far the most words he'd spoken around me since he'd returned. "I'm glad it's been such a fun experience. May I ask how you did it? I mean, such success in just a few years … I'm sure people ask you that all the time, right?"

His face became serious again, and he nodded. "Pretty much constantly." For a long moment, he said nothing. Maybe he wouldn't tell me anything. That was fair. But finally, he spoke, his mind seeming far away. "As is often the case, it was a combination of luck and hard work. Very hard work. Like nonstop work every day until my eyeballs wouldn't work anymore. I just wouldn't stop. I was … determined, I suppose."

"So did you start out in a position like mine or …" I trailed off, trying to encourage him to say more.

He chuckled. "Lower. I was an intern, not even a paid one at first. It was New York City … I knew it wouldn't be easy. I was willing to start at the bottom. I worked graveyard shifts at a hotel, plus a million hours a week at the agency trying to prove myself. Well, it worked. But I had some help," he said, a touch of bitterness in his voice.

"Somehow you don't sound happy about the help," I noted hesitantly.

"No, I was grateful … I am. But things got complicated. It's a long story. Basically, I became friends with the owner's son shortly after I started working at the agency. One day I overheard Josh saying he needed more D&D players, so I volunteered. You might remember I … never mind," he said, lowering his eyes for a moment before inhaling and exhaling slowly. "So I was in the right place at the right time. The friendship opened a lot of doors, and I moved up through the ranks quickly. Before I knew it, I was part of management thanks to, well, luck and connections. And I did work hard too. I basically did nothing but work. I became really close with the family, not just Josh but also his dad and his sister Jem."

Kylan swung his gaze from the ceiling to me and took a deep breath. "And you're wondering, 'OK, but how did you get from being a manager in the agency to *owning* a bunch of agencies,' right? Well, Josh's dad had a major stroke and passed away suddenly. He ... he actually left the agency to the three of us, along with his investments. Josh, Jem, and me."

My mouth formed an *O*, but I said nothing.

"Yeah. We were all sort of numb with grief and shock, but Josh was livid. Resentful. He ... he changed. I didn't know him anymore. So, I ended up buying them both out. I didn't want to be tied to someone who was just so hostile, and Jem ... well, she had her own issues. We were never going to be able to work together. I could've sold them my part, but their hearts weren't really in the business anymore. They couldn't even deny it. So I bought out their dad's business, and then I started buying up other agencies."

My eyes were wide. "Wow, for some reason, the way you tell the story, acquisitions actually sound fun or exciting."

"It was—well, it *is*—kind of intoxicating." He exhaled softly and then paused. "So, now you know."

Our eyes locked for a long moment. "It's incredible, Kylan. Yes, it sounds like there was some luck, and some tragedy, but you expanded their business into the amazingly successful operation that it is today. From nothing. Four years ago you were just a new college grad. A lowly intern. Less than I am today. And now this. It's just ... mind boggling. Everyone who knows you has to be in awe."

"Perhaps not everyone," he said softly. His expression was unreadable, but his eyes lingered on mine for a long moment. "But I have my share of fans. Sometimes I worry that I'll peak too early though. I mean, I'm not even 30 yet." He shook his head. "What a problem to complain about, huh? Sorry."

"No, it's OK. My friend Viv said something similar about our writer friend Jack, who's kind of facing that. He's in his early 30s, but he's achieved so much success as a writer already that we worry he's peaked too soon. He seems pretty content in life—he's just that kind of person—but who knows if it will last. So much life ahead—" My eyes had been wandering but happened to land back on his face. His mouth was curved into a severe frown, while his arms were crossed in a defensive pose. "Oh, did I say something wrong? I'm sorry if—"

"No. Nothing," he said abruptly, looking away. He quickly rose to his feet. "Actually, it's time to take your temperature. Let me get the thermometer, one moment." He practically raced out of the room.

What on earth did I say or do?

I tried to think frantically, replaying the scene in my head.

I was talking about peaking in careers, and I mentioned—oh.

Oh.

Viviana.

He remembers her.

Of course he does, and now he remembers why he hates me.

Why, oh why, did I have to bring her up? We were getting along, for once.

And it was…

I didn't want to admit it.

It was nice.

Better than nice.

Before I could ruminate any longer, he was back with two thermometers. "First, we'll do the forehead thermometer and then the oral one, just to compare," he said, his tone all business.

But as he came close, close enough to place the thermometer in front of my forehead, his eyes locked on mine with something unspoken. Not just concern. Something heavier. Something that twisted in my chest.

I opened my mouth to say something—anything—but he shook his head gently.

"Don't talk," he said. "Just let me do this."

I nodded, and as I opened my mouth, his hand hovered in front of me, steady and careful. But it was his eyes that undid me—drawn to my lips, lingering just a second too long.

He's watching to make sure he gets the placement right. That's all.

Still, my pulse was racing, my breath uneven.

The way he looked at me—like he remembered every-thing—made me wonder if he was thinking the same thing I was: how close we were. How close his mouth was to mine.

The thermometer beeped softly between us, but the silence felt louder.

Like the space where a kiss almost happens—and doesn't.

He inched back slowly as he removed the thermometer and squinted at the tiny screen. "Both above 98 degrees. You're perfect. But ... are you all right?" He sat down next to me, closer this time, with genuine concern on his face as his gaze swept over my heated cheeks. "You look ... I don't know. Are you feeling symptoms of—"

Mortified, I interrupted him. "I'm fine. I think ... I'm, uh, prob-ably just tired. It's been a long day." I wasn't lying. It *had* been a long day, and I was beyond exhausted. It was a convenient excuse for blushing and nearly panting in front of him. "Can I snooze on your couch? Just for a couple hours probably, until the storm lets up. I'm sure a little nap will be enough."

"Don't be an idiot, Annie," he snapped. "You can stay the night. The roads won't magically be safe and clear within a couple hours. It would be dangerous to venture out again. And even if they were, you'll need more than a couple hours of rest before you can brave that winter mess out there."

"But I should—"

"You can stay in my sister's room. She wouldn't mind at all. There's a guest room, but it might be a bit dusty. She doesn't en-tertain out-of-town guests often, other than me."

"Oh no, I couldn't. I'll just doze here on the couch."

He gave me an exasperated look. "You're still just as stubborn as ever, I see."

I stared at him, unmoved.

"Fine," he barked, crossing his arms over his chest. "Let me get you some more comfortable blankets and pillows though."

"Wait!" I extended an arm to stop him. My hand landed briefly on his forearm before I jerked it away, realizing I probably couldn't handle physical contact like a mature ex-girlfriend. "I was wondering if I could use your phone or computer. It's just—my roommates are probably wondering if I'm dead in a ditch somewhere."

"They're not," Kylan said, making eye contact only briefly. "I called Rainn earlier, when you were bathing, and I let him know the situation."

"Oh," I said, surprised he'd thought of that. "Thank you, that was so thoughtful of you."

After a pause, he muttered, "Well, I guess I have my moments."

As he rose from the sofa and left to retrieve the promised bedding, I was left alone with my thoughts.

The very last thing I needed at that moment.

Because they were all swirling around in my head, hazy because of my exhaustion but still cognizant enough to know what they all meant.

Kylan Quinn. He had not lost his power over me.

Maybe it was more potent than ever.

Chapter 20

I turned toward Sofia slowly, my eyes reluctantly leaving Kylan's person, seated across from me in the conference room. He was oblivious, thank goodness, as his eyes tracked back and forth across several papers in front of him. I'd seen plenty of him since the fateful night of the blizzard, and I'd managed to play it cool for the most part. We'd been friendly or, at a minimum, professional. Our relations seemed to thaw a bit as he involved himself with contract negotiations, including some of Sofia's. "Sorry, what, Sofia?"

"Oh, nothing important," she said with a sigh. "I was just complaining about how I wanted to go to that new restaurant opening tonight, the one we were talking about last week. First world problems, am I right?"

I chuckled and nodded. Kylan looked up, his eyes briefly landing on me before swinging to Sofia. "Why can't you go?"

"Because it's tonight," Sofia said.

Kylan tilted his head. "So let's go tonight."

Sofia pursed her lips. "You know we can't. The dinner with Johnson is tonight. He's pretty high up there on the difficult client scale. The last thing I'd want to do is change the time or date on him."

Kylan gave me a brief but oddly intense look. "Annie can go instead."

Sofia gasped. "But I ... can't just send my assistant," she sputtered. "As fantastic as she is, you know. Johnson isn't really flexible like that."

He leaned back in his chair. "Tell him Annie's his agent now. Better yet, I'll handle it." When we both stared at him with wide eyes, he added, "It'll be fine."

"Wait," I said, my breath halting. "Do you mean—you want me—I'm to be his agent from now on?"

"That is what I said, yes," he said with a slightly impatient edge. "Isn't that part of the co-agenting and mentoring process? I thought you wanted to take on your own."

"I mean, yes, but Sofia may not—"

"I love it," Sofia pronounced. "This is perfect. I feel bad because he's not the easiest one to work with, but I've been wanting to give you more responsibility anyway. You can do this, girl. I got your back too."

Kylan nodded before returning his attention to the documents in front of him, while Sofia started humming, suddenly in a good mood.

I sat there, stunned.

This was great news—I was one significant step closer toward becoming an agent—*an agent*!

But when I replayed the scene later that evening at the barre, Rafael pinpointed what was really on my mind.

"That's great, Annie ... but it's like, how can you be happy about that, when your colleague and work bestie seems to be dating your ex, who you obviously still have feelings for?"

"What?" I turned toward him, nearly slipping as we dipped into grand plies from second. "*Not* obvious. I'm not ..." When we started the next sequence, I restarted, "I mean, it would be hard for anyone to watch. You just don't date your ex's friends. Or your friend's exes. But I haven't really known Sofia long enough to hold her to that."

"But you have known *him* long enough," Rafael said with a side eye. He frowned. "Are you sure there's something going on though? Maybe they're just friends. Even if there's a flirtatious vibe, it doesn't mean anything is happening. Or will happen."

"You haven't seen them together," I grumbled, turning to face the barre for calf exercises.

"Fair," Rafael said, biting his lip. "Anyway, they sound like a nightmare together. You do have my sympathy, girl. But I feel like he's trying to give you opportunities, Annie. He may be inadvertently helping you out. My girl's going to be an agent! You know I've already planned to take you on a celebratory shopping spree after you get the promotion. Among other things."

I smiled wryly. "I wish I could be so confident. I hope you're right."

And I hope he's right about Kylan and Sofia maybe not actually being a thing.

"Speaking of work stuff, I forgot to tell you: I need someone to cover my class next Saturday. I'm hosting the first book signing at Bookshop, with one of Sofia's newest authors actually. Can you cover it?"

Rafael grinned. "I'll do you one better. I'll get someone else to cover the class, and then I'll come to the bookstore to support you in case you're a basket case."

I breathed a sigh of relief. "You always know just what I need."

"I'm glad you're finally acknowledging that," Rafael said, his lips twisting into a sly grin. "I also think what you need is to try some wedding cake flavors with me tomorrow during your lunch break."

"Oh, I think Rainn would be so much better for that, Raf. He can eat a house—"

"But his taste isn't as discerning," he pouted. "I need *you*, Annie. Just, uh, don't plan any important meetings in the afternoon, just in case we are unable to recover from the cake coma." Rafael grinned at me, and I giggled, almost toppling over from my passé position.

On the Saturday morning of the book signing event, I stood with hands on my hips in front of the couch, where Rafael was sprawled out with a thick blanket, several pillows and heating pads, and numerous OTC meds and medicinal teas on the end table. "Rafael, you can't be serious. No one—"

"Shhh," he whispered, wincing as he removed the eye mask to look at me through squinty, bloodshot eyes. "I have a splitting headache."

I sighed, lowering my voice. "No one gets this sick from eating a little cake. I think ... you went out drinking, didn't you?"

"A little cake, Annie? A little?" he asked, his eyebrows rising.

"OK, it was a lot," I conceded. "But still—"

"I don't do overindulgences well. You know this about me."

I was silent for a long moment. Should I feel sorry for him? I did know that overindulgence tended to be harder for him than the average person ... but he also tended to exaggerate. A lot.

"*Annie*!" His eyes flew open again. "I just remembered the book event. Crap, I'm sorry. I didn't think."

I sighed, sitting next to him. "It's OK. It's not like I've been available a ton to help you with the wedding stuff either. Who am I to be asking you for favors?"

"Oh, it's not like that, Annie," Rafael said, his tone regretful. "I *wanted* to come, if only to observe the two idiots you work with who are supposedly hooking up. And maybe threaten him or something."

"And to support me professionally?"

"And that."

I grinned. "It's OK. I'll survive. I'll just—"

"Wait, what about Rainn?" Rafael interrupted as our roommate sauntered into the room. "Did you ask him to come?"

"I didn't, actually," I said thoughtfully. "It's not the worst idea—"

"Come to what?" Rainn said, his usual easygoing smile in place.

"My big Bookshop event today. The book signing." Rainn's smile faded, which was peculiar, but I continued, "Rafael was going to come for moral support, but, well, look at him. He's got a cake hangover."

"A cake-over," Rafael said.

"Would you come, Rainn?" I asked with pleading eyes. "I don't know why I didn't think to ask you before."

His jaw seemed tight, and his eyes avoided mine. Finally, he said, "I don't know."

"Oh. Uh, do you ... have other plans?"

He crossed his arms, pointing to his gym bag. "Gym."

Rafael rolled his eyes. "Please. You'd rather go to the gym than help out our girl?"

I didn't miss the scowl that Rainn shot in Rafael's direction. "It's not that. It's ... there's ..." he trailed off. After closing his eyes for a moment, he exhaled loudly and looked back at me. "Fine."

With this great start to the day, Rainn and I headed to Bookshop for our very first public event, a book signing. The store had held signings occasionally in the past, but it had been a long while, and the events had usually been thrown together somewhat haphazardly with little effort.

I regretted putting less time and effort into this internship than I'd originally hoped, but it couldn't be helped—the agent promotion was the most important for my future. I probably needed to scale back even more or give up the Bookshop gig, but ... I wasn't confronting that decision yet. I liked being busy, but I was nearly running on empty between the three jobs. At least I hadn't fallen asleep in anyone's back seat lately.

Hakeem had agreed to kick off the event. He introduced himself and me to the decent group of people gathered and then spoke briefly about some promotions and other store information. When he gave the floor to me, I gave a brief background on Sara Erickson, a native Minnesotan author who had just published her ninth historical fiction novel. After the introduction, I sat at the signing table with Hakeem and Sofia while Sara performed a brief reading from her latest novel.

My eyes wandered the room and landed on Kylan, as they often did, against my will. He was sitting in the back behind the rows of chairs we'd set up, next to Rainn. My heartbeat quickened. What were they talking about?

Calm down.

They're probably not talking at all—they're listening to the author. If they do talk, it wouldn't be about you.

Still, my eyes were frequently drawn to them, and Sofia had to repeat my name several times to get my attention after the reading when the signing had actually began.

"Oh, sorry, Sofia, what was that?" I asked.

"I'm just giving you props, girl! This event, you did all this? On top of the agency stuff? Mind-boggling. This will be a big boost to Sara's local sales, which she said was really key for her earlier books when she worked with Laina." Apparently Laina was her original agent, but she was reportedly much happier with Sofia. I'd smiled upon hearing that. Laina was smart, successful, capable, tough ... but abrasive. Laina and I still hadn't warmed to each other. Fortunately, I didn't have to work with her that much longer, so I was able to smile and nod through all the busywork the senior agent dumped on me.

"I'm not sure if it's the publicity or the author herself, but the turnout is far higher than I allowed myself to imagine," I said, smiling with satisfaction. Again my eyes drifted over to Kylan and my roommate, and this time, they *were* talking. Possibly enjoying a joke. Both in a good mood? Interesting. Kylan was rarely in a good mood in my vicinity, and Rainn had been grumpy all day for some inexplicable reason.

Once the event concluded and the author had been sent home happy, I strolled over to the manager, who was tidying up some handouts on a display table. "Hakeem, hey, don't worry about cleanup! My friends and I from the agency can take care of it all."

Hakeem glanced up, scrunching up his brows. "Not on my watch. The bookstore staff can clean up. *You* can go home."

My smile faded. "Oh. Um. Well, thank you ... for the opportunity today."

His sharp eyes landed on me again. "Thank me? All I did was speak to a crowd for like 30 seconds. You did all of this."

"Oh, uh ..." I trailed off, confused. Was he thanking me? Or blaming me for something?

"Thank you, Annie. Great job." He sighed loudly. "Sorry, I should've led with that."

My face relaxed into a slight smile. "Yeah, probably. You're welcome, but also thank you. I'm glad you gave me this opportunity."

Hakeem nodded stiffly. "Sai's around here somewhere. I'll get her to help, or one of the shelvers. Speaking of Sai, well, I don't like to beat around the bush. How do you feel about slowly transitioning the coordinator duties to her? When you first came to me for work, you didn't have any other job, but now you do, and it sounds like a pretty demanding one. I thought you might be looking to offload this obligation at some point, but we hadn't really spoken about it yet."

He's so direct. If only everything else in my life were so clear and direct.

"You're right. I was vaguely thinking in that direction too. Do you think Sai is interested? I think she could handle more responsibility."

"She's interested." Hakeem looked to the side and then back to me. "Look, we'll talk about this next week or soon. Right now, I want you to go relax or celebrate with your friends, and I'll handle my bookstore. Got it? Manager's orders." He even offered a small smile.

"Yes, sir," I replied, my eyes twinkling. "Have a good night, Hakeem."

When I turned around, my friends were approaching.

Rainn was the first to reach me. "Amazing job today, Annie. Not that I'm surprised at all." He leaned in for a tight hug before pulling back. "Sorry I was less than eager this morning, despite having, well, nothing to do today ... but I'm glad I got to witness all your hard work firsthand. You rock at this, no surprise though."

I smiled, squeezing his shoulders before pulling away. "Aw, thanks." Before I could say more, Sofia and Kylan joined us and added their own praise—hers was likely genuine, whereas his was merely polite—as well as gratitude for the opportunity to help one of their own clients.

"We really have to give most of the credit to the author," I said. "People wouldn't show up for a crappy author. They showed up for an awesome one."

"*Yes, yes, yes*, so true," Sofia gushed. "I wish I could take credit for discovering her, but that was all Laina. I'm surprised she wasn't here today actually." She paused, her expression thoughtful for a moment before it lit up with excitement. "Anyway, drinks, anyone? I think it's time to celebrate!"

I gave an apologetic look. "Sorry, Sofia, I can't. It sounds fun, and everyone knows I could use some fun, but I need sleep more. Juggling all this has been ..." I halted, glancing at Kylan quickly. What was I thinking? I was aiming for a promotion! I shouldn't imply I couldn't juggle lots of demands. "I'm just a little worn out, so I need to rest up."

Sofia stuck out her lower lip. "I get it. I don't like it, but I get it."

"I'm afraid I can't either," Kylan said, his deep voice cracking a bit. "My sister's flight is landing tonight, so I need to pick her up. Another time though."

Sofia's frown deepened. Feeling bad for her, I pointed to my roommate. "Rainn, that leaves you. Think you can handle drinks with the lovely Sofia tonight?"

Sofia looked at Rainn with mild interest, but he shook his head as his brows furrowed. "No, I don't think so."

"Oh, you said you didn't have anything going on—"

"I do." His response was curt, and a muscle was ticking in his square jaw.

"Oh, all right," I said, biting my lip.

This is awkward. Why's Rainn being weird?

Sofia stared at the floor for a moment before looking up with an overly enthusiastic laugh. "Well, there's always my favorite drinking companion ... me." At our dismayed expressions, she added, "Lighten up. I was joking. I've got other friends. Or else I'll see if my sister needs a hand with the baby."

As we all left the store, I eyed Rainn from the corner of my eye, trying to pinpoint why he was acting strangely. He seemed to still really dislike Sofia, and it was unlike him to dislike anyone without good cause. Even if he did occasionally dislike a person, he never hurt their feelings—and in front of others! It had been so painful to watch. I made a mental note to ask him what on earth that was about—and perhaps to pull Sofia aside sometime too and apologize for him. But for now, all that mattered was getting some sleep. And I could rest easy knowing that Kylan and Sofia weren't together tonight, at least.

Chapter 21

I swiveled in my desk chair, back and forth, my forehead creased as I stared at the only part of my desk that wasn't covered in files, notes, and books. I was working up the courage to march into Sofia's office and ask for a massive favor but hadn't quite figured out how. I chewed on the pen I'd been twirling around in my fingers for at least ten minutes. If only I could wait a few weeks to ask for the favor—until after the promotion was decided—just in case it made things awkward at work. But after seeing Viviana in tears over lunch *in public* today, I couldn't resist offering to help. I'd spit out the first thing that came to mind. Sure, I'd help her find an agent. I'd use my connections, flimsy though they still were, being new to the business.

With a deep sigh, I placed my feet flat on the floor to steady the chair. I rose and walked directly to Sofia's office, knocking lightly first.

Now or never.

"Hey, Sof—"

"Annie, hey! You are not going to believe the deal we got for Campton's next trilogy. He'll be kissing my—" She stopped short, her eyes widening as she scanned her computer screen. "Oh, hold on. Just a minute, OK?"

I nodded, stepping further into the office.

After a blitz of furious typing, Sofia met my eyes, but she looked disoriented. "Sorry about that. Where were we?"

I needed to jump right in before I could change my mind, remembering the look on Viviana's face yesterday when she'd imagined herself failing as an author. I'd seen that devastation on the faces of at least a dozen authors at work, in addition to the hundreds or thousands who never made it out of the slush pile. It was ten times worse when the author was my friend. "So I wanted to talk to you about something. Actually, I ... ah, I have a favor to ask. Kind of a big one."

Sofia turned fully away from her computer monitor and rested her chin on her hands. "OK, I'm listening."

"You can say no. Especially if it's a conflict of interest. I am hoping it's not, but I'm not sure. I ... this is awkward. I hope—"

"Annie, you've known me a while now. When I want to say no to someone, what do I do?"

"You say no," I said, and we both chuckled. "Point taken. OK. Well, all right, here's the short version. A close friend wrote her first novel, and she wants me to help her find an agent. I wanted to ask if you'd be willing to read it. First 30 pages, or less, whatever you can squeeze in." I spoke rapidly but then paused. "Again, you can say no. I just—"

"Sure."

I inhaled sharply. "Sure, as in you'll do it? Or—"

"Of course."

Relieved, I smiled, relaxing into the chair near Sofia's desk. I should have known Sofia wouldn't let me down. She never let anyone down.

"Given how crazy things are now though, could I put this on my planner for sometime in the fall, maybe as early as September? With you vouching for her, I'm sure I'd want to take her on, but I want to give her the attention she'd need."

My spirits deflated. This wasn't surprising. Sofia had been closed to queries for almost a month now since she was so swamped. "Oh, uh …"

She eyed me curiously. "Ah, wrong answer? Is your friend in a hurry?"

"Not in a hurry so much, but … well, you know how it is for new authors. Her confidence has really taken a hit with some early querying. I was hoping a quicker uptake could help her feel better. But you can't fit her in now. Of course you can't—I know your schedule." I shook her head. "Sorry, you gave me a totally reasonable, generous answer. I just wish I could help her more myself. Please don't stress about fitting this in."

"I'll help," said a voice from behind. I'd know that voice anywhere, but I turned around to confirm. Or to … ogle. Kylan was dressed in gym shorts and a casual blue shirt, his brow glistening with sweat.

I tried not to stare. "Uh, hi, we were just—"

"Sorry, I overheard," he said. "And sorry about the sweaty gym clothes. I had an urgent business meeting that came up while I was working out, so I didn't have time to change and shower—well, you get the picture."

"Oh, we get the picture," Sofia said, her voice low. "And you needn't apologize for it."

Oddly, Kylan blushed at that. Only slightly, and it was barely noticeable on his already sweaty and slightly flushed face, but I still noticed. It was surprising, with all the time they'd spent together lately, that he'd be embarrassed about a flirty comment. Maybe only because it was spoken in front of me.

I sighed. "I was just going to head back to my desk anyway—"

"Wait," he said in his commanding voice, placing a hand on my forearm as I went to move past him. I stepped back immediately, putting a couple feet of distance between us. "I mean it. I can help. You have a friend looking for an agent for their first manuscript, I gather?" When I nodded slowly, he continued, "I'll take it home this weekend and read it. Or tonight."

My eyes widened.

I can't be hearing this right.

Before I could protest, Sofia replied, "I'd love that, Kylan. Sort of a screening to save me some time?"

Kylan looked back and forth between us a few times. "That isn't going to ultimately save you much time though, since you have to read it anyway if you're going to represent someone. How about this: I'll read it, and if it's not trash, I'll represent the author."

I gasped. "As in ... yourself?"

"Yes."

"But ..." I looked between them, unsure how to reply, stunned that he would do this. "You, uh ... you're—"

Sofia chuckled. "You're the big guy in charge, Kylan, so we're a little surprised. But I think I can speak for both myself and Ms. Tongue-Tied over there and say that we'd be really grateful, if you think you have the time."

I cleared my throat, embarrassed. "It's just—well, I didn't know you represented authors yourself. Anymore."

"Not often," he admitted, giving us a half-smile. "It's not a big deal though. I like to stay involved at various levels of my companies."

I nodded and then froze. He couldn't know yet who the author in question was. Mentioning her name was the last thing I wanted to do, but I needed to tell him now, so he had a chance to change his mind. My voice shook as I said, "You need to know, the aspiring author is my friend Viviana Cantwell. She's—"

His face didn't change, but his voice was quiet. "I remember." He glanced at his watch quickly. "Give her my email address and have her send the manuscript. I've got to run." Before I could blink, he was heading out the door with a quick wave.

I sank into the chair nearest to her.

After a moment of silence, Sofia spoke up. "Annie? I know this is a little irregular, but it's fine. Take it as the gift that it is." She smiled. "Think of the connections he has. He could get her published anywhere, probably."

Sofia was right. This was a gift. I should be overjoyed or at least relieved. Instead, worries swirled around in my mind as I forced a smile for Sofia. This was a blessing, I reminded myself again.

But Viviana doesn't like Kylan.

And he sure as heck doesn't like Viviana, and with good reason.

How can this possibly work?

And why is he doing this?

I needn't have worried about Viviana's reaction to the shocking news. Sure, she'd been astonished, as anyone would be, and she didn't believe me at first. Shock had transitioned into mistrust and even a hint of the old scorn, until Jack reminded her of how powerful Kylan had become in this industry. After Jack said, "I've never known you to be a snob, love," Viviana softened, nodding in acceptance.

By the time we'd met for lunch the following weekend, Viviana looked ready to jump out of her skin with excitement as she grinned at me. "I have an agent! I'm going to be a real writer with a real agent and a real published book!" I'd just sat back and smiled, glad I could have a role in connecting them and only a little sad that I hadn't successfully done so years ago, when it mattered most.

It was a warm Tuesday in late June when my phone buzzed with a surprising text: another gushing thank-you text from Viviana, but with an interesting revelation. Not only was Kylan proving to be invaluable as her new agent, but he'd even volunteered to use his influence in publishing to knock down Gregory a peg or two. Hearing that Kylan was angry when he heard how Gregory had treated Viviana was almost as surprising as the fact that they'd even talked about the situation at all. Were they somehow becoming friends?

My heartbeat sped up when my eyes drifted to my computer screen and landed on a new email marked Important. I was requested to appear in Francis's office in ... now. I jumped out of my chair.

Francis cared about promptness, and this could be the all-important news.

My heart thudded in my chest, and my stomach roiled as I walked quickly to the boss's office. At the doorway, Francis called out in a clear, authoritative tone, "Don't keep us waiting, Annie."

I walked in quickly, and my eyes widened as I saw two other assistants in the room. One seat was empty near Francis's desk, and the other seats were occupied by two of my fellow assistants.

Once I'd sat down, I stole a glance at the others. To my right, Jessa's foot was tapping out a silent but steady rhythm, and her brows were drawn together as she fidgeted. To my left, though, Ambrose looked confident, cocky even. He probably had a right to be. He was the most experienced assistant, likely a shoo-in for the promotion. Still, I lifted my chin in determination.

After what felt like hours of fraught silence, Francis finally spoke, "No doubt you've all figured out what this meeting is about. I won't delay. Congratulations." Francis looked at us with what was the closest thing to a smile that I'd ever seen from our boss.

The assistants and I glanced at each other with unease, and Ambrose was the first to respond. "Thank you. I'm honored to be chosen, given the top-notch competition from my peers here." The last part he said with a faux-gracious smile to Jessa and me.

"Indeed, the competition was fierce, and it was impossible to choose." Francis paused while we all held our breath. "So we didn't. One of Kylan's goals has always been expansion, so adding new agents was a natural choice. The three of you will all become agents, and we'll open up a fifth assistant role to support the additional work."

Ambrose gasped before arranging his expression into a polite smile. "Congratulations to my two junior colleagues as well then, Jessa and Annie," he said, again with the faux-gracious tone.

I didn't much care about Ambrose's reaction though.

I'm going to be an agent!

As shock coursed through me, I glanced over at Jessa, who appeared terrified but excited.

I'm becoming an agent? What? Me? Me!

After just a couple months of learning the assistant job, I was being promoted. *I*, Annie York, was becoming an actual agent. It hardly seemed possible.

"As you know, Laina will be leaving soon. Annie, you will move into her office and take on many of her clients. This decision was based only on practicalities. You are already familiar with Laina's clients and organizational methods. Jessa and Ambrose, you'll move into your positions in the fall, when we have new offices prepared and new assistants hired and trained." Francis paused. "You'll all no doubt have more questions, but that is all, for now." With an air of finality, Francis stood, tilting their head briefly in the direction of the door.

I rose quickly and thanked Francis, knowing they didn't like to waste time. Ambrose and Jessa followed, a bit more sluggishly. Ambrose had a distinctly disgruntled air about him as he walked out of the office, and Jessa still seemed to be in a daze. For me, it was all I could do not to literally run to Sofia's office with the news.

And not long after I plopped into a chair in her office with a mile-wide grin, a familiar voice rang out. Or more like sang out.

"Happy agenting to you, happy agenting to you, happy agenting to Annieeeee—"

"I think she gets the picture," said Rainn, cutting off our roommate as he laughed. "Stick to dance, Raf."

Rafael sighed dramatically. "I'm an amazing singer. You just have poor taste."

"Then I guess everyone else in the world does too," Rainn said, his lips twitching.

Before Rafael could come up with a suitable retort, I cleared my throat loudly and said, "Hey! Um, hi?"

Both men turned to me, nearly falling over themselves to apologize for the clumsy entrance and to congratulate me on the promotion. I chuckled as I watched them, my heart feeling full for the first time in ... forever.

"I found out about the promotion yesterday," Sofia said. "So I called them up this morning and told them to come on by for some news."

I gasped. "So *they* found out before me?"

"She didn't tell us you were promoted. We knew when we heard 'news,' it had to be that," Rainn said, an oddly shy grin on his face as he looked between Sofia and me.

I crossed one leg over the other, a thoughtful expression on my face. "But Sofia *could* have been calling you here to comfort me because I didn't get the job."

Rafael burst into laughter, and to my absolute shock, Rainn and Sofia joined in. After he stopped laughing and wiped his damp eyes, Rafael looked at me in disbelief. "Oh, come on. You had to know the job was yours. Like they could really pass up the opportunity to promote *you*. There's no one better than *you.*"

"I love you guys," I said, warmth flooding through me. "But you're a bit biased. I thought the promotion was a long shot, honestly. But ... whatever. Who cares. You guys, I did it. I did it!" I jumped out of the chair and nearly bowled them over with a long group hug, and when I finally tore myself away, I found Sofia waiting for one as well, which I was happy to oblige.

"Sofia," I said. "I couldn't have done this with you. Any of this. Ah, ah—don't say anything. You don't get to object. You're an awesome mentor. Own it, girl."

She eyed me thoughtfully and then smiled. "You're so right. We're both brilliant, you know. And these guys know it too."

Rafael nodded, grinning back at us. After a moment, Rafael nudged Rainn, who jumped back.

"Oh, hey, sorry, I zoned out a bit," Rainn muttered.

Rafael gave him a strange look before turning back to us. "So, we're of course throwing you a big party to celebrate. Joel's parents' house, Friday night."

My eyes widened. "Oh, I don't know if I—"

"Don't bother arguing. You don't have time to plan a party, I know, but you can make time to go to one, girl. You love parties.

Don't you worry about anything—we'll handle all the planning and invite some friends. We're going to tear it up one last time before you get serious as our new Agent Annie."

"That has a nice ring to it," Sofia said, biting her lip with a smile. "Should we invite anyone from here or—"

"Eh, I lean toward no," I said quickly, "Or at least very few. You're my only cool friend here, Sof. At least, the only friend who isn't more of a rival. And Rainn … I guess you could invite your buddies in IT or HR if you want." I tried to think of a way to say 'don't invite Kylan' without sounding rude or suspicious, but I came up short. Hopefully Sofia would realize the last person I wanted to celebrate with was my college boyfriend. Ex-college boyfriend.

Chapter 22

Alas, it was too much to hope that Sofia wouldn't bring Kylan to the party as her plus one. Sighing, I watched him enter the large poolside backyard area set up for the party at Joel's parents' house.

They're probably dating, after all, so of course he'd be Sofia's plus one.

My thoughts were glum as I sipped my first cocktail of the humid summer evening and averted my eyes. I always loved parties, so this feeling of wanting to skip out was unpracticed.

Rainn nudged me with his elbow. We were sitting at the small outdoor bar, while other early arrivals, mostly friends of Joel and Rafael, were lounging poolside. "Who's the woman on his arm?" His voice was a strange mixture of worry and intrigue.

I reluctantly glanced back toward the door. "I have no idea. But there's Sofia too. Maybe it's his sister?" I stared at the unfamiliar woman, whose sandy blonde hair was swept back with an orange hair tie that matched her simple, flowy sundress. Simple but classy—I had to approve. "Yeah, look! She has his smile."

Rainn squinted. "Really? I don't see it. And when does that guy ever smile anyway?" He gave me a sympathetic look. "I guess before ..."

I shook my head, giving him a warning look before returning my attention to the new arrivals. Joel was shaking their hands as Rafael made introductions.

It has to be his sister. But why would he bring her?

Are Sofia and Kelly becoming close?

For one alarming second, I felt moisture start to pool in my eyes. *Stupid, stupid.*

"So how much redecorating are you going to have to do?" Rainn asked. "You moved into her office today, right?" I couldn't help but smile at this change of topic. Laina's last day was yesterday, and I'd wasted no time moving into my new space.

"Assuming you mean Laina's office, it needs a massive makeover. She had horrible taste. Maybe not in books, but definitely in office decor. Though I'm not feeling perfect harmony with her client list either. Sofia said occasionally some trading happens in this situation. I imagine sometimes the clients look elsewhere too, if they aren't keen on being transferred to a newbie agent."

"Ah, what's this drivel I hear?" Rafael's voice came up behind us. "I'm sure you've gotten to know her old clients somewhat. Anyone who knows you even a little would want to keep you, Annie."

I inhaled sharply and glanced around, worried that Kylan might have overheard that. I breathed out a sigh of relief though when I saw Joel leading him and his guest toward the other group by the pool.

Viviana and Jack arrived soon after, along with Jenn Weston. As usual, I felt happy to see Jenn but also uncomfortably ... wistful. If only we could be closer, I heard myself thinking. The recent rift with Viviana hadn't helped, as I'd shied away from all our mutual friends during that period. Well, except Jack. A tall, unfamiliar woman walked alongside them.

Viviana tugged on the woman's arm and made a beeline for us, with Jack and Jenn trailing behind. "Annie, I am so excited for you!" she exclaimed, pulling me up for a startlingly strong hug.

"Thanks," I said as we stepped back, and I smiled politely at the newcomer. "Hi, I'm Annie. Obviously."

Viviana gasped. "Sorry, I should lead with introductions, but I never do. Annie, this is Jane Alton. *The Jane* from Duluth!"

Jane chuckled, her long blonde ponytail swaying as she leaned forward to extend a hand in greeting. "Great to meet you, Annie. And congratulations are in order, I hear. I've heard great things about you."

"Same," I said, smiling but also wondering if it was fully true. After all, Viviana had met and befriended Jane at a literary conference in Duluth in early spring when she and I weren't speaking, so Jane might not have heard the greatest things about me initially. Still, I could mend that impression, surely. I was pretty good at charming people.

Usually.

Well, until recently.

"*The Jane* is a bit much though, Viv," Jane said, eyeing our mutual friend. "I tend to reserve that for Jane Austen, don't you?"

Viviana grinned. "I did, until I met you. Annie, Jane here is as much of an Austen fan as I am. Maybe more."

"Doubtful that anyone could be *more* of an Austen fan than you, Vivi," Jack said, stepping forward as he casually placed an arm across her shoulders.

"I have to agree with your man, Viv. And I still can't believe I'm calling him your man," Jenn said, laughing as Jane nodded. She turned to me then and smiled widely. "Congrats, girl. This is so freaking awesome for you."

"Thanks, Jenn. And Viv, you and Jane can have all the Austen," I said, a slight smile gracing my face. "I mean, she's fine, but I'm all about the contemporary authors. As you'll see from my new clients ... Oh, *oh*, you guys, I'm going to be an agent!"

Everyone laughed before commencing a round of hugs and congrats again.

When Viviana came in for another hug, she whispered to me, "We're going to return to the whole 'she's fine' comment about Austen later on, Annie. For now though, let's go get our drink on!" Laughing, we linked arms and ambled over to the bar.

The party was proceeding smoothly, with Rafael and Joel introducing me to a lot of their friends and Sofia introducing some friends and siblings she'd brought. Rainn had brought a few friends as well, whom I knew only a little. Kylan and his (likely) sister kept their distance, probably because they were constantly surrounded by a crowd of people who wanted to meet them. Or him, probably. He was basically a celebrity.

And then disaster struck.

After disappearing for a bit, Joel and Rafael returned, clad in their swim shorts, their impressive ballet physiques and matching tattoos on full display. Rafael cleared his throat, and Joel let out a shrill whistle until a hush fell over the crowd.

"Thanks for coming out, everybody, but don't be shy. Get in the damn pool. It's scorching out here, am I right?" Rafael wiped his brow and grinned at Joel. "But first, speech time."

My mouth formed an *O* as my eyes widened.

How drunk is he?

But I didn't have to wonder long, as he soon launched into a rambling monologue that was both sweet and hilarious and had me in tears, both of laughter and of a deeper emotion. He even had Joel bring Charlie outside for a brief appearance. The kitten took one look at the pool and hissed before darting off toward the house, back to the cozy cat house where he'd been set up in luxury for the evening.

"OK, you're all starting to nod off. I'll shut up. Annie, congratulations, you amazing, gorgeous, talented lady. I love you, BFF," Rafael said with a smile as he lifted a glass to me. "Now let's—"

"Wait, my turn!" Sofia stood abruptly. "I haven't known Annie very long, so I'll keep this short and sweet. Girl, you've been on fire since you started at the agency. Since you showed up for your dang interview. Anyone who knows me knows I'm kind of, well ... competitive toward my peers. I'm a woman of color in a world that doesn't make space for people like me, so, well, I got to make space for myself, right? But with you, Annie ... I couldn't be happier to have you as both a peer and a friend. I'm so glad you decided to change careers and landed at our agency as my assistant—and didn't stay as an assistant for long. Though replacing you is going to be impossible. Anyway, I promised not to ramble too much, but how much booze is *in* these drinks, guys? So, congratulations, Annie. You're amazing." She smiled warmly, and I beamed.

I wished I hadn't been sitting so far away from Sofia and Rafael because these amazing speeches called for massive hugs in gratitude.

Sofia looked immediately at Kylan, who was seated near her. "Do you want to speak too?" He shook his head quickly. Sofia looked like she was about to speak but then apparently thought better of it and turned back to Rafael with a half-smile. "All right, guys. Proceed."

Without warning, Rafael and Joel glanced at each other and grinned and then dove into the water, splashing nearly everyone around them.

Kylan snubbed me.

Publicly.

He refused to speak on my behalf? To congratulate me at my party? Why was he even here then? He could've just said something simple, gracious, polite. But to just ... decline. It hurt. A lot. I wasn't getting this promotion to impress him, yet ... it hurt.

Before I could continue this depressing line of thinking, though, I realized everyone around me was either jumping into the pool or heading into the house. I turned to Viviana, who was just rising beside me. "Where's everyone going?"

"To put on bathing suits, I imagine. Some people are just jumping in, clothes and all, but some of us aren't so keen on that. Like Jack." She laughed. "We're headed inside. You coming?"

"Oh, uh, I'm not sure yet," I said, my heart thumping in my chest. "You go on without me."

This was it.

The moment I'd feared. The fear that had driven me to almost skip out on my own party.

Breathe.

Panic.

Breathe.

Maybe if I just hadn't fallen into the pool—

Can't breathe. Panic. Breathe. No. Don't swallow water.

"No, it wasn't my fault," I whispered to no one. "My mother should've been watching her only child more closely. Or at all."

Did she save me because she loved me? Or because she was trying to impress her boyfriend?

Did she ever love me?

Breathe.

In, out.

In, out.

I'd done this before. Pretended I wasn't terrified of swimming. Pretended my throat wasn't closing up at the very idea. Pretended I hadn't experienced a horrible childhood trauma. I'd done it convincingly, apparently, because even Rafael didn't know.

But it had been a while. I'd successfully dodged most invitations to go to pools and beaches in recent years.

I was out of practice. My breathing, my heart rate, my eye movement, all going faster and faster while I desperately tried to slow it all down. I gripped the bottom of the garden bench I sat on, holding on for dear life. Alcohol was supposed to dull the senses, wasn't it? But I couldn't stop feeling ... everything.

In and out, just breathe.

Sweat beaded on my forehead. I nearly jumped out of my skin when I heard the warm voice, distant yet close, so close.

"I haven't gotten a chance to congratulate you yet."

I blinked several times, trying to force my eyes to settle on Kylan as he sat next to me on the bench. "Uh ... yeah." It was all I could manage as I tried desperately not to let it show how hard it was to breathe, to think, to do anything.

"I wanted to congratulate you one on one. A speech in front of a group might have hinted at some kind of favoritism—" He stopped speaking and rubbed his jaw. "Or something."

I took some slow breaths as the panic started to subside, but the word "favoritism" coming from him sparked a different kind of feeling. Surely he hadn't meant it *that* way, right? I managed a shaky smile. "Thank you."

Kylan studied me intently. "Are you all right?"

I bit my lip and inhaled slowly. "Maybe? I, uh … this is going to sound ridiculous, but I don't swim."

"I know." He paused. "Don't look so shocked. It wasn't that long ago that we were close, Annie. I did wonder if you, well, since you were having a pool party in your honor that maybe you'd changed your feelings on swimming in recent years, but … obviously not."

I frowned. "Obviously?"

"Well, obviously to me."

"Only to you?" I tilted my head, doubt on my face.

Kylan looked around. "Everyone else is far too busy getting drunk and enjoying the pool. I doubt anyone noticed your panic attack."

"No one but you."

He nodded.

After a long silence where I couldn't form any coherent thoughts, I said, "You can go swimming, you know. I don't need anyone to stay with me and cover for me. I'll just, like, tell everyone I have my period or something. And it's a heavy flow day."

Did I seriously just talk about menstruation with my estranged ex and the hottest guy on the freaking planet?

Unfazed, Kylan stretched out his long, tanned legs, leaning back a bit. "Nah. I didn't bring my swim shorts, and I don't feel like swimming anyway. I don't even like it."

I narrowed my eyes. "Liar."

He flashed a grin—and it was just as irresistible as it'd always been. "OK, I like it a little."

"You did swim team in high school and part of college."

"Ah, so I'm not the only one with a meticulous memory for swimming-related knowledge about each other," he said, his eyes twinkling with something unspoken.

He shouldn't be this appealing. It wasn't fair.

Look away!

I couldn't.

But Sofia solved that problem, shouting and waving at Kylan and me from the other side of the pool where she was swimming with her friends.

I sat up straighter. Was that Rainn with Sofia? How odd. I squinted in their direction. Rainn was always so surly toward her.

But they were laughing together in the pool. Standing very close.

"Not in the mood to swim, Sof. I'm just going to relax here for now," Kylan replied. When Sofia and Rafael called out threats to throw me in the water, he stiffened and shook his head. "She isn't swimming." Something in his expression must have warned them away, as no one asked further.

"Kylan," I said when Sofia and the others had turned their attention to someone else.

It's now or never.

I need to nip this in the bud now. Before I fall for him all over again.

"Yeah?" he said, meeting my gaze.

My heart was beating erratically now, but I had to say it. "Why are you being so nice to me? It might be ... easier if you're not."

He stared at me for what seemed like an eternity. "You think ... I should be ..." He tilted his head in apparent confusion. "Annie?"

I opened my mouth and then closed it, shaking my head. "I just—" Suddenly I spotted a flash of orange coming close, not far behind him. "Your sister?"

"My—" He looked sideways as she came to stand next to him. "Oh, hey." He looked somehow both happy and unhappy to see her, oddly. "Kelly, this isn't the best timing, but I really wanted to introduce you to the guest of honor, so—"

His sister raised her eyebrows. "Oh, I can come back if I'm interrupting—"

"No, you're fine," I assured her, pasting a wide smile on my face. I needed Kelly to stay, instead of continuing the awkward conversation I'd stupidly started. "Please, sit. I'm Annie York. Kylan's told me about you!"

"Likewise, Annie, I've heard great things about you. I'm Kelly, the little sister. I'm so excited to meet you. I love your fashion sense already—maybe you can help Ky with his! Seriously, congratulations on your new position!" She seemed so genuine. What had Kylan told her about me?

"Thanks, it's a dream—I'm so grateful for the opportunity. Beyond excited. A few months ago, I was facing a career I didn't like, a cheating boyfriend and a consistently terrible mother, an ex—er, I mean, a falling out with a great friend, depression and booze … now here I am. I not only found my dream job but I got it. It's—" I clamped a hand over my mouth. "I am so sorry for the verbal diarrhea. We just met, so much TMI. I think I've had one too many of these." I nodded toward the empty glass on the table next to me.

Kelly grinned. "I love it. You're fine. I'll go next, OK? If my hovering brother can make himself scarce."

Kylan sighed. "All right. I know when I'm not wanted." He started to walk away and then turned back, meeting me with mysterious grey eyes I couldn't look away from. He might as well be staring into my soul. "Maybe we can talk later?"

My breath caught, and all I could do was nod slightly. With superhuman effort, I forced myself to turn toward Kelly, who began to tell me all about herself. It was easy to focus on his sister though. She was one of those people who were ridiculously easy to like. But of course she was. Everything in the universe seemed to be conspiring against me in the goal to get some safe distance from him—and from all the reasons I should've never walked away from him.

Fortunately or not, Kylan never found me alone again. I was dying to know what he wanted to say—but also terrified at the same time. Lucky for us, Jack had stayed sober and driven me along with Viviana and Jane to Viviana's place for a girls' night/after-party after dropping off Jenn, who claimed to be exhausted after only two drinks. I probably should've abstained, but we were celebrating, right? We teased Jenn that being married with children suited her, as much as she liked to complain about it.

"Annie, I am so excited to finally meet you. And so excited for you, seriously," Jane gushed, her eyes lighting up as she leaned forward on the worn-in couch in Viviana's one-bedroom apartment.

I giggled. "You might have mentioned that, uh—"

"Four times. No, five!" Viviana said, holding up fingers. "Jane's such a cute drunk, I swear. The cutest I've ever seen. If only I were into ladies, we'd be a perfect match."

"I'm only tipsy, not drunk," Jane said with a smile. "I actually dated a fellow Austenite once, and you'd think it would be amazing, right? But nope. Most boring relationship I've ever had. We were too much alike, I suppose, at least at that age, when attraction was, for me, all about romantic tension. I'd settle for comfortable and easy right now." She frowned, tilting her head back as she took a long swig from her champagne glass. Viviana was quick to open a new bottle and ready to pour some more.

"Jane, you'll find the one. You're far too sweet and amazing and interesting and, just, *everything* not to find someone who's just as awesome," Viviana gushed, leaning over for a hug but landing on Jane's side instead. They both laughed as Jane pushed her upright.

"I think we're all a little more than tipsy," I chimed in. "Though my opinion is probably worthless since I just met you, you seem awesome, so I think your Mr. or Ms. Right is still out there."

"Aww, thanks, Annie. I can see why everyone loves you so much."

I nearly spit out the champagne swirling in my mouth. "Everyone loves me so—"

"Oh come on, Annie, what do you think tonight was all about? And the promotion? And just ... come on, don't look so surprised," Viviana said, her brows furrowed in confusion.

I eyed them both warily. After a long moment of self-doubt, my lips slowly curved into a smile, and I laughed. "Of course. I'm amazing."

And *there* it was, the confidence I'd lost in these past months—the confidence that had surfaced only rarely lately but had still gotten me where I was today, a star rising quickly in a new career.

"You ladies are amazing too." I wiped a small tear from the corner of one eye and sipped my champagne. Or perhaps it was more than a sip. "OK, I have to confess something. Like I have to tell someone or I'll scream. Can we just make it, like, *that* kind of girls night? Please?"

"Yes, so much yes!" Viviana nearly shouted. "I need that kind of girls night."

Jane smiled. "Yes please."

"So, I'm going to come right out and say it because I'm drunk. Yeah, you heard it. Drunk, not tipsy." I took a deep breath, wondering if I was crazy for doing this. For *feeling* this. "I am, uh ..." I trailed off, squeezing my eyes shut.

Could I actually say it out loud?

If not now, when?

"You're ..." Jane prompted me.

Taking a deep breath, I spit out the words. "I'm still in love with him."

"With—" Viviana asked, her tone cautious.

I stared at my lap. "Kylan."

Viviana exhaled softly, and I cautiously looked up to see a small smile on her face.

"Are you ... you're not disappointed?'

"I was afraid you might say Brandon! So, I'm relieved." Viviana smiled, holding up her glass before taking a long swig.

I watched her closely. "But ... you don't like Kylan."

"That's not true. I don't dislike him. I just … disapproved. That sounds awful when I say it aloud, yeesh. But anyway, that was the past."

My heart started beating even more quickly. "And now?"

"Now, he's getting me a book deal with one of the biggest New York publishers. He's been fantastic to work with. I thought he might hold a grudge from the past, but … I've seen no sign of it. And he's never spoken ill of you. He's been wonderful." Viviana bit her lip and then smiled. "So, I approve."

My jaw dropped. "Oh … uh. Thank you? But I don't think I have a chance with him now. So …"

"Wait, why not?" Jane interjected. "I saw the two of you talking. He seemed pretty interested."

I tried to swallow the lump in my throat. "I broke his heart four years ago. He has resented me ever since. I don't think he ha–hates me anymore." I choked up as tears started to form. "But our chance has long since passed. He's been dating Sofia."

Viviana winced. "Oh, Annie, I'm so sorry. That has to be painful to watch. Does she know?"

"She knows only a little about our past, and I told her it was no big deal."

"I'm getting the sense it's actually a very big deal though." Her expression turned somber. "That maybe … maybe I was wrong to persuade you to let him go."

"To let him go where?" Jane asked.

I took a steadying breath. "He was graduating from college a year earlier than me, and he wanted me to go with him to New York to pursue his dreams."

"While you were still getting your degree?" Jane made a face. "That's not cool of him."

"Right?" Viviana said. "That's what I thought."

"But I didn't even know for sure what I wanted to major in," I said quietly. "I probably could've transferred schools relatively easily since I was still technically undecided."

We were all quiet for a moment, pondering this. Then Jane sat up straighter, her eyes bright. "This is *Persuasion*! Kylan is *so* Captain Wentworth. Right, Viv? And Annie ... well, she's Anne. We have another real-life Austen on our hands, I think."

Viviana's face slowly transformed into an expression of wonder, then glee. "Jane, you genius. How did I not see this? You're right. This is *so Persuasion*!" Then she frowned, the joy fading from her eyes. "Wait, does that make me Lady Russell?"

Jane winced. "I think so."

I shook my head slowly. "I haven't read any Austen since college, so I don't remember that character. Regardless, I'm afraid I'll disappoint you all because the real story here isn't a happily ever after. He doesn't want me. He's made that clear."

The three of us were silent for a long moment.

"Are you sure? Maybe he's just afraid to get hurt again, so he's hiding his real feelings," Jane started.

"Or, like Wentworth, he doesn't realize you still love him," Viviana said, her hand over her heart as she sighed dramatically.

"He *doesn't* want me. He's dating my work bestie, remember?" I sucked my lips between my teeth. It hurt to say that aloud. Before they could reply, I waved my hands to stop them. "Can we talk about something else? Someone else's turn? Jane, tell us all about your fabulous life in Duluth. How's the shopping there?"

Jane burst into laughter, and as the seconds ticked by, Viviana and I looked at her curiously. "Sorry," she said once she caught her breath. "It's just ... my life is anything but fabulous. Duluth is great, for sure. I love the city, always have. But not my life."

I frowned. "Sorry to hear that. Want to vent or no?"

"She's not really the venting type," Viviana said. "Trust me, I've tried."

"No point," Jane said, waving her hand. "You all don't need to hear the boring details. Because it's boring. My life isn't terrible or even bad, really. It's just boring. Dull. I'm basically middle-aged, and I'm a proofreader. And I hate this word but I'm going to say it anyway ... lonely. I'm single, I don't have children, I don't own a home."

"And there's nothing wrong with that, if that's how you choose to live—"

"It's not though. I'm not single by choice. I'm not stuck in this job by choice. I'm not ... ugh." Jane stopped as she covered her face with her hands. There was clearly more, but we weren't about to pressure her.

"Well, I think we've established that I'm a total mess when it comes to love, so I have nothing to offer on the single problem," I said, chuckling. "But maybe I can help with the job thing. I recently reinvented myself. Maybe you just need to do the same!"

Jane eyed us warily. "I'm almost 40 though—"

"So?"

"What am I going to do? I don't want to go back to school," Jane said, crossing her arms.

Viviana smiled gently. "There are lots of things you could—"

"What are you interested in? What is your dream job? I just met you so I have no idea, but surely you've thought about it," I prodded.

Viviana nodded slowly. "If you could do anything, what would it be?"

Jane licked her lips and started to speak and then stopped. After a few long moments, she said, "There's so much to love about journalism. I'm just tired of proofreading other people's work. I think I want ... to create. To—you know what? It doesn't matter. It's pretty unlikely at this stage of life, and anyway, I have obligations that would get in the way. Family. Personal stuff."

Viviana and I raised our eyebrows. With a doubtful tone, I pressed on, "You have personal obligations that prevent you from pursuing a new career?"

Jane nodded, her voice becoming somber. "I do. My dad ... he's not well. I won't bore you with the details right now, but suffice to say it's a big consideration for me."

Viviana lunged forward and hugged her, and I joined in.

"Sorry for prying or overstepping," I said. "Especially when I barely know you."

Jane laughed. "And me comparing your relationship with the head of your agency to a Jane Austen love story wasn't overstepping? You're fine, Annie." Then she turned to Viviana with a growing smile. "It's your turn, Viv. Spill."

"Spill what?" Viviana asked, tilting her head uncertainly. "I'm practically an open book these days."

"She got the guy, the exciting new job ..." I pointed out.

"True," Jane said, narrowing her eyes while also smiling. "But there must be something. How's the bedroom—?"

"Amazing-but-that's-all-I'm-going-to-say," she said in a rush of words as she flushed, looking downward.

Jane and I laughed.

"That good, huh?" Jane said.

"'Good' doesn't even begin to—" At our widening eyes, Viviana reddened further. "Nope, not going there."

"Such a tease," I said, and we all giggled.

After a pause, Viviana spoke up, "All right, there is one thing."

We glanced up with eager expressions as Viviana filled another champagne glass and took several sips.

"I ... am ... oh, I don't know—"

"*Viv*, just say it," I said impatiently. Jane nodded.

She bit her lip, looking pained. "This can *not* leave the room. I don't even know if I'm thinking straight at all right now—"

"You're not—we're all hammered, Viv," Jane said, laughing.

"But *nothing* is leaving this room," I insisted. "We all agree on that."

"Fine," Viviana muttered. "I'm thinking about proposing to Jack."

"Proposing marriage?" I asked, my voice rising.

Jane giggled. "What else would she propose to her boyfriend?"

"Well ..." I clamped my mouth shut and then smiled. "*Viv*! You're getting married!"

"She's getting married!" Jane shouted, and the two of us stood up and began dancing around in a drunken circle, hands clasped together until we fell in a heap onto the couch next to Viviana, who looked mortified.

"I said I was *thinking* of proposing! I have no idea if I will or if he'd say yes. What if he—" She stopped when Jane and I erupted into a fit of giggles, unable to sit up straight on the couch. Crossing her arms over her chest, she cleared her throat loudly. "As I was saying—"

"Viv," I interrupted her, out of breath. "You—you can't be serious. That man adores you. Worships you. I'll be surprised if he doesn't beat you to the proposal."

Jane nodded rapidly. "He's probably already planning something romantic. If you want to out-romance him, you'd better make it amazing."

"I mean, it's not a competition," Viviana said. Her face morphed into a smile, with stars in her eyes. "You think he is? You think ... he wants to marry me?"

"Nothing could be more certain," I said.

Jane nodded, "I barely know him yet, but that man would follow you to the ends of the earth and back. But, hey, that gave me an idea. You two should have your wedding in Duluth. I could help you plan it!"

"A destination wedding ... I never thought of that," Viviana said thoughtfully. "But do you really think he'll say yes?"

While Jane hugged and reassured her, I rolled my eyes.

Of course Jack would marry her. And I was genuinely happy for my friends.

Love was wonderful, even if it was only for other people to experience. That would have to be enough.

Chapter 23

"Make it stop."

"Annie."

"Annie!"

"Please, make it stop!"

The words infiltrated my brain slowly, in broken pieces, just like my broken head. At least, it felt broken. Broken shards of glass or rock or ... ouch.

The Imperial March.

My stomach started churning at the song as the dread set in, and I knew it wasn't just the hangover as I opened my eyes slowly. When my hand found the sound, I reluctantly swiped left.

"Hello, Mother."

"Anastasia, my word! Why did it take you so long to answer? Did I teach you nothing about good telephone etiquette?" Jacqueline paused for just a breath. "Never mind that. Where are you? We are at the hotel. We sent a messenger to fetch you from your home, but no one answered the summons."

I took a deep breath, steeling myself as both my head and chest pounded. "Mother, I didn't know I was to be *summoned* today.

You're in town—" I stopped myself. Was I supposed to know that they were visiting this weekend? I couldn't recall whether my mother had sent me the travel dates already, and I realized it was best not to act surprised. I didn't need yet another lecture on being reckless or forgetful.

"Well, I—you—" she sputtered. My mother never sputtered. "I am shocked, Anastasia. It sounds as though you are not even sufficiently prepared for our visit. I hope I am wrong. Though we both know that rarely happens."

What was I supposed to say to that? "Uh, welcome to Minnesota, Mother."

"Being the magnanimous mother I am, I shall overlook this careless oversight this morning, but please do consult the itinerary. No slip-ups this weekend, darling. I need you on your best behavior, do you understand me?"

With my brows furrowed almost painfully, I forced the words out. "Yes, Mother."

"So, we'll see you at brunch in one hour. Goodbye." The call ended, and I exhaled in relief.

Then the panic set in.

I have to see her.

My mother is here. In town.

"I think I'm going to be sick," I mumbled hoarsely, stumbling out of the tangled bedsheets, speaking to whoever was with me in Viviana's room. I couldn't recall who had crashed in the bedroom and who'd been stuck with the couch; by the time we'd decided to sleep, we'd been hardly able to stand.

Racing to the restroom, I braced myself, but after I stared in the mirror for a while, my stomach seemed to settle, if only slightly. I splashed water on my face. My head was spinning, and I looked horrendous. I had to meet Jacqueline in under an hour. And her latest boyfriend and his ... daughter, I think. What were their names? Chris, maybe. Or Christine. I shook my head slowly as I swished some toothpaste around in my mouth and tried to run a brush through my hair. Staring at my rumpled appearance, I decided to text Rafael for help.

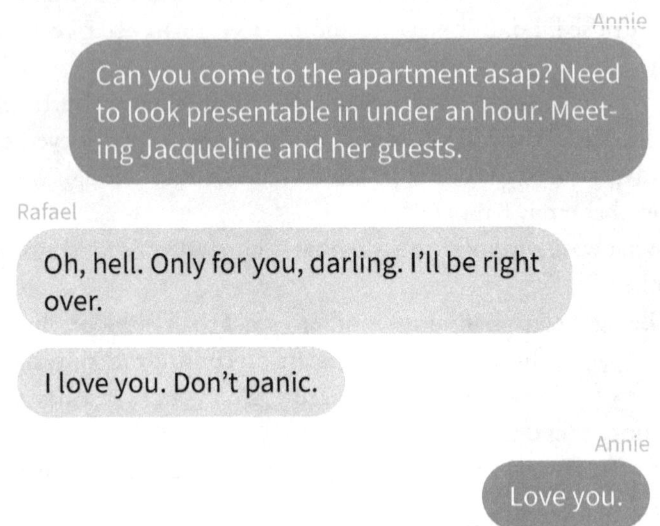

An hour later, I was speedwalking into the Four Seasons, my head still swirling with pain and a bit of queasiness that I barely noticed, so deep in thought about what was coming. Years had passed since I'd seen my mother, who refused to visit me in what she called the pitiful Midwest.

"Darling," called a high-pitched voice. That was Jacqueline's socialite voice, the public one that she thought sounded more sophisticated and philanthropic than her real voice. Or at least the one she used with her daughter—who knew the real Jacqueline. It was strange that she spoke so differently in different settings, but I'd long ago grown accustomed to it. "This is my darling Anastasia. She is late, but we will kindly forgive her, of course. You know I am kindness itself, dearest Ricardo, am I not?

"Indeed," said Ricardo, assessing me from head to toe in a leisurely fashion. "How could anyone not forgive such a beautiful face ... that is so like her mother's?" He smiled at Jacqueline and linked arms with both her and the younger woman on his other side. "Anastasia, I am Ricardo. I'm sure your mother has told you much about me and Caroline, my lovely daughter."

Caroline was apparently the other woman on his arm, and she yawned. "Hi, nice to meet you."

I forced a bright smile. "It's nice to meet you, Ricardo and Caroline. And Mother, you look well," I added politely.

Her eyes flashed. "*Well.* Yes. Do show us into the restaurant, Anastasia. We are quite famished."

My brows furrowed as I looked around.

Does my mother assume I'll be their damn tour guide?

I've been to the hotel before, since Brandon stayed here, but—oh, man, I hope he's not still here now.

After a beat though, I realized I didn't care that much one way or the other. I was long over him.

"Anastasia, did you hear—" My mother's voice became a bit more shrill.

"Yes, sorry," I mumbled. "Right this way, everyone," I said like a tour guide, pointing in the direction of the only restaurant within sight.

As the morning hours passed, so too did my enthusiasm for, well, anything. Even the news about my literary agent job hadn't impressed my mother. In fact, she seemed disgusted by the turn of events. Caroline had looked a bit sympathetic and had congratulated me, while Ricardo had merely smiled and eyed me with an odd kind of interest. Jacqueline's reaction shouldn't have surprised me, but for some reason I'd always held out hope that I could one day secure that elusive approval from her. Didn't everyone want that? Apparently working was beneath us, especially working on commission.

"It's so ... common," my mother said, wrinkling her nose.

My hand shook as I sipped my drink, wishing it was stronger. "If by common you mean *normal*, then yes." I wanted to add that many people would kill for a job in publishing. I didn't consider it a cutthroat industry per se, but one needed a hefty dose of both luck and talent to succeed.

"Don't be obtuse," Jacqueline said sharply. When Ricardo and Caroline looked startled, she smoothly changed her tone to one of honey and innocence. "Why work so hard and waste your youth, your beauty, for pennies? At least Caroline will be working for a good wage as a surgeon," she said. She looked around, appearing to be genuinely confused as to why I would pursue what she deemed a dead-end job.

I wanted to scream that publishing jobs were coveted, that they were far from a *waste*, that I wouldn't be working for pennies—though it wasn't about that. "Mother—"

"Did you not follow my advice with that wealthy young man from New York—"

"No," I said, fighting back tears. "He isn't a good man. I told you that. He *propositioned* one of my best friends. While I was sick."

"Well—" Jacqueline started, and then apparently she decided to change course because her tone became quiet and scolding. "Let us not speak of such coarse things at the table, Anastasia. I raised you better than that."

Somehow I survived the rest of the meal, only to be dragged along to a jazz concert in the park, of all things. Caroline's idea, probably. She seemed normal-ish. I was mortified when my mother insisted on an elaborate setup with several large beach umbrellas and ornate wooden chairs, while the rest of the attendees sat on blankets or cheap folding chairs.

"Anastasia, I need to powder my nose, and I believe you do as well. Please show me to the ladies' room."

I was about to reply that there was no ladies' room in the park—and that I didn't need to powder my nose—when Caroline stood up. "I actually need to pee. I'll take you to the bathroom, Jacqueline."

My eyes widened as I watched my mother smile graciously at Caroline, who linked arms with her. If I ever uttered a word like "pee" in my mother's presence, I'd have been blasted with her disdain. Apparently Caroline could get away with it though, since Jacqueline was trying to impress her rich father.

I don't care anyway.

And this is good—it means I don't have to be alone with her.

And then it dawned on me. I was alone with Ricardo instead.

"Anastasia, I hope you've been enjoying the concert," came his deep, grainy voice, far too close to my ear. I realized he was mere inches from me, leaning as far as he could over the arm of his chair.

"Uh, it's Annie," I said, my voice shaking.

And I knew immediately that my words were a mistake.

"*Annie*," he said, his smile growing as his eyes swept over my chest. "Yes. I'd be happy to be more, uh, familiar with each other."

When I felt his fingertips brush my knee lightly, I squeezed my eyes shut.

This day couldn't get any worse, could it?

"Actually, I do need to powder my nose after all," I said, rising abruptly from the chair and nearly tripping. I didn't bother to turn back and see his expression but merely strode in the direction I'd seen Caroline and Jacqueline heading earlier.

On the way there, I encountered them. "Mom, I need to talk to you," I said firmly, placing a hand on her arm.

My mother's eyes widened. "Darling, I'm sure it can wait. This is terribly rude to Caroline, who was just telling me about Ascott's plans for their move here—"

"That can wait," I said, trying to pull her aside.

Caroline looked between the two of us and smiled politely. "Jacqueline, I'd love to catch up a bit later. We have all weekend, right? I don't want to monopolize it."

When she'd walked away, Jacqueline wrestled her arm out of my grip and hissed, "See? She takes care not to monopolize every situation. You could learn from Caroline, you know."

I glared at her. I didn't know whether to scream or sob, but I needed to say what I came to say. "I'm going to get straight to the point, Mother. Ricardo hit on me. Your boyfriend. I left right away, of course."

Jacqueline stilled, staring into my eyes with an unreadable expression.

When she didn't speak, I added, "I just, uh, thought you should know."

Her lips were thin and her voice cold when she finally spoke. "I shouldn't blame myself for how you've turned out. But I can't help but feel at least a little bit responsible for the failure you've become, Anastasia. I know that I have been an outstanding mother, though, beyond reproach. If I've erred with you, I've probably been too soft, too indulgent, and you have taken advantage of it. Now this is how you've turned out." She straightened and started to walk away.

"What?" I shrieked. "That's it?"

"Lower your voice, child," Jacqueline hissed before composing her features into a fake smile. "What have I told you about being so melodramatic? It doesn't suit a York woman, darling."

She spun on her heel, leaving me with my jaw hanging open so long that my mouth became dry.

I blinked, once, twice, and licked my lips.

I have to get out of here.

Before I could analyze what just happened, my feet were already in action, my vision blurred, my mind unseeing, not knowing where I was going as long as it was in a different direction than *that woman* had gone.

My arms were crossed over my head, my eyes on the dark floor as I mumbled, "I thought you'd have to teach this morning."

"No classes because of the holiday weekend," Rafael said quietly, coming to sit cross-legged beside me on the floor of my walk-in closet.

And there we sat, without speaking, without moving. Eventually, Rafael gently clasped my hand and scooted a little closer.

Finally, in what might have been ten minutes or one hundred, I choked out, "She—she couldn't even be happy for me, n–not even a little." I stopped to catch my breath. "My new line of work seemed to—to disgust her."

Rafael stiffened beside me. "Go on."

"She asked me again why I wasn't b–back with Brandon, and then instead of being outraged by how he treated me, she was offended by my 'coarse' words." I turned to my best friend briefly, though I didn't meet his eyes. "I've never used *truly* coarse words with her. I wouldn't dare."

"I know."

"And then her slimy rich boyfriend—he, well, he hit on me. When I told her about it, she basically turned to ice and told me what a massive failure of a daughter I am."

Rafael breathed out slowly and, in an icy calm voice, asked, "Annie ... is there more?"

"Those are the highlights. And I know, I *know* she isn't always right to say these things, but—"

"Annie—"

"But I am such an idiot for imagining, for *hoping* this could've ended any other way. I should know better. I must be so deluded, but then I wonder, what else am I deluded about? Is she ... could she be right about some things?" I inhaled a shaky breath, staring down at my knees. "I've been sitting here thinking maybe this promotion, this job thing is stupid after all. I've already written my resignation email in my head. It's just—"

Rafael gave my shoulders a gentle shake. "*Stop.* I can't let you keep talking."

I slowly raised my head, my bloodshot eyes finally meeting his. "Raf—"

"I'll sit here all day with you in this closet if you want to. But I can't, for a second more, let you believe anything out of that *horrible* woman's mouth."

I inhaled sharply.

"She gave birth to you, I know, but I'm done pretending she's anything but a vile, abusive, self-centered monster."

I stared at him, and for some reason my eyes watered. Why? He wasn't saying anything that I didn't know or agree with. I didn't resent him for saying it. Before I knew it, tears were streaming down my face, and my entire body was shaking.

Rafael enveloped me in his arms, and he stroked my hair lightly until I stopped shaking.

"I—I'm not—" I started.

"I'm sorry if that sounded harsh. I don't mean to be hurtful. Not to you anyway."

"No, I'm not ... I can't defend her. I don't want to. How could I? She has no redeeming qualities, that I know of." I fell silent, thinking of everything I knew about her mother. "She did have a difficult childhood, I think. Neglect, emotional abuse, for example. She never talked about it much, but I know it shaped her. It's not an excuse, but ..." I let the words hang in the air.

"At the very least, she probably has narcissistic personality disorder. I looked it up after your last call from her. Maybe other issues as well. And you know what, Annie? She isn't going to change. This is who she is." He squeezed my hand to soften the blow of his words.

After a few steadying breaths, I said quietly, "Logically, I know that."

Rafael squeezed me tighter into his side, and we sat quietly for a long time.

I debated internally whether or not to confess my other messy personal disaster to Rafael.

Why not?

This is my year of rock bottoms, apparently.

"That's actually not the only reason I'm doubting my future at the agency." I exhaled in relief at having forced the words out.

"Oh?" He turned to face me and sit cross-legged, so we were sitting perpendicular now instead of side by side.

"Yeah, um," I started, squeezing my eyes shut. "It's kind of embarrassing, but I realized I'm, uh, still in love with—"

"Oh, that," Rafael interrupted, chuckling. "Duh."

I elbowed him. "You knew? Wait, I didn't even know myself until recently."

Rafael raised an eyebrow. "Who do you think you're talking to?"

"I should have known." I sighed and then bit back a smile. "If I want to know how I feel about something, I should just ask you, eh?"

We both laughed, and it felt good, cleansing, for a few minutes.

But I sobered, recalling what we were discussing. "So, yeah, I don't know if I can keep working for him. And he's been *nice* to me lately. It would be easier if he was mean and I could try to, like, hate him. In fact, I told him so, basically."

"I get it," Rafael said, nodding slowly. "But you can't let this guy, *any* guy, get in the way of this job. I've never seen you so excited about a job before. Not a job, a career. You're becoming what I've always known you can be, passionate and focused and ... you can't give that all up because of a guy."

I tilted my head thoughtfully. "Similar to the advice you and Viv gave me years ago, to let him go."

"Wait, what?" Rafael raised his eyebrows and his hands in protest. "That was all Viviana. I didn't agree with her."

My eyes widened. "*What?*" My brow furrowed as I tried to process this. "You so did."

He bit his lip, his eyes pointed at the corner of the ceiling. After a few slow breaths, he said, "I can see how you might've thought that. I wasn't vocal about it. I wanted you to follow your heart, and I thought ... well, things are different now. You didn't know what you wanted then. And now you do. You were a kid then, and now you're a career woman."

I felt the corners of my mouth tugging upward. "Uh, it wasn't that many years ago."

"Mm-hmm." He smiled and squeezed my hand briefly. "Annie, please. If you take anything away from this chat, let it be this: you are amazing, and you can't let anyone, whether it's your mother, your ex, or even me, dictate what you do with your life or how you feel about yourself. Except, well, you need to listen to *me* when I say you're amazing. Got it?"

My eyes pooled with unshed tears, but my lips curved upward into a sad smile. "Love you to the moon and back."

"Love you to the barre and mat," he replied as he always did. "Hey, let's go get our ballet on."

"Said no dancer ever," I said with a groan. "Do I have to?"

"Yep," he said, pulling me up by both hands. "I spent enough time in the closet, you know?"

I smiled ruefully and let him lead me out of the dark. For now.

I blinked. How long had that spider web been in that corner of the ceiling?

And how long had I been lying in bed staring at it?

I blinked again, several times in succession. My eyes burned from crying yesterday.

The weekend that I should be celebrating the new life I'd begun making for myself? I'd spent it sobbing in a dark closet. And sleeping—

Holy crap.

The alarm clock said 7:00 pm. I'd slept all day? How was that possible? Rafael must have slipped me a sleep aid last night. Or was it this morning? I vaguely remembered it being dark outside when he practically carried me and tucked me into bed.

Then again, I'd barely slept for weeks. Months, really. Maybe my body needed it. My brain certainly did. In fact, I just wanted to sleep some more, to forget, to mourn the dream fulfilled if only for a fleeting moment ... a fantasy of a happy life for myself, really. Of making something of myself. Of being ... worthy.

Just sleep, need to make it all stop. Sleep until tomorrow, at least.

Where is that sleep aid?

There must be more of it somewhere.

Or alcohol.

And somehow, another thought arose, if only quietly at first.

No.

Not anymore.

New rule: Self-pity stops at 24 hours.

I sighed, dragging myself up to a sitting position and stretching my arms overhead.

The last bout of sleep and booze and depression had done nothing for me. "Not your style, girl," I said to myself aloud. "Get the hell up." I almost grinned as I added, "Talking to yourself is underrated."

In the shower, the hot water blended with the salty tears running downward. But these were angry tears. The time for sadness and self-pity were over, replaced by molten fury flooding my veins.

Settled back onto my bed in a thick robe, I picked up my phone, ready to send my mother a scathing text message, to tell her to go straight to hell.

But as my fingers were poised above the screen, I exhaled slowly, feeling my heart ache once more.

No.

I'm not my mother. I don't need to be cruel, just to be cruel.

Even if she deserves it.

Even if—

No.

I counted my breaths for a long moment.

I had to cut ties. Jacqueline would think that was cruel regardless of how I said it. But I had to speak my truth, as neutrally as I could. Email was probably best, so I could explain. A phone call or in-person conversation would be kinder for most people, but I knew what would happen. She wouldn't let me speak. She'd interrupt and belittle me until I forgot what I wanted to say, until I no longer felt worthy of speaking at all.

An email would have to suffice.

Dear Mother,
Please do not contact me at all anymore. After en-
during years of emotional abuse from you, I can no
longer handle seeing or talking to you. I need to take
care of myself. I would consider reconciling if you were
to undergo extensive mental health treatment, both in-
dividually and together, but I make no promises.
Best Wishes,
Annie

It sounded kind of awkward, but maybe that was the nature of a communication like this, with a woman like her? Should I tell her I'd be blocking her number? I copied the email into a message for Rafael and Rainn to get their input.

Surprisingly, I didn't feel the weight of sadness I'd experienced yesterday. I didn't really feel anything, except ... maybe lighter. Perhaps it would hit me later, or perhaps I'd wanted this to happen much longer than I'd realized.

The feeling of lightness vanished though when my other problem surfaced in my mind.

Oh, Kylan.

I sank back into the bed.

It was pointless to try to ignore them, the feelings that had been building, growing louder, every day since we'd become reacquainted.

It was time to be truly honest with myself. Had I ever stopped loving him, wanting a life with him, however impossible, regretting the decision to let him go?

I couldn't say for sure. Did it matter now? Maybe not. I was hopelessly in love with him. Maybe I always would be. The thought was painful.

Unlike four years ago, he wasn't in love with me. He might not even *like* me. We were basically business associates.

He's my boss.

I flattened myself on the mattress again and covered my face with my hands.

He was far up the chain, of course, like my boss's boss's boss. But my boss nonetheless. He could end my career if he wanted, but ... he wouldn't. He wasn't a jerk.

I sat up slowly.

Am I the jerk here?

First I broke his heart, and now I'm taking up space in his company. Should I quit?

I felt tears forming in my eyes again and wiped them away, frustrated. This was not the time for another emotional breakdown. I needed to think. And figure out what to do.

I mulled that over for a while, but when I was no closer to a decision, I sighed in frustration and picked up my phone.

Where are my roommates anyway?

While firing off a text to them both, I jumped at a sharp, loud sound and glanced out the window. Fireworks.

Crap, it's the Fourth of July. All my friends would have plans tonight.

I didn't want to bother them with my morose state of mind and impossible decisions. It could wait until another day. I briefly considered watching a movie and opening a bottle of wine but decided against it. I'd known for a while that I seriously needed to ease up on the drinking.

I could just read in bed until I nodded off. I was exhausted—who knew that creating boundaries like an adult and dealing with emotions could be so draining?

Chapter 24

Fumbling for my keys in my bag, I stopped just outside my apartment door the next morning. It was still well before lunch, but I'd decided to work from home for the rest of today—a benefit I'd rarely taken advantage of since starting at the agency, in part because the job of an assistant was much more tied to being present in the office. As a new agent, I had more freedom, in a sense, though I was still going to be juggling some assistant duties until they'd hired and trained my replacement.

The truth was, I didn't want to risk seeing Kylan today. I still felt very undecided about my future, and seeing him would only complicate things. And if I happened to see him with Sofia, well—I didn't know if I could handle that today, on a rainy Monday no less. I was already on my way out when I noticed Sofia was out of the office. Guilt swept through me, as I felt only relief at not having to say goodbye to my friend, who was really an awesome person but hard to see right now, given the situation.

The ... situation.

Sighing, I turned the key in the lock and opened—

"Uh."

"Girl!"

"What, Sof—"

As I stepped into my *own* apartment and shut the door absently behind me, my coworker tightened the towel—the *bath towel*—around her bare limbs. "Yeah. Hi." In both words, she drew out the vowels, her eyes flitting in every direction.

"You're in—in my apartment, wearing a towel," I sputtered, my eyes like saucers and my mouth gaping. I vaguely noticed some candles at the dining table and the faint smell of wax in the air. "What is happening? Am I ..." I put my fingers on my temples. "Am I finally having an actual meltdown?"

Then a familiar male voice called out, "Sofia, are you having trouble finding the ... *oh* ..." Rainn trailed off as he entered the room, clad in a bathrobe, and saw me. He closed his mouth, reopened it, and then closed it again.

No one spoke for a moment. "Rainn?" I squeaked. "What's going on?"

He flinched. "I was going to tell you, Annie. Sorry, I really was. It's—this—" He pointed between himself and Sofia. "We're—"

"This is new," Sofia cut in, coming to stand by him. "We were going to tell you soon."

I turned my widened eyes to Rainn. "Is *she* the one you were talking about all those months ago?" He winced and nodded, his cheeks turning red. "Why didn't you tell me?"

"Aww, I didn't know you'd been crushing on me that long," Sofia said, smiling at him and nuzzling his shoulder. "Sorry, is that super weird? I'm really into your roommate, Annie."

I looked back and forth between them and shook my head slowly. "Honestly, it's not as weird as you being really into my ex."

Sofia looked at me blankly for a moment before recognition dawned, and she laughed. "Oh, right. Kylan, yeah, that was never going to work out. He wasn't really interested—"

"Wait," I said, not really listening to Sofia's words. "This means you and Kylan aren't a thing."

"It definitely means that." Rainn grinned. "What are you gonna do about it, Annie?"

I opened my mouth at the blunt question, but it was a moment before any words came out. "I—I don't know what you mean."

Rainn's grin only widened. "OK, sure, but can you do me a favor and get out of here? You can come back tonight." He pulled Sofia close to his side. She laughed, seeming not to notice me in the room anymore.

I backed out, mumbling something incoherent as I left the apartment. Once out in the hallway, I stopped and leaned against the opposite wall.

This means…

Kylan's not with Sofia.

This…

I leaned heavily against the wall, breathing hard.

This is everything.

"Annie York! How dare you text me at a time like this?" Viviana demanded after I picked up the ringing phone.

I laughed, which helped only slightly in dispelling the tension in every single muscle in my body. "I thought you might be busy with Jane's visit."

"Oh, she went back home today. Her boss—wait, it doesn't matter. So, wow, Sofia and Rainn? Didn't see that coming. Meaning she and Kylan aren't …" She paused, and her eyebrows shot up. "*Kylan is single!*"

"Well," I said cautiously. "We don't actually know that. I only know that he's not with Sofia."

"But you haven't seen him with anyone else."

"No."

"And neither have I. I've actually seen him a lot while we've been working to get my novel ready to shop around to publishers. He's never said a word about his love life. I think … well, we haven't talked about you often, but when your name comes up, I sense there's something there."

"Something, like what? Bitterness? Resentment? Reluctant lovers-turned-coworkers feelings?" I asked, my voice full of anxiety but also a little hope.

"No, none of that. Well, maybe a little of the last thing. But it's more of ... I don't know, a softness. I think—" She paused. "I think he may still have feelings for you. But I can't be sure."

I tried to tame the hope fluttering in my chest. "Yes, well, anything is possible, but we don't really know—"

"*Annie.*"

"Viv?"

"You can't let him go again."

"But I don't even know if—"

"So what? This is *Persuasion*, Annie. By Jane Austen! Except you're not quiet and modest like Anne Elliot. You're Annie York, my fearless younger friend who is usually the most confident person I know. Give it a shot."

I swallowed with some effort, and after a few shallow breaths, I replied, "You're right. You—this isn't like me. I go after what I *want*—always. And what I want is ... love. And a career."

Viviana cheered. "Yes! You and me both. By the way, I have some news myself."

I gasped. "Did you—"

"Yes! He said *yes*!"

"As if there was *ever* any doubt that Jack would jump at the chance to marry you. He's been yours forever, Viv."

"Aww, Annie. Sometimes I still can't believe I'm this happy—well, we'll talk more about that later. Anyway, just wanted to share the big news." She paused, sounding emotional for a moment. "But back to *Kylan*, go get your man! It's my turn to be the rom-com movie sidekick character right now, and I'm loving it."

I giggled. "I guess that makes me the heroine." I sobered up quickly. "I need some time to think about how to go about this. I haven't ... well, I really haven't allowed myself to think about getting back together, to have hope that he could return the feelings. I *still* don't know if it's possible ..."

"Of course it's possible. You could write a letter, like Wentworth does in *Persuasion*. It would be a cool gender reversal. Captain Quinn, you pierce my soul—"

"Is that from the book? I'll have to reread that section. It's been years since I read Austen." Ignoring Viviana's *tsk-tsk* sound, I continued, "Thanks, Viv. I'd be lying if I said I wasn't a little terrified, but I'd also be extremely angry at myself and the world if I lost another opportunity with him. So ..."

She inhaled audibly. "So?"

"So I'm going to make an idiot out of myself, probably, but oh well. Please tell me you'll be around tonight in case I need to cry on your shoulder and forget he exists. Or help me pack and move to another continent."

"Always," Viviana said with a chuckle. "But something tells me you'll be doing something very different tonight."

Chapter 25

I was never more grateful that I'd moved into an office with a door I could close, rather than an open cubicle where anyone could come upon me. Slinking into the office with a takeout lunch in my bag, I'd gone straight to my office and, fortunately, hadn't run into Kylan or anyone else on my way in. He probably wasn't even in the office today; I hadn't seen him or any of the leadership team that morning. I knew there'd been an off-site leadership event planned for sometime this week—maybe it was today.

Having closed my door firmly and set my sandwich on the desk next to me, I opened a blank document on my computer and breathed in deeply.

But after staring at the screen for several minutes, I hadn't written a word. Perhaps I should read the famous letter from *Persuasion* as inspiration, even though I wasn't convinced my love story was going to end like Anne Elliot's. I wasn't that optimistic about my chances of success, despite feeling determined to *try* and then live with the consequences.

"He's worth the risk," I whispered. My decision was made.

Finding Captain Wentworth's famous letter online was easy, and I choked up while reading it.

*I can listen no longer in silence. I must speak to you by
such means as are within my reach. You pierce my soul.
I am half agony, half hope. Tell me not that I am too
late, that such precious feelings are gone for ever. I offer
myself to you again with a heart even more your own
than when you almost broke it...*

I had to stop reading, or else the tears would freefall. I needed to keep my wits about me to write this letter.

Or maybe I should just talk to him in person. Or a phone call?

No, if Viviana says I should write a letter, I should write a letter. If anyone knows romantic overtures, it's Viv.

It would also save my dignity a bit, in case he thought my feelings ridiculous or offensive.

Oh, who am I kidding? My dignity, or what's left of it, has no chance of survival after this.

My fingers trembled. This wasn't just a letter. This was everything I hadn't said in four years, and it had to be enough.

With a bittersweet chuckle, I began to write, but this time I put pen to paper. Crisp, white paper. No more impersonal documents on a computer.

This time, the words flowed out of me, onto the page. Some of Wentworth's, but mostly my own. I was stopping to reread my last sentence, over halfway down the page, when suddenly my office door burst open, rattling the hinges.

I nearly jumped out of my skin, dropping the inky pen on the paper. I looked up, and my breath caught as my heart did flips and sprints. "Ky–Kylan," I managed, barely able to speak.

He. Was. Here.

I blinked, and for a second I wasn't in my office—I was twenty-two again, standing outside the campus library, watching him walk away with his jaw clenched and his heart breaking. I never let myself linger on that memory. Until now.

This man I loved studied me for a long moment. As though he'd been running, he seemed out of breath as his steps slowed, but he continued in the direction of my desk. "I was hoping you'd be here."

My heart lodged in my throat.

This was it.

He stopped in front of my desk. "Annie, I–"

"I am half agony–"

"Half hope," he said.

I gasped, my hands flying to my mouth. As he stood just feet away, I saw moisture pooling in his eyes. Those beautiful grey eyes.

"Can it be?" I whispered, standing up on shaky legs. When he swallowed and started to nod, the corners of my mouth turned up slightly. "Only half?"

His intense expression turned to one of confusion.

"Only half hope?" I clarified, putting a hand on my hip.

He nodded slowly as his shoulders relaxed. But instead of speaking, he walked around the desk, never breaking eye contact.

This better be the kiss of all kisses.

I licked my lips, but he merely took my hands gently after stopping in front of me. Our eyes had locked since the moment he barged into the room. "Annie York, you pierce my soul."

I let go of his hands, throwing them up in the air. "I was going to use that line! I was writing you a letter. See?" I pointed to the desk. "You ruined my dramatic moment," I said with a watery laugh, wiping at my eyes. "I was finally going to be brave."

He stepped closer. "You are brave, Annie. You always were. I just didn't know if you still wanted me."

"I do," I whispered. "So much."

Kylan's gaze dropped to the letter on my desk, and he smiled, the kind of smile I hadn't seen in so long. Four long years.

"I love you, and I always have," he said. "I loved you when we were just college kids, and I love you even more as the woman you've become. Annie, there wasn't a day I didn't think of you," he said quietly. "But I had to learn how to live without you, or I thought I did."

My knees went weak, and I had to lean against the desk. I'd dreamed of hearing those words, but I never imagined they'd still hit with the same force, the same wonder.

"I have loved none but you," I said with a smile, quoting Wentworth again. "I thought you'd never forgive me—that you'd never give me another chance. Even when I convinced myself I was over you, I wasn't. Far from it. You're the one, Kylan."

Don't cry, don't cry, don't cry.

I placed my hand on his chest. "Now, kiss me before I change my mind."

But as he leaned in, I pulled back and licked my lips. "Better yet, let's go close those curtains and lock the door. I plan on making up for four lost years—starting now."

"Hell yes," he said with a husky laugh. "Yet another reason I'm glad you were promoted with your own office."

I turned back after closing the curtains. "Then again, you probably have a more comfortable office. We could go there—"

"I can't wait that long, love," he said just before our mouths and bodies collided in a kiss so sweet, so perfect in every way that I'd remember it every day for the rest of my life.

"Well, I bet Anne Elliot never did *that* with her captain," I said while grinning and putting on my cardigan. "And I bet Laina's office has never seen this kind of action before."

Kylan laughed. "True, on both counts. Well, actually, Austen's Anne and Frederick would've been passionate kissers—and then lovers, once they married. Don't you think?"

I considered this for a moment. "I suppose. I'm still in a state of disbelief, Kylan. That I have you back ... Hey, I have an idea! Maybe Viviana's next book could be inspired by us. Since she wrote her first book based on both Austen and her real-life love story, you know?"

His face was pensive as he slipped on his shoes. "Maybe. I'd have to pass her along to another agent though, or else that would be really awkward." He laughed but then turned serious. "We should probably talk about work though. Talk to HR. I mean, our relationship—that is, assuming you want to be with me—" Doubt flickered across his face.

I elbowed him. "Of course I do. But you're right. How terrible does that look, getting promoted right before I start dating the boss?"

"We'll figure it out. I can always quit." He grinned at the shock on my face. "What, it's just a job."

"*Just* a job?" I echoed. "You've worked so hard, and you've been wildly successful. Hardly just a job."

"But I got the girl. That's all I really wanted."

I stared at this man, the only one I'd ever wanted. Words were hard. "I ... you ... this was—all for me?" When he nodded, I clasped his hands and whispered, "I love you, Kylan. You were always enough for me, just you. I should've told you that." I paused with a soft smile. "You and Charlie."

I chuckled at his suddenly thunderous expression. "You haven't met my cat yet." He narrowed his eyes, and I smiled. "Sorry."

"No, you're not, but that's one of the things I love about you. When it comes to joy, you're unapologetic. You've so much more joy than I think you ever realized." When he captured my lips in another kiss, this one was soft and slow, tender and full of longing, all the longing of ages. As I tried to pull him closer, he broke the kiss and gently pushed back. "Wait, I wanted to share some news. I have a publisher interested in Viviana's book. You're the first to know. I was going to tell her tonight. We could even do it together if you want."

I squealed. "That's such great news! She'll be so happy and—oh, I have news about her too. She proposed to Jack. And obviously he said yes. They're getting married!"

Kylan smiled. "Good for them. Always knew they'd end up together."

"You did? Wow. Anyway, uh, so you two are cool then? You don't ... resent her?" I bit my lip, still nervous whenever the subject was my past mistake, all the hurt I must have caused him.

"Not at all. She was just looking out for you, and I love that. I mean, I didn't always feel that way, of course, but we're friends now."

I couldn't stop looking at him, every bit of that handsome face, the face of love. My mouth curved into a grin. "Good, because you're going to be my date for their wedding, you know. In Duluth."

"Duluth, eh? Isn't that where her new friend lives? Jill something, who visited recently?"

"Jane Alton, yeah, she's from Duluth. An Austen fan just like Viviana. She's pretty cool actually." My breath caught as he stepped closer. He didn't need to say anything—his eyes, full of something unspoken and sure, said it all. I swallowed. "I, uh, I think you'll like Jane when you meet."

"Looking forward to it, love, but the last thing I want to do is talk about Viviana and her friend. Or anyone else but you." His eyes flashed in that I-burn-for-you way before landing on my lips. "Kiss me again, my sassy Annie Elliot."

<h1 style="text-align:center">Epilogue</h1>

ONE YEAR LATER

The warm, early-summer air hung heavy with the scent of roses in Duluth's Leif Erikson Park as I laced my fingers through Kylan's. The soft green satin of my dress brushed the sun-warmed stones beneath my feet, and I turned to him with a smile. "This place—it's truly something else, isn't it?"

Kylan gave me that easy grin I loved. "Yeah. Feels like the kind of place where stories begin."

I glanced at Viviana standing in the gazebo, glowing with nervous excitement. Her groom was calm and steady beside her, like he'd always belonged in this exact spot. She told me once this was the very spot where she'd realized she loved Jack—on a solo trip last summer, when everything changed.

My eyes swept to the sides. Viv's and Jack's sisters stood close as attendants, their quiet support anchoring the moment, while her nieces scattered petals like bursts of sunlight and her nephew charmingly took his ringbearer duties very seriously. I didn't know Lillian very well, but her children were adorable. And Belinda was radiant as ever next to her big brother. It was all so ... perfect. Complete. The kind of perfect in a way I'd never experienced.

Jenn, Kieran, and Choua leaned in close and laughed softly in front of us, and Rainn nudged me from my other side with a lazy smile. I knew he was thinking of proposing to Sofia, and I was 100% on board. In this garden full of people who meant everything to me, I felt lucky. Chosen family was sometimes the best kind.

As the ceremony carried on, my thoughts drifted briefly to Jane—in a seat on the far side, her tablet in hand as she took notes for a work assignment she'd been so excited to get. Her ex was the photographer, a lovely Japanese American woman who'd seemed even more excited about the opportunity. And not far off, a man with furrowed eyebrows stared at Jane. She'd whispered to me earlier that he was probably spying—or hoping she'd fail, so he could report back to her new boss (also his best friend). *Why else would he attend?* she'd asked us. But there was something in his posture, if not his expression—something waiting to unfold beneath that guarded surface.

Watching Viviana's wedding unfold in this place that had changed everything for her, I felt the quiet thrill of new beginnings. Because true love stories—like Anne Elliot's in *Persuasion*—weren't always neat or easy, but they were worth every twist and turn.

I should know.

Later, when the music floated through the rose-scented air and guests mingled beneath rose-gold string lights, Kylan sidled up beside me with two nonalcoholic drinks.

He leaned in and brushed the corner of my mouth with his lips before handing me a glass. "If this wedding thing wears you out ..."

I laughed and shook my head. "Not a chance."

He shrugged playfully. "Then I'll just have to marry you. Right here. Right now."

Something fluttered in my chest, and I smirked, squeezing his hand. "You're going to have to work on your pitch."

He pulled me close, grinning. "Soft launch."

And just like that, with the warm weight of his hand in mine and the gentle hum of life all around us, my heart did that ridiculous thing it always did—full and scared and stubbornly hopeful. This time, I'd get my own happily ever after, hard-won and real.

As Kylan spun me gently beneath the stars, our eyes locked.

When he looked at me like that—as if I was his, always—I finally stopped wondering if I deserved this kind of love. This bliss. I just held on tight.

Acknowledgments

Writing every book is a journey, but *Austen Persuaded* took me down a different kind of path.

This was a story I wasn't sure I could—or should—tell. Annie is not the kind of heroine I usually write. She's not the reserved, introverted Anne Elliot character you might expect from a *Persuasion*-inspired retelling, either (and I do love the original Anne Elliot). From the very beginning, Annie York fascinated me. She came to me as someone deeply flawed and deeply human: shaped by very difficult circumstances both in childhood and in young adulthood, unsteady around alcohol, clinging to a shallow narrative about herself and, tragically, unsure whether she deserved more. Her second chance isn't just about romance—it's about friendship, purpose, healing, and learning to trust her own voice again.

And somewhere along the way, I realized I was still finding mine, too.

Although this is my fifth published book, *Austen Persuaded* is only the second full novel I ever wrote. I returned to this novel after a few years of growing (a lot) as a writer, determined to revise it with more honesty, depth, and heart. In fact, I penned over half of this book during National Novel Writing Month, previously an annual challenge that encouraged writers to draft an entire novel each November. I only attempted the challenge once. Just once. But it gave me exactly what I needed: not chaos, but clarity. I wasn't rushed—I was focused. Passionate. I couldn't stop thinking about Annie and her journey. I wanted to get it right.

Like all my books, this one straddles the line between rom-com, women's fiction, and contemporary romance. It's tender in some places, sharp in others, and a little messy in between. I've learned to love that in-between space. It's where the real stories live—my favorite ones, actually (a-hem, Katherine Center). Thank you, dear reader, for stepping into this space with me.

So many people helped bring this story to life and then to the world.

To my assistant and proofreader, Melissa Martin, I'm endlessly grateful for your tireless work in supporting *my* work. Thank you for being the steady, calming presence behind the scenes—making sure things didn't fall apart while I had my head in the clouds (or in revisions). To my editor, Dr. Laura Murray, thank you for your thoughtful comments and gentle nudges once again.

To every blogger, bookstagrammer, and tour host who helped spread the word about *Austen Persuaded*—your support is a gift I will never take for granted. Thank you for taking a chance on an indie author!

To my early readers and street team, thank you for reading early, posting generously, and cheering this book into the world. You make me feel like I'm not launching a new book alone ... and that my writing is worth reading. Special thanks to my earliest (beta) readers, Julie, Rebekah, and Melodie.

To my author friends, like Amanda Darcy (check out her amazing Austenesque books too!), and my author idols, like Katherine Center, Mariana Zapata, Emily Henry ... and of course, Jane Austen.

To Mr. Highbury and our children, thank you for your patience, your love, and your willingness to let me disappear into writing mode for "just a few more minutes" (that somehow turned into hours). You already know you're everything to me, but I will never stop shouting it from the rooftops.

And to you, dear reader: thank you for letting Annie's story into your heart. She is not perfect. She struggles, she laughs, she stumbles, and she keeps going. If you've ever wanted a second chance—not just at love, but at life—you're in good company.

About the Author

Alana Highbury is the bestselling author of the *Austen Inspired* and *Love & Holidays* romance series. Her novels blend rom-com, contemporary romance, and women's fiction, and she brings two decades of professional experience and a master's in English. When not writing, she's usually found reading, cross stitching, board gaming, or hanging out with her family, which includes a writerly husband, two children, two beautiful, lazy cats, and a feisty cockatiel.

Visit Alana's website at **alanahighbury.com**, or follow her on these platforms:

Facebook • Instagram • Goodreads
Amazon • BookBub • Bluesky

Also by Alana

***Austen Inspired* series**

Austen Inspired
Austen Persuaded
Austen Revisited

***Love & Holidays* series**

Meet Me on Christmas Eve
Snowed In on Valentine's Day
Dance with Me on New Year's Eve